Karl Gilmore thought he knew every way the human mind could break.

The first thing to interrupt the whirlwind of Karl's thoughts was realizing Mrs. Labine had come in with the big group that started all of this.

The second was her fingers digging into his forearm.

"Don't miss it." Her voice was a high-pitched hiss; the repeated words so fast they ran together. "Dontmissitdontmissitdontmissit."

Karl covered her hand with his own. He was sure she was drawing blood.

"It's okay, Mrs. Labine. What do you think I'm missing?"

"No one ever looks, no one ever sees," she whispered, her face twisted into a grimace, pale blue eyes narrowed. "It's the stealing that does it. Too much, too much, stealing too much. Stealing the night. Everything breaks."

"Nothing like that can happen here, okay?" he said. "Everybody's safe now. I won't let anyone hurt you."

She pulled against her thick leather restraints, trying to reach him with her other hand. He wasn't in any danger from her, but letting a new patient get too upset threw everyone into an uproar.

"Nothing works when the thief is about. Nothing, nothing, nothing. Everything breaks, no matter what you do. Stealing my bloody sleep away after everything else. Don't. Miss. It. Don't miss it. Dontmissit..."

The Dream Thief

Published 2016 by Spiral Publishing, Ltd.
www.spiralpublishing.net

Book and cover design copyright © 2016 by Spiral Publishing, Ltd.
Cover art copyright © 2016 by Andrey Kiselev | Dreamstime.com and gremlin |
istockphotos.com

Print ISBN-13: 978-0-9908875-2-2
Library of Congress Control Number: 2016915454

*To Sean, Johnny (and Dave), and everyone involved with Fiction
Unboxed and Engine World.
Thank you for Building the door to such grand adventures and for sharing
the key.
What a delightful playground we have here!*

THE DREAM THIEF

KARI KILGORE

SPIRAL PUBLISHING, LTD.

Chapter 1

Karl Gilmore stepped off of the clanging trolley while it was still moving, but only just. His mother's long-ago admonition to never do such a thing lodged too clearly in his mind for him to jump off like teenaged boys seemed to do at every stop.

The heady sweet lilacs seemed to fill his whole body, while a thousand memories of growing up on this street filled his mind. Victorian houses, every available surface embellished and decorated with sometimes gaudy colors, stretched as far as he could see in both directions. His family's a couple of blocks away stood out as the only three-story version, Karl's boyhood turret room towering above everything else at the front. He'd seen far finer homes in posh districts where various Ministry Directors lived, but none as charming and odd to his eyes as the Gilmore residence.

He walked far enough to get out of everyone else's way before he stopped and took a deep breath, same as he did every time he made the trip to Waldron's Gate. All the other passengers, either boarding or exiting the crowded car, had continued on to their destinations. Karl stood alone on the sidewalk warmed by the morning sun, waiting for his habitual signal to walk the rest of the way.

The dark green cotton shirt and brown pants his sisters bought him for these visits felt stiff and uncomfortable from rare use. A bit of discomfort was better than scaring people with his normal charcoal-gray work clothes. That uniform was so well known that he didn't need the badge that let him into and out of Joffrey Columns, the asylum where Karl had worked for more than ten years now. Just about anyone out here in the world would shy away from the uniform alone.

The brick clock tower several blocks away chimed the hour, and Karl's feet started moving without his brain's input. Ten in the morning. Time to go. No need to cause extra stress by arriving early. And definitely no need to arrive late enough to upset his parents. The smoother these visits went for everyone, the better.

Karl's eyes found the Blunderbuss in the distance, the massive chrome bell end not putting out as much white smoke as usual on a Sunday afternoon. His father and most of his brothers and sisters were Builders at the Ministry of Manifestation, using the mysterious power of the Blunderbuss to create just about everything the citizens of Waldron's Gate and other cities throughout Alterra needed.

From viewboxes and talkboxes to train rails and parts for enormous airships, and just about everything in between, the Blunderbuss provided. All it required was the talent, the ability to receive plans and designs from the Aether and send them into reality.

Karl had inherited his father's great height and strength, his nearly perfect memory, and even the hazel eyes that had marked Builders in his family for generations. Following in Arthur Gilmore's footsteps had been almost a foregone conclusion throughout most of Karl's childhood. After all, every one of his brothers, sisters, and cousins who had those eyes had that same ability.

But despite his family's expectations, and his own, and no matter how hard he tried in training, Karl didn't have the slightest trace of Builder talent.

He turned up the pale brick walkway toward his parents' broad porch, noticing changes in the discrete area where his mother tested out new color combinations. Anyone who didn't know where to look would miss Mrs. Gilmore's experimental corner, appropriately exposed to sun and shade during the day. From her neat squares painted close together, Karl suspected the current purple, gold, and light brown were about to give way to orange, blue, and pink.

Sometimes he was relieved to live in an unchanging sprawling red brick building along the outskirts of Joffrey Columns. As he knocked on the purple door, he corrected himself. He was relieved most of the time.

"Hey, Karl!" Andy, his little brother, grinned from ear to ear. "Glad you could join us for a change."

"Yeah, kid," Karl said, catching his brother in a quick hug. "Tell me you won't be out the door the second Mother gives the okay."

"Sooner if I can manage. Fair warning. We've got a bunch of cousins here for brunch."

Karl tried not to frown as he followed Andy toward the dining room at the back of the house. The thick flowery rugs did feel good under his feet instead of the wood, stone, and concrete he normally walked on all day long. But the knickknacks, photos, and various collections on every surface looked way too cluttered and congested compared to his nearly empty apartment.

"I wouldn't call that warning fair," he said to Andy right before they turned the corner. "Wish you'd gotten word to me before I left '

"That's exactly why I didn't." Andy stopped, hands on his hips. He was a smaller, nearly perfect duplicate of Karl, from the messy hair to the easily tanned skin to the promise of height to come in his lanky fifteen-year-old build. "I need to talk to you about something, Karl."

"A letter or the talkbox not good enough?"

"No," Andy said. He stared at the rug for a few seconds, tracing the outline of a rose with one bare foot. "Got to do this face to face, and not where someone else can listen in. Make sure we get the time before you leave."

Before Karl could ask questions, his normally cheerful and carefree brother turned the corner into the swirling mass of noisy relatives. Karl couldn't think of anything to do but follow him.

DOING his best to keep up with family chatter left Karl exhausted long before the cook had the famously huge Gilmore family brunch on the table. Even when he attempted to give his brain the day off, it was determined to catalog every bit of gossip and news with the person who delivered it.

Who'd been promoted, who had a dispute with a neighbor, who was falling into or out of love. The benefit was he didn't have to pretend to be interested whether he wanted to be or not. And staying quiet in a crowd like this was the best way to keep his own life private.

That only lasted until all the cousins went home. Their traditional Sunday afternoon gathering in the second-floor family room gave Karl's mother the perfect chance for a bit of affectionate cross-examination. Of course if he visited more often, or called, she might not have felt the need to investigate him so thoroughly when she had the chance.

Karl remembered playing with puzzles and toys, or later reading on the colorful pillows piled up at one end of the room during these long afternoons. He'd watched his older brothers and sister sitting in the wingback chairs and sofa around the fireplace with their parents, envious and wondering what the quiet conversations were about. Andy still joined their youngest sisters sometimes, but he usually stayed close when Karl was around.

When Klia Gilmore set her delicate pink teacup down with a sigh, Karl knew he was in her sights.

"Karl, you seem so tired today," she said. "Have you been getting enough days off?"

He decided not to mention the mass of socializing he'd just been through.

"We normally get enough days off, sure. Longer hours than usual lately. That's all."

"Maybe you just need a change of scenery," his mother said. Her slow smile and blush warned Karl he wasn't going to like the next words. "I hear there's a new house going up over on Juniper Street, set up for young single men your age. And a house a couple of blocks over for single women, too."

"That would be a long trip every day, Mother," Karl said.

"Housing out at the Columns isn't exactly luxurious, but it's free. You know that."

Something in his tone made Karl's father glance up over the edge of his broadsheet. Arthur Gilmore didn't tolerate any sort of sharp talk, certainly not in the evenings. Karl had lived away for ten years, but he still knew when to smile and keep his mouth shut. He did both.

"Maybe I should move over there," Andy said with a grin.

Karl couldn't stop himself from grinning back.

"Not quite yet, young man," their mother said. Her pursed mouth said more than her words or the brisk shake of her head. "You'll stay here until you have eighteen years, same as all your brothers and sisters."

She picked up her teacup again, noticed it was empty, and refilled everyone's with sweet, mint-and-bergamot-flavored water.

"That reminds me," she said. "I heard from Rethia this morning. She went to the doctor, and the baby is strong and healthy as ever. She was hoping they'd say she could keep working, but she's on leave just like the first time. I told her the Ministry would manage just fine without her. The baby will be a lot healthier for it. I think she's happier when she can fret about something."

Karl glanced at their father to make sure he was buried in his paper again, then winked at Andy. As was almost always the case on these obligatory visits home, his little brother had rescued him from their mother's clutches. Or at least from her questions. Karl's impending niece or nephew, the eighth so far, was much safer territory.

"Arthur," she said, her hand on her husband's arm. "Andy had the highest talent scores in his class last week. He might be at the Ministry before he's sixteen."

She beamed at her youngest son, but her face fell when she turned back to Karl. He tried to keep his own features neutral, and he was usually pretty good at that. No matter what he told himself or saw out in the world, he was terribly self-conscious as a non-Builder in a family loaded to the gills with them.

"Way to go, Andy!" Karl said. "You'll be moving up the ranks before you're twenty." Karl stood, glad to take the excuse his mother's embarrassed silence gave him. "I'd better be on my way. New trainees tomorrow. Have to get an early start."

Klia Gilmore's red cheeks shifted from embarrassment to a flush of pride in an instant. Even if Karl wasn't following in any of the approved family career paths, anyone as high up in the Ministry of Decorum as she was knew bragging rights when she heard them.

"That's wonderful," she said. "How much of the training do you handle now?"

"All of it for these new orderlies," Karl said. "And most for junior nurses. I made head trainer a few weeks ago."

"Oh, why didn't you tell us?" she said, tears in her light brown eyes.

Karl winced at his mother's genuinely stricken expression. He wondered why he waited to drop these good news bombs until he was ready to leave. Some kind of perverse need to run down his own accomplishments? His excuse to himself about not wanting announcements in all the papers didn't make sense when he didn't even live here anymore.

"I'm sorry, Mother. I just forgot. We've had a lot of new recruits lately. Probably could use more days off with so much going on. Lots of great bonus pay, though."

To Karl's surprise, that got his father to look over the edge of his broadsheet again. Mr. Gilmore raised his eyebrows just a tiny bit and nodded, but everyone at the grown-up end of the room saw it. That was the biggest approval Karl or anyone else was likely to get.

Andy and their mother turned to Karl, the admiration plain. Not so much over the pay. Only his father would be impressed by that. Everyone else was impressed at those eyebrows and that nod.

"In any case, I need to get back," he said. "Thank you for brunch, Mother. It was great to see all the cousins. Give Rethia my love, and let me know about that new niece or nephew. Has she been to a psychic to see what she's having? She's due in, what, a month or so?"

Everyone knew Karl didn't believe in psychics or fortune-tellers any more than he believed some Imp cavorted in The Pit or Jonah circled a great mythical ocean surrounding Alterra. But most everyone played along with those games when someone was pregnant.

"She's due in eight weeks," his mother said, getting to her feet. "But we'd better see you before then. She doesn't want to know which it is, silly goose. I keep telling her that takes so much of the stress away, but you know how she is."

She caught Karl up in a great, tight hug, then stepped aside so the others could do the same.

"That I do, Mother," Karl said. "I think she just likes surprises. I'll get back as soon as I can."

Klia managed to wipe her eyes discretely before she smiled at her middle child. Rethia was the other one Karl would like to see a lot more often. He'd have to make time to do that when the baby drama was over.

"Surprises always suited the two of you better than me," Karl's mother said. She caught Andy in a one-armed hug as he tried to pass by. "And this is another one just like you. See you again soon, Karl?"

He nodded, then grunted when Andy caught his arm and pulled him forward.

"I'll walk you to the corner, big Brother," Andy said. "Be right back."

He almost pushed Karl out the door before anyone else could respond.

SEVERAL PEOPLE WERE out for Sunday afternoon strolls when Karl and Andy stepped onto the porch. Young couples not much older than Andy, married couples not much older than Karl. Pushing brass-and-leather strollers, pulling brightly painted wagons, walking hand in hand, huge colorful dresses contrasting with dark jackets. The peaceful scene sat uneasily alongside whatever was bothering the younger Gilmore.

"What's up, little Brother?" Karl said.

Andy shook his head, dark brown curls floating over his high forehead. Karl kept his unruly hair a good bit shorter, but otherwise he could have been looking into a mirror. A younger, better rested mirror.

"You know how it is," Andy said. "Can't say a word without

Mother overhearing or Father disapproving. I just wanted a minute or two with someone I can talk to."

Karl smiled with one side of his mouth, and though Andy tried to fight it, the two of them burst into laughter. From the day Andy was born, Karl felt a year or two older rather than more than ten. In that moment, he felt like they were exactly the same silly age.

"Out with it, kid."

Andy was still smiling, but his eyes were serious in a heartbeat. He looked over his shoulder to make sure no one was watching as they walked away from the house.

"I hate to bug you about work," Andy said. "I know you can't say much of anything anyway."

Karl counted ten strides while he waited for his brother to go on. When they were too far from the house for anyone to see them, he detoured onto an ornate wrought iron bench against the row of lilacs.

Unless someone hiked up to the tallest point in their parents' house, the tiny window in Karl's rounded turret bedroom, no one would know where they were. Andy sat beside him and sighed in perfect imitation of their mother.

"Come on, what's going on?" Karl said. "You were out of there like a shot before Mother could say a word."

Andy smiled, but this time it was worried rather than amused.

"It's just...I've been hearing a bunch of talk, probably mostly bull-shit. But it's been going on for a long time."

He stopped again, looking at the slightly less grand row of houses across the street. They were painted just as elaborately and kept just as neatly, but most were one floor, too small for more than a couple of people.

"Talk about what?" Karl said.

Andy turned to him, barely fifteen but looking a lot older in that moment. He squinted into the distance and chewed his lower lip.

"I suddenly know a lot of people with family members out at the Columns, Karl. A lot."

Karl tried to hide it, but he knew his maddeningly observant brother caught that brief twist of his mouth. Again, Andy was just like their mother.

"You know I can't—"

"I know you can't say much. I do," Andy said. "But hear me out, okay?" He waited until Karl nodded. "I'm used to people having to go every now and then. We all are. But this is different. I've counted more than ten in the last month, and I know I haven't caught all of them. A lot of people keep it really quiet, you know?"

That was how most folks outside of their family felt and acted about Karl working out at Joffrey Columns. Don't talk about the crazy house at all, or it might happen to you.

"I know. Ten people isn't all that unusual, Andy."

"No, that's not all of it. I heard you say you've been busy lately, and I'd bet it wasn't just from new trainees, was it?" Karl looked into his brother's eyes, not trying to hide his scowl. This was definitely crossing the line. "Let's try this. If you weren't extra busy with new patients, what are all the new trainees for?"

"You got me, kid," Karl said. "We've had a heavy workload lately, sure. I'm not sure why you're so worried about it, though. Our family isn't exactly susceptible to that kind of trouble, not for a long time."

"This is more than that," Andy said. "Do you get to see the paperwork, the intake, whatever you call it? The things that have to be filled out when someone new gets there?"

"I see it for my new patients, yeah," he said. "But not for everyone. That's not exactly my department."

Karl was more than a little nervous now, and he had to force himself not to look over his shoulder. That oath of secrecy he'd taken when he got the job at the Columns was burning in his mind, brighter than the sun.

"Well, you might want to look around a little bit," Andy said. "A whole lot of kids I know, kids from right around here, have had parents or brothers or sisters heading out your way over the past few months. And none of them had much of a history of crazy in the family, either."

Karl blinked, and before he could stop it his mind was spinning through the names and faces he'd come across since his own birthday three months ago. No one he knew, not personally. He had an idea the Director kept that from happening for a very good reason.

But now that he thought more about it, he had seen a few more family names that he recognized than usual. And since families tended to stay in the same neighborhoods...

"You have seen something," Andy said.

"You know I—"

"Yeah, I know. Listen, I'm not asking you to say a word. I'm just asking you to take a look around. That's all. I'm not the only one who's getting a little worried. No one's sure if it's the newest Builds, something that went pear-shaped during a big push on a new project, or maybe something in the water. Hell, it could be something as simple as a bad batch of Crumble, not that that wouldn't be a disaster. But I'm getting more than a little bit worried. Our whole family could get caught up in whatever this is."

Karl tried to let that roll off his shoulders, knowing Andy didn't mean to hurt his feelings like other people in the family sometimes did. But it did hurt, just a little.

When he was back here, surrounded by the handsome old houses and breathing in the sweet scent of lilacs from this street, he never forgot for even one second that he was no Builder. Everyone in his family could get caught up in something going wrong.

Everyone but him.

"Sure thing," Karl finally said. "I'll keep my eyes open, okay? Don't worry so much. You'll be old before your time."

Andy closed his eyes, and his shoulders sagged. He nodded and smiled.

"Thank you, Karl. I appreciate this. You better run, or you'll miss the last train out. Don't want to end up in Mother's clutches overnight."

Chapter 2

Loretta Schofield placed a black leather bag on the cafei table in front of her. Like everything else in this massive house, the table was the finest available—for any amount of rittern. The expanse of deep brown oak was carved into an elaborate scene complete with elves, dragons, and the mysterious robed figures of Alterra's distant past. In properly devout fashion, the glittering Crown rode high in the sky, and Jonah the whale god swam in his heavenly ocean surrounding the land. A perfect sheet of glass covered the whole thing, the shimmering effect creating an even stronger sense of fantasy.

She tried not to shudder at placing such a horrific object, far more suited for nightmares than fairy tales, on top of it.

Mrs. Roma Norwood was one of her wealthiest, and therefore best, clients. The chubby woman, just shy of old age but doing her best to fight it, opened the bag and pulled out a glass case with brass fittings. She let out a deep sigh and cradled the hideous thing Loretta had just given her against her substantial bosom.

"I simply cannot understand how you're able to do this over and over again, Ms. Schofield."

"It's my pleasure, Mrs. Norwood," she said. "This one was difficult to locate, but I hope it's everything you were looking for."

Loretta had long ago stopped wondering why people wanted the things they did, wanted them so badly that they'd pay a fortune for something they only dared show a few others. Friends and neighbors as caught up in this sick mania as they were. As long as they paid well, and paid reliably, she didn't care.

"And you've never seen another one like it?" Mrs. Norwood said.

The woman stared at Loretta, her eyes heavily painted and made up, but pretty enough. That kohl and powder did help distract from the thick layers all over the rest of her face.

"No, Mrs. Norwood. Neither I nor any of my suppliers have ever seen anything like this before." Loretta leaned closer, the black leather around her waist and torso creaking. "None of your neighbors will have, either."

Those eyes were wider for a second before proper Mrs. Norwood leaned back into a most girlish fit of giggling.

"Oh dear, you've once again read my mind," she said. "If we're to be on such intimate terms, please do call me Roma. May I ask you a question? About a silly rumor I've heard?"

"Of course you may, Roma," Loretta said, bracing herself for whatever nonsense was to come. "One of the ways I keep my trade healthy is by keeping up with what my neighbors are most excited about."

Mrs. Norwood leaned forward and whispered.

"I've heard some of my friends talk about special items that come all the way from Aerohead, hidden away in the haunted houses there. That's why they're so rare and take so long to find. Do your treasures come from there?"

Loretta smiled, amused by the question. She'd started that little rumor herself a long time ago.

"You know Aerohead is dangerous," she said, shivering. "I imagine anyone brave enough to venture to that lost city would find wonders without number. If they survived."

She winked as she looked up at Mrs. Norwood.

Roma Norwood covered her mouth and giggled again before getting to her feet in a rustling, perfumed bundle.

"I'll just go speak to Mr. Norwood about the payment. May I take this little treasure with me? You know how seeing a thing helps men to understand the value. Poor dears."

Loretta inclined her head, and her smile was genuine. Neither Mr. Norwood nor any of the other spouses ever argued about payment, or the prices she charged. At least none of the houses she visited more than once. A husband, or a wife, who argued about such things would lose the services of Ms. Loretta Schofield—permanently.

"Of course you may," Loretta said. "I know I can trust you, Roma."

The older woman grinned, looking years younger despite the powders and potions caked onto her skin. She made a show of arranging her fashionably cumbersome rust-colored dress before she swept through the broad lattice-topped archway toward the back of the house.

Loretta took in a deep, perfume-free breath as soon as she heard the door to Mr. Norwood's study close. If the lady of this fine house hadn't wanted to take the thing with her, Loretta would have insisted.

She knew it was like any other treasure she mysteriously found, created in the night from whatever substance floated down out of the Aether and through a Builder's mind at the Ministry of Manifestation. It could just have well have looked like an ancient pocket watch, a stolen sheaf of top-secret military papers from Stensue, or a bundle of pressed flowers from a long-ago first date. All of the fake trinkets she peddled came from the same place.

The fact that the occupants of this particularly wealthy household were happy to believe she'd somehow procured the petrified left hand of a deformed child—a child with seven perfect fingers and a double-jointed thumb—was more than enough for Loretta to want the damned thing far away from her.

These negotiations between Mr. and Mrs. Norwood could go on for ages even though the outcome was never in doubt. Loretta stood and walked around the room, looking at the more conventional collection displayed all around her. Every little bit of information helped in her line of work.

Coin was never an object inside the walls of these fine old houses, by far the finest and most elaborate in all of Waldron's Gate, probably in all of Alterra. Loretta knew which houses held Directors, but what they directed made no difference to her. She was much more interested in what they, and their spouses, desired.

A burst of giggly, girlish laughter floated from the back of the house. Loretta rolled her eyes and continued her investigations. No matter how desperately her clients longed for anything new to set them apart from their peers, their routines inside their own homes rarely varied. She didn't want—or need—to know the particulars.

She knew the rittern would be forthcoming, and that she had at least another ten minutes to wait. She gathered her heavy black skirts and stepped closer to the fireplace.

The mantels might seem to hold the most important items in any of these houses, and in this case that meant the most expensive. The most expensive things the residents were willing to have on public display, at least.

Mrs. Norwood kept her decor fresh and surprising, with something different out on every visit. It never occurred to Loretta that Roma might have done that to impress her with what she already owned.

The only thing that ever impressed her in her clients' houses was the payment and how quickly it moved into her hands. The current seemingly careless arrangement of gems and stones, including a precious dragon stone, red at the heart and blue around the faceted edges, made no impression. She'd seen the real treasure vault only a few weeks ago, during her last visit.

That generally took at least four deliveries, sometimes more, but the people eager to engage Loretta's services were always just as eager to share what they already had. The premise was to make sure she understood what sort of things they liked, and of course to make sure there was no duplication. She never had any doubt that these wealthy collectors were as excited to show off to her as to any other trusted guest. Quite likely more so.

Her quick eyes and quicker mind noted the color scheme in this public area of the house: warm violets, yellows, and tans. The Norwoods had carefully, if not consciously, reproduced that same palate in the most private room in the house, but they'd shifted the hues.

That room, hidden behind a massive bookshelf filled with real, and rare, books, was decorated in much deeper purples, golds, and browns. The lighting in that secure inner room was tasteful yet effective. Every single macabre curio was displayed to its best possible advantage.

On the wall opposite the fireplace, Loretta found another clue to the hidden desires of this most demure and socially acceptable couple. A huge shadowbox, larger than Loretta could have lifted by herself, was filled with perfectly lifelike insects, every one pierced through with a color-coordinated enameled pin.

Some of the specimens were too foreign and strange to have come from nearby, and Loretta wondered if some of them had come from far distant corners of Alterra. She wasn't the only one trading in such strange and exotic items, even if she was by far the most successful.

Loretta had the advantage of never being limited by her clients' desires or their imaginations. She was only empowered by them.

She was leaning closer to a display of what looked like pressed flowers and leaves, wondering if any were of more dubious origin, when she heard the study door open.

Loretta settled herself on the sofa, arranging her skirt and her features appropriately. Not too eager, not too concerned, and definitely not showing too much leg. Polite interest was far more effective than smug certainty, and flirting wouldn't get her anywhere with Mrs. Norwood. With some of her neighbors, certainly, but not here.

Loretta had to bite the inside of her cheek to keep that carefully distant expression when Mr. Olsen Norwood walked in.

Mr. Norwood, Director of the Post for all of Alterra, Loretta reminded herself. He was not overly tall or large or even overly bald or pompous-looking like so many Directors were. This man was past middle age and not trying to hide it, and everything about his appearance was decidedly average. Short gray hair, perfectly tailored pants and jacket, polished black shoes.

Everything except his eyes. Cold and green, Mr. Norwood's eyes bored right through to Loretta's soul.

Roma was again beaming, her hand on her husband's arm and an entirely natural flush on her cheeks. Loretta got to her feet as gracefully as she could.

"Ms. Loretta Schofield, I'd like you to meet my husband, Olsen Norwood."

"Mr. Norwood," she said, this time with a proper bow of her head. "I'm very pleased to meet you, sir."

"Please, dear lady, do have a seat." Mr. Norwood appeared to fuss over his wife, helping her arrange her voluminous skirts, but his gaze never left Loretta's. He sat across from both of them in a high-backed upholstered chair. "We've been so well pleased with your efforts on our behalf over the past few months. I thought it was high time I met such a talented procurer. I did not expect such a lovely young maiden as yourself."

This time, Loretta felt color rising in her own cheeks. She was nowhere near Roma Norwood's age, but she was hardly what anyone would call young. And maiden was not a term she or anyone else had applied to herself since she was barely out of play clothes.

"You are too kind, sir," she said. "I have a strong and loyal network of suppliers who range far and wide for my most valued clientele. Such as yourself."

Mrs. Norwood giggled at Loretta's words, but the only reaction her husband showed was the twitch of an eyebrow. Flattery wasn't gong to work with this one, and flirting with him in front of his wife would likely be disastrous.

"I'm certain that would be an interesting gathering," Mr. Norwood said before he finally focused on his wife. Roma took his blatant cue.

"Ms. Schofield, speaking of gatherings, we're having a sort of a party here in a few weeks' time," she said. "An after-hours affair, if you take my meaning. When I showed this most delightful addition to our collection to my husband, he was so pleased he suggested we invite you to join us."

She raised her hands, and the light of the fire caught the glass case. Loretta had been so focused on Mr. Norwood that she hadn't noticed the woman was carrying that hideous thing. He cleared his throat, regaining her full attention.

"I can promise you would make the acquaintance of a most interesting circle of friends," he said.

Those disquieting green eyes flashed back to Loretta, and she forced herself to look back without flinching. Nothing about this man put her in a social or relaxed mood. In fact, everything about him had her wanting to get out of here and never darken the door again, no matter how well and willingly he paid.

"Mr. and Mrs. Norwood, I certainly do appreciate the thought and the invitation." She bowed her head again as she got to her feet. "One thing about my endeavors is my clientele are generally eager to remain...unaware of each other. And I am duty and honor bound to respect their wishes. I'm sure you can appreciate how awkward it would be for those who were not in attendance at this party if I were to be recognized in a social situation."

Roma seemed disappointed, but her smile was sympathetic. She put the deformed hand gently on the display table in front of her and drew out a silvery beaded and embroidered purse.

Loretta turned back to Mr. Norwood, who was also standing. His smile was slight and not the least bit sympathetic. His eyes pinned her as effectively as those enameled insect pins. The light green even coordinated with the black of her garments.

"We all must run our businesses as we see fit, Ms. Schofield, of course," he said. "I do hope we'll be seeing you before too terribly much time has passed."

He held out his hand, and Loretta could think of nothing else to do but offer hers. His grip was strong, just on the edge of painful, but not as uncomfortable as his gaze.

"Indeed, sir," she said. "That would be my pleasure."

He stared at her until his wife finished fumbling in her purse, and Loretta remained frozen to the spot. When Roma spoke, her husband abruptly dropped Loretta's hand, turned on his heel, and strode out of the room.

"Thank you again, Loretta," she said. "I look forward to our next visit."

Loretta grasped the older woman's hands, mainly to hide the way her own were shaking.

"Thank you, Roma. I'll be watchful for your next treasure."

Loretta made her escape, walking as quickly across the huge porch and down the stairs as she dared. Once she was out of range of the windows, she increased her pace until she was almost running.

Nothing particularly sinister had happened back there, but every hard-won survival tactic and instinct was on full alert. She had no intention of ever darkening the door of that grand home as long as she lived.

That conviction lasted until Loretta was seated on the trolley and feeling calm enough to open her own black leather purse. She blinked, certain she had left her last payment in there by mistake. No, she remembered clearing out her purse the same way she always did before she headed out for a delivery.

Mrs. Norwood had given her more than twice her absurd asking price for that nasty piece of work, nearly three times the ritterns they'd agreed upon. With her husband sitting right there, it could not possibly have been an accident.

Loretta closed the bag, re-secured it in the folds of her skirts, and stared out at the rows of flowers passing her by. She'd taken a lot of difficult actions in her life, and made a lot of harder decisions.

The extreme generosity of Olsen and Roma Norwood had turned an obvious choice into a decidedly more complicated one.

Chapter 3

KARL JUMPED when a harsh buzzer sounded through the train. He'd gotten so far into pondering Andy's fears that he had no idea where he was. Almost everyone sitting around him in the first passenger car was quiet or downright grim. Hardly the usual ride through the country-side on an early Sunday evening. The only times he'd encountered groups who could be so somber or weary were heading out to the working-class neighborhoods of the Doer District back in Waldron's Gate.

The people who'd been talking or seeming to enjoy themselves left the train as the shudders and jolts of detaching rear cars rumbled under Karl's feet. Most were no doubt bound for the fishing village at the end of the public train line. Only a handful ever rode farther. The obvious reason was the restricted access leading out to Joffrey Columns, of course.

Karl knew there was another, deeper explanation, the same reason people who lived in Waldron's Gate hardly ever went to the Convenience. They both dealt with used up, discarded, often ruined things no one wanted to think about if they didn't have to.

The Convenience dealt with garbage. The Columns with minds.

A larger crowd than made sense for a remote fishing village walked under the Swan's Gate sign in the middle of the narrow wooden platform, heading toward those empty cars. Neither the villagers nor the train conductors would pay any attention to how those women, and a few men, seemed to disappear once they were away from the station every weekend.

Karl knew without asking that quite a few of them would be going to the other end of the train line, then taking the trolley out to the Convenience. Employees at either extreme of society often didn't have the energy or optimism for relationships, especially at the Columns. That didn't mean certain physical needs went away. Quite a few people worked at one place or the other—likely both—filling those needs.

The head conductor, her dark blue uniform accented with generous amounts of brass echoing Constable Law back in the Gate, strolled through the nearly empty car. Karl held his badge in his hand, but she recognized him and most of the rest. She nodded at them, only checking the identification of a few before closing the front door of the car behind her.

The much lighter train, now only the engine and this one silent compartment, jerked back into motion. Karl closed his eyes, relieved that only the last fifteen minutes of a nearly two-hour journey remained. He had no desire to watch the empty, marshy grassland passing by after so many trips over the years.

When Karl opened his eyes, the train was approaching the towering front wall of Joffrey Columns. The dark gray stones were easily three times Karl's height, broken only by a passage large enough for the steam locomotive to pass through. A metal strip circled the opening, the top black with soot from countless smokestacks. A heavy lattice gate made of the same metal stood to one side to allow passage.

On his first tour of the grounds before he'd ever taken the job, Karl had asked about that odd metal strip. It didn't anchor the swinging gate, and it didn't look thick enough to reinforce the stone blocks that were already wider than Karl's long arms. That was his first experience with asking one too many questions out here, a habit he still struggled with.

After a sharp reminder to not ask about things that did not concern him, Karl hadn't argued with the explanation of a solid steel floodgate hidden inside the top of the gate. The towers and massive pulleys at the very top that Karl decided not to ask about matched that story. The thing was no one had heard of a flood that high for hundreds of years.

Karl suspected those gates were built to be closed for other kinds of trouble, much worse than high water. No one he'd ever spoken to remembered them being closed for anything but safety drills.

The three-story brown stone building in front of Karl didn't quite block out the twisting brick columns in the distance when he stepped off the train. He'd never been out to that part of the Columns, where the worst of the patients lived. Human and otherwise. The nurses, orderlies, and flat-out hired muscle who worked out there mostly kept to themselves.

That was about what he'd expected when he took the job at eighteen: an escape from disappointment in himself and a life of abusing his body for not much pay. Getting the chance to use his mind had been a surprise, as was the odd sort of family he found when he left his first one behind.

Back then, Karl had enjoyed watching the giant platform turning the train around like an overgrown child's toy, pointing it back toward the real world. Now he only joined the silent group streaming through employee entrance, decidedly less grand and intimidating than the one the train would pass back through. Karl had to duck to fit through the wooden door, and unlike the main gate, no one bothered guarding this one from the outside. Karl had passed through a matching gate on the other side that morning.

A few people murmured to each other on the long walk down the blandest corridor in all the land. The walls and ceiling were narrow strips of dark wood that had never been varnished or even sanded, the floor pale stone worn into tracks by countless shuffling feet. No one bothered upgrading to even the oldest dim electrics, leaving dingy gas lamps decades past their prime.

Karl suspected no one wanted the exposure of bright light here.

The end of the line, for this hallway at least, went far past bright to blinding. A scarred and battered wooden desk sat below several painfully glaring electrics, a bored guard behind it. Karl also suspected the bright lights here were on purpose, and that the guard was paying far closer attention than anyone knew.

Five plain wooden doors took up the large wall behind the guard desk, each with a rotating circle in the middle. Green or red, depending upon whether someone was inside for the inspection phase of returning to such a lovely workplace.

"Nice visit?"

Karl blinked, surprised anybody had spoken to him. He usually stood in the line, followed directions, got searched, and went on his way. No one had ever asked him anything so seemingly innocent.

The guard, a young guy Karl had never seen before, even smiled. He did take Karl's badge and record the number in one notebook before he crossed it off of another.

"Sure, same as usual," Karl said. "Family, you know. I live out here for a reason."

"Same here," the guard said, nodding. "Sometimes I wonder if we have the right people on the inside. Go on through. Room three is open."

Karl nodded and walked over to the door with the green circle. The guard waiting inside the small room was an older man he recognized.

"Gilmore," Davis said. "You know the routine. Turn out your pockets and strip. Anything strange happen?"

"No, sir. No more than a typical visit with my family. Didn't take anything out or bring anything in."

He emptied his pockets: a ring stuffed with too many keys, his badge, and some spare coin. Karl got undressed as quickly as he could. He didn't love this part of the routine, but it was indeed routine.

"Arms out, turn in a circle."

Karl did, watching Davis shake out his clothes. He'd thought a few times about telling his parents he wouldn't be visiting anymore because this took way too long. Annoying as the inspection was, that would be a bigger lie than he was comfortable telling.

"Get dressed and back to your apartment," the guard said. "Bit restless in there all day. They're asking for people not on shift to stay out of the way."

KARL STEPPED into the far busier main corridor, wondering what could have happened since he'd left that morning. He saw more gray-uniformed people walking past in both directions than usual for early Sunday evening, and they all seemed more than little bit nervous. It wasn't a full lockdown. Those were rare enough to fade to rumors, but telling folks to stay in at all was hardly normal. Whatever had the guard anxious was hitting everyone.

Andy had asked him to keep an eye out. Well, this might just be a good time to look around if everyone was distracted. He walked until he should have turned to the left to go to the staff apartments.

Without a backward glance, he turned right toward the medical records offices instead.

Karl stood up tall and walked with a purpose, wanting to look like he had somewhere to be even in his street clothes. He was getting a bit tired and frustrated with his job lately, but he didn't want to get fired or demoted for snooping, either.

He saw lights through the windows of several office doors he passed, but thankfully the records office was dark. He looked over his shoulder to make sure the hall was empty, then tried the door. Locked.

Karl pulled out his ring full of brass keys out and sorted through them. A buddy of his, another escapee from an all-Builder family, worked in maintenance and supply. Just a few weeks ago, he'd given Karl what he claimed was a master key, a special one that would open nearly any door in the place.

George Wood had been trying to work out how to make one for weeks, though he never would say why. Karl hadn't believed a word of it, but he hadn't tossed the key. He slid it slowly into the lock, expecting the key to break or nothing at all to happen. After a little shifting, the lock turned.

"I'll be damned..."

Karl opened the door and slipped inside, turning the lock again. He was in here all the time turning in new patient files or getting information, but he'd never been all that interested in looking around. The only thing he really wanted to learn more about was housed elsewhere, in the experimental medicine wing. He'd never manage to sneak into there.

And he couldn't get Andy's worried eyes out of his mind.

He started one of the gas lamps away from the door, leaving it low so it wouldn't be obvious someone was in here. The electrics were far too bright. The skylights let in more light than he expected, so it didn't take much.

The vast room was full of wooden-and-brass cabinets as far as he could see, and every one of them had several thick brown folders stacked on top. The whole thing was an overwhelming mess—one Karl had no idea how to start digging into for answers.

The huge number of new cases a couple of weeks ago that drove everyone to exhaustion could work in his favor. If the towering piles on every cabinet were any indication, this office was as short-staffed as Karl's nursing department.

He walked deeper into the huge office, lighting lamps as he went until he got closer to the windows. The sunset was still an hour or so away, and plenty of light was streaming through. Even with that, Karl couldn't get a handle on how things were supposed to be organized. Some of the labels seemed to be alphabetical, but the system started over again and again. He finally saw the cards tucked into brass holders on the cabinets at the end of each aisle.

They were organized by what was wrong with the new admissions, then alphabetically. Karl frowned, wondering if they possibly had that many patients to organize. He hardly ever went outside his own section, so this huge number he was unfamiliar with was entirely possible.

Karl kept walking, still not sure what he was looking for. He found sections for the people he usually cared for. Mania. Hysteria. Obsessive disorders. He knew what those were and exactly which of his patients suffered from each. Without more to go on, he'd never find anything.

His broad shoulders brushed against the stack of folders on top of the end cabinet for depth syndrome, the insanity that struck Builders who lost the way back to reality after getting too far into their work. Karl barely managed to keep the whole stack from falling over and going everywhere. Several of the folders did land at his feet, thankfully without spilling their contents. He picked them up, glancing at their covers.

"Hang on a minute..."

None of them had the same name, so these weren't just spillover storage. Karl pulled another stack down without seeing any kind of pattern. He was normally great at that if nothing else, spotting a pattern where no one else could see it. These patients had nothing at all in common. Unless...

Karl flipped through the folders again, this time looking at the dates of admission. That was it. These were new patient folders, in order by nothing more than those dates. And unless he was misunderstanding a strong hunch growing in his belly, he was looking at the big surge he'd noticed over the past few weeks. The same surge Andy had spotted.

He grabbed a few more folders and carried them to a long table by the window already overflowing with paperwork. Once they were laid out where he could see them all, another of Karl's talents he didn't give himself credit for kicked in. His memory was beyond good; it was as extraordinary as any Builder's. He recognized several family names he'd known all his life, and a few of the individuals.

Andy was right. Out of almost twenty new patients in a couple of weeks, more than half were from their neighborhood.

Karl got though the stack to the bottom before he realized he'd been straining to read the last couple. The sun had nearly set. He'd been digging through the files for over an hour. Cold sweat broke out all over his body at the thought of a watchman or someone on the cleaning crew walking in and catching him with confidential folders scattered everywhere.

Even worse, there was no rule at all to stop a new admission from coming in at any time during the day or night. If a Director walked in instead, Karl might be on the next train back to Waldron's Gate for a permanent stay.

He managed to get everything stacked up in the same order he'd found it, and remarkably close to the same twisted and tilted arrangement. He thought about grabbing a few pieces of paper so he could write down the names, but that seemed as bad an idea as hanging around here long enough to do it.

Better to just trust he'd remember the names when he needed to than to get caught with the lists. He doused the lamps one at a time behind him as he walked back out.

Karl stepped out into an empty hall, but he could still hear people hurrying around close by. He shook his head, not sure what had possessed him to do such a crazy thing to begin with. Almost as crazy as his patients.

That curiosity, the same thing that had gotten him in trouble as a kid and scolded as a green orderly, had apparently followed him into adulthood. That was all well and good until it got him fired. It was far past time to make himself scarce tonight.

If nothing else, he couldn't even ask questions if he ran into anybody. They'd just ask why he was wandering around the administration building if he wasn't supposed to be here.

He knew exactly who would gossip and who wouldn't on his shift in the patient residential areas and treatment rooms. Tomorrow would be soon enough to find out more. Especially if it meant keeping his job.

Chapter 4

Loretta paced back and forth in her study, turning her head with every turn of her body so she never looked away from her wall. Several lamps were on full brightness, and she knew the map better than she knew her own face.

Still she paced.

Maybe she was worried about going out into the night again, into the risky business of Building. Maybe this was part of her routine, what she needed to get herself and her nerves steeled. Maybe she was just giving her own excitement and anticipation the chance to get to a delirious fever pitch.

The only thing she truly still needed was full dark.

The map of the Builders' neighborhoods in Waldron's Gate was the largest she'd been able to find in any of the shops in town, nearly five feet to a side. She'd often wished for something a bit bigger, though this did serve her purposes quite nicely. Several colored pins and matching lengths of thread decorated the otherwise plain map, spiraling out from individual houses.

Loretta didn't need such a visual representation of her nocturnal adventures, but it pleased her greatly to have it.

A false wall with a boring but flawlessly executed painting was pushed back behind the bookshelves to her right, all the traps and warning devices disabled. She'd never had to put any of them to use since no one had ever entered her study. Again, she was pleased and reassured to have them.

Right now she was not reassured by the amount of time she had available to her. So many Builds, so little time.

She normally worked on Builds for at least a month, often longer if she had as many requests as she did right now. Her encounter with Olsen Norwood kept her uneasy in her bones. None of her other clients or anyone else acted strangely, but that didn't lessen Loretta's sense of danger all around her and her need to complete these Builds as quickly as possible.

She finally walked over to the map and touched the only pin with no thread yet attached to it, the head a rich, dark green. So far, she'd matched the pin to the main paint color of the first house in her circuit. That match was not always an easy thing with such elaborate decorating styles all the rage over the past few years. Sometimes it was simply a matter of picking the one she liked best out of half a dozen choices.

Loretta knew the Labine household well, as she did all of her best repeat customers. Her last visit had moved the resident Builder squarely onto the top of Loretta's target list. Mr. Labine, a clothier to many of the wealthiest families in Waldron's Gate, had finally trusted her enough to let her see their entire stomach-turning collection. Far too many of the items were unfamiliar to her. Even Loretta didn't want to speculate about how many of them may have been genuine.

What caught Loretta's attention was the private chamber's location right across the hall from the master bedroom, where she now knew the lady of the house slept every night. Mrs. Labine happened to be a high-ranking and well-respected Builder. She'd even confirmed Loretta's decision by helping her husband with the detailed description of the next curio they were seeking. The woman's strange wishes and desires would further Loretta's own ambitions. She'd sunk the green pin into her map that very night.

With one last glance at the street names surrounding her target, more to calm her nerves than to set it in her mind, Loretta closed the fake wall and reset the security devices. She turned to make one last check over her tools and supplies. She was already wearing her most critical disguise, a solid black leather garment that fit her tightly as any glove, as scandalous in that tight fit as in being formed into pants instead of a skirt.

The hide was nearly as soft as Loretta's own skin, so it wouldn't creak as she moved. The skinsuit was well reinforced with bone and steel where it counted. Her long, curly black hair was tightly braided and pulled into a low bun. She opened the matching black bag she would carry across her back even though she knew everything was inside.

The most important thing, her Dragon, was safe in a fitted case, with her gyro-compass tucked inside. Another small case held her headgear, matte black like everything else. A map she never needed and a large flask filled with cold water were the only other items.

Her clothing held pockets for all the weapons she could comfortably carry, though she'd never needed any on her Building nights: knives, a garrote, hypodermics, and a leaded club.

Her specially made tripod, expandable to taller than she herself stood, designed to be silent and nearly invisible with the wood and brass painted black, was folded into a cane.

Nerves worked off and appetite worked up, Loretta was ready.

Her most trusted guard was the only one allowed on duty on Build nights. Bess knew better than to ask too many questions. Her loyalty was unquestioned, and so was her participation. She was already hidden away in the secret compartment on the porch when Loretta locked her front door, held up one hand in silent thanks to the guard, and stepped out into the darkness.

LORETTA WALKED SLOWLY, confident she would be alone, but alert to anyone else out and about. Her eager mind switched from remembering which turns to make to running down the list of the night's Builds.

Loretta hadn't attempted the full nine her table could accommodate for a few months now. Losing a reliable Builder to insanity and

Joffrey Columns had been more of an inconvenience than she would have imagined.

Her inner unrest drove her to take the risk, and to risk her new Builder's mind.

Her breathing was quick by the time she reached the house, the dark green of the roof, shutters, and scroll work looking as black as her clothing in the dim gaslight. Neither exertion nor anxiety quickened her lungs, but anticipation had. Keeping herself calm for the first Build after a long time away from it was always a pleasurable challenge.

She walked around the grand three-story house in a slow circle, watchful for any movement or lights within or without. Seeing, and sensing, nothing, Loretta stopped just below the bedroom window.

She slipped a brass catch free, and the three legs of the tripod separated. Loretta pushed them solidly into the ground before she raised the pivot to what she was certain from long practice would be the right height. With everything locked into place, she shrugged out of the pack and set it carefully on the ground. The Dragon was first, fitted against the tripod. She'd wondered why it had two bell ends unlike the massive Blunderbuss, but not enough to ask her wild Tinker grandmother.

Her version was infinitely more pleasing to look upon, with symmetry and balance to match the sleek black. She snapped the gyro-compass onto the middle like a sighting scope on a rifle. One bell end swung slowly toward the giant magnet of her house. This gross adjustment Loretta allowed without intervention. Mental fine tuning to the spaces on her goal—an intricate metal table hidden in her basement— would come soon enough.

As one end of the Dragon found her house, the other targeted the window above her. The Builder's strange power drew the Dragon as surely as her house did. When the motion stopped, she pulled out her headgear. The thin straps of soft leather fit her skull perfectly. Nearly invisible wires through and around the straps caught the faint moonlight.

From tales she'd heard of how the Blunderbuss worked, this was essentially one of their cradles made small enough to wear. Her grandmother had never said such a thing, but her words were often strange and unreliable. As long as her devices worked, Loretta had little concern over why.

With the black cable fitted into the Dragon, Loretta lifted the cap to her head. She breathed deeply, calming her racing mind and heart. Satisfaction, much needed and long overdue, would only come if she could focus. By the time Loretta felt the pull of the Dragon, her heart beat slowly.

Small puffs of white smoke rose from both ends of the device, the only thing she hadn't been able to adjust to suit her need for near-invisibility. Thankfully the mist was light enough to dissipate only a few feet above Loretta's head.

She'd often wondered if Builders felt this same tingling anticipation warring with calm as they settled in their cradles, preparing to Build with the towering Blunderbuss instead of her tiny Dragon, barely the length of her arm. Somehow she doubted it was the same.

Working as a group with the Blunderbuss did not require such risks and thrills, nor did it offer the seductive tingle of theft.

Loretta knelt on the ground, settling against her leather shoes. Not as stylish or big enough to hold knives like her boots, the flats were silent and far more comfortable for a long night's work. She took a deep breath and closed her eyes.

As she always did at this moment, she spared a thought for her grandmother, Gemma, vowing to send coin from these Builds for her upkeep and safety. That was a vow she never failed to keep.

The horrid object the Labines were going to pay her very well for, a necklace made of toes, swam before her mind's eye. She turned the thing, looking at details, locking it into the unemotional center of her focus. Loretta pushed, reaching out to the sleeping mind she needed in order to Build.

With a rush of power that made her lightheaded, she made contact. Knowing the Dragon made the actual connection didn't change the sensation. Loretta held the thing up in her mind, moving it forward a millimeter at a time. This time she felt the secure click of a well-made lock striking home.

The image in her mind, while still unpleasant, was no longer faint and hard to hold. Now she felt as if she could reach out and touch it as the Builder's talent took over. Each small toenail, each tiny wrinkle and hair, each half-decayed fold of dead flesh grew vivid and sharp. The necklace itself started to change, and Loretta watched instead of interfering.

That was one of the advantages of working with the Builder who made the request. The Builder knew what she wanted more than she could ever had explained in words. The rough twine cord shifted to a silver chain, and the order of the toes rearranged themselves until they went from largest to smallest, all the way to examples that had to be fetal beside the clasp. When the changes stopped, Loretta shifted her push.

Now she saw the necklace settling on the far edge of her target table, in the space she thought of as One. She saw it exactly as the sleeping Builder had just specified, down to the dirt under the largest nails, coiled up in the circle. Loretta slipped into the only role she could play in a Build.

Conduit.

The Dragon drew from the Builder, the Dragon sent through Loretta, the Dragon aimed for the table. The energy and movement flowed through her like the frightening amounts of electricity her grandmother commanded at will.

Every part of her—her heartbeat, her thoughts, her breathing, the very blood in her veins—moved to the rush and rhythm of that circuit.

The shift hit her as a physical change, the tipping point between pleasure and release. Loretta had no need to double check, to make sure the Build was complete. She felt the manifestation from Builder to Dragon to reality, passing through her in an almost painfully exhilarating burst.

Careful not to let the connection drop, Loretta slowed the energy from the Builder. This woman was powerful, nearly as strong as the one she'd lost to Joffrey Columns months before. The nine builds tonight should be no problem.

She would have to move on to another house tomorrow night to be certain Mrs. Labine didn't get pushed over the edge into burnout and insanity. Losing a strong Builder she was comfortable with and having to find a new one took far too much time and effort.

She had no time to bask in the afterglow of creation, not tonight. The next object floated into Loretta's mind, a gynecological horror greatly desired by the respectable couple three doors down.

In some cases, this was harder since she had to keep the Builder focused and not allow changes. Most of the time, though, they were cooperative with things they didn't want themselves. The main difference was Loretta's focus on space number Two on her table.

She wondered sometimes if the things she forced them to Build ever showed up behind their sleeping eyes, even though she knew she was likely the only person in all of Waldron's Gate who didn't take Crumble. She might be the only one who *could* dream.

Hours later but with dawn not yet breaking, Loretta opened her eyes. The house in front of her was still dark, as was everything else around her. Nine dreadful objects waited in her basement, the closest possible match to their future owners' dark desires. The deliveries, and the payments, would wait for another day.

Loretta packed up her tools and stood, stretching her back and arms. The cool night air settled into her bones more than it used to as she got into her thirties. She might have to procure a coat or cushion of some kind to protect her from the damp chill.

The Builds had been good; she could feel it. On the rare occasion when the Builder had awakened or had simply not been strong enough, or perhaps had missed a dose of Crumble, Loretta felt the failure right away.

Everything could not have gone more smoothly tonight. With any luck, tomorrow's Builder would be as powerful and easy to manipulate. Once she'd cleared her table and prepared herself, another nine Builds awaited.

Loretta turned toward home and her own uninvaded sleep.

Chapter 5

THE NEXT DAY was so hectic that Karl barely had time to breathe, much less ask around about all those new admissions. The overwhelming workload forced him to rush eleven raw trainees through their orientation in record time. His guilt at that sank deeper into his gut when they followed him on rounds later that morning. After watching their frightened expressions as they dealt with dozens of terribly distressed patients, he expected fully half of them to quit that afternoon. At least no one seemed to know he'd been snooping around looking at records the night before.

The only sense he could make of what people muttered as they struggled to keep up was that something strange had happened yesterday. He was still too nervous about all his sneaking around to ask more.

Whatever the disruption was had managed to filter through the entire facility, as things like that seemed to do. Karl couldn't figure out how doctors, staff, and patients in this building could possibly know what had happened several buildings away, but they did. His whole day was spent trying to keep his confused recruits from panicking, help the doctors keep patients and other staff calm, and clean up the mess when all of that failed.

By the time he took a very late lunch, it was all Karl could do to put one foot in front of the other in the food line. To top everything off and make a stressful day worse, the mechanical food conveyors had broken down. A fractured copper steam pipe filled the whole cafeteria with heavy, damp air, but the queue was too long to let the mechanics shut everything down to try to fix it.

A group of sweaty, sullen low-level orderlies had been recruited to serve as a human conveyor belt. Karl kept his head down, took his food without looking to see what it was, and plodded toward an empty table.

He was staring at his chipped white plate, wondering if the grayish gravy-covered thing in the middle was more meat or mystery, when another wooden tray slammed down beside his. George Wood fell into the chair beside Karl's hard enough to make the legs creak. He didn't say a word, just took off his round glasses and sat with his head in his hands.

George was a contrast to Karl in nearly every way. Short and round where Karl was tall and angular, charming and funny where Karl was serious and too often shy. The close friendship they'd found growing up together back on Lilac Row helped keep Karl going.

"Tough day, Georgie?"

"You have no idea." George ran his fingers through his messy brown hair, but he didn't open his eyes. "Does that look as bad as it smells?"

"I don't even know what it *is* today," Karl said. "If this was ever alive, it was a long, long time ago."

"Yeah, they're having trouble in the kitchens too, not just out here." George finally looked at his plate with a matching slab of something right in the middle. His mouth turned down, and he closed his eyes again. "I could throw a rock and hit the lake where they get fish. Fresh off the docks every day. Meat can't be more than an hour or so older. And somehow, they turn it into this. The sad thing is I'm so bloody hungry I'm going to eat it anyway."

The two men ate in silence, and Karl was relieved that the most offensive thing about the gray blob was a lack of any sort of discernible flavor. He thought he might regret eating whatever it was in a few hours, but for now it filled his middle.

"What's going on around here, anyway?" Karl said. "I was out all day visiting the family yesterday."

"You must have left before word got around," George said. "One of the monsters got out night before last. A bad one. Did a lot of damage before they finally got it under control again."

"Aren't the 'sters supposed to be restrained? Or at least locked down?"

"Supposed to be, yeah," George said. "If you can answer the question of how this one managed to make such a mess, you'll be Director of that wing in a week's time. I hear the job will be open after this little disaster. They nearly had to kill it."

Karl stared at George, not sure what to think, much less say. The 'sters out here were a secret so well kept that he hardly knew anything about them. He did know they were bad news. Having to kill one of them would be a mess big enough to get any Director shown the door.

"I've never even seen one of them. Have you, Georgie?"

George's dark brown eyes stared at something Karl wasn't sure he wanted to imagine. Those eyes were sunken and bruised-looking with exhaustion, more than Karl had ever seen.

"A few times," he said. "Most of the time when I was supposed to. The other night when I wasn't. I wish I'd been back at the Gate with you, even if that meant visiting my own family."

"Do you know where they really come from?" Karl whispered. He didn't want to upset his friend, but he was in the grips of that terrible curiosity once again. "I've heard everything from the Fog to caves to some kind of Build gone wrong."

"Not quite that dramatic," George said. "Though they wouldn't be such a big secret if any of that were true. Listen, I know we've been friends for a long time. I'm not supposed to know any of this, much less tell you or anyone else. It'd be the sack or worse for both of us if someone found out."

Karl did think about it, or at least he tried to. He was right up against one of the most important things about working at the Columns. You didn't ask, you didn't tell, and you did your level best not to remember. That had been drilled into him since he met with the first recruiter, after he got the job, and at every evaluation or promotion meeting ever since. He'd told his new trainees the same a few long hours ago.

Keep your mind on your job while you're at work, then forget it. All of it. The less you know, the better your chance of keeping your job instead of getting a lifetime pass to join the residents on the other side of the restraints.

Not telling was usually easy for Karl, and forgetting was too, at first. Not so much lately.

Not asking had been the toughest thing for him since day one.

GEORGE STILL HESITATED, and Karl had a childish certainty he wasn't going to let him in on the secret after all. Knowing it was childish didn't stop him from reacting.

"I understand, George. I'm not going to say a word to anyone. I found a couple of strange things myself yesterday. All about our old neighborhood. Maybe we can help each other."

George blinked and sat back in his chair.

"I don't know that more secrets to keep would actually help me out, Karl. I have to admit I'm curious, though." He sighed, then leaned closer and lowered his voice. "The 'sters aren't found or captured or made, not the way you're thinking. They're birthed. Just like you and me."

"Horseshit," Karl said before he could stop himself. "I'm sorry. I didn't mean to sound..."

"That's exactly what I said when I first heard it myself. But that's exactly what happens, always has. You've heard about the things in the Fog, right? The things we're not supposed to know about?"

"Well, yeah," Karl said. "I heard before I was out of short pants. That's a little different than whatever you're saying. Do you mean they're born, like from a woman?"

"No, not like that. Sorry, man." George shook his head, scowling at the same time, but his face was turning red. "I'm out of my depth here a little bit, but I don't think they come out quite that way. What I've heard is they have a special birthing room for the 'sters. That could all be rumors though, and no one is likely to admit the truth to the likes of us anytime soon."

Karl was surprised and a little relieved that his friend had said a little more than he knew. He was glad to know he wasn't the only one. Gaps in his friend's knowledge or not, this was way too big a mystery to pass up.

"What do they look like?" Karl said. "The ones you've seen?"

The flush in George's face faded until he was paler than before.

"I've only seen a few," George said. "All different. They look like walking nightmares. Not a nightmare I'd ever want to have. The worst part, though, is there's always something human about them, Karl. Something twisted and sick and broken, but human."

"But how do they look?" Karl said. "That one last night. What did you see?"

George stared out the window at the spiraling brick towers that stretched as far as the eye could see. Karl knew whole floors of those towers were full of 'sters, but he'd never seen one. George didn't turn back to Karl when he finally spoke.

"That one was like candle wax," George said. "That's the best I can do. Not solid, not like a candle that could stand up. It was red like blood, but it moved, like it was trying to fall apart the whole time. You know those aspics our mothers are forever shoving down our throats, the things that make the food here taste fantastic by comparison?"

Karl nodded, afraid to try to speak. If he said the wrong thing, George might stop.

If he said the wrong thing, George might *keep* talking.

"It looked like one of those that was halfway melted, you know?" George said. "It moved, sort of lurched around, but there was nothing solid about it. Except for one thing." George rubbed his face before he looked into Karl's eyes. "It had a perfect mouth, Karl. Perfect, like a woman's mouth that couldn't stop screaming. The sound was closer to water screaming than to any woman, but it couldn't stop."

"Did it..." Karl stopped and took a deep breath, not wanting to revisit the cool gray lunch he'd forced down. "You said it did damage."

"Oh yeah, that's the best part," George said. "This one didn't just scream and scare everyone. Whoever it touched, at least when it touched bare skin, they started screaming too. Whatever that cne's made of takes skin off, right down to the meat. It just disappears in the perfect shape of how it touches them."

George pushed his own tray away, his face nearly as gray as the splatters of gravy. He swallowed and kept talking.

"I saw a bunch of the people who first tried to stop it before they figured that part out. Whole hands with no skin, a few forearms. A few people had it on their stomachs or backs or legs where their clothes raked up when they tried to grab it. The worst ones, the ones I really wish I didn't see, those were the faces. One woman's whole face, not a scrap of eyebrows or lashes or anything else left. Just her eyes."

KARL WAS SWALLOWING CONVULSIVELY NOW, desperate not to lose that dreadful lunch in front of his friend. He was a nurse in a bloody insane asylum. Things he'd seen people do to themselves and others were surely worse than this. And the things he'd seen doctors do to some of the patients—that was definitely worse.

But he couldn't get the image of the woman's eyes, rolling and bare in a mask of raw flesh, out of his mind.

"How did they stop it?" Karl said.

"That's how I saw the thing," George said. "And I still wish I hadn't. Some of the night shift docs wanted to throw a bunch of blankets on it and knock it down, but the Director was afraid that would kill her. It, kill it. In case it dissolved or something. It seemed plenty solid when it broke through a few doors to get out into the hall, but what do I know? So a few of us had to volunteer. You know how we're encouraged to volunteer around here. We had to put on heavy coats and tuck in everything we could, and we just grabbed it. Once the Director was convinced our arms wouldn't go all the way through, they put a big cloth around it. We all dragged it back to a new cell. I hope they threw away the damned key."

"Merciful Crown," Karl whispered.

He clapped his hand over his mouth, horrified at what had just come out of it. He sounded like his grandmother. George shook his head, but he didn't look upset.

"No, don't feel bad," George said. "You'd be amazed just how many people were saying a lot more than that. The thing certainly looked like it came straight from The Pit. The loudest and most elaborate calls for mercy didn't seem to help any of them a damned bit. I'll tell you the worst part, even worse than that poor woman. I wish they'd told us to block up our ears. I haven't stopped hearing the way she screamed. The way *it* screamed, I mean, especially after we got hold of it. I'm afraid that sound did something to my brain as bad as what happened to people's skin."

Karl couldn't argue with that even if he'd wanted to. That was the worst part of the experimental medicine wing, part of his rounds after his latest promotion. The part he'd never take new recruits along for. Even with the supposedly soundproofed doors, the screams came right though.

"I'm sorry, Georgie. I didn't mean to drag all that up."

George shrugged. "Eh, I guess I need to talk to someone about it, and everyone else who wasn't there would want me strapped in a jacket for even trying to explain it. I just hope I never see another one of those things. But I know..." Karl waiting, holding his breath. He wasn't sure he wanted to know. "I know with as many monsters as we have here, there probably are worse ones all around us."

"Are they okay?" Karl said. "The ones who got hurt, I mean?"

"Too soon to tell, I guess," George said. "I don't want to imagine how much worse it would have been if that thing got out during the day. They're doing everything they can, but regrowing skin is never going to be an easy thing, is it?"

He glanced around and leaned closer to Karl again. "What I was up the rest of the night wondering is how much is it true that what goes around comes around? I mean, if these 'sters are linked to whoever made them, did that person have some kind of breakdown and that made the thing go nuts? Or did the thing going nuts have an effect on the person walking around out there like nothing could ever go wrong?"

"Is that why we're not supposed to kill the things?" Karl said.

"That's what I've heard," George said. "The way the Director was freaking out once she came on shift yesterday didn't give me any reason to think otherwise. My first thought was definitely to kill the thing, if nothing else to put it out of its misery."

Karl shivered, sure he wasn't hiding it very well. "If they're matched up, shouldn't we warn whoever it is? Out in the Gate?"

"I don't know if they are or not, but if they're not, refusing to kill it doesn't make a whole lot of sense. Certainly not if you heard..."

George jerked his chin at something over Karl's shoulder, and Karl turned to see the lanky, bearded lead mechanic walking toward them.

"Hate to break it up over here," Tommy said. "But we gotta fix that damned leak sometime today. It's gonna get a lot worse in here before it gets better. The way things are going, you might want to head out in case something blows up."

"Sure thing. Thanks, Tommy." George nodded at the mechanic, then picked up his tray. "Listen, Karl, if you want to tell me about whatever you found, I'm ready to listen. Nothing about yesterday made me a more loyal employee of our fine Columns here."

Karl grabbed his own tray and followed George.

"Want to meet me after dinner?" Karl said. "The commons in my building is usually deserted by about nine unless there's a critically important card game going on."

"Make it tomorrow night, and you've got a deal. I have to at least try to get some sleep tonight or they'll have to lock me up in here."

Chapter 6

The next day was a lot calmer, but a full day with his nine remaining trainees left Karl wearier than ever by the time he escaped to the commons area between the residential wings to wait for George.

Even more than his own meager apartment, Karl was glad his mother had never seen these rooms. The scuffed and dull hardwood floors were clean enough, with sanitation crews sweeping through every few days same as in the rest of the non-patient buildings. The fireplace in each adjoining room brought a much-needed coziness even if the tools and fittings were sturdy black steel rather than his family's gleaming brass.

But the most careful cleaning wouldn't hide the sofas hopelessly out of fashion. The scratchy fabric and shapeless design were never the highest quality to start with. Karl suspected the heavy wooden tables and chairs scattered around for card games or quick meals were older than he was.

The best thing about this shared space, about any of the spaces where he'd spent the last decade of his life, was the books. Each room in the commons had at least one wall covered with shelves full of dozens of well-worn volumes in a dizzying array of subjects.

The fact that the collection had no discernible pattern of arrangement or age made browsing for something to read even more satisfying. A brand new pulpy fiction title next to a fifteen-year-old anatomy text next to an ancient history of Alterra kept Karl's curiosity fairly under control.

The books weren't going to do a damned thing for him tonight, though. His mind had been relentless, churning and twisting and rearranging the things he knew so far. He had a dull headache and a grumpier than usual mood to go along with his worries about keeping everything secret.

Deep down inside, though, a part of Karl that had been dulled and bored to tears was wide awake. That part could not possibly have been happier with the way things were going.

"Behind you!" someone said right beside his ear.

Karl jerked back upright nearly fast enough to dump himself onto the floor. George wasn't quite smiling, but he looked less gloomy and exhausted than the day before.

"That was hardly necessary," Karl said, rubbing his face and wishing it weren't way too late for cafei.

"Not my fault. You were sleeping too hard to resist. Want to do this another night?"

Karl shook his head and looked around. No one else was in the room or in any of the other rooms he could see and hear through the arched doorways. They might have to wait a while to get this chance again.

"Now is good," he said. "I couldn't sleep last night wondering about all of this. Someone else to listen and tell me if I'm crazy or not might help."

"I might not be the best judge of that lately." George sat on the low brown sofa next to Karl with a loud sigh. "But I'll do my best. Anything strange happen today?"

"Not today, no stranger than usual," Karl said. "Patients on my rounds seem to be a lot calmer. Staff, too. Yours?"

"Sure, they always settle down pretty fast after this happens," George said. "Patients and 'sters both."

"Wait, how often does this happen, George? I probably just never got out and about at the right time before, but I'm sure I would have heard about something like a 'ster going crazy before now."

George shook his head slowly. "Not necessarily, buddy. Unless it happened in your building or on your shift, I doubt it. You work the day shift, and the bad shit always seems to happen at night. That's one of the many things the Directors work very hard to keep from getting out. How well would you sleep if you knew something like that could break down your door in the night?"

"My door? There aren't any 'sters in my building, at least I don't think so. How do you know about all of this, George?"

GEORGE GLANCED AT KARL, one thick eyebrow raised. Instead of answering right away, he got up and walked over to the fireplace. He took an unreasonably long time stirring and adjusting the coals. After a dramatic inspection of the waist-high pile of logs, he finally tossed two of them onto the fire. He spoke without turning.

"That's one thing about all us buzzards in maintenance and supply, one of the few good things. We don't get paid much, and the benefits ain't great. But we probably know more about what goes on around this place than all the Directors put together." He sat beside Karl again. "And I don't think there are any 'sters over here, no. Most of them are kept separate from patients, out in the older Columns."

Karl knew he was as out of line as Andy asking him about new admissions, probably even more. He asked anyway.

"If you know so much," he said, "tell me how often that happens? One of them losing it, I mean?"

George shrugged, shaking his head.

"I wouldn't say I know every time, but pretty close," he said. "Word does get around. They get restless every month or so, sometimes more often, sometimes less. But I only hear about one of them losing it about once a year. To tell you the truth, it had been a while since the last time, though. Probably a couple of years."

"One of those damned things gets out once a year? How the hell do they keep that much a secret?"

"I'd guess that's one reason we're encouraged to keep to our own buildings," George said. "And why most of us don't transfer. Once we're here, we're here. Not that much different than the patients o∼ the 'sters, really. Now, to prove I'm crazier than anyone we have locked up out here, tell me what you found out the other day."

"No crazier than I am, Georgie," Karl said. "Remember tha∼ big bunch of new admissions a few weeks ago? When we had to hire new people to deal with it all? I used your fancy master key and took a look around in the records room when everyone was in such an uproar and not paying attention. Turns out a whole bunch of them are from our old neighborhood. More than half."

George scowled. "Well, I'm glad to hear that key works for someone besides me, but why would you even do that? If you get caught in there, you're out on your ass in a heartbeat."

He didn't say it, but Karl knew what he was thinking. And if they asked you hard enough, you'd eventually tell them I gave you the key in the first place.

"I'm not gonna rat anyone out," Karl said. "Don't worry. It was my... A friend of mine from home." Karl was a little shocked at how close he'd come to being the rat himself, and with his own brother. "He noticed how many locals were coming down with death syndrome all at once, asked me to look into it. He was right."

"How many?"

"More than half of that twenty," Karl said. "That can't be any kind of accident. And it's way too close to home for both of us."

"You have a point there," George said. He leaned forward with his elbows on his knees. "I might not plan to ever spend a second longer there than I have to, but I want them to be safe. Most of them, anyway. What else did you see?"

"I haven't seen anything else yet, but I know I'm missing something. You say the 'sters getting restless is every few weeks, and my friend noticed a bunch of new people getting hauled out here a few weeks ago. What if they're related?"

"I don't..." George looked at him, scowling. "Well, I hadn't thought about it, but you could be right, Karl. Even if it's not something we can stop, maybe we can at least let people know. I don't know who would possibly believe the likes of us, but it might be worth a try."

"You said they do everything they can to keep trouble with the 'sters a secret," Karl said. "Do you think there's any record we could look at? Something like the admissions records I found?"

George opened his mouth, then closed it in a frown.

"Not anything official," he said, "not that either of us could get hold of even with a master key. But when one of these things really blows its top, assuming it has a top, shit's gonna get broken. I'd bet there are records of the repairs and replacements somewhere. Infirmary records might help, but that's probably harder to get to. One thing I don't have to go looking for. That bunch of new patients you were talking about a few weeks ago?"

"Yeah?"

"They didn't just hire new nurses to deal with that," George said. "Our workload was crazy then, too, and not only from making sure new beds were ready. We had a bunch more repairs and replacements, way more than we could keep up with. Most of them out where the 'sters are, Karl."

Karl tried to force himself to slow down, but his brain was running away with him. The last thing he needed was to freak out or just annoy one of the few people he could talk to, but he was certain they were about to stumble onto something huge. He didn't quite know what it could be yet, and that long-numb part didn't care.

"I'd just about promise that won't be the only time this all matches up," Karl said. "I think I can get back into admissions, probably early in the morning. I'll just see when those jumps seem to happen. When can you get a look at the supply records?"

George shook his head, but he was smiling. "Tomorrow. I'm one of the saps who has to make sure we're ordering what we need. Not nearly the honor my boss seems to think it is, especially when I have to help haul a few boatloads of it in from the docks or off a supply train. But it might come in handy for once. You sure you want to get into this mess? It might be a one-way ticket into a lot more trouble than losing our jobs."

Karl closed his eyes, trying his best to put that whirling, ravenous part of his brain aside for at least a few seconds. Why had he gotten into all of this to start with, once he put aside his own desire to finally do something that mattered?

Andy was generally a levelheaded kid, way better at dealing with family dynamics at his age than Karl was at nearly thirty. He didn't get worried over nothing. That fear had been real, and finding out there might actually be something to it did nothing to discourage Karl.

"I'm sure, George. I'm not even going to pretend the chance to do something different, something interesting, for a change isn't part of it. And I doubt I could forget all about it now. Could you?"

"No, I couldn't," George said. "Whatever made that 'ster in the first place was bad enough, but what it did the other day was too much for me. I don't want to see anything like that again as long as I have a marble or two left rattling around."

Chapter 7

Karl jumped when someone touched his shoulder at lunch the next day, barely managing to keep from dropping his food. It still wasn't spectacular, but more than the mechanical conveyor seemed to be working better in the cafeteria.

"Mind if I join you for a minute?" George said.

"Sure thing, Georgie. Over here by the window again?"

"Works for me."

George's own tray held only empty plates, but he carried it to the table anyway. Karl couldn't remember his old friend looking so lively for a long time. He looked almost as excited as Karl felt.

"So, how'd your morning go?" George was smiling, but he raised both dark eyebrows and glanced from side to side.

"I...uh..." Karl said, scrambling to follow his friend's lead. "I think a pattern is becoming clear, a lot more than I thought it would. I may be onto something. You?"

George nodded. "The same old thing just keeps happening over and over again. Seems like it's been going on for a few years now."

Karl lowered his voice and leaned in.

"Any reason for the codes?"

"I don't know, maybe," George said. "I need to do a little overtime tonight, starting around seven. Think you can get free to go with me?"

"Yeah, sure. Where?"

"Meet me at your commons. What I need to work on is in your building, as a matter of fact." George grabbed his tray and stood, and he actually winked at Karl. "See you then."

The rest of the day was a blur to Karl, his mind focused on what could have possibly been so exciting that George wanted to meet him early. He barely paid attention to what he was doing until nearly time to clock out and get ready.

His next to last patient was a woman who hadn't been there long. The first thing to interrupt the whirlwind of Karl's thoughts was realizing she'd come in with the big group that started all of this.

The second was her fingers digging into his forearm.

"Don't miss it." Her voice was a high-pitched hiss; the repeated words so fast they ran together. "Dontmissitdontmissitdontmissit."

Karl covered her hand with his own. He was sure she was drawing blood.

"It's okay, Mrs. Labine. What do you think I'm missing?"

"No one ever looks, no one ever sees,' she whispered, her pretty face twisted into a grimace, pale blue eyes narrowed. "It's the stealing that does it. Too much, too much, stealing too much. Stealing the night. Everything breaks."

"Nothing like that can happen here, okay?" he said. "Everybody's safe now. I won't let anyone hurt you."

Karl tried to keep his demeanor calm while he was stroking her hand. She didn't look nearly strong enough to be hurting him so badly, but that was how it seemed to work once people ended up in here.

He was usually the best at keeping patients settled down. This one seemed to be getting worse.

She pulled against her thick leather restraints, trying to reach him with her other hand. He wasn't in any danger from her, but letting a new one get too upset threw everyone into an uproar.

"Nothing works when the thief is about. Nothing, nothing, nothing. Everything breaks, no matter what you do. Stealing my bloody sleep away after everything else. Don't. Miss. It. Don't miss it. Dontmissit..."

"I won't miss it, Mrs. Labine, I promise. I'll keep a close eye out. If you let go of my arm, I'll get you something to drink."

He was thinking his own stash of illegal whiskey George got for him, far more effective than the insipid Thunderbolt back at the Gate, might be the best thing for a situation like this.

Starting out with a nice cup full of strong Crumblewater would make more sense. She pulled him closer for a second, staring so hard that it felt like a physical touch. He nodded and smiled. She finally closed her burning eyes and let go.

Karl stood, rubbing his bright red arm, surprised to see no blood. Felt like it would bruise, though. That was exactly what he deserved for not paying attention, especially with someone he didn't know well.

He normally didn't like the other nurses' habit of calling patients heads or blowouts or empties any more than he liked the Directors calling them visitors or guests. Once they checked in, they never checked out. No one here for something as brief as Mending ever made it to Karl's building in the first place. Mrs. Labine might be closer to a blowout than he wanted to admit.

And whoever left the poor woman in such bad shape without an IV full of Crumble slurry deserved a week of scrubbing bedpans. Karl intended to do whatever it took to make that happen.

"Just another day in paradise," he whispered, walking out into the hall.

Cold or hot water with medical-grade Crumble dissolved in it, so much that not another speck of the gray ash would fit, was such a constant need that it was in every hall of the patient wings. He didn't know this woman well enough to know if hot or cold would work better, or if she'd prefer honey or mint to mask the flavor. Karl filled a metal cup with lukewarm water flavored with both.

He debated adding one of the sedative drops he was newly allowed to carry with him on his rounds, part of his last promotion to lead nurse. He went back to her room instead, hoping this big a dose of Crumble might do the trick until he could get the situation sorted out.

"Mrs. Labine," he whispered, making sure he was out of her reach. "This will make you feel—"

Karl stared at her chart, hanging just far enough over her head that she wouldn't be able to read it. A note written in a looping hand he recognized as his new supervisor's dominated the top of the notes.

Crumble ineffective. DO NOT administer without direct orders.

Karl stepped backward so quickly he nearly tripped over his own feet. Thankfully the woman still hadn't opened her eyes, but he held the cup behind his back just to be safe.

He'd heard of a few rare cases of bad reactions to Crumble, usually children who didn't last long, but this was an adult. He reached up and took the chart, taking care not to make a sound, before he walked back out into the hall.

He started to drink the water down himself before he remembered his plans to meet with George that evening. Maybe he didn't want to be overly calm and tranquil for that meeting after all. He put the cup on the table with the rest of the Crumblewater and walked back toward Mrs. Labine's room.

"That doesn't make a damned bit of sense," he said under his breath.

Karl looked around to make sure he was still alone. Mrs. Labine had been a Builder. There was no possible way she been off Crumble for any length of time, not with a job like that. Builders had to keep their levels especially high to avoid falling into their own talent and ending up here with depth syndrome. Everyone else needed Crumble to prevent the more common insanity of a terribly disordered and broken mind.

He flipped over to the personal information page to see if there was a note of her having problems in the past. All the air left his chest at once. Mrs. Labine was not anyone he'd ever met before, but she was from his neighborhood. She'd moved there just a few months ago, to a house just one block over from his parents.

One block away from Andy.

"Gilmore! Aren't you supposed to be off shift by now?"

Karl jumped and barely managed not to drop the chart. That could only be his previous boss.

"One more stop, Mr. Willer. Just verifying the orders for this patient."

The scrawny older man was standing with his hands on his hips at the intersection of the next hallway. They'd gotten along just fine until Karl had accepted this latest promotion, before Willer thought he was ready. He decided to take a risk he wasn't willing to with his new supervisor.

"This one is strange," Karl said. "Never heard of a patient taken completely off Crumble. You?"

"I don't make it a habit to question the doctors about their orders, Gilmore." He crossed his arms and lowered his pointy chin. "I suggest if you want to keep that new job of yours, you don't develop that habit yourself. No matter how many books you've read."

Karl managed to smile, knowing it wouldn't fool Willer or anyone else.

"I'll keep that in mind, sir."

"Wrap it up, then. I doubt Ms. Curtis wants to pay you overtime any more than I did when you worked for me."

"I'm sure you're right," Karl said under his breath as he walked back into the room.

He glanced down to make sure she was still asleep or passed out or whatever it was before he hung the chart back up. The sooner he could compare notes with George, the better. Whatever this was had hit far too close to home already.

Chapter 8

George finally showed up nearly half an hour late, cheeks flushed and hair even messier than usual. Karl was pacing the creaky wooden floor, walking from one common room to the other and back again. Thankfully the rowdy group who'd tried to recruit him into their own variety of trouble had continued on their way.

"Where the hell have you been, Georgie? I'm going nuts in here."

"Sorry, had to duck a couple of other guys wanting to have a few drinks. We might be better off doing that, but I guess it's too late now."

"Yeah, I guess so," Karl said. "We should probably go somewhere else tonight. Too many people wandering in and out."

"Way ahead of you, Karl. There's something I want you to get a look at anyway."

George walked toward the exit door to the lawns, Karl trying his best not to walk on his heels.

"Why are we going outside?" Karl said. "I can get us wherever you need to go through the tunnels or corridors."

George shook his head and kept walking. "Like you said, buddy, too many people wandering around tonight. We'll go through the maintenance doors. No one watching those this time of night with no supplies coming in. What's got you so jumpy? Besides the obvious."

"One of the new patients," Karl said. He'd gotten more unnerved over Mrs. Labine, not less. "She came in with the big bunch a few weeks ago. She lives one block away from my parents, George. One block. And something strange is going on with her. They're not giving her any Crumble at all."

"None?" George slowed enough for Karl to walk beside him, and Karl shook his head as they passed under a bright electric. "What makes you think so?"

"It's on her chart," Karl said. "Crumble ineffective, with orders not to give it. She's restrained, so she's not getting any on her own. Someone that disturbed is generally on high doses of medical Crumble, right into their veins."

George grunted. "That's a good way to make her crazier than she already is. They give too much Crumble around here if anything, not too little. Is she out of it?"

Karl shuddered, remembering the woman's gaze that was almost like a touch.

"She seems to come and go. Just about ripped my arm off this afternoon."

He was surprised when George laughed.

"I'm sorry, Karl, I just can't imagine anyone ripping your arm off, much less a woman. You're big as an ox, man!"

George had a point, since he did stand almost a head shorter than Karl.

"They're stronger than you think once they get inside," Karl said. "Trust me. Have you ever heard of that, denying Crumble to an adult?"

"No, can't say that I have." George slowed to flip through his massive keyring. He handed Karl a folder he hadn't noticed the other man carrying. "That's not what we usually hear much about in my line of work, though. Hey, do you have that master key still? Never mind, here it is."

Another bright bulb lit the bold and intimidating sign on the door. *Maintenance Only. Restricted.* It cast enough light for Karl to flip through the folder. It was exactly the kind of information he'd been afraid to copy on his own explorations, but it would be a lot harder to understand what this meant. No names or conditions, only dates and what seemed to be a record of damages repaired.

"George, these dates match what I've been seeing."

"Surprised? I'm not."

With a twist and a sharp shoulder to the door, they were inside. The corridor was dimly lit, the flames barely visible in the lamps stretching down the hallway. The walls, floor, and ceiling were the same dingy brick as the passages Karl was more familiar with: the tunnels hidden beneath their feet.

"Did you bring a lamp?" Karl said. "I think they turn these off in an hour or so, don't they?"

"Sure do. I just so happen to know where maintenance keeps the lamps for this building. We won't be in this low-class corridor for long, though."

George grinned back at Karl as he stopped at the fourth door on the right. Sure enough, they stepped into a far better built and maintained stretch of the administration wing. Polished wood gleamed all around them, the brass and glass burnished to a bright sheen.

Karl easily read the letters painted in gold on the window of the door George stopped in front of, though it didn't make a bit of sense to him. *Director of Public Relations.*

"What could they possibly have in here that can help us?" he said. "I don't even know what public relations would do for a place like this."

"Pipe down," George said. "Let me get the lights on. I was just in here for the first time a couple of months ago, helping finish up the very thing we need."

George lit one of the lamps along the wall, then pulled the shade over the door glass. When he turned the light up higher, Karl gasped.

The room was as neat and tastefully decorated as Karl's family's house, with none of the clutter and disorganization that seemed to be taking over the rest of the Columns. Two sofas and two chairs, all intricately carved and upholstered in finer fabric than Karl had ever seen took up the outer space. A thick, colorful rug covered with flowers lay underneath. Klia Gilmore would have been proud to have that one in her own house.

Beautifully framed paintings hung on the walls, and fresh flowers in heavy glass vases sat on the marble mantelpiece. Only a small desk, just as expensively made and decorated, gave any indication that this was an office rather than a Director's private residence.

"What do they do in here, Georgie?"

"This, my dear Karl, is where the Director and his staff convince other Directors out in the rest of Alterra, and the rare and regretful family members who manage to get out here to ask, that everything will someday be all right. They probably believe it at first. Or at least they finally decide to stop asking."

Karl breathed in the soft scent of flowers and a recent wood fire, such a contrast to the sharps smells of cleaner and cloying stench of madness that his nose and the rest of his head felt confused. He wasn't quite able to put this room together with Joffrey Columns.

George walked across that gorgeous rug to a dark wooden door that again seemed out of place, with carvings and brass fittings rather than a plain slab of wood. What Karl most wanted to do was take his shoes off and sink his toes into the mass of color on the floor. He hadn't done that since he was a kid in his parents' house.

"So sorry to disturb you, Karl, but wake up. We'll be perfectly safe in here for a while, but we don't have all night." Karl shook his head and joined George. "A supply closet is right across the hall if we need lanterns. We probably should be out of here before they turn all the lamps down. I doubt you'll need that long with that big brain of yours."

"Big brain?" Karl said, following George. "What are you talking..."

PART OF KARL was amused to feel his own jaw dropping. The rest of him was frozen halfway through the doorway, too busy staring in awe.

"I'm talking about that massive lump you carry around between your ears," George said. "You don't look like you have a thing up there right now. Even when we were back in school, I never saw you write a word down, Karl, but you never forget anything either. I'd be willing to bet this will be more than enough of a push for you to crack this whole mess wide open."

Karl blinked, looked at George, then walked closer to the wall in front of him. He heard the door close, and he was distantly grateful for the brighter light as his friend switched on electrics, but he was focused on the map. Not just any map, but by far the largest and most detailed one he'd ever seen.

The wealthy residential areas of Waldron's Gate covered the wall from floor to ceiling, with every single street, house, and landmark illustrated in full color. The streets weren't just names; they were surrounded by the flowers the name had come from. Karl wouldn't have been surprised to smell roses, hyacinths, or lilacs as clearly as his eyes could see them.

"Where did this come from?" he said.

"An artist came in here and painted the whole thing," George said. "Right onto the wall. All we did was put the frame around it. The painting took more than a month."

"There's our house."

Karl had his nose almost against the map, but the illusion was still perfect. He could tell that house was taller than the others, and he could even see his turret bedroom standing out against the roof.

"Yep, and mine just a few blocks over," George said. "Now show me where your patient today came from."

Karl opened his mouth to ask what patient before his brain lurched back into motion. That's why they were here, sneaking around after hours in violation of every single rule and regulation he'd ever heard of.

They were here to try to figure out the bunches of new patients from the neighborhood he was almost inhaling. Much as he might want to, he wasn't here to examine every square inch of this incredible painting.

"She was from one block over," he said, moving his finger along the street without touching the wall. "Right here."

George walked up beside him.

"Okay, good. I don't have any addresses in my list, only dates. Did all the dates match what you found this morning?"

"They did, every one," Karl said. "The records I saw started about ten years ago. Same thing you found?"

Karl finally turned away from the map to look at George.

"Exactly the same," George said. "The dates get closer together, and the damage worse, up until about two years ago when it got really bad. Then everything quieted down again until a few nights ago. Whatever it is might be starting again."

Karl turned back to the map, his mind pulling up the addresses he'd seen as clearly as the papers in George's files.

"Well, from just the last month, we have one here." He pointed to another house, several blocks away from his parents. "Here. And here."

Karl kept going, unconsciously sorting the addresses by the date the patient was admitted. Before he was finished, chills ran from his scalp down to his thighs.

"Do you see that, Karl?" George whispered.

"I see it. A bunch of spirals, looping around neighborhoods where Builders live. If we could use pins and yarn, it would be close to perfect. A few are on either side of the loops, but with so many matches that's probably just normal depth syndrome."

"When did..." George stopped and swallowed. "Your patient today, when did she come in?"

"She was right in the middle, before this one. And this one." Karl's finger crossed almost over his own home's roof, just one house away. He would have sworn his legs no longer reached the ground. "It's the next loop that's going to be the real problem, Georgie. Whatever this is seems to shift one house to the south each time."

"Merciful Crown, Karl. We have to figure this thing out, or at least warn them."

Karl dropped his hands to his sides and turned to face George. His friend was paler than usual, his whole face clenched up. Karl knew he didn't look any better.

"That woman today," he said. "She said the stealing did it, the stealing at night. If someone's behind this, whatever it is happens at night."

George shook his head. "We can't take the word of a blowout. Sorry, I mean a patient. They're in here for a reason."

"Yeah, and whatever the reason is, it's headed right toward my family," Karl said. "I can't stand most of them, but I can't let this happen without even trying to warn them."

Karl was seized by a deep and terrible urge to laugh, to guffaw until he was reduced to grasping his sides and crying.

"Hell, George, if nothing else, I can't take the risk of them ending up in here when I worked so hard to get away from them."

A ghost of a smile, so brief it would have been easy to miss, flitted across George's face.

"You have a point there, but we can't just go rushing off into the night either. Maybe we can ask one of the doctors, see what they have to say. This is pretty clear evidence even for some of them."

"Evidence of what?" Karl said. "Of both of us sneaking around and breaking into restricted offices in the middle of the night? You can give that a try if you want, but I'm going to see if I can't do something besides lose my job."

George stared at Karl for several seconds.

"What are you going to do, Karl?"

"The only thing I can think of, at least right now. If this pattern holds true, and I can't see why it wouldn't, whatever it is should start here next time." This time Karl did touch the map, and he would have sworn he felt a tingle. "Maybe it's just a bad supply of Crumble or something, or water, or who the hell knows what. But one thing I do know is it will get to my parents' house just a few days later. I have to try something."

"I can't argue with you," George said. "You're too damn big to try to stop. At least let me get you some decent lanterns and supplies before you jump into this."

Chapter 9

Loretta slowed as she approached her own house, far smaller and less grand than those of most of her clients. The exterior matched the proper Victorian style, with green, black, and copper paints chosen specifically to hide the unusual amount of metal trim on a modest one-story design. It was more than enough for her, though, easy to keep in order and remote enough for privacy.

She hadn't built her house to attract attention, and nothing that really mattered was visible except to the observant eye. Even the most observant wouldn't understand what they did see.

The young man she'd hired just a few weeks ago to keep an eye out should have already left for the day, leaving the most trusted guard in his place. Before Loretta could finish her thought, a shadow moved across her porch.

Bess was tall and slender, her red hair pulled back and out of the way. Her black close-fitting shirt and pants that would be scandalous if anyone else ever saw them.

"Good evening, ma'am," her guard said.

"Good evening, Bess."

"Did everything go well?"

Loretta walked slowly up onto the small space, the difficulty of her long day of deliveries catching up with her all at once.

"Well enough," she said. "Anything strange here?"

"Everything is normal. I checked inside about an hour ago. All is well."

"Thank you, Bess. No deliveries tomorrow. Please let the day guard know."

Bess stepped back into the early evening shadows, nodding once. "Sleep well."

The inside of the house was as appropriate and low key as the outside, sturdy dark cottons rather than the bright silks in her customers' homes, and the same paint colors designed to draw attention away from an unusual amount of metal sculptures and fittings. Her day guards had lit electrics in the living room and a gaslight in the hall. Loretta doused them both as she headed back to her bedroom.

A small light was on in there as well, and her far more decadent and expensive bedclothes had been turned back. Loretta smiled, appreciating her guards as she so often did.

Loretta opened her closet door, then sat on a low bench against the wall to remove her black leather boots. When she put the second one by the door, her nose wrinkled. That wasn't something she'd stepped in or gotten on the hem of her long skirts on the way home.

She'd only smelled that stinking mix of cheap cologne, expensive cigars, and too much whiskey in one other place. Before she could draw breath or stand, a heavy hand fell on her shoulder.

"Not one sound, darlin', or I'll cut your lover girl's throat and use her guts to bind your wrists for you."

"Rhysto," Loretta said. "Always did know how to treat a lady."

The hand squeezed, digging into the tender front of her shoulder until Loretta had to grit her teeth to keep from drawing away.

"I do know how to treat a lady, sure," Rhysto said. "I know how to treat the likes of you, too."

He finally let go, and she sat back, forcing herself to stay calm. Rhysto walked out of her closet and stood in front of her, his thumbs hooked behind his wide black leather belt. She remembered that belt far better than she wanted to.

Not all of her memories were unpleasant.

He was standing so close that Loretta had to lean back to see his face. His beard was still long and thick, though his brown hair had been cut not too long ago. The smirk on his face was exactly the same.

"What do you want?" she said. "I paid you off a long time ago."

He stepped closer, and now Loretta could smell his sweat. If she'd had any mind to, she could have leaned forward just an inch or so and touched his groin with her forehead. Right now she'd rather touch it with her teeth.

"You paid me, sure," he said. "I thought we might have a little fun for old time's sake. A little fun and a little information, just between friends."

"You were never my friend, Rhysto. You did a job, and I paid you well. That part of my life is over now. I don't have any information I'd be willing to share with you."

He squatted, and Loretta wished he were still looming over her. His dark, heavy-lidded eyes were worse than his vaguely threatening crotch.

"That's where we'll have a difference of opinion, I'm afraid," he said. "You'll tell me what I want to know, we'll have our fun, and I'll go along my merry way. If those things don't happen, I might have to visit your lady friend after all. After I deal with you, of course."

Loretta summoned the appearance of nervousness she was not feeling. She knew very well how to deal with Rhysto. The solution would be more pleasant than not if her memory of how to direct his mood served. She was certain it did.

All he could get out of her was the payment, and only the one she'd just gotten. Her safe was well hidden and protected enough that he'd never possibly find it.

"How did you get in here?" she said.

He grinned, showing far too many teeth. "Ah, that. I explained the situation to your young man, and he understood what I was trying to accomplish. He understood that getting in the way would lose him more than his job. How does he do in your bed? Better or worse than the young woman?"

Loretta shook her head, not having to feign her disgust. She only hoped Gus was still loyal and not too frightened to return after any sort of conversation with Rhysto. Her guards didn't know enough to betray her. Not even Bess.

"I don't know, since I've never been with either of them," she said "There's not a chance of that if he sold out for you. Just ask me your questions and get it over with, rudder mouth. I have other things to do tonight."

~

RHYSTO LAUGHED, a big booming sound that didn't match his intimidating appearance. Not for the first time, Loretta thanked her insistence on soundproofing this room for her frequent daytime sleeping habits. Bess didn't know the history between them, and neither of them would react well to a confrontation. He finally stood and moved away.

"Well, good thing for you I'm in a generous mood tonight," he said. "I'll be glad to let that smartass remark go. Deal with your turncoat however you want to tomorrow, if you can. Tonight you'll be dealing with me."

Loretta wished she still had her boots on, with easy access to her sharpest knives and one of her tiny clockwork revolvers. The knife hidden in the back of her corset might do, but she'd rather have the gun with someone like him.

No matter, as long as she kept control of the situation, Loretta knew how to distract him. And please herself at the same time.

"Answer my question first, Rhysto, then we'll see about yours. How did you get in here? The guard you spoke to doesn't have a key. I know you didn't get past the woman."

She slowly leaned forward, reaching toward her boots.

"I didn't have to get past anyone," he said, strolling around the room. "Your fancy clockwork locks, the kind no one else in your neighborhood has any need of? Who do you think brought them down from the Northlands to begin with? I always know how to unlock anything I carry on my shaw, and that includes people." He pointed to her fingers, barely an inch away from the revolver, his gesture far more casual than his words. "Touch those boots and you lose both hands."

She slowly sat back, putting the gun out of her mind. She couldn't get it, so it no longer mattered. Loretta did have other means of keeping herself safe.

"I'll ask again," she said. "What is it you think I know?"

"Kick those pretty boots into the closet. Then sit down here with me and we'll talk about it."

Rhysto sat on her bed and patted the space beside him. His other hand lifted his vest just enough for Loretta to see the revolver and knives.

"I can hear you just fine from here," she said.

She kicked the boots away and closed the closet door. He had certainly investigated for a safe in there, but it didn't hurt for him to think something valuable had escaped his attention. He'd just moved himself into range of her best, and far less messy, weapons.

"Ah, but this isn't about you, now is it?" he said. "Resisting is a different game when we're out of our clothes and our imagined roles as civilized people. All it does right now is cause you more trouble in the end."

Loretta sat as far away as she could, her hip against the carved oak pillar at the head of her bed. She might be able to move fast enough to get him with her short knife if other methods failed, but that revolver forced her to wait. He'd have too much time to pay her back for her many, many sins.

"That's so much better, isn't it?" Rhysto's long arms had no problem getting to Loretta's face, and his rough, calloused hand scratched across her cheek. She refused to flinch away. "Now, we'll have plenty of time for our play while the rest of your quaint little neighborhood goes on about their evening. You can answer me nicely, and things will go a bit easier for you. Refuse to answer or lie to me, and even you can't imagine how long the fun will last."

"I don't know, Rhysto. I seem to remember what you consider fun going on for a long damned time."

He laughed again and caught a handful of Loretta's hair, pulling just enough to let her know he could pull harder.

"You flatter me, my dear," he said. "My skills have only increased in the time that's gone by. And nothing motivates me more than a juicy secret. Unless a juicy woman is the one to share it."

That huge hand slid from her hair, to her cheek, along her neck, to her exposed cleavage. His fingers slipped under the top of her corset, and Loretta didn't dare move away when they caught her skin in the tight fit. His rough fingertips were like sand across her flesh, but he didn't pinch. Not yet.

The danger between them had always been a huge part of the fierce attraction. Loretta never forgot how easily that danger could get out of hand, even when she was in her own safest place.

"Now," he said, his voice far smoother than his appearance "I don't normally listen to the useless chatter of the other pilots who look to me for protection, much less the weakling shopkeepers they supply. As long as they pay me their due, I could not possibly care less what squabbles they get up to among themselves."

The hand on Loretta's breast, squeezing her flesh under the steel and bones of the corset, started to pull. Ever so slightly, but steady enough to let her know he wasn't going to stop. She moved, staying within arm's reach of her headboard.

"Lately, though," he said, "I've been hearing a complaint often enough that it's been annoying me to no end. I've found the only way to stop a complaint like that, to get the lazy buggars to shut the hell up, is to get to the bottom of it. That brings me to you, darlin'."

"What could I possibly have to do with shaw pilots?" Loretta said. "My feet haven't left the ground since you dropped me off here years ago."

"Well, that's what piqued my curiosity, you might say. Seems a few of the merchants have been getting requests they simply can't fill. Requests of a more distasteful nature, at least to the delicate sensibil-ties of my fellow pilots. Turns out not much is too distasteful for the residents of your fair community."

～

RHYSTO REACHED DOWN and drew one of his smaller blades, solid black with copper wire wrapped around the handle. That hand went behind her back while the other slid under the top of Loretta's corset again.

"Once an appetite for that sort of thing gets started," he said, "seems folks will go to any ends necessary to get what they're after. And that, my dear Loretta, is what brings me to you." He was looking into her eyes, but she felt the knife moving along the curve of her shoulders, touching light as a feather. "Much as it would pain you to admit it, you and I have more in common than not. Both of us will do what it takes to survive. Am I right?"

Loretta stared into his cold black eyes until she felt that knife, somehow cold instead of warmed by his flesh, pushing a bit harder against the bones in her spine. He hadn't drawn blood, but the promise had been made.

"Yes, Rhysto. We're more alike than I care to admit. I'll do what it takes to survive."

He smiled, showing his surprisingly white, even teeth. She remembered those, too. Just as with his belt, many of her memories were inappropriate, and pleasant.

"So glad to hear it!" he said. "I wondered to myself, who would be willing to supply such fine citizens with their unpleasant items, creepy curios, if you will, for a very fine price?" The knife lay flat against the flesh of her upper back for a moment. "And only one person came to mind."

She heard a whispery cut, and for a moment she thought he was cutting her hair. After another soft slice, she realized he was cutting through the ribbon holding her corset tight. Once he took that off, she'd lose her own blade hidden there, but she'd be able to breathe and move much more freely. She was hardly defenseless even without her weapons.

"So I did a little asking around over the past few days," he said. "Very discretely, of course. Turns out I was right. Tell me, darlin'. Exactly where do you find the ghastly things you peddle? Who brings you these little treasures?"

Loretta forced herself not to smile. That was it, the angle he was after. And the angle she needed to control him. Rhysto didn't want her working with shaw pilots who weren't afraid enough to pay for his protection. Her wariness turned to deep, hot anticipation.

"I'm not working with scab pilots, or any of the independents," she said. "If that's what you're thinking, put your mind at rest. Most of them come from right here, hidden away in someone's attic or basement or other cozy hiding place. You'd be surprised what our forbearers did to amuse themselves, Rhysto. They made these little collections seem tame and boring. Once people realize they can make a small fortune selling the macabre, they seek me out. It's easier than you might think, though not nearly as profitable as your various operations."

Rhysto turned his face away from her, half-closed eyes and compressed mouth saying more than words could have.

"You expect me to believe these things are just lying around here under their noses," he said, "and you happen to be there to liberate them?"

The corset was loose enough to slip over her head now, but he continued to slice the ribbon into smaller and smaller pieces. His right hand pushed her thin black cotton shirt away as he worked, exposing more of her chest.

"For a price, as you say." Loretta pulled the useless corset forward until the last of the blood-red ribbon slipped free and dropped it carefully beside the bed. She wanted the knife still hidden in the garment within her reach. "Word does get around once a trend like this settles in. Almost like a mania among people with nothing better to do. Who am I to judge?"

Rhysto shook his head, but he was smiling. He still held the knife behind her back. Loretta pulled her loose undershirt free and over her head, leaving her naked to the waist. No matter how intensely satisfying the next few hours turned out to be, she was determined to send him out of here with nothing more than half-truths in his possession.

"When this hidden supply of horrors runs dry?" he said, his voice rough. "How will you maintain yourself in such a lavish lifestyle?"

He cupped her left breast in his rough hand, then her right, squeezing each nipple hard enough to send heat coursing through her body. The high color in his cheeks let her know he hadn't lost his weakness for flesh. Her flesh in particular.

"My lifestyle is hardly lavish," she said. "Out here on the edge of the Fog in this tiny little house. But if it runs dry, I might have to recruit an associate to alternate visits with me. See if we can't set up a little bidding war and split the profits. These people like nothing more than having something their neighbor doesn't, especially if they paid a lot more than necessary to get it."

"Well then, darlin', sounds like I should send one of my own associates around to keep an eye on you, make sure no one with less-than-pure intentions decides to separate you from your hard-earned treasure."

Loretta arched her back and drew in her breath, giving up on hiding how much she was enjoying his rough manipulations. The words didn't matter, not now. All she wanted was for him to drop that damned knife. That and the sheer bulk of him put her at too much of a disadvantage. She raised both arms and pulled him into a bristly, whiskey-reeking kiss, then pulled his face toward her breasts.

"I certainly appreciate your concern, Rhysto. I do." She gasped at the heat of his mouth, and more at the surprisingly gentle pressure of his teeth. "I take very good care of myself and my treasure."

"I can see that you do." His breathing was faster as he bit the base of her neck, a spot that never failed to turn up the nerve endings throughout her body. "But I'd hate for anything bad to happen to such a dear friend."

Loretta grabbed the front of his jacket and slipped it down over his shoulders, not wanting him to think she was after his weapons. She was deploying her own weapon quite successfully.

He finally moved the knife away from her back and pulled his jacket off. She ran her fingernails through the hair exposed at his chest, then moved lower until she grasped the bulge in his pants. She felt heat even through the thick wool.

"I don't think anything bad is going to happen to me for the next few hours, Rhysto." She whispered against his ear before she bit his earlobe, paying close attention as he dropped the weapon belt on top of his jacket on the floor. "Nothing bad that I don't want, anyway."

He shifted away from her, holding her shoulders a little too hard. She couldn't forget even for one second how dangerous this man was, even when his mind was half-crazed over wanting to plunder each and every inch of her.

"Things will go very badly for you if I find out you're employing my competitors, Loretta. For you and for them. We'll all be so much better off if you tell me anything I need to know right now."

"Stand up," she whispered.

Putting herself into such a vulnerable position made her skin crawl, but she knew of no surer way to get him off this track. Her flesh and her senses knew what was coming and demanded she keep going. Loretta reached for his heavy belt. Rhysto got to his feet, never looking away from her eyes.

"You can ask every shaw pilot from one end of Alterra to the other," she said. "Ask every peddler and cart dragger besides. I'm not working with any of them."

She unbuckled the belt, knowing he would use it later no matter how agreeable she was right now. The hell of it was she wanted him to use it, very badly. Around her wrists or ankles, across her ass, sometimes even around her neck.

Her mind might have worked very hard to put the desire for this part of her life behind her, but her body had not cooperated. And her body was starving for what no one could do better than the man in front of her. She pushed his pants down, exposing the clearest proof that he felt the same.

"Do you swear it?" He was breathless now, his hands in her hair, lips parted. "Don't make me punish you, Loretta. Really punish you. Not the kind you like."

She leaned forward and ran her tongue along the length of him, and his whole body jerked toward her.

"I speak the truth, I swear it," she said, breathless herself. "Investigate all you want to. You'll see I'm not working with any of them. No one knows the kind of punishment I need better than you do."

Chapter 10

Karl opened his eyes in his dark apartment, as wide awake as he'd been fast asleep the second before. He heard no noise, and no part of his body hurt or needed to be emptied. He was simply awake.

He turned onto his back, glancing toward the window. No, not a trace of dawn. He'd only been out for a few hours, but he didn't feel like he had a chance of falling asleep again. He sighed and folded his arms under his head, trying to figure out what had bolted him awake.

He normally slept like a log, as did most people he knew who weren't permanent residents at the Columns. Most of the residents were liberally dosed with enough Crumble during the day to help. That woman, Mrs. Labine, she might not sleep well.

Crumble not effective.

That didn't make any more sense to him in the middle of the night than it had standing beside her bed, and he hadn't had a chance to ask about it yet. Instead of settling down, Karl's mind ticked over each of his other patients, relentlessly scrolling through their names, faces, disorders, one after the other. Besides Mrs. Labine, each and every one of them was probably sound asleep.

Why wasn't he?

He turned onto his side and shoved at his pillow, rearranging it as if that had been the problem. Minutes crawled by, and he wasn't feeling calmer or even enjoying a brief time alone with his thoughts.

Karl was on edge, an internal alert growing stronger. He finally recognized his twinge, his gut feeling when something was not right around him.

Some of the other nurses who'd been around a while seem to have it, too. Just a sense, maybe some kind of caregiver's instinct that something disruptive was about to happen. No one had any illusion that sort of thing could be taught. All anyone could do was recognize it and learn to trust it.

Karl himself was pretty good at catching it in others, young nurses and orderlies alike. He sometimes caught a lack of it in doctors, but he'd learned to keep his mouth shut in those cases.

"I'll ask about Mrs. Labine tomorrow," he said. "I will."

Sometimes that helped, promising himself out loud that he'd do something about whatever was bugging him most. That strange woman raving about a thief had never quite left his mind since he'd wrenched his arm from her painful grasp.

Trying to figure out what to do about the pattern he and George seemed to have stumbled onto wasn't helping. Too many things competed for space in a head that should have been filled with the emptiness of deep sleep.

He considered swallowing a half dose or so of the Crumble Mrs. Labine was denied. He was far from the only one working at the Columns who took the lightest dose possible. Keeping his internal levels of suspicion and paranoia on the higher side kept him safer in the midst of so much madness. Still, tonight it might help him sleep.

Whatever was going on with that pattern around his family's house was too important to risk dulling his observations and reactions.

Karl shifted again, curling into a ball with the blankets pulled over his ears. He'd gotten into that habit sleeping in a noisy house as a kid. His lofty turret room conducted every whisper and creak from the three floors below.

Once he'd moved out here into this strangely quiet apartment, it had taken him a few weeks to adjust to the silence. Now he couldn't imagine sleeping somewhere so noisy.

"Okay, I'll pay a visit home soon, talk to Andy again. See if he's noticed anything else. I really need to get some more sleep. If I'm right, we're in for a hell of a day tomorrow."

That whispered vow finally did the trick. Karl's inner alarm continued, but he could put it away for now. At least enough to sleep.

❧

BEFORE KARL WAS HALFWAY to midday, he was grateful for those extra hours of rest a thousand times over. Getting up in the middle of the night wouldn't have helped anyone as it turned out. Constant challenges and stress didn't prepare him for what was coming.

Hell didn't truly break loose for Karl until nearly the end of his terribly long day.

All of the patients were on edge and restless, almost as badly as when the 'ster had had a meltdown a few days before. Karl didn't see George at lunch to ask how the rest of the place was doing. He didn't take that as a good sign.

Hours later, when Karl was hoping to finally finish up and find George, his friend stepped into the doorway of a patient's room.

"Hey, Karl? I need to talk to you."

"Just give me a minute, Georgie. This one's had a bad day. I have to change his bedding."

"This really can't wait," George said. "I'll help you."

The hesitant sound of his friend's voice brought Karl's earlier alarm back full blast. They worked silently, shifting the sedated man, cleaning him up, getting new clothes and sheets in place.

"Thanks, I appreciate that," Karl said. "He wasn't in any shape to cooperate." He followed George out into the hall before grabbing his shoulder. "What's so urgent? I've got three more to check."

"I got Karen to cover for you," George said. "Don't worry about them. There's something you have to see."

"Come on, what's happening? You're scaring me, George."

George nodded. "Good. Let's go."

Karl followed without another word, not sure what he'd say if he could manage to speak. Unfortunately, his imagination had always been better at scaring him than anything or anyone else. Andy's words and his own kept coming back, building on his worry about whatever was going wrong catching up to his family.

That didn't make any sense, but neither did calm, dependable George marching him out before his shift was over. They left Karl's building and headed across the plain grass lawn, toward the older section of the Columns. Toward the twisting brick towers where the 'sters were supposed to be.

"George, I can't go out here. I'm not authorized for this."

"Well, you weren't authorized to dig through records either," George said. "Any more than I was to get us in to see that map. No time to get scared on me now."

George tried to smile, but it looked horrible with his worried eyes. He pulled out his official master key and opened the heaviest black iron gate Karl had ever passed through, standing between the newer, cleaner towers where patients were kept and most people lived. Karl had only ever heard rumors about what lived out here.

"Is it... Are we safe out here?" Karl whispered.

He hated to sound like such a coward, but he wasn't feeling nearly as adventurous as he usually did when he actually did something new. His troublesome curiosity had no interest in this, not with George so nervous.

"Safe enough," George said. "We're not going to where they keep the really bad 'sters. This one's brand new. Just birthed last night."

"But why?" Karl said, close to shouting. "Tell me what the hell is going on!"

Karl grabbed his friend's arm again, and this time George stopped and turned to face him. The worry was still there, but anger was pushing it aside.

"Listen, I'm not going to try to explain this to you," George said. "But you have to see. I'm sorry, Karl. I really am. Doing this with no warning feels like a really shitty way to act. I can't think of anything else to do. Now please, just come with me."

After George was a few steps away, Karl finally got his own feet moving. His lungs were useless for breathing or anything else except clenching up around his pounding heart.

Karl was afraid he was going to pass out for the first time since his first few days at the Columns, that some poor green orderlies were going to have to haul his huge carcass back to the infirmary. Having to explain what he was doing out here in the first place might be easier than whatever he was walking toward.

~

GEORGE WAS WAITING beside a heavy steel door, corroded and scarred, probably older than the two of them put together. When Karl finally stood beside him, he turned the handle.

The first thing that hit Karl was the smell. A thousand times worse than the soiled sheets he and George had changed, and punctuated with sweat and blood and fear.

Worst of all, this didn't smell like it had just happened today, this week, or maybe this year. The stench was thick enough that Karl could taste it at the back of his throat.

"Doesn't anyone ever shovel this place out?"

"I doubt they have time," George said. "If they did, it would smell this way again in a day or two. They bring it with them."

"Who?" Karl said. "Who brings it?"

"The 'sters, Karl. These are the new ones, too. You should smell where the old ones live sometime."

Karl covered his nose with his sleeve, hoping he never had that opportunity as long as he lived. He was wondering how human beings could possibly work in this when George stopped beside a huge wooden cabinet. He pulled out shiny black things with tubes dangling all over and handed one to Karl.

"What the hell is this?"

"It's a gas mask," George said. "You won't last long in here without one, and it'll help cover your face anyway. Here, I'll show you..." George held the glass pieces shaped like goggles up to Karl's eyes, squeezing another part against his mouth. "No, don't jerk away from it. Just breathe. It won't smell nearly so bad. Once you're still, I'll adjust the straps."

Karl forced his breath to slow, holding the heavy mask with both hands. After several seconds, George reached up. He pulled several straps tight against Karl's head, tugged on the mask, and adjusted the straps again. Once he was finished, he turned away to get his own.

Karl let go, expecting the heavy thing to hurt his neck or just fall off, but it wasn't as bad as he thought. And George had been telling the truth. The awful smell was still there but the mask cut it down to almost nothing. Karl would have put up with a lot more discomfort for that.

He followed George for a few minutes down a narrow, dimly lit hall. The sides and roof were rough, dark gray stone, the floor the same but worn smooth in a path down the middle. Various types of doors lined the hall on both sides. Dark, aged wood with open barred windows, solid wood, black metal with glass windows.

Karl was relieved enough to be breathing almost normally that he almost forgot why they were here. Something urgent that he had to see, that his normally gossipy friend was not willing to describe.

He still wasn't curious, not one bit.

Karl wished any of his supervisors, old or new, would walk around the next corner and demand he get back to his own side of that huge fence. George stopped in front of a metal door with no window and lifted his mask for a second.

"You ready?"

Karl shook his head, but George opened the door anyway. The room seemed empty at first, and Karl dared to hope whatever it was had already been taken somewhere else. Bars stretched from wall to wall, floor to ceiling just in front of him.

Nothing was in the cell but a large ceramic bowl sitting on the bunk. It was oval like a bassinet, the kind of thing Rethia would bring his niece or nephew home in before much more time had passed, but Karl couldn't imagine putting a baby in such a hard container. He took a step toward the bars, and the basket jerked.

"Is it in there?" he whispered, his gaze locked onto the bed. His own voice sounded distant and distorted through the mask.

"They're small in the beginning," George said. "Just like we are. I'm sorry, Karl. I'm really sorry."

Karl took another step forward, but George stayed by the door. He finally stood close enough to touch the bars, and close enough to see what needed to be locked up before it was one day old.

The 'ster, if that's what it was, looked like a perfectly healthy newborn baby. It was naked, with pink, perfect skin and wispy blond hair, and Karl couldn't help noticing it was a boy. He turned around to ask what kind of sick joke George was up to, and the metal buckle on his belt sang out against the bars.

The baby opened its eyes.

They looked normal at first too. What took Karl's breath was the color, the exact same hazel he and so many in his family had. Before he could say a word or look away, the green grew deeper and more vivid. The same way everyone's but Karl's did when they were Building.

The baby's skin darkened, turning red as if he were upset. Karl stepped away from the bars, not wanting him to start crying. This had to be some kind of monster or it wouldn't be locked up in here. The red deepened further, now looking like the bricks lining the tunnels under their feet. The baby didn't cry or move, just kept staring at Karl with those glowing green eyes.

Patches of skin turned ashy, then started to pucker and wrinkle. When those spots started to burst open, Karl realized what he was seeing. The baby was burning, all over its body, as if it were being roasted over an open fire.

He opened his mouth, but only a clicking noise came out. If the baby was indeed in a Builder's trance, and it certainly looked like it was, it was Building itself into an inferno.

When the remaining flesh started to turn black, George grabbed Karl's shoulders and pulled him back. Karl stared into the baby's eyes until his friend closed and locked the door between them.

"Karl? Are you okay? Karl?"

George shook his shoulders now, but Karl could only stare straight ahead. Burning itself; it was burning itself alive. A sharp noise drove through his head what seemed like several seconds before he felt the pain in his cheek. George had slapped him, gas mask and all.

"I'm sorry," George said. "We have to get out of here. Someone will be in to check on it before long. We can't be here. You can't be here."

"Its eyes, Georgie. Its eyes."

"I know. That's why you had to see. Come on."

Karl didn't notice his surroundings until they were back outside, his body moving because his legs decided to. He managed to hold himself together until they passed through that giant gate, the gate Karl had never known how thankful he was for until now.

He fell onto the first bench he saw, shaking too hard to keep walking. George sat beside him, watching him closely.

"What happens to it?" Karl said. "When it closes its eyes?"

"Just what you're thinking, I'm sure. Its skin grows back when it sleeps. As long as it sleeps, it's just fine. As soon as it opens its eyes, that happens again."

Karl rubbed his eyes hard, trying to force the burning flesh out of his memory.

"Kill it," he said. "They just need to kill it. No one needs to see something like that. Nothing needs to *live* like that."

"They can't," George said. "You know that. The 'sters are linked to whoever birthed them. If they kill it, the person dies."

Karl stared at George, sure he understood what the other man was saying and more sure he didn't want to.

"Do you mean... Did that thing come from someone in my family? Is that what you think happened?"

George looked back at the stone building, one of the few that wasn't brick in the whole place. He rubbed his upper arms.

"I'm not a doctor," he said. "Or even a nurse. But I've been around you and your family my whole life, Karl. I've seen them focus too hard on something. I don't have to be a Builder any more than you are to know what I saw."

"But what can we do?" Karl said. "We can't kill it, I get that, but what am I supposed to do?"

"I think you might need to check on your family," George said. "See if anything strange is going on. We both think the 'sters and the patients getting so riled up could be linked to that pattern you saw. Maybe it hit too close to your house after all. Maybe the pattern changed. That thing just came in this morning, born last night. Maybe one of them will remember something."

Karl got to his feet, swaying a second before he caught his balance.

"No, George, the pattern didn't change. I'm such a bloody idiot."

He walked toward his building as fast as his rubbery muscles would carry him.

"Hang on!" George shouted. "Where are you going?"

"I missed it," Karl said without slowing down. "Right there in front of my own damned eyes, and I missed it. It's my sister, George. Rethia. She doesn't live at home anymore. She lives right in the path of whatever the hell this is. And she's pregnant, due any time now, stuck at home because Building isn't good for the baby this late. How could I have missed it? I've got to get home, right now."

Chapter 11

LORETTA TURNED over without opening her eyes. There was no need to. She had all the information she required. Rhysto was gone, no doubt to make sure she knew he could come and go as he pleased.

He hadn't taken anything of real value with him, except her will to resist him. Now she just had to figure out how to deal with his return to her life.

She stretched carefully, checking herself over for bruises, sore muscles, raw places. She'd definitely felt worse after time spent in his bed. At least an hour after she'd gotten home, maybe longer, she'd asked him to leave no marks. He was far gone enough in the twisted passion they made together that he might not have heard. She'd have to make sure before anyone else saw her.

When she finally sat up enough to start the lamp beside the bed, Loretta groaned. The whirring table clock said half past noon. She'd slept far later than she usually did, no surprise after the late-night activities. Good thing she had no deliveries planned for today.

Ignoring the protests of her stomach and back muscles, Loretta picked up her discarded clothing. Her knife was still hidden in the disabled corset.

That knife, that damned black knife. Even if she did still crave his attentions, she was determined not to be surprised like that again.

Much to her surprise, her purse was still in her skirts, and still stuffed full of ritterns from her last delivery. For all his bad habits and questionable business practices, she supposed Rhysto wasn't much of an out and out thief. He preferred to exert control and get paid that way.

Loretta crawled back onto the bed, tapping various hollow spaces on her massive headboard and the columns that supported it. Invisible drawers slid open, revealing they'd been no more disturbed than her purse. Her own tiny knives, another pistol, a garrote, and more than one numbing brass hypodermic were all intact. The larger drawers hidden under the bed skirts were similarly undiscovered.

He hadn't found any of them. Her resolve to get him out of her bedroom had faltered once she gave in to her own body's demands, but she was still relieved he didn't know her options. She closed the drawers and walked slowly into the bathroom.

She had to try three times to start the tiny boiler underneath her tub, but she didn't want to ask her day guard in to take care of it. Talking to Gus, possibly having to fire him, was going to be unpleasant enough already. Even after what had happened, she hoped he'd be able to stay on.

If nothing else, Loretta was going to need an additional guard to keep an eye on that damned back door for when Rhysto decided to return. Neither Bess nor anyone else could watch two doors at once, and he'd proved he could defeat her locks and probably any others she could buy locally.

Her grandmother had warned her about back doors, but Loretta had been too afraid of being trapped inside with only one way out. She could see the advantages of that now.

While the water heated up, Loretta stood over the toilet and used the uncomfortable tubed contraption and stinging solution the chemist refused to supply to unmarried women. His sympathetic wife was happy to provide that and the herbs and medication to back it up. Rhysto didn't bother himself with such things, but Loretta never failed to. She had no desire to have a child, certainly not one who would certainly have countless half-siblings scattered all over Alterra.

Necessities completed, Loretta stood in the middle of her three tall mirrors and turned from side to side. Rhysto had stayed true to her wishes, mostly. The bruises on her ass were only going to get darker over the next day or two, but all the other red marks would disappear by the end of the day.

Rhysto's attentions always left her feeling a bit the worse for wear the next day. Her consolation, besides all that exquisite pleasure, was she was quite certain she'd left bruises with her own handiwork. He hadn't asked her not to leave marks, after all.

She turned the valve, and hot water poured out the brass spigot into her copper tub, custom-made larger and deeper than she'd seen anywhere before. Extra copper could only be a good thing in this house.

Loretta turned the temperature up just a touch, added a long pour of healing elixir from a purple glass bottle, then opened the slow circulating flow. She wanted a good, long soak, and the water needed to stay hot.

Loretta sucked air in through her teeth when her toes hit the steaming surface, but she kept going. Now was not the time to get dainty and reluctant. With both feet in, she gripped the high sides of the tub and lowered herself as slowly as she could.

She couldn't keep from groaning when her privates went under, but her lower back welcomed the heat. She leaned against the curved tub, closing her eyes and sighing. She'd let a few lovers share in her bath and the amazingly fast and unlimited hot water supply, but she could never tell them where such wonders came from.

That was a secret too deep for even her basement to keep.

Rhysto seemed to believe her tales of finding things in plain sight, at least for now. She'd told no lies for him to detect or disprove. She still didn't believe for one second that he'd turned up after seven years for nothing more than a good roll, even one as spectacular as they'd had.

He'd be back, and possibly with much harder to answer questions. Worse, he could decide she needed to go back into her old line of work and bring a steady stream of pilots to sample the wares. That thought was enough to convince Loretta that something would have to be done. Whether she'd enjoyed herself or not didn't matter. She never wanted another surprise visitor hiding in her closet.

After an hour of soaking, gentle washing, and making sure any traces of her evening activities were gone, Loretta got out and drained the tub. Even if she hadn't been staying in today, her ribs and breasts were in no shape for a corset. She knew her figure was just fine without one, but bruises and sore muscles did limit her choice of clothing a bit.

She'd go with one of her nightgowns and put a long coat over it to speak with her guards. She did drop one of her dainty but effective pistols into one pocket and a knife in the other. She doubted Rhysto would come back right away—far better to keep her off balance.

Loretta had never been one to take chances.

LORETTA GLANCED at the indicator on her living room wall as she passed through. She had to admit that was one of the more clever ideas her grandmother had come up with.

Anyone who didn't know better would see one of several elaborate metal sculptures, like many others inside and outside the house. Even if a guest looked very closely, that's all the uninitiated eye would ever see. The only thing anyone could notice was one of several glass jewels scattered throughout the looping metal.

The one that mattered switched from red to green when the guard was in place.

She'd doubted such a simple device could be effective, but Loretta had come to rely on it over time. As soon as a guard walked into the hidden room around the corner of the porch, the corner that faced the Fog, and closed the door, a wire flipped the glass around. When the door opened, it was reset.

Such devices, scattered throughout the house inside and out, were the simplest parts of Loretta's life. She gathered up her leather delivery bags embroidered with fine gold threads and carried them into the kitchen

The kitchen seemed far grander than a woman from the rugged and rural Northlands, especially one who lived alone, could justify.

Loretta was an unnaturally quick study. Her clients demanded a certain appearance, even in places they would rarely see.

The most important facade was one of the most subtle.

When she opened the cabinet to get out her cafei mug, Loretta reached past a large bottle of Crumble. A dish sat on the stone countertop with tiny silver spoons made just for that purpose laid out in a holder nearby.

She encouraged her guards and visitors alike to use her supply, and they did so without hesitation. She even made her pills available to the guards, telling them she didn't want them to ever worry about forgetting them or trying to stretch out the time between doses on her account.

The real reason was Loretta hadn't taken Crumble herself for many years. Having a fluctuating supply of it was just another way she avoided drawing attention to herself. Someone, probably Rhysto, had helped himself to a large supply of both forms.

Cafei in hand, Loretta slid the pantry door into the wall, stopping to light the hanging gaslight before she closed it behind her.

This was another unusual extravagance in her small house, a pantry large enough for two or more people to walk into. The large variety of food was certainly nice after a childhood and young adult life full of worry about where her next meal was coming from. Only Loretta and one other person knew the true value of the space.

She stood two paces in front of the lamp and slowly pulled it down to her chest level. Before raising it again, she flipped what looked like a useless brass ornament on the front from horizontal to vertical. She raised the lamp up to its normal position just above her head.

The floor under her feet looked like nothing more than the shorter pieces of wood used in a utility space until several of them started to sink. The motion was smooth enough that not a drop of Loretta's cafei spilled. The relatively new technology of hydraulics was responsible for her slow descent through the jagged hole in her pantry floor.

Loretta made a mental note to pay a visit to her grandmother in the blasted Northlands as soon as she could get Rhysto and his spies off her trail. Adding a guard station to her back porch suddenly seemed a lot more important, as did a few more security devices.

When the moving floor sank into a matching hole in the basement, Loretta started a lamp within her arm's reach and well within the light from the one in the pantry. She had several lamps down here, but she hardly ever lit more than one. The gleaming copper floor, walls, and ceiling reflected more than enough to light her way.

She stepped off and pushed a bronze button on the copper column nearest to her, and the floor moved back up into place. She could hear the counterweights shifting to keep everything from moving too fast, but only as the slightest whisper.

That was one trick neither Rhysto nor anyone else would likely figure out or be able to defeat. The weights were keyed to Loretta's own body weight.

Even if someone else knew how to activate the moving floor, it would not respond to someone much heavier or lighter than her. She had no intention of sharing the secret of the built-in override with her guards or anyone else.

The other secrets underneath her modest little house were far too valuable to take that risk.

THE BASEMENT WAS as large as the first floor, and at the moment it was emptier than Loretta would have liked. Copper-wrapped shelves lined most of the walls, and a huge table covered with gold took up most of the center of the room. That was one exception to the solid copper used everywhere else.

The table had inlays of various other metals: bronze, copper, and electrum primarily, in nine concentric circles with bars of lead pointing to their centers.

Loretta knew essentially how the various arrangements worked, functioning as specific targets all inside the larger one of the house itself, but she preferred to let her grandmother worry about of that. They worked, and that was her only concern.

A far bigger concern was the dwindling supply of objects on all those shelves. Loretta counted seven distasteful curios waiting to be delivered to the collections of her enthusiastic clients. That was only a few days' work if all went smoothly, and this was the part she had no trouble at all letting Rhysto learn all about.

He could watch her make deliveries all day and all night. Gathering new inventory once this modest supply ran out would be a much bigger problem.

Loretta finished her cafei, wishing she'd brought more down here with her. This was the hardest part of shifting from delivery to building inventory, at least before Rhysto's little intrusion. Changing her sleep schedule wasn't as easy as it had been just a few years ago. That was the whole point of these days off to help adjust.

A very late night and a long sleep had done her a favor, but she still had to stay up later than usual while finishing these remaining deliveries. She put the empty cup and delivery bags down and walked over to the wall opposite the hanging lamp.

The shelves here were kept empty most of the time unless she had a particularly large supply of goods awaiting her attention. She hadn't felt comfortable Building that many things at once for a couple of years now, but that might have to change with Rhysto's threat of surveillance.

Loretta reached under the shelf at mid-thigh height and pushed an unseen button fitted seamlessly into the copper. The barest sigh, more like breath than steam, was the only result for several seconds.

The pipes in this part of the house had to be remarkably well built and insulated to avoid corroding everything around her, or spoiling the things she and Gemma had gone to so much trouble to make possible.

The whisper subsided, and the shelves folded sideways upon themselves. When the wall was exposed, Loretta stepped forward onto another spot with a scale built in. She stood forward on her toes, being careful not to touch the retracted shelves or the wall in front of her. The security features down here were a bit more serious than upstairs.

With that same faint sigh, the wall to her left split and moved to her right. That seam looked no different than the others at regular intervals around the room. Not even Loretta herself could spot the important one. When the wall had fully retracted, she lowered her heels, counted to three, and stepped forward into the room.

All the lamps in this small chamber were electric. She'd agreed with Gemma that gas would be too dangerous in such an enclosed space even though she found the light terribly harsh and bright. These walls were lead instead of copper, and most of the room was taken up with a floor-to-ceiling safe.

The combination was simple and easy to remember as long as the operator knew exactly where to place her feet and where to touch the handle of the safe. If any of that were not done properly, the enclosed space would become a gas-filled coffin before the thief realized anything was wrong.

The lock clicked, and Loretta pulled the heavy door open. Inside were shelves, but none of these were empty at the moment. Coin was by far Loretta's preferred method of payment, but she'd been known to accept rare gemstones or jewelry on occasion.

She added the contents of her bulging purse to the glittering arrangements, keeping only enough coin to carry her through the next few weeks. Even with all of her safeguards, coming down here while Rhysto threatened to appear without warning was a risk she'd rather avoid.

With her safe locked and the shelves back in place against the wall, Loretta turned her attention to her inventory. She recalled where each item would be delivered as she placed them in the bags, wrapping them in black silk if they were fragile.

She never wrote such things down, a habit she'd picked up a long time ago. Even if her need, and her desire, for secrecy weren't so great, carelessly dropping a list of who had requested these sorts of items would be the quick end of her business. Bags loaded and mental notes made, she turned to the one remaining item on the shelves.

This wasn't anything so common or distasteful as a shriveled tongue or a coat made out of carefully matched human scalps. And no price, not even the considerable contents of Loretta's safe, would come close to what her most treasured possession was worth.

She touched one of the bell ends of her Dragon, then ran her finger along the length, careful not to dislodge or break any of the tiny gears, pulleys, or hair-thin water pipes.

The time to Build again was close, and so was the desire to throw herself into the thrill and excitement of the work. Building suited her personality and needs far more than socializing and selling, but one truly could not exist without the other. Loretta sighed, caressed the opposite bell end one more time, and turned back to her curios.

No shaw pilot, not even one as powerful and well positioned as Rhysto, could stay on the ground forever. Business and temperament kept them all from lingering in Waldron's Gate. Odds were good he'd be on his way again before the week was out. That would give Loretta plenty of time to make her deliveries and gather up new requests.

She already had many nights' worth of Builds stored up in her memory for when the time came. With attention newly being paid to her activities, she might have to push the schedule more than she wanted to. Despite Rhysto's barely veiled threats, Loretta had not forgotten the scare Mr. Norwood had given her, either.

Moving so quickly, with so many Builds packed into each night, was hard on her, and far harder on the Builders. But until she could find a way to get Rhysto permanently out of her life, Loretta would have to take her chances.

She opened the column in the middle of the floor and put the bags on the large scale hanging inside. Weights clinked into place above her head, enough to offset the load she was carrying now. Loretta closed the column and pushed the bronze button again.

When the floor moved down enough for the pantry lamp to light her way, she extinguished the lamp beside her. She made sure she had a good balance before she stepped onto the pieces of wood and pushed the button one more time. Loretta gazed at her Dragon as she and her few remaining deliveries ascended back into the light.

Chapter 12

The tendons in Karl's forearm ached from holding on so tightly, but he could only force himself to relax for a few minutes at a time. He'd made the trolley ride from the hectic train station to his old neighborhood hundreds of times. He knew every stop, every turn. The journey had never taken as long as today.

Over and over again, he stepped down, let others get on or off, and stepped back up so he could be close to the exit. He wasn't sure if being a few steps closer was going to make a bit of difference by the time he finally did get there, but he couldn't seem to stop now. The movement kept at least some part of his mind and body distracted.

That damned map, the one he'd wanted to stare at for hours on end instead of concentrating on what really mattered. Every landmark the trolley passed—distant Ministry building, street, or house—lit up in Karl's mind. He remembered wishing he and George could mark the houses in some way so they could see exactly where this thing had come from and where it was going, this wave of people losing their minds.

If they had done that simple thing, even with the finest thread they could have easily removed, Karl might have noticed his sister sitting right in its path.

He knew the comforting words and gestures for people feeling guilty. Hardly anyone ever came out to visit people who were sent to the Columns, but Karl had run into them a few times out here in the world. He knew how to say it wasn't their fault, nothing they could have done, nothing at all caused this to happen, all the clichés that floated naturally out of his mouth. He also understood why people were never comforted by them, and why most never spoke of their loved one again.

The trolley slowed to a stop where he usually got off when he was visiting his parents on his monthly guilt-induced trip, the scent of lilacs drifting through the open windows, but Karl stayed put. He didn't want to risk anyone seeing him since they'd all be getting home right about now.

He'd only stopped by his apartment long enough to change clothes, not wanting to wear his stained and stinking uniform out in public. He thought he might have to burn that one to ever have a chance of getting the reek of the 'sters out of the fabric.

He'd barely leaned into his supervisor's office, mumbling something about an emergency with his pregnant sister and needing a few days off. Ms. Curtis hadn't been happy, but she hadn't questioned him the way Mr. Willer would have. Karl had until the end of the week to try to figure all of this out.

Karl had one foot dangling just above the street before the next stop, hearing his mother warning him to never do any such thing when he'd first been allowed to ride alone at age nine. For the first time in nearly twenty years, he ignored her voice in his mind. He was several paces down the sidewalk before the trolley clanged to a halt, his eyes on his sister's house a block away.

He'd heard their mother call it a cozy place to start out, but never in Rethia's earshot. What Klia Gilmore meant was the house was far too small to live in for more than a year or two at most. Two full stories with some of the most elaborate woodwork in the neighborhood seemed like a mansion to Karl.

He walked slowly up onto the porch, torn between needing to know if she was okay and not wanting to disturb her. Her first two pregnancies had been rough at this stage, leading her to sleep a lot more than usual. Karl was too afraid to walk away. He knocked on the door, newly painted a deep orange. Before he could knock again, his youngest sister, Janie, jerked it open.

"Karl! What are *you* doing here?"

She stood with her hands on her hips in a comically accurate imitation of their mother, lips pursed, head tilted to one side, blue eyes narrowed. She even wore a perfectly fitted lace apron exactly like Klia Gilmore's. Unlike their mother would have, however, she made no move to let him in.

"Hi, Janie. I got to leave work a little early today. Thought I'd come check on my soon-to-be niece or nephew. What are you doing here?"

She rolled her eyes and sighed with every ounce of exhaustion a spoiled twelve-year-old could manage.

"Someone has to watch the kids while Rethia takes a nap. Again."

"Well, good," Karl said. "I'm glad you're here for her. I need to sneak up and see her, okay? I promise, I won't make too much noise. Are the kids asleep, too?"

Karl squeezed past and glanced up the stairs. Janie didn't quite step in front of him, but he was certain she wanted to.

"Yes, of *course*," she said. "They're in the living room, so you be quiet. I don't think you should go up there, Karl. She needs to get her rest."

"I know, little Sister," he said. "You're great to help out so she can. I just need to talk to her for few minutes. Grown-up stuff."

Janie shook her head, pursing her lips again before she crossed her arms.

"Fine, whatever you want to do. Don't blame me if she gets mad at you."

Karl was halfway up the stairs before he answered over his shoulder.

"Not a chance."

THE STAIRWAY HAD a flowered carpet a lot like the big one in the Gilmore house going down the middle and anchored with brass bars.

The whole family had pitched in to get it as a housewarming gift when she and Gerald moved in here. As far as Karl was concerned, the best part was it was kept his shoes from making any noise.

The last thing he wanted to do was wake up his niece and nephew and bring the wrath of Janie down on his head. He was a little worried about her mentioning his visit to their parents, but she was easier to deal with than his prickly brother-in-law.

"Rethia? Ree?" Karl hoped he wouldn't have to knock again.

"Who's there? Gerry?"

"No, it's Karl. Can I come in for a minute?"

He waited, trying not to drum his fingers against the wall. He heard slow footsteps right before she opened the door.

"Hey Karl," she said, beaming. "What brings you out here in the middle of the month?"

She softened her words with a smile, and Karl couldn't help smiling back. Rethia was his favorite of what he thought of as the first half of the family, just as much as Andy was of the second.

Karl hugged her, trying not to squeeze too hard. "Just got a hunch I needed to check on my niece. Or my nephew?"

"You and Mother," Rethia said. "Driving me crazy with that psychic stuff. You don't even believe in it. Come on in."

Rethia's hair was as curly as Karl's and most of the rest of them, but she had the unfair advantage of being able to wear it long. Instead of fighting constantly trying to keep it under some kind of control, she and the other girls could let it fall loose and free and lovely.

When she turned to sit in a chair by the window, Karl saw she looked great in general, not nearly as tired as with the last two. Her embroidered dark blue velvet housecoat set off the glow in her cheeks and fit perfectly around her huge belly.

Karl sat on the window seat beside her.

"You look wonderful, Sis. How've you been feeling?"

"Thanks, I feel like some kind of great beast," she said. "I'm fine, getting bored of sitting around here all the time. You look like I could knock you over with a feather duster. What's going on?"

Rethia was much more like Karl and Andy, not nearly so given to putting on grand airs like their mother and Janie. He blew out a breath through puffed cheeks, trying to figure out where to start. Obsessing about what to say all the way out here hadn't done him a damned bit of good.

"Busier than usual out at the Columns," he said. "For a couple of weeks now. I actually got the rest of the week off just today. My boss thinks I look rotten too."

"Oh come on," she said. "The way you keep getting promoted, they seem to think the sun rises and sets on you. When did you last get a good night's sleep?"

"That's exactly what Ms. Curtis said when she told me to take the time off," Karl said, laughing. "I will, I might even stay with Mother and Father for a few days, unless you have the space here."

"We do, but my kids are a lot younger than Mom's, remember. You'll stand a better chance of sleeping at all over there."

"Listen, Ree, how have you been?" Karl said. "Sleeping okay?"

She looked out the window and chewed her bottom lip. Karl remembered that little tic from their childhood. She didn't want to answer, but she probably would anyway.

"I'd been sleeping pretty well, considering this block of lead in my belly." She looked at her hands on her stomach, not meeting Karl's eyes. "I had kind of a rough time last night, though."

Karl was relieved she wasn't watching him. He was quite sure his face had turned white. Hearing about her night might be more than he could stand after the thing he'd seen that morning, but he couldn't ignore the coincidence.

"What happened?"

"It was strange, Karl. The baby woke me several times, for one thing, more than usual for nighttime. Even when I could sleep, though, I felt like I was almost seeing things, almost doing things. Gerald said I would toss and turn, settle down for a few minutes, then toss and turn again. I can't remember anything like that happening before."

Karl's throat was dry, as if he'd swallowed a bale of cotton balls.

"What kinds of things?" he said. "Could you tell?"

"I never could quite see." She scowled, her hazel eyes seeming to glow in the sunset. "I didn't want to, though. Even if I could have, I just didn't want to know more. Are you here to take me back with you?"

Karl stared at her, most of him sure she was joking, but a terrified streak right down his middle feared something like that would indeed happen. After watching that baby burn itself just a few hours ago, he was afraid he'd end up a permanent resident himself. Rethia finally laughed, and after a second he joined her.

"Your face, Karl, you looked like you actually believed me! I was kidding, at least about going back with you. I'm sure it's just my body going crazy dealing with this little one here. I'm not any crazier than I was yesterday."

Karl had to chew the insides of his cheeks to keep himself from an honest reply that wouldn't help either of them. He said the first thing that he could catch out of the mess in his mind.

"Why aren't you able to work? I don't know all that much about Building. Does it cause some kind of trouble?"

"Well, I don't know much of anything about what you do," she said. "I know you're damn good at it. Not every woman has trouble. Some women go right through with no problems at all. I did my second time. But not with the first or this one. It's the strangest thing. Everything seems fine until about the seventh month, besides trying to fit into the Building cradle with all this extra ballast. Then one day I settled in to Build, and it felt like some kind of party was going on in there. Every single time after that, the same thing."

"There's nothing the doctor can do?"

"Not a thing," Rethia said. "She said when women try to keep going, the movement just gets worse, to the point that it's really too painful to relax enough to even try to Build. And my midwife is convinced it hurts the baby somehow. Much as I hate sitting around here, I figure it's not worth the risk."

"You're probably right," Karl said. "Moving around like normal today?"

"Oh yes, back to normal twisting and turning." She shifted in her chair before resettling her hands on her belly. "As uncomfortable as that can be, it's quite an improvement over the dancing and kicking all night long. What do you think, Supervising Nurse Gilmore?"

"I think my complete lack of experience with pregnant women is showing," Karl said. "So I proclaim you both perfectly healthy. Seriously, I've bothered you long enough. You already said you didn't sleep well last night."

Karl stood, too distracted by the absurd thoughts running through his mind to keep still. He held out his arm so Rethia could lean on him to get to her own feet.

"To tell you the truth, I just needed a bit of peace and quiet," she said, grinning. "I should get back downstairs. Mother's trying to help by sending Janie, but our little sister can drive me crazy. She's Mother made over."

"That she is," Karl said. "Feel up to dinner at the big house tonight?"

"You know what?" she said. "That would be a nice change of pace. Let her know we'll all be there, will you? Including you, that makes five unexpected guests and no chance to plan ahead. Mother will be delighted."

Chapter 13

Karl paced around his boyhood bedroom, feeling like he'd never sleep again as long as he drew breath. Not a thing had changed since he'd moved out at eighteen. The plaster walls were the same dark blue he'd painted them at twelve, and white pinholes from several posters still clustered in rectangular patterns. He doubted anyone made the climb up here to notice unless they had to.

None of those posters had been worth saving, mainly because Karl didn't care any more about his surroundings as a kid as he did in his own apartment. He hung a few because he felt like he should. He'd only bothered to change them when they got frayed enough for his mother to complain.

The room was only a few of his adult strides across, with four small windows breaking the curved walls. He'd asked Andy a few months ago why he'd never moved upstairs to get away from the clatter and drama of two younger sisters. Andy made the excellent point that as the only boy left at home, he had a much larger room to himself on the third floor. He also didn't have to climb down narrow wooden spiral stairs in the middle of the night to get to a bathroom.

The biggest problem about being in his parents' house, one he hadn't counted on when he decided to come home, was not having George or anyone else to talk to.

His gut feeling, the same one that had alerted him to trouble the night before, was certain Rethia's restless night had not been random. He kept coming back to the 'ster, Building before it could have possibly known how.

All of this was assuming monsters knew how to Build, something Karl had never considered before, and he didn't want to consider, ever. He didn't have room for one more thing to worry about. He nearly jumped out of his skin when someone knocked on one of the wooden stairs.

"Yeah," he said. "Come on up."

"You got some kind of parade going up here, big Brother?" Andy was smiling, but he was dressed and ready for bed. "Your sisters are about to organize a lynching party. They sent me to give you a chance to beg for mercy."

"Shit, I'm sorry, Andy. I'm so used to my apartment, I never even thought."

"Quite all right by me." Andy sat on the one chair that would fit into the room, a wooden desk chair Karl had long since outgrown. "I was getting a kick out of listening to Janie complain. Lucy was just glaring at the ceiling when Janie called me in, but I think she's trying to curse you. Something on your mind you didn't want to tell me earlier?"

"A lot on my mind I wish I could tell you or anybody else now," Karl said, sitting on his squeaky old bed. "I can't 'til I figure at least part of it out. I wasn't kidding. All George and I can find are hints. Anything you didn't want to tell *me* earlier?"

"Same thing as before," Andy said. "A couple of people have gone out to the Columns this week, but you already know that. You sure whatever you found has been going on for a long time? Maybe this is something different."

"I'm not sure about anything," Karl said. "Less than I was a week ago. Maybe I should just get out of everyone's hair and go."

Andy snorted. "One thing I am sure of, Karl, is Mother would fillet you and serve you up for Sunday dinner if you just disappear like that. She's too excited to have you here even for the night."

"I know," Karl said. "I didn't think I could possibly feel guiltier about never visiting. Just one more thing I'm wrong about. At least I'd keep everyone fed for a while."

"I know I'd get sick of the leftovers." Andy got to his feet and stretched, his fingertips just brushing the ceiling. "I might catch you yet."

"I'll keep it down up here," Karl said. "I promise. See you tomorrow, kid."

After trying his best to sit still, probably for at least three minutes, Karl walked over to the window at the front of the house. At least he could get a little bit of fresh air. Something else he'd forgotten was how stuffy the top level in a house could get, even with four windows. His overheating brain wasn't helping.

Before he'd talked to Rethia, he'd thought the 'ster coming from his sister would be the worst thing he could imagine. Now he was terribly afraid it had somehow come from her baby, trying to Build in the womb.

Was that even possible?

He shook his aching head. So many things he didn't know. And the list was getting longer, not shorter. He'd just about decided to try lying down again when movement caught his eye.

The streets below were empty, dimly lit with everyone in Alterra once again asleep but him, but he was sure he'd seen something. A couple of blocks down, not far from his usual trolley stop. His mind happily switched to something it could easily sort through, and Karl felt a dizzying shift in perspective.

He saw his neighborhood from even higher up, just like he had with that amazing map in the Director of Public Relations' office. He picked out Rethia's house, and that led him to the other ones he'd matched up with admissions over the past few months. He let the ones in between, the ones that didn't quite fit, slip out of his mind. Karl could just about hear a ticking sound as his eyes moved from one house to another, marking each of them in the overlapping spirals.

From Rethia's, he shifted to what should be next, another house with a smaller rounded turret up the street. If the pattern held true, and he still hadn't seen any reason to think it wouldn't, whatever was happening would happen there next.

"There!" he whispered, leaning forward, the windowsill digging into his ribs.

That time he was sure he'd seen someone walking down the intersecting street. Whoever it was wore dark clothes and blended into the dim light almost well enough to be invisible. Nighttime walkers, certainly past midnight, were exceedingly rare in Waldron's Gate. It just wasn't done.

His mother would surely have been able to give a good reason from her work at the Ministry of Decorum, but Karl suspected it had something to do with Crumble. He had a brief thought that his wakefulness might have been because he couldn't remember when he'd last had any. He saw the shape again, turning the corner toward the next house in the pattern.

"To The Pit with this."

He sat down again, long enough to put his shoes back on, and grabbed his jacket on the way out. He walked as quietly as he could down three more creaky flights of stairs, hoping the house was still as noisy settling down at night as he remembered. He stood for several seconds with his hand on the cool brass of the front doorknob, listening to see if he'd disturbed anyone. If he had, they were being quiet about it.

Karl stepped out into the night.

As FAR AS Karl could see on a moonless night, the only illumination was the greatly reduced streetlights, turned down low to conserve gas while everyone slept. He went out to the center of the trolley tracks where hardly any light reached and tried to keep his steps quiet, wishing for grass to walk on.

The figure had looked small from four floors up, and Karl hoped that was the truth. He had no restraints or anything at all to subdue someone who tried to resist whatever it was he thought he'd be able to do. Nothing beyond a stern "Stop that!" was coming to his mind at the moment.

He didn't see anyone now, but he knew exactly where the dark figure would be heading. Assuming Karl wasn't too far past his last dose of Crumble and imagining the whole thing, of course.

Or maybe he d just find another person who couldn't sleep and had decided to wander around at night. For no reason. When no one else ever did.

He'd just about convinced himself to turn around and go back to bed when he caught motion out of the corner of his eye. Someone crossing the yard of the house he'd expected, walking away from him and turning the corner out of sight.

Karl froze, not sure if he should chase the guy or try to hide. If he stood right here, whoever it was would see him on the next turn. He walked as fast as he could into the deeper shadow of a big tree in the next yard over.

He waited, holding his breath, still not quite convinced he'd seen anything at all. Tales of hallucinations and other strange things happening when people missed too much Crumble were persistent enough that he couldn't quite dismiss them, though he'd never been brave enough to test it on purpose for himself. He hadn't missed much, but stress and sleeplessness made everything worse. He'd decided to walk around the house to make sure when the shadow moved around the far side of the yard.

The person was small, and he didn't see Karl crouching beside the tree. He carried some kind of stick, one that looked heavy enough to do some real damage if it contacted Karl's head, for example. Karl drew back when the stick sprouted three legs.

The stranger slung some kind of pack off of his back, and Karl's jaw dropped. The twisting movement made it clear he wasn't watching a boy or a small man. This person clad in all black, skulking around in the middle of the night, was a woman. He had to restrain women all the time, and he'd been attacked by more than his fair share. He knew how strong women were, but he relaxed a tiny bit.

She pulled something out of the bag and raised it onto the tripod. Woman or not, Karl's heart sped up at the sight of it. He hadn't seen many, and he'd never touched one, but he was certain that was a revolver.

He'd never seen anyone outside of Waldron's Guard or Constable

Law carrying any sort of blaster, and he'd certainly never heard of a revolver people used at night. Karl was pretty sure even the official Bronzed Revolvers did not swing around slowly and aim themselves, but that didn't matter. All worries about his sister and even the horrifying 'ster forgotten, Karl crept forward.

She bent to get something else out of the bag. Karl was sure she hadn't heard him, and now he was walking on soft grass. Part of his early training and experience, before he or anyone else realized he'd ever be more than a huge and strong orderly who could subdue the tough ones, was how to take patients down without hurting them or getting himself hurt.

He couldn't see any weapons, but it was possible she had something other than a gun. If he ran at her from the right angle, he could knock her to the ground away from the tripod and whatever was on top of it. Safer for both of them that way. Karl got himself into position a few feet away, still hidden by the shadow of the house.

Before he'd taken three steps, he knew this wasn't going to go well.

The woman wasn't focused on whatever she was doing, and she wasn't frozen in fear either. She was turning toward him, and she held one of the weighted sticks some of the guards out at the Columns were too fond of using.

Karl turned his body, launching himself in the air before he'd planed to. The agonizing blow landed on the meaty part of his thigh rather than his kneecap, and he landed on top of the woman.

"What are you doing out here?" he whispered, struggling to pin her arms before she could knock a hole in his skull with that thing. "Who are you?"

She continued to twist underneath him, and Karl twisted along with her. Trying to subdue someone who wasn't screaming into his face was oddly disorienting. He managed to wrap both legs around hers, but her leather-clad arms slipped away from his hands.

"You can't get away," he said. "Stop fighting me!"

"You call this a fight?"

She managed to swing the club around and hit Karl in the middle of his back, forcing his breath out in a hoarse cough. She dropped the club and reached for her side. Whatever she was trying to get could only make things worse.

Karl grabbed the club and rapped the back of her hand, hard enough to make it go numb but not break it. She swung at his face anyway, barely missing his eye.

"That's enough, settle down!" Karl pushed the club against her throat, leaning his weight against her chest at the same time. "I'm not going to hurt you, but I'm not going to let you hurt me either. Now stop!"

When she continued to struggle, he moved the club up to her jawbone. She resisted for a few more seconds before she finally relaxed.

"What are you going to do to me?" she said.

"I don't want to do a damned thing to you," he said. "I just want to know what you're doing out here. I am going to get whatever you were after out of your pocket."

Karl moved the hand not holding the club down along her side until he felt the loose flap of leather. Inside he touched loops of metal, cool glass underneath. He drew out a small hypodermic.

"Going to drug me, were you?"

"Just let me go," she said. "I won't come back this way, I swear it."

"Can't do that," Karl said. "Sorry. I know why I'm out here. Now you need to tell me why you are."

"Get off of me first, you great oaf. You're crushing me to death.'

Chapter 14

Loretta forced her arms and legs to be still, letting her racing mind take up all the excess motion. This giant seemed to come out of nowhere, just a few feet away under a tree when she finally noticed him. No one else had ever caught her on her nighttime visits, not in a decade. She reminded herself to be grateful this man hadn't waited until she was in her own version of a Builder's trance.

"If I let you go, what are you going to pull out next?" he said. "Another revolver? A knife? You're not exactly defenseless."

"You have my only club," she said. "I'll show you where my knives are. I can't breathe!"

He only watched her, and Loretta was sure he would stay where he was until she blacked out from lack of oxygen. He was quite purposely crushing his barrel chest against hers and choking her with her own damned club.

He nodded and moved slowly away. When he sat back on his haunches, he held up the club and the syringe, as if she needed reminding.

"I'm going to sit up," she said. "I'll keep my hands flat on the ground."

He nodded, and he didn't move when she did. Loretta finally caught a deep breath, and the pounding need for oxygen started to let up. No one besides Rhysto had ever managed to control her like that. And he hadn't attacked her at all; that was the frustrating part. He gave her nothing to counter.

"I have two knives," she said. "I'm going to get them now."

"Put them on the ground." He pointed to the space between them with her club. "I don't want to use this or whatever you have in the hypo, but I will."

Loretta pulled a knife out of each of her thigh pouches and dropped them on the damp grass. She could get to them before he did, but he'd outreach her with that club. She had no intention of revealing her small revolver or garrote, or the knife hidden in her tripod. Those might still come in handy later.

"Great," he said. "Now what are you doing out here?"

Loretta shook her head. "We can't sit in this yard and make small talk. I have a couple of things I want to ask. You've had some kind of training. You didn't accidentally manage to pin me down like that."

He sighed. "You're not exactly my first. I live a long way away from here. No way to get there until morning."

Rhysto walking out of her closet flashed into Loretta's mind. This man looked to be several inches taller than the shaw pilot and probably at least thirty pounds heavier. Not an ounce of wasted flesh from what she'd been able to feel, either.

With whatever training he had, he could be exactly what she needed to make those particular worries a thing of the past.

"Keep the club and hypodermic," she said. "Take one of the knives if you want, but I'm keeping the other. We can talk at my house. We might have a lot to offer each other."

He smiled and shook his head, pushing curly hair back off of his forehead.

"I don't know what you think you're going to get out of me," he said. "But I do want answers. Pack up your kit. Keep your hands in sight. If that goes well, we'll see about going somewhere else."

Loretta watched as he picked up one of the knives and got to his feet. He slipped it into his belt and held the club and the hypo. He stood even taller than she'd thought.

If he had any kind of brain to go with those broad shoulders, he could be a fierce ally, indeed. She turned toward her tools.

"Bloody Crown, look at this mess!" she cried.

"Keep your voice down, we don't... Oh. I'm... I hope it's not broken."

The tripod was in the grass with the legs collapsed, and the Dragon was about a foot away. Loretta's guts clenched at the thought of any of it being broken. She had a rare moment of not wanting to find out, of wanting to pretend none of this had ever happened. She scrambled closer and picked up the Dragon.

"I should slit your throat for this," she said.

"Look, I didn't mean to break whatever it is," he said. Big as he was, he sounded about five years old. "No one will be slitting anyone's throat. Let's get it picked up and see if it's okay."

"No, don't you touch it. Stay back. Just stay there."

She picked up the Dragon, afraid to even run her hands over it until she had better light. She rotated it enough to fit into the case and gently put it in. Loretta ran her fingers over the grass, hoping the gyro-compass hadn't gone far.

"Is part of it missing?" he said.

"I don't know," she said. "I can't tell. I need to find something else. Don't panic. It's not a weapon."

When her fingers finally brushed over the gyro, Loretta wished it were a weapon instead. The delicate centerpiece was snapped, and she could feel several of the wires had been broken when the two ends separated. She'd never be able to get everything realigned.

"I can get the tripod," he said in a quiet voice.

"Don't touch it! You've done enough damage already. Stand still, okay?"

She heard the huge man sigh again and shook her head. What a Build night this had turned out to be. Not one single thing finished, one of her most crucial tools broken, and now this stranger was determined to follow her around.

Even if she could get past that club, she'd have a hell of a time disposing of a body this big out in the open. Loretta carefully put the twisted compass into her pack, then collapsed the tripod. Thankfully all of its pieces still moved properly.

"Don't forget that other knife," he said. "Someone will find it for certain."

Loretta stared at him, wishing she could see his face. He could easily outreach her, and the club was a lot more effective than her cane. Still, reminding her to grab another weapon said a lot about his confidence, just as much as not wanting it to be found did about his brains. He could come in very handy.

"It's about a ten-minute walk," she said, getting to her feet. "Neither one of us is going to trust the other, so we'll just split the difference and walk side by side."

"Fine. It's darkest in the middle of the street."

Very handy indeed.

NEITHER OF THEM spoke on the quick walk to her house, and nothing else moved in Waldron's Gate. Loretta needed to know more about him before she could decide if he was worth the risk. She had to get him safely past Bess to have a chance of that.

Her most loyal guard was understandably more paranoid after hearing even the bare minimum about Rhysto. Walking up on the porch unnoticed would be impossible. Responding to the challenge without the man beside her noticing she had a guard—beyond unusual in their proper, perfect city—would probably be equally difficult.

He'd already been the first person to notice Loretta after a decade.

"You can't simply walk into my house," she said.

"Loyal husband waiting at home?"

"No." Loretta watched him. "Loyal guard."

He stopped, adjusting his grip on the club but not raising it.

"I'm not going one more step," he said, "and neither are you until I know a little more. Why should you need a guard? To keep you in or to keep me out?"

"That's not quite what I expected you to ask," Loretta said, trying her best not to smile. "This one is to keep you out, I assure you. My turn. To get you past her, I'll have to know your name or something close to it."

"Karl Gilmore. Yours?"

He'd spoken too quickly to make something up. Loretta had more than one identity she could easily assume, but now was not the time. She would either be working with Karl Gilmore, or he would not survive the night.

"Loretta Schofield. I can't say I'm pleased to meet you, but here we are. We're going to the last house on the right. I'd appreciate it if you wait on the sidewalk until I speak to my guard."

"Sorry," he said. "Don't think so. One or both of you might have a blaster, and I'd be an easy target. I'll walk up if it's all the same to you."

"It isn't, but I'm not going to argue the point. Stay to my right, and keep still if you want to see another day."

She turned to the left, where her guard would be watching. After a few seconds, Bess stood beside her. The black uniform and silent movement made the woman's appearance seemingly from nowhere even more startling.

"Ma'am."

"This is Karl Gilmore," Loretta said. "He's an invited guest. I've had some equipment problems, so I'm afraid I'm in for the night."

Bess glanced at Karl.

"He's armed, ma'am."

"Yes," Loretta said. "He knows both of us are too. I'll alert you to any trouble."

"Very well."

Bess disappeared again without a sound. When Loretta turned to Karl, he was staring with wide eyes.

"Where did she come from?"

"Don't worry yourself with such things, and our association will go much more smoothly." Loretta unlocked the door, stepped inside, and held it open.

"Why don't you turn on a light or two before I go in?" he said. "I'd hate to trip and break something else."

~

ONCE THE ROOM WAS LIT, Karl finally walked inside, his hazel eyes taking in every detail. She had a feeling those eyes didn't miss much.

"If we're to pretend to have a civilized conversation, can I get you something to drink, Karl? Cafei or Thunderclap? Whiskey from the Northlands? Not quite legal, but not poisoned, I promise. I'll even drink first."

"I'll pass, thanks," he said. Both of them sat, Loretta on the sofa and Karl in a chair close to the door. He held the club and the hypodermic across his long legs. "Why did you bring me here, Loretta?"

"Just what I said back there," she said. "We might be able to offer a lot to each other."

"Such as?"

"I might be able to work with someone as strong and smart as you are," she said. "There are far less pleasant characters than me wandering around Alterra. They're in Waldron's Gate more often than I'd like."

"How could that possibly benefit me?" he said. "I don't even live in the Gate anymore."

"The profits of my work are considerable," Loretta said. "Not just in coin. Where do you live?"

"You can find out easily enough. You have my name. I work out at Joffrey Columns with some of those unpleasant characters. That's where I live."

Loretta sat back, crossing her arms. "Now that *is* interesting. What do you do there?"

"Not so fast," Karl said. "What is this work of yours?"

"You can find that out easily enough yourself. I locate and sell curios, items that are in high demand in certain circles."

Karl crossed his own arms.

"That might be," he said. "But what were you doing out there tonight? I didn't see any other dealers in antiquities."

"Soon enough," Loretta said. "What do you do at the Columns?"

Karl shook his head. "I changed my mind. I'm not going to sit here all night playing this little game with you. Either you're willing to tell me, or you're not. Here's what I've got. I'm a nurse, head nurse in my section. Yes, I work with insane people, for about ten years now. My family is almost all Builders. I'm not. No wife, no kids. I live alone. Not a whole lot more to tell."

Loretta studied Karl, considering. She didn't know any more about Joffrey Columns than most citizens of Alterra. She did know she'd accidentally sent at least one person out there by using her too much. She'd often wondered if the insane Builders could still Build.

If they could, Karl might be able to offer her a lot more than protection. Their mental states could even prove to be a benefit with the things Loretta needed for her clients these days.

And if she needed to, she and Bess could dispose of him together quite easily. It wouldn't be the first time.

"All right, Karl. I was out there tonight because one of my buyers lives in that house. The easiest way to get what these people want is to use them to Build it. I was getting ready to do just that when you showed up."

"Use them?" he said. "Do you mean you force them to Build while they're sleeping? Is that what that thing is, a miniature Blunderbuss?"

He leaned forward, eyes narrowed, one hand gripping the club. That was the first flash of anger she'd seen or heard tonight. It didn't scare her, not with him across the room and a tiny clockwork revolver hidden in the small of her back.

She liked it, though, very much.

"That's the general idea, yes," she said. "I've learned to be careful over the years so I don't cause them too much stress. They're quite pleased with the items. After all, they Build exactly what they ask for."

"So you take their ritterns for what their talent creates." Karl took a deep breath, scrubbing his fingers through his hair. "You either have no idea, or you don't give a shit. Just because you don't see it doesn't mean there's no stress. You're stealing from them. That always shows up somewhere, Loretta."

She shrugged. "We can argue about that another time. I won't be Building again anytime soon. That little tussle back there broke my gyro-compass. Until I can get that repaired or replaced, I'm out of business."

"Good," he said. "The damage you may have done..."

"You're right," Loretta said. "I have no way to know past the trouble I had when I didn't know any better. Maybe you can help me figure out a safer way to do it."

"You could just bloody stop, you know!" Loretta saw the muscles in his jaw flexing. "From the looks of this place, you've made plenty of coin already."

"Could you just stop, Karl? If you had the power to Build? To make something appear, right out of the air? To make something wanted or needed that no one else could?" Loretta hesitated, but she needed to take the chance. She needed to turn him from anger to interest. "Like the rest of your family does?'

KARL SCOWLED, but the risk paid off. His eyes lit up, almost as if he were actually Building.

"Okay, I'll bite," he said. "What kinds of things do you Build? This hypodermic? I've never seen one like this."

He held the glass-and-metal device up, and Loretta noticed he held it at the ready. Fingers through the brass loops, thumb on the plunger. Probably something he used every day in his work. No standard-issue medical hypo had a spring-loaded cap over the needle, though, at least not like hers did.

"I didn't Build that," she said. "You might like it for your job, though. A button just under your thumb activates a burst of steam that numbs the flesh. No one ever feels the needle go in."

Karl half smiled, turning the needle end of the hypo, then the plunger, close to his eyes.

"And is everything you Build so useful?"

"No, not at all," she said. "Most are no bigger than a bottle of

Thunderclap and just about that effective. I probably could make something larger, but I've never tried. Partly because what they've asked for has been small. Partly for the same reason you don't like this. I don't want to hurt one of them."

"Is what you're selling illegal then?"

"No, not illegal," she said. "I'd imagine if more people knew what residents of Waldron's Gate were so eager to collect, it might be. The worst you could say for it now is most would find it distasteful. I certainly do."

"And yet you supply these things," he said. "By stealing from Builders."

"You wouldn't want legitimate suppliers of things like this, Karl." Loretta leaned forward and stared into his eyes. "What I do keeps a trade in flesh you don't want to imagine from taking over. And if you could help me find a way to do this without damaging the Builders I need, that can only make your job easier."

"Sounds to me like you've got it all figured out except for me helping you become a better..." His face went pale, and he closed his eyes for a second. Loretta could only wait, but she wouldn't forget that reaction. "A better thief. If I can't agree to do that, and I'm not making any promises, what do you need me for?"

"Once you think about it, you might change your mind about that part," Loretta said. "But I could use your help for other things too. I'll have to get my gyro-compass repaired, and that means a long and dangerous journey from here. I need protection. From what I've seen tonight, you could easily do that."

"What I could do or not doesn't matter," Karl said. "I'm not going to agree to a damned thing tonight. Let me see that compass, or whatever you have that's broken."

He still looked unsettled for whatever reason, but he didn't sound like he was refusing her. Not yet.

"I need to get it out of my pack," she said. "There by the door."

"Then do it. Don't make any fast moves, and I won't have to."

Loretta wasn't unaware of how his eyes followed her when she knelt by the door. Nothing about her body was hidden by the soft leather. Even with almost no skin showing, the view was scandalous and more than a little titillating.

Karl could look all he wanted. As long as he didn't want to look too closely at the Dragon, she was willing to share.

Loretta dropped the mangled gyro-compass into his hands. The brighter light made it painfully clear she needed a replacement, not a repair.

He turned it carefully, examining the broken and twisted wires

"And this stops you from doing whatever you were trying to do tonight?"

"Whatever I Build would be lost," she said. "The gyro-compass helps me send it to the right place."

"Would it work for anyone else?"

Loretta was glad Karl wasn't looking at her, his eyes still focused on what couldn't be repaired. Of course. A non-Builder in a family full of them. That might work to get around his distaste.

"That one is tuned to work for me," she said. "No one else could use it even if it weren't broken. I don't suppose you're good with wires and magnets and such?"

"No, that's not me." He shook his head before giving the compass back. Loretta dropped it back into the pack and closed it. "So you're saying as long as you don't have this thing in working order, you won't be out stealing from Builders?"

"That's exactly what I'm saying, Karl. I'll also say if you help me, if you go with me to get this one replaced, it's quite possible another can be made. So far I've only Built obscene playthings for the idle class. That doesn't mean we couldn't do something far more useful."

"If they Build what they want for themselves," Karl said, "that could be more of a strain on them, not less."

"You may be right," Loretta said. She wasn't yet sure if his quick mind would be good or bad for her. "Maybe we can figure that out together."

"Maybe," he said, closing his eyes for a second. "That's enough for one night. I don't see why I should believe a word you've said with no proof of any kind. For all I know, that black tube really is some kind of blaster or spyglass. With this thing broken, you'll say you have no way to prove it. Right?"

Loretta couldn't do anything but nod. His brief smile didn't reach his eyes.

"We're going to have to come to some kind of arrangement here anyway," he said. "I need to get back before dawn. I doubt even your guard would want to face my mother if I just disappear out of her house. We each know the other's names. I don't have any other loyal guards, but I do have the option to turn you in."

"You do," she said. "Though I'm not sure what they'd prosecute me for. As you pointed out, I can't do a thing without my gyro-compass, including incriminating myself. You know I have the option to call Bess in here right now."

"And yet you haven't." He got to his feet, holding the club and the hypo. "I'm not going to turn you in. At least not yet. You have a lot more to tell me, and you still want to try to persuade me to do what-ever you really want. Can we hold that truce until later today?"

Loretta permitted herself a smile, a small one he would most likely not understand. He didn't realize it yet, but Karl was going to do what she needed. He was still interested enough to be listening and wanting to ask more. And she was getting a much clearer idea of the tiny little pushes he would need to make the right decision.

"We can indeed," she said. "I'm not going anywhere else tonight. I have no reason to. Six in the evening, perhaps? I'd invite you to dinner, but I have a feeling you'd decline."

"Make it seven. And dinner won't be necessary." He put the club and the syringe on the chair and held up his hands. "Will I be getting out of here with or without a fight?"

"Without. I'll inform Bess if you'll wait here for a moment."

Loretta could easily have called her guard inside, but that was far too much for Karl or anyone else who was going to live out the night to see. She stepped out onto the porch. Bess was beside her in a few seconds.

"Mr. Gilmore is leaving," she said. "There's no need to follow him. He'll be back this evening. He may be able to help solve more than one of the little problems we've been dealing with."

Loretta leaned in the door. "It's fine now, Karl. You won't be followed."

"Never even considered the possibility," he said as he walked past her.

He left without another word or a backward glance, leaving Loretta wondering if he was being sarcastic. She decided he was. Karl Gilmore pleased her more than anything or anyone had for a long while.

Chapter 15

Karl turned up the sidewalk toward home, the tense muscles in his arms and shoulders relaxing the slightest bit. If the woman or her guard were planning to attack him, they wouldn't have waited until he was so far away.

He still had no idea what was going on or what he was going to do about it, but it seemed like he was going to survive the night.

Could any of this be true, or even possible? Loretta showing up at the correct house on the correct night, and in the middle of the night dressed all in black, didn't leave much room to doubt she was involved in the pattern Karl and George had spotted. And he had to admit forcing Builders to work all night long might very well lead to insanity. Enough of them ended up at the Columns without being used like that.

He shook his head and closed his eyes for a second. That was another part he couldn't ignore even if he wanted to. What Mrs. Labine had said about the thief, about stealing, breaking everything.

If any of the rest of this turned out to be true, Loretta was the reason that poor woman was one of Karl's patients now. Who knew how many others as well? What he needed to do was turn her in, no more questions asked or answered.

Sure, that made perfect sense.

Turn her in to the soldiers who worked at Parliament. Or maybe haul her out to Stensue and turn her in to the military. Perhaps drag her out to the Columns, see if his new supervisor knew how to handle it.

Oh no, the best option had to be his own mother. After all, even if stealing from Builders wasn't inappropriate, Loretta herself believed the things she Built were. Surely a woman as highly placed at the Ministry of Decorum as Klia Gilmore would be the perfect choice.

Karl wished even more that he could talk all of this over with George, see if anything he was thinking made sense outside of his own head.

His relentless mind kept trying to turn back to what she'd offered, no matter how much Karl tried to resist, no matter how he concentrated on putting one foot in front of the other as quietly as he could.

This strange woman claimed she was no Builder herself, but she could direct them. She could hijack that incredible power somehow, trick them into Building the things they most wanted. Karl knew his father, brothers, and sisters weren't free to Build whatever they wanted.

He'd known that for years, since long before any of them suspected he would be the only one with the look to lack the talent.

They Built what was sent to them, delivered in the Aether, and that was that. Some insecure and heartbroken part of him had long believed they only told him that so he would feel better about not being able to do it, to find out the truth for himself.

Assuming Builders truly had no power over what they made, that only made what Loretta was able to do that much more enticing.

Could it be possible that Karl's lack, the missing part of him that had always made him so much less than, was what let him have a power none of the rest of them did?

He clenched his fists, wishing he could dig that idea out of his brain. He'd seen suffering with his own eyes, cleaned wounds and waste with his own hands, suffered various scrapes and scratches and bruises with his own body, at least in part because of whatever Loretta did. He couldn't stand by and let her continue, much less get involved in creating more misery.

He turned the last corner toward his parents' house, looking down the street to where all this craziness had started when he first spotted Loretta. That felt like days ago.

Craziness, yes. But what if her idea about him helping her learn how to do it with less damage was possible? Used for good, Building consciously could be an incredible power for all of them.

And what if one of Karl's long-held and long-concealed ideas were true?

From his earliest days out at the Columns, he'd wondered if *not* Building made the insanity worse. Not being able to Build certainly had a huge impact on his own life. If these people were born with such a great ability and then forced to never use it again, that couldn't help how their minds and bodies deteriorated over time.

No one ever got better once they came under Karl's care, his or anyone else at Joffrey Columns. They only ever got worse. The one time he'd dared mentioned his idea, barely a couple of months out of his first promotion from orderly to nurse years ago, the doctor he'd spoken to had made it clear the whole idea was nonsense.

Not only nonsense but a horrible way to create false hope for Builders and their families. Karl knew without being told that bringing it up again would reverse his upward path, probably permanently.

He stopped across the street from the house, looking at all of the windows, trying to see if anyone was up yet. He seemed to be safe. By the time he dragged his weary body upstairs, Karl was surprised to feel more than tired or sleepy. He was utterly exhausted. It was all he could do to get out of his shoes and street clothes and collapse onto the worn out mattress.

Tired as he was, his brain kept going. That had to be the lack of Crumble. Trying to make up doses in the middle of the night when he had to talk to Loretta again might not be the best idea. He fell back on one of his oldest mind tricks.

"I'll talk to her and learn as much as I can. If she seems trustworthy at all, I might even take her out to the Columns to try it out. If she doesn't, I'll figure out who to report her to. But I can't do any of that tonight. I have to get some sleep."

As soon as the words were out, Karl felt the familiar dark cloud overtaking his brain. He had no idea what was coming or what to do about it. All he could do now was try his best to get ready.

Chapter 16

Karl walked toward Loretta's house, noticing the exteriors of the houses with a bit of daylight left. He had a faint memory of his mother being annoyed about the new neighborhood a long time ago, but he didn't understand why. The yards were neat, the houses perfectly charming if not as big as the one where he'd grown up.

He slowed as he approached the end of the row, wanting to be sure the guard had plenty of time to see him. None of this business made any more sense to him than it had the night before. A restless night and jittery day pretending to have a normal visit with his family hadn't helped much.

That morning he'd taken even less than his usual small dose of Crumble. He didn't want to suffer through another sleepless night, but he had the strong feeling he needed his most paranoid imagination here even more than out at the Columns.

He stepped onto Loretta's porch, trying to look everywhere at once. He wanted to see where that guard was hiding.

"Mr. Gilmore."

The shadows weren't nearly as thick as during the night, but he couldn't see where the voice was coming from. A curious echoing effect made it sound like the guard was speaking all around him.

"Yes. I'm here to see Ms. Schofield."

"You're expected. Go on in."

He had no idea what to do, so he nodded and opened the door.

The room was as brightly lit as the night before, and this time he'd been invited by both the owner of the house and her enigmatic guard. But Karl couldn't keep his eyes from darting around, wondering which direction the threat would be coming from.

The furnishings and decorations were as well made as the outside but not showy. The twisting metal sculptures on every wall had seemed odd to him but not particularly ominous. Now they looked like hibernating snakes.

"Mr. Gilmore. What a pleasure to see you again."

Loretta stood in the doorway opposite Karl, dressed in a stylish full-skirted purple gown his mother would have approved of, for the most part. The neckline might have been a little bit low and the corset a bit aggressive in displaying Loretta's cleavage, but this was far more socially acceptable than her skintight black leather. It was equally enticing, if in a different way.

"Ms. Schofield. I think we can skip the formalities and pretending like either of us is glad I'm here. I did bring whiskey if you'd like a drink. I'll warn you this is real stuff made out at the Columns, not Thunderclap."

Karl put the full bottle on a low table in the middle of the sitting area, full of heavy clear liquid rather than the bright green of Thunderclap. He sat in the same chair from the night before.

"I for one appreciate the lack of formalities, Karl," she said. "I'll try to return the favor. Let me just fetch something for this." She walked through in a cloud of rustling fabric and perfume Karl tried to ignore. She returned from what he assumed was her kitchen with two small glasses. "Shall I pour for both of us?"

Karl nodded. "I'll even drink first."

Loretta filled both glasses to the brim and picked one up when Karl did.

"To our future joint adventures," she said with a smile he didn't quite trust.

She drained her glass at the same time as him, then sat on the couch, her dress arranged to frame her perfectly. Karl did wish her hair were still pulled back against her skull. The last thing he needed right now was to imagine how the long black curls would look spread across a pillow, or feel trailing across his chest and stomach.

No matter how she looked, or how long it had been, he couldn't forget for one second he wasn't on a date. This woman had been perfectly willing to kill him the night before. And no doubt perfectly capable of following through.

"Never mind joint ventures just yet," he said. "You gave me an idea last night, but I'm asking again anyway. How can you prove what you're saying about using Builders?"

"I doubt that's going to be possible," she said. "When I was first learning how to do this, several Builds were lost, either to the Fog or just never found. That was with my gyro-compass. Without it, I'd have no way to know where anything went."

"You said you get them to Build these things they want them-selves," he said. "Can you make anything else?"

Karl wanted to believe this smile was genuine, but he couldn't get past the gleam in her violet eyes.

"That's an excellent question. Sometimes they Build the unpleasant things someone else wants. I'm sure they could create things they wouldn't have to hide. And you and I together could Build what people really need rather than waiting for inspiration from the Aether."

"We'll see," Karl said. He forced his racing mind back to practical matters. "Where did you get the things you use to Build? You say you need to travel to get the gyro-compass repaired? I've never seen Tinkers make anything like that, here or out at the Columns."

"My tools come from the Northlands," she said. "From a different sort of Tinker in the mountains. Not exactly a trolley ride away from here."

Karl raised his eyebrows and sighed. He didn't even know how distant the Northlands really were, only that no one he knew had ever been so far from Waldron's Gate.

"No, it's not," he said. "How did you get there before?"

"I traveled with shaws before," Loretta said. "One was not a kind man. Even after I paid him well, he continues to scheme against me. He's after my business and anything else he can take."

Her downcast eyes and flushed cheeks left no doubt what she meant. Karl tried to stop his mind, but the images flashed up anyway. Under different circumstances he might go to great lengths to possess a woman like Loretta himself, one with strength, intelligence, and such a body. Again, those thoughts were not helping him right now when he had no way to trust her.

Perhaps the whiskey had been a mistake.

"The trains then?" he said. "Or passenger airships, legitimate ones?"

"Rhysto and anyone else can too easily trace official transport," she said. "Far too risky. I must find a pilot not in league with the worst one. Do you know any shaws you trust?"

"I can't say I do," he said. "We don't often see them out at the Columns. Mostly trains or boats."

"Of course not," she said. "I apologize. If you were to ask around about one named Rhysto—carefully, I might add—you'd hear he controls much of the trade in and out of Waldron's Gate. A few remain independent, but I'd fear for my life traveling alone with him and his allies about."

Karl tried to sound braver than he felt.

"And if I were to speak to this Rhysto myself?"

"He's out on runs right now," she said. "That's the only reason I felt safe enough to Build last night. I don't think you'd enjoy talking to him any more than I do. His last visit here was most unpleasant. He'd gotten it into his head that I'd been working with another shaw as a supplier. For obvious reasons, I couldn't tell him the truth of what I do. He was displeased."

Karl shook his head, staring at the fireplace to avoid her eyes. He wasn't sure if it was his growing paranoia or his practice at reading people, but he was almost certain Loretta was lying.

He got the feeling she was afraid of Rhysto, and that he probably should be as well. But he didn't think she'd minded his visit as much as all that.

"If you actually do work with another shaw," he said, "won't he get even worse?"

"In all likelihood, he will. But with my gyro-compass broken, I don't have much choice, do I?"

"This place seems a palace to me," Karl said, looking around the room. "It's not huge, but you hardly seem destitute. Do you have to keep doing this business, legitimate or not?"

Loretta leaned forward, and Karl thought it wasn't entirely to emphasize her breasts. She clasped her hands together and stared at him.

"What you see isn't funds I can easily draw upon, Karl. I do own the house, yes, and I'm fortunate in that. But with someone like Rhysto likely to show up at any time, I must have protection. The coin I need for that is more than you'd imagine. I don't have the training or experience you do. How many other options do you think there are for a woman in my situation to earn a living? Legitimate or not?"

KARL DIDN'T HAVE to ask what she meant. He'd seen those women. Never in Waldron's Gate, of course, at least not out in the open. Such things simply were not done. But as a much younger man he'd heard about how different life was out in the countryside, or even as close to home as the Convenience.

Disposal of garbage and waste wasn't the only thing residents of Waldron's Gate preferred to be kept out of sight in that far end of town.

And like so many other young men, he'd visited the Convenience a few times. Years ago, but he wasn't the kind of man to deny the existence of what he himself had taken advantage of.

"All that may be," he said. "But there's still the matter of whether any of what you claim is possible. All I saw you do was set something up. I need some kind of proof before I can even consider this. How do you propose we do that?"

Loretta sat back. "I could take you to some of my clients, see if they'd be interested in showing you what they've bought from me over the years. That might not prove anything to you, other than how shallow the appearance of civility can be. You'll hope the things are not authentic, but I can't prove they're not. I suppose we could try to Build something and hope we can retrieve it. We just need to know where a Builder sleeps. '

Karl took a deep breath, tilting his head from one side to the other. No matter how much he might want to, losing his temper wasn't going to help anyone. He was painfully aware he'd already told her most everyone in his family were Builders.

But if he lost his temper, he wouldn't have to follow the horrible question that had just flashed through his mind. Or the other questions he'd thought of during the long night and day.

"We need to get one thing straight right now," he said. "You're not going to show up outside houses where the Builders I know sleep. One of the main reasons I'm here is to stop that from happening. Understand?"

"Of course, Karl. I don't want to hurt your family or anyone else. I hope you can help me figure out how to avoid that."

"I need to ask you something else," he said. "I'm not sure I want the answer. But I'm asking you to tell me the truth."

"You should never ask a question you're not ready to have answered."

"That's my concern, not yours," he said. "Have you ever used a Builder who isn't a client, Loretta? Does every house you visit have one of those collections?"

"Have a certain one you're concerned about?"

Karl shook his head. "I'm not giving you any new targets. Describe the house you were outside of the night before we met."

"I get the feeling you already know." She described Rethia's house down to the smallest detail. "Match what you expected?"

"Just tell me if anyone there is a client," he said. "That's a simple matter, isn't it?"

"I suppose it is," she said, shrugging. "No one in that house is a client."

"Either you're lying to me now, or you were lying to me last night. That's another simple matter that makes a very big difference."

She looked at him for several seconds, then she leaned forward and poured two more glasses full of whiskey. Karl surprised himself by drinking his down, and by managing not to stare at her breasts. When she sat back, her cheeks were flushed.

"I didn't say one way or the other last night," she said. "But I do sometimes use Builders who aren't clients. It's a little harder, for me and possibly for them, but I do it. Fair enough?"

"It will do unless I find out otherwise," Karl said. "So you already know whether they can Build something they don't want themselves."

"I didn't exactly lie about that either, but yes, they can. What I don't know is if it's harder on them or not. Now I need you to answer a tough question for me. How did you know I was at that house, Karl? If someone you care about lives there, I can't imagine you saw me and waited until the next night to join me at a different house."

Karl settled his hips lower in the chair, deciding to be as honest as he could whether Loretta was or not. Despite the situation, George's booze had him feeling decidedly more relaxed.

"This is part of the damage you might not know about," he said. "I noticed a pattern in some of our recent admissions, one that hasn't deviated for a while now. You've been busy lately. Couple of weeks on, couple of weeks off. Right?"

KARL WAS GRATIFIED when her blush faded away in an instant. He couldn't tell if she was upset by hurting Builders or by getting caught, but he didn't care about that yet. He was glad he'd managed to get to her, even a little bit.

"I had no idea that was happening," she said. "I truly didn't. I thought... I thought that wasn't a problem anymore. Did something happen to anyone at the house you told me to stay away from?"

"Luckily for your sake, no," Karl said. "The Builder in that house seems to be fine, at least so far. That doesn't mean using them like this isn't causing trouble none of us understand."

Glowing green baby's eyes and the heavy, sickening scent of burning flesh tore through Karl's mind. Suspicions or not, he couldn't know for certain whether the horrors she sent through his sister's mind, and perhaps through the baby's, were involved in the monster's birth.

"If they're not all clients," he said, "how are you choosing them?"

"What shape was the pattern you saw?" Loretta said. Karl blinked, not sure he understood the odd question. "You said you noticed a pattern. What did it look like?"

"It was a spiral. Bunches of them, really. I thought the house you were outside of last night would be next on the list. It was."

Loretta got to her feet quickly enough that Karl drew back. He could see both of her hands, but he was nowhere near trusting her.

"Wait here," she said over her shoulder. "I need to show you something."

She disappeared through a heavy wooden door beside the swinging door to her kitchen. Karl moved forward to the edge of his seat, hoping he wouldn't regret that second shot of whiskey if she charged back in with a weapon. She called through the closed door a few seconds later.

"You can come in. Everything is safe now."

Karl wondered if her last words were meant to reassure him as he opened the door. The small room looked like a study, with a desk, wooden chairs, and several bookcases. On the wall directly behind the desk was a huge map.

It was nowhere near as grand as what he'd seen in the Director of Public Relations' office, but no less effective. The pattern of threads on this smaller version made Karl's head swim. It was an exact match to what he'd seen in his mind.

"How closely did you guess my pattern, Karl?"

He stood beside her and touched the pin sunken into his sister's house. He didn't feel that vaguely magic tingle of the larger map. The green enamel felt like solid ice.

"None of this looks out of place to me," he said, his voice barely above a whisper. "I had it exactly right."

Loretta sighed. "I'm not exactly pleased anyone was able to track me like this, but you're certainly as observant as I'd hoped. A little more so."

He turned to her, unable to look away from those eyes.

"Why are you showing me this?"

"Honestly, I'm already far more exposed than I ever wanted to be. I needed to see how good you were, what all you'd been able to figure out. No one else has ever seen this map. Not even Bess. I do hope we can work together."

Karl heard the words as clearly as if she had said them out loud. *Otherwise I'll have to kill you.* This was a display of equal parts confidence and threat, and she understood that as well as he did.

If his curiosity, need to protect his family, and a few other desires he wasn't so eager to admit to didn't have him in too deep already, what he learned about Loretta in that moment did the trick.

"I don't know if I can do what you want, Loretta. Certainly not until I know exactly what that is."

"You want proof of using a Builder's power," she said. "Neither of us wants to do that here, not until we know more about how to do so safely. I need to stay clear of Rhysto and other entanglements for a while. Can you get me into Joffrey Columns?"

"Can I..." Karl had to force his mouth to start working again. "Are you serious? People don't normally want to get in there on purpose, Loretta."

Karl turned away and sat in one of the hard wooden chairs in front of the desk. He didn't want her to see his face when she already had so much leverage.

If she could connect with one of the insane Builders and he could watch...

"I don't mean as a permanent resident," she said. "But this would solve problems for both of us. You see proof of what I'm doing, and I'd be out of Rhysto's line of sight for a while. Then when he returns, when we know where he is, we both go to the Northlands. The same person who can repair and tune my gyro-compass may be able to make tools for you, Karl."

"You have no idea what you're asking me." Karl rubbed the back of his neck, wishing he could reset his life to before Andy had asked him the first question. "It's not the sort of place you just walk into. Not if you want to walk out."

Loretta sat beside him. Without asking for his permission, his nose breathed in her sweet, lovely scent.

"Are you telling me men and women never find their way inside?' she said. "Men and women who can look like they belong there, and offer a service once they're inside?"

Karl looked at her through his fingers.

"That has been known to happen," he said. "At least in the residential areas. Getting you closer to the patients would be impossible."

But Karl knew it wouldn't be. Between his knowledge of who and where patients were and exactly when doctors made rounds and George's master key and access to uniforms, getting Loretta in would be dead simple.

"I'm quite sure you can manage, though," Loretta said. "Is there some way you could be convinced?"

Karl sat back, watching her. She was way too smart to be talking about the obvious things she could offer him, whether he kept getting distracted by impure thoughts about her body or not. They each already had far too much at risk to get caught up in such pointless games.

"I'm going to mark a few houses off-limits," Karl said. "Can you respect that and leave them alone?"

"Yes," she said without hesitation. "Even when we figure out better ways to do this, I will not target your family for Building."

"And if we go to the Northlands, you'll talk to this Tinker friend of yours about making something for me? Something I can Build with?"

"Yes," she said. "Repairing mine will have it fresh in her mind, assuming she can repair it. You may find it suits you, Karl."

He shook his head. "Another time. If you're honestly willing to go to Joffrey Columns on purpose, you have to be ready to leave tomorrow evening. No promises, but I'll go back in the morning and try to get a few things arranged. I'll need help on the inside, from a guy I'd trust with my own life. The Solstice Celebration on Monday gives us a long weekend to do this. Or at least try it."

"I can be ready whatever time you say," she said. "I appreciate what you're risking. I truly do. The rewards will be well worth it."

"Ever been on a boat?" Even though he was more than interested, Karl had to try one last time to stop this disaster. "I don't mean a calm little river cruise or paddleboat, either. The only way you'll get into the Columns and back out again is over the lake on a fishing boat. There's nothing calm about that water, even before it gets to the rocks."

"I've been on more than enough shaws in a high wind with no trouble. I'll take my chances."

Karl stood, and Loretta stood with him.

"No reward will matter if I see or hear of you going after my family," he said. "Are we clear?"

She nodded. "Are we clear that one word of any of this to a single person you don't trust with your life means all agreements are off?"

"We are," he said. "I won't be saying one word more than I have to. I don't want anyone else to know about this, either."

Chapter 17

Karl closed his apartment door and leaned against it. Returning a day early hadn't stopped his boss from glaring at him for the time off every time he saw her. He glanced around the postcard-sized living room, kitchen jammed along one wall, fading sunlight from his bedroom, the only window in the place. Even a few days spent in the vivid surroundings of Waldron's Gate made this dump look like a glorified faded brown closet.

Plain wooden floors that needed polishing, scuffed walls, a rundown blue couch and chair the last occupant abandoned. A couple of scarred tables, nothing to speak of for decoration. He'd always meant to get a rug for the floor when he came back from spending time in his parents' tastefully decorated home. A few paintings for the walls. At least a tablecloth for the minuscule kitchen table. And then he fell back into his routine and forgot all about it.

The bedroom beyond wasn't much better. Hardly anything but his gray uniforms hung in the wardrobe. He came back from the Gate with new sheets when someone in his family got worried enough about him and shoved them into his hands. Same with new street clothes or shoes. He still had all the same kitchenware his mother gave each of her children for their eighteenth birthdays, his rarely taken out of the cupboards.

His adult apartment was a bit larger than his turret bedroom but every bit as neglected. George had managed to turn his similar space in the maintenance wing into a pleasant little home. Maybe Karl should hire him to do the same here.

At least everything was fairly neat. There wasn't enough here to get messy.

Karl had a feeling his dull, predictable life was about to get terribly messy.

He closed his eyes, seriously considering ignoring that and everything else and going straight to bed—until a knock on the door rattled his teeth. That could only be one person this time of day.

"What are you getting me into, Karl?" George said when Karl opened the door. "If you want a little on the side, there are easier ways to accomplish that."

He looked as doubtful as Karl had ever seen him, but he was carrying a huge brown bag.

"Good to see you too, Georgie. If it were something that simple, you'd be the last one I'd ask for help."

George dropped the bag at Karl's feet and walked inside.

"Bring anything good back?" George said. "Anything that won't give me a new disease?"

"Bottle of whiskey from the Northlands in the kitchen. I hear it's strong enough to sterilize whatever you drink it out of and still tastes better than that rotgut you make." All manner of clothes and shoes and badges were in the canvas duffel, everything Karl had asked for and more. "How many people do you think I'm dealing with here?"

"Just wanted to be sure I wouldn't have to go back in for more," George said. "When does this bad idea arrive?"

He handed Karl a cafei cup filled with an unwise amount of the dark, almost oily spirit Loretta had provided as a bribe. Karl barely managed not to cough at the explosion of heat in his throat and belly.

"Watch that stuff," he said, proud that he wasn't wheezing. "They could use this in surgery. She'll be on the nine o'clock train to Swan Gate, and she'll smuggle in on a fishing boat just like everyone else who isn't supposed to be here. It's up to me to get her past the guards."

George nearly collapsed onto the couch beside Karl, managing not to spill his own booze before he finished it without so much as a grimace.

"I'm tougher than I look," he said. "This won't be your first time doing that, right? Bringing in entertainment for the evening?"

"Yeah, actually, it will be," Karl said. "I've never smuggled anyone in or out of here. I'm not quite the charity case you think I am."

"I never thought that at all," George said. "I just thought you were cheap. Seriously, do you have this under control?"

"I am cheap. You got me there." Karl drained the rest of his whiskey. "Just look at this place. I'm also the most careful cheap bastard you'll ever meet. I know the routine as well as anybody does. The guards don't seem to bother watching too closely as long as we're not idiots about it."

George snorted. "Mainly because most of the guards *are* idiots. I've never seen a single one near the docks unless we have a shipment coming in. Listen, Karl, you were right about one thing. Since you left, things have been calm around here. No new admissions, and the 'sters have been quieter than they've been for a long time."

Relief at the improvement hit Karl as hard as the whiskey, followed immediately by horror at more proof of the damage Loretta had done.

"At least I managed to accomplish that much," he said. "I don't want to get you any more mixed up in this than you already are."

"Don't worry," George said. "I don't plan to be. Just don't get yourself caught. Almost time, lover boy."

"Bloody Crown, you are an asshole." Karl pulled out a long, dark coat like he'd seen outside maintenance crews wearing before. "Appreciate the help anyway."

"You'd better," George said, getting to his feet. "I might visit you in here after you're finally locked up, but I'm not going to risk my neck if you get packed off to Stensue or something. To tell you the truth, I'm glad to finally be figuring this thing out, doing something. The past few months were grinding me down to the bone. Let me know how it goes."

"Sure thing. Thanks, George."

Karl had to admit he hadn't seen George with such a spring in his step for quite a long time. If nothing else, breaking that damned gyro-compass and getting Loretta away from the Gate for a few days would let everyone out here catch up on their rest.

Too bad Karl could never take the credit. He knew he'd get plenty of blame if things went wrong. He walked in the opposite direction, toward the exit.

~

SEVERAL PEOPLE WERE MILLING around on the close-trimmed lawn, moving between the towering trees and clumps of flowering bushes, trying to seem more casual than they were. Typical for sundown on a Friday evening.

Karl knew he'd be one of many heading out to meet a weekend visitor. Anyone with a fishing boat—and a valuable contract to supply the huge population at the local asylum—wasn't going to be stupid about who they brought in and took out after hours. Quite a few were willing to earn a bit of extra coin doing just that. And on the inside, as long as certain rules were obeyed, like not letting anyone who didn't work here into the patient areas and making sure they were out before Monday, everyone looked the other way.

Karl was going to break those rules and more.

He did his best to stroll, not wanting to draw any attention to himself, while keeping a close eye on the others doing the same. Several men and a few women randomly headed in exactly the same direction, toward the intersection of the massive stone wall that protected the front of the Columns and the iron fence that surrounded everything else.

There was no reason someone as obviously smart as Loretta shouldn't be able to follow the crowd up from the docks, not unlike what he was doing across the lawn. Karl knew he wouldn't relax until she was safe in his apartment. He barely caught himself before he laughed out loud at relaxing anywhere near that woman. He covered a fake cough with his hand and leaned against the cool stone. One among many who weren't fooling anyone.

After a very long ten minutes, he heard a far too perfect bird whistle from beyond the fence. If she'd followed his directions and paid attention, Loretta would be somewhere in the middle of the crowd outside the seemingly unbroken stretch of thick metal.

The passage of time, lack of maintenance, and a bit of stealthy assistance had left a well-hidden gap where the stone wall joined the shorter iron fence. One by one, the shadows around Karl moved away from their hiding places and walked toward that gap. He waited until he guessed about half of them had gone.

By the time he reached the corner, no one was standing beside it. Karl passed through, not having to hunch as much as he'd expected. The support pole for the fence was still firmly anchored to the wall, but several small stones were missing at the bottom.

A small group of women and men stood together on the other side, not taking nearly as much care to look uninterested as those on the inside.

He stepped forward, hoping Loretta would recognize him before he had to say anything. She wouldn't be able to see his face in the fading light, but he stood several inches taller than almost everyone else he worked with. After a few seconds of silence, he heard footsteps across the gravelly sand. A small form stood beside him.

"George?" she whispered.

Karl smiled. She had been paying attention.

"That's me. Right this way, ma'am."

He was surprised to feel her hand in his, warm and holding tight. Before he could stop himself, he turned his head to the side and caught her scent, that mix of hair and perfume and flesh he hadn't been able to get out of his mind. The sharp hints of saltwater only intensified the effect.

Karl didn't much like Loretta, and he knew he'd never be able to trust her. He couldn't imagine the two of them ever being friends, much less involved in a relationship.

That didn't change how badly he wanted her. The fact that she didn't trust him either only made that desire worse.

"I'm glad to see you, George."

"You too, Bess. I hope the trip wasn't any problem."

"None at all. Everything was exactly as you said. Didn't even get seasick."

Karl stepped though the gap first, and Loretta held onto his hand until she was through. He took her bag, much heavier than the one George had brought, and gave her the coat. A woman passed by on the way out to retrieve her own company for the evening.

"I'm afraid you'll be staying in my apartment," he said. "Not much else is available that won't be searched. It's nowhere near as comfortable as your house."

"It will suit me just fine."

Karl tried to ignore the smile he heard in her voice.

"I doubt we'll be stopped," he said. "Guards hardly ever bother on Friday evenings. More than a few are waiting their turn. Button up your coat, and if anyone asks, I'll answer."

No one said a word to either of them all the way back. Karl hadn't been out much on Friday evenings, partly to avoid all the sneaking around, but he was fascinated at how people around him behaved. No one even looked up, much less spoke or made eye contact. Everyone out on the lawn had turned into ghosts.

When Karl opened the door at the end of his hallway, he was dismayed at how this all must look to Loretta or any other woman. There was a rug running down the middle, but it was threadbare and worn. His practically bare apartment was sure to look even worse to her.

"This is it," he said, fumbling for his key. "No security to worry about now. Nothing worth stealing in here."

He held his door open as Loretta walked through. He cringed as she looked around, wondering how drab and awful this dump must look to her. He avoided noticing when he could.

She turned toward him, her violet eyes catching the dim light. That was one thing he was glad he'd never gotten around to, scrubbing the glass around his gaslights. Brighter light usually wasn't a good thing around here.

"You can sleep through there in the bedroom," he said. "The bed's new, my mother's way of hinting that I need someone to share it with." He felt his cheeks blazing red, not the first time his mouth had mortified the rest of him. "I'll...uh, I'll take the couch. The bathroom is two doors down on the right, back by the door we came in. I'm afraid there isn't much food. I usually just grab meals in the dining hall. No one notices if we take extra over the weekends."

"I'm not worried about that, Karl. We'll manage." She walked to the open bedroom door and looked inside. At least he'd remembered to put clean sheets on the bed. "It's early for going to bed alone. What do you do out here for entertainment?"

"Not much. We have a library in the common room, so I read a lot. Sometimes I play cards with a bunch of guys I work with. To tell you the truth, I guess I study more than anything else."

Loretta walked over to the wall opposite the couch where four long shelves held all the nursing and medical books Karl had been able to get his hands on. That was about the only thing he did spend his salary on these days. He read way more than he thought was normal, but it was a great way to pass the time.

"Looks like you're just as curious as I am, Karl. Always wanting to learn something new."

She ran her fingers along the cloth spines as she spoke, their colors easily the brightest thing in his whole apartment. He tried to stop imagining her dark red nails digging into his back.

"Yeah, that's gotten me into trouble most of my life," he said. "I'm sure it will again. Can I get you anything? We'll get started on what we need to do tomorrow. I'm not up for anything like that tonight."

Loretta hung the dark coat on one of the hooks beside the door. Her dress was plain black, with no corset or flared skirt, but it fit her body perfectly. She sat on the couch and watched Karl, not saying a word. He felt like his flesh was going to burn itself up like that baby 'ster.

He sat in the chair across from her, forcing himself not to look into her eyes. He did his best not to fidget like a nervous teenager.

"Are you up for anything tonight, Karl?"

"Only for trying to get some sleep. It's going to be a busy few days."

"Have I misread you?" she said in a low voice. "I get the strong impression you'd like to join me in your bedroom."

"No. No, you haven't misread me. But this isn't the night. We'll see how it goes from here." He got up and grabbed his small toiletry bag. "I'll just be a minute, then the bathroom is all yours. No one will complain unless you're in there for a long time. I doubt you'll want to be."

He left before she could say anything else, closing the door behind him.

"Get a grip, Gilmore," he said under his breath. "At least keep it in your pants for one more night."

Karl was certain he'd be a lot safer with his clothes off in his own bedroom than in Loretta's house, but it seemed like a spectacularly bad idea no matter where they were.

A bad idea he wanted very much to think a lot more about.

Chapter 18

Loretta watched Karl close the door, shaking her head. She couldn't remember encountering a man who was more maddening and more compelling at the same time.

He wanted her here, he obviously wanted to take her, and he still wasn't playing along. He'd even stacked up blankets and a pillow at the end of that awful, beat-up couch before she got here. She could see the lumps in it, and it wasn't nearly long enough for those legs of his.

No matter. There were plenty of ways to get through a little resistance.

She walked around the apartment, looking in the few cabinets and drawers and the small wardrobe in his bedroom. He was right. There wasn't a damned thing worth stealing or investigating in the whole place. She needed barely two minutes to figure that out. Figuring him out was going to be more of an interesting challenge.

By the time he came back, she was in the lumpy chair, reading one of the few fiction books he owned. Historical fiction, as a matter of fact: a fanciful tale about the original brave citizens who discovered the Blunderbuss, and the handful who supposedly lived forever.

"That's a good one," he said. "No one knows who writes those. Some of the others are really out there, full of dragons and unicorns and mechanical people."

He went into the bedroom and closed the door, coming back out just a few minutes later wearing the plainest pajamas she'd ever seen. They were a dark green that brought out his eyes, and the fabric wasn't cheap even if it had no designs or embellishments on it. Even the buttons blended in. Still, they suited Karl so well Loretta had no doubt one of the women in his family had forced those on him at some holiday or other.

He jerked his chin at the shelves. "Read whatever you like. I think I've finished everything in here. No one's in the bathroom if you need it."

"You don't make a whole lot of sense to me, Karl Gilmore," she said, putting the book down and getting up.

"You're not the first to say that. I don't make a whole lot of sense to me either. I don't quite know what we're getting into here, but I'm glad to be doing something instead of letting everything happen around me."

When Loretta came back to the apartment wearing her chaste pink nightgown and sensible dressing gown over it, he'd already laid out his makeshift bed. He was still awake, flipping through one of the medical books.

"Found a cure for whatever I'm doing yet?" she said.

"No, I don't think there is one. I was just looking at the section about depth syndrome. That's what it's closest to, but it doesn't quite match. It seems like Crumble fails them, like they're taking nothing at all. Or like some kind of allergic reaction. That reminds me, do you need a dose?"

Loretta opened her mouth, ready with her normal denial routine. With everything Karl already knew about her, the lie was too absurd to tell.

"I don't take Crumble, Karl. I haven't for a long time. That's another one of my dirty little secrets no one else knows."

"Why did you stop?" He didn't look nearly as alarmed as she'd expected. "Don't you have trouble with that?"

She sat in the chair again, watching him.

"I used to take it, when I was a kid," she said. "Some of the people I hung around with once I got a little older weren't the nicest. Even worse than my family, which I never thought was possible. I needed all the paranoia I could get. I think it helps with the Builds, too. It definitely helps with being up all night."

He shrugged. "Hard to argue with you there. A lot of people out here take a light dose. Seeing plots around every corner can help with some of the patients. Some of the staff, too. I've never gone completely off it, though."

"I've been off for over ten years now," Loretta said. "I feel like my mind's more my own. Might be worth taking the chance if you're going to run with the likes of me."

Karl laughed, put the book on a scarred wooden cafei table, and stretched out on the couch. Loretta wondered if he had any idea how that thin green fabric showed off the muscles in his chest and legs.

"I hope all my practice with people in here helps a little," he said. "I guess if I use you as an example, getting off the stuff doesn't make you as crazy as they say.'

"That probably depends on who you compare me to." Loretta stood, running her fingers down his chest. He caught her hand, holding it for a second before he let go. "Any chance you'll change your mind?"

"Not tonight. Too much going on around here already. Sleep well."

Chapter 19

Loretta was quite surprised to find Karl awake when she opened the door in the morning. The room had been quiet and the bed comfortable, and she'd slept far better than she expected. Someone else bought him such quality sheets, too.

Surely he hadn't slept well cramped up on that couch. Something smelled better than she expected, too.

He'd pulled the tiny dining table toward the center of the room, and two breakfast plates were already there. More importantly, so was a huge pot of cafei.

"Are things busy out there today?" Loretta said, sitting across from him.

"No, they've all been calmer for a few days now. Since..."

"Since you got me off the streets."

He looked into her eyes without a trace of apology. They both knew it was the truth.

"Right," he said. "Listen, I need to know a little more about how all of this works before we try anything. The compass aiming it in the right direction I understand. What is it aiming?"

"The other part is the Dragon," she said. "That's what does every-thing, or at least makes it possible. I use it to Build using the Builders.

It seems to work sort of like the Blunderbuss does, just on a much smaller scale."

Karl scowled. "Seems to work? How did you copy the Blunderbuss?"

Loretta looked away and took a long drink of the hot cafei. She'd always been uncomfortable with how vulnerable this part made her, how dependent on her grandmother. Until Karl tackled her, it hadn't really mattered.

"I didn't make it. It was made for me. I know how to use it, but I couldn't make one myself. Do you understand how all the medicine and machines here work?"

"Well, most of them, yeah." She was surprised at how embarrassed he looked, as if he'd been caught stealing something. "I told you I read a lot. I haven't made things myself, but I understand probably as much as the doctors. None of us know how the brain breaks, though."

"Why aren't you a bloody doctor yourself, then?"

"I don't know," Karl said, staring at his hands. "I've thought about it. I guess I never saw the point of years of school so I could stop doing what I'm already pretty good at. Listen, who made these things for you?"

Loretta shook her head. "I'm not going to tell you that unless I have to. If you go north with me, and if she agrees to it, you'll get to meet her. That's all I'm going to say."

Gemma would likely be more than happy to meet Karl, especially if she thought Loretta was in love with him. Yet another fact best kept to herself.

"Okay, tell me how this Dragon works," Karl said. "I saw you pointing it at the window that night. I don't know much more about the Blunderbuss than any other non-Builder, but I know the basics. Explain the Dragon to me."

"I told you I didn't make it, Karl," Loretta said. "I know how to use it, probably more than the woman who made it. It focuses the talent of the Builders like the Blunderbuss, but I can direct it more than they can. That's all I can tell you no matter how many different ways you ask. If you go with me, you can ask her. I doubt she'll be able to explain it herself, any more than Builders usually do."

Karl stared into her eyes for several seconds, then he sighed. He finally concentrated on his food instead of on her.

No one had ever known about the Dragon's existence before, much less had the chance to ask questions. Loretta was not enjoying having her lack of knowledge pointed out.

"So you think you'll be able to use the Dragon here to Build," he said. "But without your gyro-compass, you can't say where it will go. And you need to be fairly close to the Builders to try it out. Is that much right?"

"That much is right. And none of this works without me, the way I put the image in the Builder's mind. That may or may not work for you even with your own Dragon."

"Fair enough," he said, pushing his chair back. "I have a couple of people in mind, but I need to make sure they're calm this morning. There are some clothes in that bag for you. I think the usual doctor's uniform would be best, the gray one. This place can never shut down, but not as many people are around on the weekends. I'll be back in about twenty minutes."

He walked over to the door, then turned back.

"When the gyro-compass was working, where did you send your Builds, Loretta?"

She shook her head again. That was way too much for him or anyone else to know. Not even her grandmother, the one who'd designed and set up her basement, understood all of it. He shrugged.

"I'm taking the key," he said. "I can't imagine why anyone would, but if someone knocks, don't answer."

Chapter 20

KARL HARDLY RECOGNIZED Loretta in the uniform George had smuggled in. Her hair was once again pulled back against her skull and hidden, and the bland gray skirt and jacket hid her figure.

With the badge and the proper bored attitude, she'd easily pass as a member of the medical staff. As long as the halls were as deserted as usual on the weekend, they'd be fine.

Karl had to believe that to have a chance of getting through the next few hours. He stood with his hand on the door to his apartment, wondering if he'd make it back there tonight or get himself fired. Or worse.

"Loretta, you need to listen to me. While you're in here, you have to play by my rules. If we get caught, we'll be in more trouble than even you've known before. You need to do what I say, when I say it. No questions. When you're using the Dragon, you're in charge, but not before. Understand?"

"I don't have any desire to join you here on a permanent basis. I'm quite an expert at keeping my head down. Get me in there, and I'll handle the rest."

Karl set a quick pace through the empty halls, but Loretta had no trouble keeping up with his long strides.

"Where are we going?" she said.

"First is a man who's been here for a while. Mr. Otis is calm most of the time, very friendly. What got him sent up is he hoards things. If we don't watch him every minute, he'll pick up everything he can touch and hide it somewhere in his room. When someone finally went to his house after not hearing from him for a few days, it was so packed full they could hardly walk through."

He was silent for several seconds, wondering if this particular patient might be the worst choice rather than the best.

"I'd hate to imagine what he would do if he could Build for himself," he finally said. "Anyway, the main reason I chose him is his room is against an outside wall. I figure if you aim that thing wrong, nothing will show up embedded in someone else's floor. Or their skull."

"I'll do my best, Karl, but I don't know how well this will work without the gyro-compass."

He stopped at the door to the Green patient wing, closing his eyes and listening. No one seemed to be moving around inside. He opened the door and beckoned Loretta through.

The other big advantage of starting with Mr. Otis was he lived in the calmest wing of the whole hospital, reserved for relatively stable patients with wealthy families. The hallway was far better decorated and maintained than the residential wing, with the walls and floor polished to a mellow gleam, paintings on the walls, and spotless electric and gaslight fixtures.

These folks would get their meals and medical checkups as usual, but the weekends were far more quiet here than in new admissions or around the more challenging patients.

"He's the fourth door on the right," he said. "I'll go in and sedate him if he's not already asleep." He unlocked a solid wood door across the hall. "This room is vacant. And clean. Best if you wait in there."

As soon as Loretta closed the door, Karl knocked as he opened the other one.

"Mr. Otis?"

The small man was sitting up in the middle of his bed, wearing black-rimmed glasses and dark blue pajamas decorated with bright yellow ducks. His legs were crossed under him like a kid.

A huge assortment of bits of colored paper spread out all around him, a constantly changing game only he knew the rules to. His poof of thinning gray hair looked out of place with his little boy pose.

Mr. Otis grinned. "Karl! What a nice surprise."

"What are you working on today?"

Karl held the hospital-issue hypodermic behind his back. He wondered again what Loretta kept in her syringes.

"I'm afraid I've misplaced some of my things again." Mr. Otis sounded content, but his fingers never stopped moving, shuffling and rearranging the paper. The constant motion sounded like wind through tall grass. "I thought they were all over there, but some of them aren't, so I need to have them all together."

"Good," Karl said. "I'm glad you're getting them in the right place. Would you mind if a doctor came in to visit you for a minute? She wants to try a new treatment. It won't hurt. She doesn't even have to touch you."

Karl decided in that instant to test his own theory about not being allowed to Build making the mental symptoms worse. Mr. Otis had been a Builder for more than thirty years, and when he was less agitated he talked about it constantly.

"Of course, of course," Mr. Otis said, his eyes bright but never looking away from the paper. "Over there. A new doctor, that has to be a good thing. A woman too, you say? Is she good to look upon, Karl? Will she be a pleasing sight over there for my old, sore eyes?"

"She is very good to look upon, Mr. Otis. I think you'll like her just fine. I'll bring her in."

KARL STEPPED out of the room and leaned against the wall. The hall was still empty and quiet. No one was around to stop him from using that sweet man, from possibly hurting him.

But what if it helped him? What if it could help other Builders, maybe even someday figure out how to keep them out of here in the first place?

He chewed his lower lip for a second, then pushed his body into motion. The truth was he couldn't get so close and not answer the question he'd been asking himself for so many years. His curiosity was driving on, same as it ever had.

Loretta was waiting just inside the door

"Mr. Otis is ready," Karl said. "He's awake, but he's distracted enough that everything should work just fine."

"Awake?" Loretta crossed her arms and shook her head. "I've never tried that before. If he focuses on what I'm doing, there's no telling what he'll Build."

"I'm telling you his mind is as occupied as if he were sound asleep. Just aim at the outside. If you let me talk to him and let him keep on with what he's doing, it should be fine."

Karl walked out without looking back, waiting beside Mr. Otis's bed until he heard both doors close. The whispery sound of the paper never slowed.

"Mr. Otis," he said. "This is Dr. Schofield. She's going to try something new."

The man barely broke his concentration on the paper long enough to glance at Loretta.

"Dr. Schofield, so good to see you. Over there. Everything is out of place here. I thought it was over there, right over there, just over there. I'll take care of it all, don't you worry."

Loretta stared at Karl, her black eyebrows drawn together. He nodded and handed her the pack. Mr. Otis never looked up as she set up the tripod and attached the Dragon on top of it. They were on the ground floor, so she locked it at almost level, pointing down just a little toward the wall.

When she got out the headgear he'd seen her wearing that first night, Karl's attention was finally pulled away from Mr. Otis and his obsessive movements.

The narrow leather straps wouldn't possibly fit his big skull, but he wondered if Loretta's mystery woman would be willing to make a set that did.

She settled the contraption on her head and plugged a cable into the side of the Dragon. When she knelt on the floor, Karl noticed Mr. Otis moving faster, muttering "Over there" constantly to himself now. If he got much more upset, Karl would call the whole thing off.

Loretta closed her eyes.

Karl didn't hear or feel anything, but the difference in the man in front of him was dramatic. Mr. Otis froze, his hands still held over the piles of paper. He slowly sat back, closing his own eyes and folding his hands in his lap. The anxious lines on his forehead and across his eyes smoothed out, and he smiled.

At a deep, humming sigh, Karl turned back to Loretta. Her breathing was deep but getting faster, and her full lips were parted. Her face held softness he'd never seen, and a warm blush spread from her throat up to her cheeks. Her head fell back a little.

Her breath sounded like she was just on the edge of the best orgasm of her life, and he saw the same thing on her face, twitches of concentration and ecstasy in her lips and around her eyes.

She held her breath, and Karl was sure he did too. Her eyes squeezed tight as her mouth fell open, but she made no sound other than a long, low exhalation.

When she opened her eyes, Karl realized he'd been gripping the footboard of Mr. Otis's bed tightly enough to make his arms ache. And he had a raging hard-on. No way to hide that in his work pants. He turned to the side, but he was sure she saw. He only managed to break away from her gaze when Mr. Otis let out a huge yawn.

"I'm sorry, Karl. Think I need to take a nap for a little while. Can...can you help..."

Mr. Otis lay down and turned on his side. Karl grabbed the box he kept this set of paper in and brushed everything inside right before he kicked his feet under the blanket. Karl put the box on top of several others on the chest of drawers, all holding various collections.

"Is he okay?" Loretta whispered.

Karl felt his pulse.

"He seems to be fine. Just asleep. He was still as a statue while you were doing that. I've never seen him still while he was awake. Did it work?"

"It felt like it did," she said. She took a deep breath. "When the Build is successful, I feel it, like something goes all the way through."

"Like an orgasm." Karl realized how that sounded as soon as it was out of his mouth, but Loretta only nodded.

"Exactly like an orgasm."

"Let me help you gather all of this up." Karl turned away so she wouldn't see how red his face was. "We'll, ah, we'll go outside and see if anything showed up. What did you Build?"

"I saw a string of pearls," she said. "Plain white pearls, the kind that was so in fashion a few years ago."

"Did it feel like he was trying to change anything?" Karl said as he held the pack open for her.

"I started out with black pearls, just because I like them better. It felt like he really wanted blue, so I let him shift that part."

"Was he hard to Build with? Could you tell he had any kind of problem?"

"He felt very strong but kind of blurry at first," Loretta said, her eyes distant and unfocused. "Once I was able to push toward him, he got clearer. Sounds like that's how he acted."

Karl watched her fold the tripod into a cane before he went back to Mr. Otis. He was still sound asleep.

"He calmed down right away," he said. "I don't think I've ever seen him asleep during the day, either, not without sedation. Let's find those pearls and try it with someone else before they bring lunch around."

KARL WAS RARELY outside so early in the day. He usually focused on morning patient duties or trying to catch up on his sleep. Even the lawn in this section was far more pleasant than the plain grass around his apartment, with the sun catching bits of glass in concrete sculptures and lacy spiderwebs between the tree branches and flowers.

While they searched, he finally managed to drag his mind away from the sounds Loretta made while she was Building. And the look on her face.

He flipped through the mental list of patients he kept long after they were out of his care. Even if they never found what the Builds created, he was more certain than ever that the Dragon or even someday the Blunderbuss itself could be a means of treating former Builders.

He doubted any of them would ever be able to leave the Columns and lead normal lives again, but less sedation and restraints would be an obvious improvement. He couldn't imagine anything he or Loretta could do that would be worse than what he'd heard of in the experimental wing. Not unless she did have something to do with that burning baby 'ster.

"This is where it was pointing," Karl said after twenty minutes. "Any other ideas where it could have gone?"

'No," Loretta said. "I never found my first Builds, when I was learning how everything worked. Without any way to direct it, I have no way to know."

"Strange things make the rounds in this place faster than you'd believe," he said. "If someone finds it, I'll hear about it. Want to try again?"

Loretta turned to face him, hands on her hips. Even in the drab, shapeless uniform, she was lovely in the sunlight.

"Are you going to sedate this one?"

"Not if I don't have to," he said. He started walking to avoid her gaze. "She already sleeps too much. She might not be nearly so pleasant as Mr. Otis, but I don't think she's dangerous. New arrival. Not violent, except for grabbing my arm, but she's unsettled. Just keep your distance and let me talk to her."

They went back inside and down two flights of stairs, one wood and the lower one dark brick and stone, to the tunnels. The underground corridors were lined with the same dingy red brick and dimly lit, with the flames in the few lamps turned down low.

"Do you keep The Imp out here too?" Loretta said, wrinkling her nose.

Footing was treacherous with the floor damp and puddled in spots, and even Karl had to admit the smell was not pleasant. Pushing a screaming man or woman over the jagged bricks was far beyond unpleasant.

"Not that I know of," Karl said. "He'd feel right at home, though.

No doctor or hardly anyone else is going to use these tunnels. They'll keep us a lot safer."

"Why are they still lit?"

Karl pushed a fallen brick out of the way with his foot.

"When I was a green orderly, I expected to be dragging gurneys and restraining patients for the rest of my life. Part of the training for hired muscle was moving the worst ones under here without upsetting everyone else. The loud ones. I doubt anyone else who has a choice ever comes down here."

"Why do you?" she said. "When you're not sneaking fugitives around."

"It's quiet down here." Karl smiled at her, hoping his words didn't sound as strange to her ears as they did to his. "Hanging out with the dripping water and rats is better than the alternative some days. Faster to get around than up top sometimes, too."

Karl wondered if similar tunnels ran below the older parts of the Columns, with horrifying 'sters the secret cargo. Maybe after they were birthed at the Ministry. He decided to ask George, if things ever settled down.

"We're going to where new patients are kept," he said as they walked up another set of brick stairs. "So we'll have to be a lot more careful. People come in over the weekend all the time, just not as many. They try to do most admissions during the week when more staff is here. If anyone *does* come in now, they're too far gone to wait one more day on the outside. If that happens, we'll have to call this off."

Karl stopped at the door to the ground floor, listening. He held his hand up and stepped out. He couldn't see anyone in the brightly lit hall, and the voices he heard were quiet.

He motioned Loretta forward and turned left, toward where Mrs. Labine had startled him so badly just a few days before. As he expected, they passed several people. None of them really focused on the two of them, either nodding or not even looking up from their charts.

"Hang on for a second," he said. "I need to see how she is. Just stand out here and look bored."

THE NEARLY EMPTY room was dim, with curtains pulled over the window and the lamp turned low. Karl pushed the curtains back enough to see the same woman fast asleep, though she looked like she'd aged twenty years. Her face was sunken and gray, and she was still restrained.

"Mrs. Labine?" he said. She didn't respond.

Her lunch sat ignored on a cart close beside the bed. At least no one would be interrupting them to bring it. Karl turned the chart with the bold warning about not giving her Crumble against the wall, then opened the door and turned the lamp up.

"I've seen her before," Loretta whispered. "What happened?"

"Odds are this is a result of you and that Dragon," he said. "She lived in one of the houses you visited not long ago."

Loretta didn't seem sad or remorseful, only angry.

"Then why did you bring me here?"

"If you truly want me to help keep this from happening," he said, "I have to understand what happens in the first place. We know you can Build with her. I'm not going to let you burn up perfectly healthy Builders so I can watch how their minds break. So here we are."

Loretta shook her head and looked away, her mouth compressed. Karl opened the tripod and started to take her pack. She jerked it away and got the Dragon out herself. She glared at him as she put the head-gear on and attached the cable.

"Be sure you have that hypo ready," she snapped.

Karl held it up.

"Afraid of what she'll Build?" he said.

"You don't know what some of these people wanted for their little collections, Karl. Nothing we could easily explain if it just appears in someone's bed. I remember Mrs. Labine here. She was a collector."

"Take care, then," he said, shrugging. "Make this a set of diamond earrings."

She scowled as she settled onto the floor, again sitting against her own heels. With a great, deep breath, she closed her eyes. Karl didn't want to get distracted by her face, or his body's reaction, so he watched Mrs. Labine.

For a long moment, she was perfectly still, long enough that he was starting to wonder if this was a waste of time. Then Mrs. Labine opened her eyes, staring right into Karl's. He took a step back, making sure he was out of her reach.

"The thief..." she whispered.

Loretta didn't seem to hear, lost in her trance.

"What thief, Mrs. Labine?" he said.

Her voice was low and urgent, her words nearly too fast to follow.

"Stealing my mind, breaking everything. The thief scrapes against me, grinding at my brain. The thief cannot get inside. Not anymore."

He jumped when Loretta spoke.

"Karl, this isn't—"

Loretta gripped his calf, her fingers digging into the flesh. He didn't look away, not wanting the patient to see Loretta crouched on the ground beside her bed.

It didn't matter. Mrs. Labine's gaze darted to the other woman.

"Don't steal from me." Her voice was barely audible but gaining volume with every syllable. "Don't steal from me! *Don't steal from me!*"

Karl grasped one of the frail arms and injected the full dose of sedative, hoping that it would take effect before anyone located the source of the screams.

Mrs. Labine stared at her arm, eyes comically wide. By the time she looked back up at Karl, her ability to focus was failing.

"She breaks everything. She breaks...everything. She...breaks..."

"Pack up, now," he said. "Someone probably heard her. We have to go."

When Loretta didn't move, Karl pulled her headgear off.

"I said put it away, Loretta. Now!"

He reached for the Dragon, and she finally moved, knocking his hand aside. Karl checked Mrs. Labine's pulse before he flipped the chart back over. Neither of them spoke until they were in the damp corridor below the hospital.

"What happened back there?" he said.

She stopped walking and leaned against the damp brick wall. Karl leaned against the opposite side.

"I couldn't find her," she said. "At least I couldn't find the way in. She felt like this damned wall." She smacked the bricks with her palm. "What was different with her? I've never felt anything like that, never."

"She's off Crumble," Karl said. "I don't know why, and when I asked, I didn't get anywhere."

Loretta was across the tunnel in a flash, driving both fists into Karl's chest.

"Why didn't you tell me? I'm not one of your crazy patients waiting for your experiments! To The Pit with you, Karl! That hurt!"

He caught her wrists before she could hit him again.

"What do you mean, it hurt?" he said. "Hurt what?"

Loretta twisted away from him and stepped back.

"I don't know," she said, rubbing her forehead. "Whatever it is inside my skull that does this. Her screaming hurt my ears on top of it all. Why didn't you warn me?"

Karl thought of explaining how he hadn't wanted to bias the experiment by telling her the difference, how a trial had to be properly conducted to yield useful information. He didn't need anyone to tell him that would be a mistake he'd come to regret at some point.

And he hadn't expected to hurt Loretta. He already regretted that, and he hoped Mrs. Labine hadn't felt the same thing.

"I'm sorry," he said. "I should have. I didn't know it would cause you pain. I thought... I thought you wouldn't be able to get through, that's all."

"It felt like dragging my brain across these damned bricks," she said. "Like I was rubbing my mind raw. And no, I couldn't get through at all. Satisfied?"

"Not really. That doesn't answer much, except that whoever you use needs to be on Crumble. I'd guess everyone except Mrs. Labine in all of Alterra is. Her and you. I still have no idea why she's not on it. I shouldn't have used you like that, Loretta.'

"Do not let it happen again."

She didn't have to say it, but even in the dim light Karl could see the rest in her eyes. All agreements, including not using his family for Building, would be off if he did.

"I won't. You have my word."

She took a deep breath and let it out in a harsh sigh.

"What do we do now?" she said.

"Everyone else we could try with will be getting their lunch over the next hour or so. We might as well go back to my room and do the same."

Chapter 21

Karl locked the door to his apartment and dropped his keys into his pocket. He rubbed his temples, wishing he could go right back inside and go to sleep and forget about this whole damned mess. His growling stomach got him moving.

Sure, it was fun to be doing some kind of research, learning something new that no one else was even thinking about. But he was afraid the cost would only keep going up the longer he was associated with Loretta Schofield.

When he walked into the cafeteria, he was surprised to see George sitting at the table closest to the door. His friend actually cooked in his own apartment, and he rarely ate in here off-duty or over the weekend. He'd never seen George sitting in such a high-traffic location. Karl joined him with a groan.

"How's your weekend going, Karl?" George's smug grin made it clear what he was really asking. "Everything working out the way you wanted?

"More exhausting than anything. Not nearly as much fun as you seem to think."

"Now that's a real shame. Got something here for you."

He pushed a dark purple envelope across the table. It was addressed to Karl in unfamiliar handwriting. He turned it to face him.

"Where did this come from?"

"The usual place," George said. "I stopped by to check my mail like normal folks do. Noticed this in your slot, something I never see outside of your birthday or major holidays. Those are usually pink, though, the ones from your mother. I figured with all the excitement going on, you might need to see it. Could be months before you remember to check again."

"I'm not sure if I should thank you or not, Georgie."

Karl turned the envelope over, but he found no return address. The seal was dark blue, with no initials or insignia at all. Just a flat circle.

His mother always used gray wax unless she was getting tired of not hearing from Karl. Then it tinted into light green. And Klia Gilmore had never failed to use her elaborate, stylized G seal as far back as Karl could remember.

"Hey, have you heard of anything strange going on this morning?" Karl said. "I know you're not on duty, but sometimes..."

"Maintenance rats have ears everywhere, right?" George drained his cafei and shrugged. "Eh, that's not far from the truth. I heard the 'sters were restless, but only for a little while. They didn't have time to get themselves really worked up. Anything I should be watching out for?"

"I don't know," Karl said. "Maybe. This afternoon might get interesting. I might be taking a little trip sometime over the next week or so. Family trouble up north, you know."

George knew as well as Karl did that both their families had lived in the Gate as far back as anyone could remember. Karl just wanted someone to understand if he did suddenly disappear.

"I'll keep that in mind," George said. "Better grab your food before they close up. I'll be around for the card game in the commons tonight. Come get me if you need help."

"Thanks, Georgie. I owe you one."

George stood when Karl did, a crooked smile on his face.

"More than you could ever repay, buddy. See you later."

~

WHEN KARL OPENED the door to his rooms, Loretta was again reading the battered old science fiction book. He tried to hide his smile as he handed her the envelope.

"I think you might have gotten a note."

She frowned before her features shifted into relief when she saw the handwriting.

"This is from Bess," she said. "Sorry I didn't warn you, but she wouldn't have written unless it was urgent."

"Fine by me. Hope you don't mind it being read first. Security never lets anything go in or out of here without helping themselves. They somehow manage to never break the seals."

She shook her head, already focused on reading.

"I've always assumed anything I send or...receive...could be... Bloody Crown."

Karl raised his eyebrows but said nothing. He concentrated on the surprisingly good soup and bread and waited. Loretta folded the letter and handed it to him.

"I'm afraid my timetable has been moved up," she said. "Rhysto has returned, and he's already been to my house."

"Is Bess all right?"

"Bess can take care of herself better than most anyone you'll meet," she said. "Besides me. I told her before I left to let him go on in if he showed up. He'd never be able to find anything of real worth, and he might do himself real damage if he looks very hard."

Karl unfolded the letter.

Dear Karl,

We have unexpected company, and he was asking about you. He's made himself comfortable in your room, and he's really no trouble. He's most eager to see you, though, so I promised I'd send word. Hope to hear from you soon,

Love, Mother

"Care to translate?" he said.

"It's not particularly complicated," Loretta paced around the cramped living room. "Nothing terrible has happened, but if she's hoping to hear from me soon, threats have been made. I need to find a way to deal with him permanently, but right now I need to get to the Northlands."

She tilted her head down and looked at Karl under her eyebrows.

"Forget it, Loretta. Sounds to me like the best thing would be to stay right where you are until things calm down. Even if he could work out where you are, he won't be getting in here. No one's going to let him sneak through the gap like you did."

"Rhysto has never been one for subtlety," she said. "I'm not going to be, either. I need to go, and I need you to go with me, Karl. This is the safest time to be hiring a shaw pilot. We know where he is, so no risk of running into him somewhere in the hinterlands. I do know of a few shaws who would be delighted to take us out right under his nose."

Karl crossed his arms and drummed his fingers against his biceps. Getting even more involved with this business didn't seem like the best career move for him, even if he was interested in the trip and the reasons for it.

"For a price," he said.

Loretta laughed. "Of course, for a price, one I'm quite willing to pay for both of us as far as coin goes. I'll need you to make the arrangements, and I do need your protection. You will be well rewarded. I give you my word."

"I'm not sure any reward is worth digging myself deeper into this mess. As long as you're not able to Build, things stay calmer where it really matters to me."

She joined him at the table, a faint smile on her face. She sampled the soup and bread, nodding in approval before she finally looked up at him.

"You know there's more at stake here," she said. "I'm quite sure I could find whoever I need to speak with to cause you a great deal of trouble. I'm surprised to admit I don't want to do that. I truly don't. But you would surely not be surprised to know I still would. I'd be tossed out as a prostitute. Not pleasant but not catastrophic. You might not fare as well once it gets out that I had access to patients here."

Karl smiled himself, pleased when her eyes narrowed at the sight of it. He'd resigned himself to that possibility before agreeing to bring Loretta out here. The idea didn't upset him quite as much. Now that he'd seen it in action, he did want to learn more about the Dragon and what it could do. Particularly what he could do with one of his own.

"You're right. I'd be out on my ass," he said. "I'm sure the magistrates in Waldron's Gate would be interested in your little business, especially since everything you peddle is counterfeit. Knowing your lifestyle requires guards would get their attention if that didn't."

She smiled broadly, not looking the least bit displeased.

"We're as evenly matched as I'd hoped, then. What arrangements shall we make to adjust to this new equality?"

"You pay for my passage, obviously,' Karl said. "And my lost salary for whatever time I take off work."

Loretta nodded. "Of course. I don't have that much coin with me, but I have more than enough available to me. I'm sure that's not all."

"Whenever we get to the Northlands," Karl said, "I want this person to build a compass, headgear, and a Dragon tuned to me. You'll teach me how to use it."

Loretta ate a few more spoonsful of her soup before she answered.

"The compass and headgear should be possible," she said. "I can't make promises for another person, but she loves a challenge. My Dragon took weeks to make, Karl. I have no desire to be up there for so long. Do you?"

Karl rubbed his stubbly chin, looking at the ceiling.

"I don't," he said. "Can't she come back with us? Make repairs a lot easier in the future?"

She drew back, eyebrows raised.

"That's not the best idea. She wouldn't agree, anyway. She's like many with such abilities, no matter what the field. Living closely with other people would not suit her well, nor the ones she lives near. She's had trouble with that in the past."

"You live up against the edge of the Fog, Loretta, nowhere near the middle of town. Surely a suitable house could be found or built for her out there."

Loretta leaned forward. "Can you provide her a place to stay until then? Or a place safe from Rhysto until he's dealt with? If you think my having the Dragon is a threat to people's sanity, you have no idea what horrors he would unleash with such power."

Karl walked into his bedroom and stared out at the indifferently maintained lawn behind the building. He didn't want her to see his face. He wasn't sure if his eagerness or his dread would be worse for Loretta to know about.

Having access to the same equipment Loretta used to her own advantage would be a horrible temptation. He definitely wanted the effect the Dragon seemed to have with his patients, with Mr. Otis's sudden calm vivid in his memory.

That power was likely to have side effects, though, and side benefits he hadn't yet imagined. But that power was a temptation Karl was willing to take great risks to have in his possession.

"I'll help you find a place to stay if she agrees to come back with us," he said. "In return, you convince her to make a Dragon for me."

He turned around. Loretta watched him, her head high and confident. She stood and held out her hand.

"If everything else still stands," she said, "we're in agreement."

Chapter 22

KARL HELD on to the looped leather handle, swaying with the movement of the trolley. He could see Loretta at the other end of the car, but she never met his gaze. He wasn't quite sure where George had gotten the badge she wore, exactly like his own. She'd walked through the employee exit right in front of him after the guard signed her out without batting an eye.

If he lived though the next week, Karl intended to pour George a lot more of Loretta's Northlands whiskey and get him to explain a great many things.

Taking more than a week was simply not an option, at least one Karl was willing to explore. His boss had been fairly understanding, but he had a strong feeling he'd have to produce a corpse to get any more time off. The story of his ailing sister only had to hold up a little bit longer.

Karl got off with a good-sized crowd a few stops before Loretta would. She didn't want Rhysto having any reason to suspect she'd been out at the Columns. Karl would go to any lengths to keep Rhysto from following any hints back to his family. He watched the trolley leave, surprised to see Loretta smile at him just before she was out of sight.

By the time Karl made the walk, Loretta's house still seemed deserted. He didn't like walking down this street in late afternoon, when anyone could see him, but it couldn't be helped. He doubted anyone in this part of town would recognize him anyway. Just another fringe benefit of living out of sight for more than ten years.

A familiar ghostly voice greeted him on the porch of Loretta's house.

"Mr. Gilmore. If you'd be so kind as to knock, Ms. Schofield is expecting you."

"Thank you, Bess."

Loretta opened before his second knock. She pulled him inside and closed the door behind him before she spoke. Karl was nervous enough without her agitation making it worse.

"Did anyone follow you?" she said.

"Not that I'm aware of," he said. "I'm not exactly used to worrying about that."

"We need to get out of here as soon as we can. Rhysto only left a few hours ago, and I don't know when he'll be back." She walked a few steps then came back. "I must retrieve a few things before we go, but I need privacy."

Karl snorted and shook his head. Even after everything he'd done and was going to do, she still didn't trust him.

"What do you want me to do?" he said. "Go home? Getting away from my parents before several hours go by might not be possible."

"No, that won't be necessary. The porch will be fine. I know it seems like a lot to ask."

"It is a lot to ask," Karl said, already heading for the door. "Especially when you're dragging me off to who bloody knows where."

"Karl, hang on." She touched his arm. "I'm not used to working with anyone, but that's not all of it. You can't tell him what you don't know. If you don't know anything, he may not question you all that hard if it comes to that."

She stepped over to a bookcase and moved several books aside. She turned to him with a small black revolver. Unlike the nearly arm-length bronzed weapons Constable Law carried, this wasn't much larger than his hand. She also held a leather belt with a rigid pouch.

"I want you to put this on under your jacket," she said. "Bess is more than capable of defending me and herself, but Rhysto never fights fair. He's also a typical bully in a lot of ways. If he does happen to return and sees you, and this, odds are good that will buy us time to get away.'

"Odds are also good that buys us a return visit with a lot more company with real blasters," Karl said, but he took his jacket off and strapped the belt on. Loretta slipped the gun into the pouch and snapped a strap across the back. "How long are you going to be retrieving your things? I've never touched any kind of gun, Loretta, much less fired one."

"It won't come to that," she said. "Not in the middle of the day. I'm telling you, seeing you with it will be enough, at least until we're gone from here. He knows what kinds of people go through the trouble to get these. I need about twenty minutes."

"I know what kinds of people, too." Karl said. "Not one minute longer."

Karl forced himself not to slam the door, mainly because having a firearm attached to his body made him distinctly uncomfortable. Carrying an illegal device at all was bad enough, especially in broad daylight. He knew the general procedure of shooting, but not much at all about avoiding it. He adjusted his jacket as carefully as he could, then sat on the porch swing to wait.

"I assume Loretta let you in on this little plan?" he said.

"We made the plan together, Mr. Gilmore," the floating voice said. "Far better he not know about me at all if we can avoid it."

"You didn't let him in?"

"He let himself in," she said. "He never suspected I was here.'

Karl rolled his eyes, starting to wonder if Rhysto were a figment of Loretta's imagination, one meant to help keep him in line.

Movement at the end of the street caught his eye. A broad man with a heavy, dark brown beard strolled toward the house, the arrogance in his stride unmistakable.

"Expecting any other visitors, Bess?"

"I am not," she said. "Burly, brutish asshole approaching?"

"That would be him. Do I need to let Loretta know?"

"I already have," she said. "Make sure he sees the gun. You'll be perfectly safe."

Karl tried to let the firm confidence in her voice settle his nerves, but it didn't help. He watched the man approaching and listened to his own heart beating faster. Seeing Rhysto in the flesh made him tend to believe Loretta's description of his personality.

He wore the shaw pilot's typical long black jacket with a blood-red vest and broad black belt underneath. Coarse wool pants and boots that matched the belt completed the rough image Karl's mother so deeply disapproved of. She would have been even more horrified at Rhysto's shaggy brown hair, loose in the breeze without the flat, rimmed hat the pilots normally wore.

Restraining a patient, no matter how big or insane, was one thing. Facing down a cruel, shrewd man who likely carried his own forbidden weapons and at least as many knives as Loretta did was not something he felt prepared to do. And yet here he was.

Rhysto stood at the bottom of the stairs, and one hand was indeed hovering close to his left side.

"Who the hell are you?"

"I'm an invited guest of the owner of this house," Karl said. "I doubt I could say the same about you."

"Invitations don't mean a damned thing with a certain class of woman," Rhysto said, one foot on the bottom step.

Karl leaned back and stretched one arm along the back of the swing, grasping tightly so his hand wouldn't shake. He felt his jacket shift, and more importantly, he saw the other man's eyes shift too.

"All the same," he said. "She's made her preference clear."

"Why are you here?" Rhysto leaned forward, but he didn't take another step. "Do you know what sort of woman you're mixed up with?"

"That's none of your concern," Karl said. "You can state your business, and I'll decide whether to let anyone know or not. Or you can turn around and go back where you came from. It's all the same to me."

Imitating a courage he didn't feel, Karl got to his feet and stood with his arms crossed. He was a good bit younger and taller than

Rhysto, and George wasn't the only one who talked about how strong he was.

Rhysto's hands curled into fists, then relaxed at his side. He moved his foot off the step.

"I don't know or care who you are," Rhysto said. "But I do know what's mine. You tell our mutual acquaintance that nothing between us is settled. If she keeps dodging me, it will only get worse. Understand me?"

Karl shrugged, putting his hands in his pockets. He made sure to pull his jacket back again with the motion.

"I understand the words, sure," he said. "We'll see about the rest."

Rhysto glared up at him for several more seconds. He then walked away without looking back. Karl stayed where he was until the man turned the far corner out of sight. He nearly collapsed onto the swing, making the chains sing out in protest. He jumped when Bess spoke.

"That was very well played, Mr. Gilmore. He won't forget you anytime soon."

"I'd rather he forgot the whole damned thing," Karl said. His trembling came through in his voice. "He'll be back, and you might not be as safe as you think."

"I'm safer than you know," she said. "He'd have to burn the house down to dislodge me."

"And if he does burn it down?"

"Then I slit his throat for him and go on about my life with a very pleasant memory. Ms. Schofield is ready now."

Karl shook his head, more aware than ever that he was far out of his depth with this crowd. He was also too far in to walk away, at least for now. Loretta opened the door before he could knock.

"He's gone?" she said.

"Yeah, but I doubt he'll be gone for long," Karl said. His heart was finally slowing down. "Nice guy."

"We'll be away before he returns." She stepped out and handed Karl two heavy leather bags. She carried two herself, one that sounded like it was full of coin. "Keep the revolver. We need to get out to the shaws before he has a chance to."

"I'll keep the gun if you'll show me how to use the dammed thing," Karl said. "I don't know if I could shoot it on purpose or not."

"The safety's on. You don't have any bullets. You're not likely to shoot yourself or anyone else just yet, but I'll teach you. I promise. I'll send word to you when I return, Bess."

Karl jumped again when the other woman spoke from right behind him.

"Very well, ma'am. I'll maintain current procedures until you do."

A tall, strong woman with her dark red hair pulled back stood before Karl. Her blue eyes seemed to evaluate and understand every part of him before she held out her hand. She shook his with a strong grip, nodding once.

"Safe travels, Karl."

"Thank you, Bess. Take care."

KARL FOLLOWED Loretta off the trolley, not nearly so worried about being seen. A vengeful shaw pilot knowing what he looked like made him a lot less worried about someone he hadn't seen in a decade recognizing him.

The crowds around the grand airships weren't as big as when the shaws first arrived. Karl never forgot his older brothers dragging him into those nightmare swarms of people when he was too young, and too small, to resist. He'd spent the whole time terrified of either getting trampled to death or losing sight of his brothers. He hadn't been back since until today.

He couldn't decide if he'd been too afraid to notice back then or if the designs of the ships had changed that much in twenty years. Unlike the sleek silver military airships patrolling out of Stensue, none of the ferry shaws looked the same. Some of the huge air balloons were long and narrow like the patrol ships. The ends were less pointed, the fabrics far more colorful. A few had two or more perfectly round balloons tethered together with thick ropes. Still others had what looked like one huge balloon that bulged in several places as if someone had thrown a gigantic blanket over the smaller ones.

The vessels below that carried the cargo were nearly as varied, with some wide and flat, others shaped like vast wooden tubes. Most were tall with rounded sides and flat surfaces just under the balloons Karl wondered if the shapes varied according to what they carried or simply to suit their owners. With so many of the balloons and flags matching the tents pitched nearby, in shades of everything from bright white to vivid blue to darkest black, he suspected preference played a role.

Most of the goods the long wooden ships carried had already been sent away to merchants, the rudder mouths' outlandish tales already told to starry-eyed young girls. Now the camp moved to a fairly orderly rhythm.

Instead of curious shoppers and young people, only peddlers and workers providing services to the pilots and crews moved about. Porters carried loads of food or clothing or tools for repairs. Brightly dressed men and women clearly there to take care of other needs strolled among the camps.

The noise of hammers and fires, the smell of roasting food and too many bodies, and the blur of constant motion were making Karl's head ache.

"Not all the shaws are loyal to Rhysto," Loretta said into his ear, dragging his attention away from the spectacle. "He's made nearly as many enemies as allies. I've made a point of keeping track either way in case I need transport off the official routes again."

They passed several ships with their airbags missing or collapsed for repair sitting on curved wooden cradles, broad rear propellers nearly touching the ground. A few were airborne and tethered to spindly looking wooden or metal towers with chains or ropes.

Karl had never been off the ground for any reason. He wasn't looking forward to finding out if he got airsick or not.

Loretta continued out to the edge of the camps, where a small group of ships gathered apart from the others.

"I'll talk to them," she said. "You stay back when I say. I want to be sure they see you, but they'll know who I am."

"You said you needed me to make the arrangements."

"Bess has been busy since she sent that letter," she said. "She s been in contact with the pilots I can trust. They know to expect me. Since they don't know who you are yet, this will go a lot faster."

"Make sure they see the hired muscle," Karl said, trying to keep it under his breath. "Even if he doesn't have a clue what he's doing."

"Something like that."

They walked toward a camp that wasn't flashy, loud, or filled with hangers-on like many of the ones they'd passed, but quiet and organized. The black ship perched on a dark wooden cradle was clean and well maintained. The bottom looked flat enough to land on the ground, and the sides curved out and up. The front narrowed to a point opposite the broad, flat back with the propellers. The red-and-black, three-chambered airbag looked brand new. Karl guessed the main part of the ship was three stories tall, with two smaller flat levels full of windows at the top.

A young man, clearly not yet out of his teens, stood outside a matching red-and-black tent. A pole only a few feet taller than Karl stood in the middle, with four smaller ones around the edges. Flags with crests of different cities of Alterra rippled in the warm wind, with Waldron's Gate highest.

When the teenager saw Loretta walking toward him, he ducked his head under the tent flap.

"Wait here," she said under her breath.

She set the bags she was carrying down at Karl's feet, keeping a smaller purse for herself. After a few seconds, he walked back out to greet her. Karl couldn't hear what they said, but he did see some sort of coin pass between them.

The boy nodded and ducked into the tent again. The pause was longer this time, but when he stepped out he waved Loretta over. She smiled at Karl before she disappeared into the tent.

Chapter 23

LORETTA STOOD INSIDE THE TENT, trying to see everything without giving away her uneasiness. She'd known Bill for a long while now, but she hadn't spoken to him for nearly a year.

He certainly wasn't aligned with Rhysto, but she had no way to know what other arrangements he might have made. A deep voice floated out of the dim space.

"Loretta Schofield. When my man Rullin told me you were at my door, I was certain he was deceiving me. To what do I owe this distinct pleasure?"

"Bill. Do raise the lights so I may look upon you. It's been far too long."

She heard the rumbling laugh she remembered quite well, and the lamp in the middle of the tent grew brighter. A wiry man with fine, dark features sat on the ground beside a low table. He wore loose clothes not much different from Rhysto's, but these were new and perfectly clean. He got to his feet easily, standing only a few inches taller than Loretta.

"You're looking quite prosperous," he said. "Life in Waldron's Gate must suit you."

"You seem to be doing well yourself. Handsome as ever."

She walked over to him, holding out her hand. Instead of shaking it, he kissed it before pulling her forward into a quick hug.

"I always hope to see you when I'm anchored here," he said. "If anyone could tempt me away from my wandering ways, it would be you. Please, come sit with me. Tell me what brings you to my side again after so long."

Bill poured two glasses of what looked and smelled like his favorite spicy whiskey from the Midlands, and he held his up. Loretta did the same.

"To dear friends," Loretta said.

"To warm memories and new adventures," he said.

"I'm glad to see you, Bill, but I come asking a great favor. One I'll pay you well for, of course. I need transport. To the Northlands."

"Only you?" He smiled as he poured another glass for each of them. "Or you and the great brute of a man with you?"

"Both of us," she said. "He's an associate of mine, helping me with a project we both have serious interest in."

"You know as well as I do that transporting passengers on a shaw is illegal, Loretta. I would stand to lose everything if we're caught."

She smiled and leaned closer to him.

"I've never known you to get caught, Bill. And you know the same can be said of me. We'd prefer to stay off the records of official transport."

"Of course you would," he said. "When do you need to leave on this illicit trip north?"

"Looks like you've unloaded all of your cargo," Loretta said. "Your ship is in fine running order as always. We'd love to depart tonight or tomorrow morning. I can offer you a great incentive to leave tonight."

Bill threw back his head, and that rumbling laugh filled the tent.

"I'm quite sure you can," he said. "Would your gentleman friend object to the incentive you offer?"

"In this case, absolutely not. The incentive I offer is coin. More than enough to make it worth your time and effort."

"Only coin, then?" he said, smiling. "Not even time spent together for old time's sake? Your fellow must be the jealous sort."

"I'm sure he would be," she said. "Alas, he hasn't had the opportunity to find out for himself. Can you manage to see this as a business transaction, one between two friends? Or shall I take my commerce elsewhere?"

Loretta shifted the heavy purse so the coins within rattled.

"You know I'm happy to work with you on whatever terms you set, my dear. Any other cargo to transport, or is it just you and the rather large man?"

"Just us and the bags we carry," Loretta said. "We may have a third passenger upon our return, a small woman who'd be even less trouble than we are."

"If memory serves," he said, "being less trouble than you often have around you isn't all that difficult. Is this woman more likely to want to share the pilot's bed than you are these days?"

"She may very well be willing, Bill, but I doubt you will. She's easily twice your age."

"Ah, well." He got to his feet and helped Loretta to hers. "I must admit, though, I would be the last one to turn up my nose at such vast experience as a woman that age may have. How long will you need before we can return?"

"Give us two days if you can," she said. "We just need to speak to her and help her pack up her belongings. That may take up a bit more room than the two of us do, but again, your time and trouble will be well rewarded."

"In that case, we must make ready." Bill kissed her hand again. "Leaving tonight will put us in a bit of a rush, but I believe we can manage. And this reward you speak of?"

Loretta smiled at him as she opened her purse. She counted out a bit more than she'd intended, but less than half of what she carried.

"This should serve to get us off the ground and underway," she said. "There will be more when we arrive safely in the Northlands, and double that amount when we return here."

Bill counted the coins, then slipped them into his pocket. He put a hand on her waist as they walked toward the door, but he didn't try anything more.

"We'll be ready to leave in an hour, my dear. If you'd like, you and your friend can wait on the far side of my camp. Whoever you're running from won't be able to see you back there. You'll have to make do with quarters in the cargo hold, but you'll be comfortable enough. No maid service, I'm afraid, but I'll get you to your destination. Rhysto keeps his camp in the main section. He won't see you, or us, until we're already airborne. I'm sure you'd rather take fewer chances than more."

"You're right about that, Bill. I appreciate you taking the chance to help me, my friend. You'll be glad you did in the end."

Chapter 24

Loretta took three paces and reached the far wall of the hold. The rough-hewn wood throughout was scuffed but clean. Storage racks lined the three walls, and the ceiling bristled with metal hooks. A huge box, like a rectangular coffin with the lid removed, sat at the end. Coarse tan burlap covered whatever was inside, but someone had left sheets and a blanket at one end.

Karl stretched out his long arms and touched both sides. He didn't quite look comfortable, but he wasn't as nervous as he had been.

"Bill was true to his word in this case," Loretta said. "We're nothing more than cargo. At least we each have our own rooms."

"There are bolts of fabric in mine," Karl said. "Let me know if you need more for bedding. How long do we have to enjoy such luxury?"

"Charming coming from a man who lives in splendor out at Joffrey Columns. We'll be three days in the air. Not nearly as fast as the transport ships, but quite a bit faster than walking."

Karl put his hands on his hips, then shrugged.

"And we're out of Rhysto's grasp for now," he said. "I guess I'll be next door if you need anything."

Loretta sat on one of the bundles and realized Bill had given her the more comfortable space after all. This was filled with some kind of loose, soft material, maybe loose wool. Almost as good as a mattress if she didn't mind the scratchy surface under the sheet. She'd certainly slept in worse places.

Much as she hated to admit it, she was weary. She wasn't sure if it was the stress of having to leave so quickly, the rocking motion of the shaw, or the constant noise of the propellers and fires keeping the airbag inflated, but she was ready for sleep herself.

The door to her cargo hold was hardly secure, and she wasn't confident Karl would be much of a stand-in for Bess. It would have to do.

A creak woke her, a strangely distinct sound in the general noise of the ship. That didn't sound far enough away to be the door.

She'd turned the tin reflector attached to the gas lamp toward the door before she fell asleep to try to prevent this exact problem. The lamp was brighter now, and aimed toward her. She couldn't see a thing in the pitch black beyond where she lay.

Loretta reached under her makeshift pillow for her knife. A hand shot forward out of the dark and closed over her wrist, squeezing hard enough to hurt.

"Don't think so, sweetheart. You'll have to move faster than that."

That wasn't Bill, and she knew it wouldn't be Karl. She tried to shift just enough to get her other hand to the knife, but he was faster.

A cold blade was against her throat. She recognized the young man who'd been guarding Bill's tent.

Rullin.

"I've heard enough of Bill's tales to know what sort of woman he offers passage to," he said. "You're no different, except you made the mistake of not going to his bed or bringing that oaf you're with to your own. That leaves you for my purposes."

"And if I'm not part of the payment?" Loretta said. "If I've paid plenty of coin to Bill, and he'd be none too pleased at what you're trying to do?"

"What Bill doesn't know won't hurt him," the boy said. "But seeing as you have nowhere to go that doesn't involve dropping a hundred feet or more to the ground, anything Bill learns from you *will* hurt you."

Loretta knew there were far worse fates than having to open her legs for some stranger, but she'd worked for years to put those days behind her. If she could just keep this one distracted long enough, she'd get to his knife or her own.

"Do what you will, and let me get back to sleep then," she said, forcing her muscles to relax. "I doubt you'll take long enough to cause any real disturbance."

"Just as I expected," Rullin said. "Already on your back and not good for much more." He shifted his weight to hold her body immobile under the sheet, but he didn't let go of her arm. "Well, I'm not interested in diseases a woman like you could offer. What you're going to give me is information. Where you're going, what you're doing, who you're working with. Do that quickly and well, and I won't have to hurt you. Not unless you go running to Bill."

Loretta heard that same creak and gritted her teeth. She couldn't let someone working with Rullin join in the fun. His weight on her chest kept her from drawing a full breath. She couldn't shout for help.

If he would just move for a second, just one second, she wouldn't need anyone's damned help. One of her numbing hypos was mere inches away from her fingers. Rullin would never know until she followed the needle with her knife.

The weight lifted as if he'd been yanked on a rope, and her attacker let out a strangled shout.

"He has a knife!" Loretta shouted as she grabbed her own.

"Got it." The lamp flared bright, and Karl was holding Rullin, one arm around his throat, the other holding the wrist with the knife. "Did the lady invite you to share her bed this evening?"

"There's no lady here."

At the young man's croak, Loretta jumped forward, holding her knife against his smooth cheek.

"Perhaps not," she said. "There is a woman here who will slit your throat for you and sleep like a baby. Just couldn't wait to start your career as a raping bastard until you grew hair on your balls?"

"Who said anything about rape?' Rullin said. "I wouldn't soil myself with the likes of you."

Loretta slid the knife just enough to draw blood before Karl twisted away.

"We need to take him to the pilot," he said. "Let him deal with this."

"The pilot's my bother, you bloody worthless oaf."

"In that case," Loretta said. "I should just save him the trouble and spill your guts on the floor right now."

Loretta leaned forward, the knife held against Rullin's gut. Karl twisted away with him, squeezing the younger man's wrist until he dropped his blade.

"No, no one's spilling anything," Karl said. "Get his knife and come on." The boy tried to shift enough to kick Karl's shins, but the larger man leaned back until Rullin's feet dangled and he choked. "Want some air? Then settle down."

Loretta darted forward and grabbed the knife at their feet just as Karl let the boy down.

"We're making a mistake," she said. "Bill could put us off the ship for this."

The boy continued to twist, but Karl's grip never changed. He looked like an adult holding a child's doll.

"Is he any less likely to do that if we murder his brother, Loretta?"

"Murder?" Loretta smiled and shook her head, taking a step toward the door before she was pushing Rullin against Karl's body again. This time her knife made a clear indentation in the boy's throat. "Not until we get *information*. Why do you care where I'm going? Did Rhysto send you?"

"Loretta, we—"

"Shut up, Karl!" She reached down and grabbed the boy's balls, squeezing until he grimaced. "I asked you a question, Rullin. Karl can't get you away fast enough if I decide to cut your throat or crush your balls for you."

"I'm not working for bloody Rhysto," Rullin said, his voice strained. "Not for lack of him trying right under my brother's arrogant nose. Rhysto's a bigger asshole than Bill."

Rullin's face was dark red, but the disgust in his voice was real.

Karl stepped back, and Loretta moved with him, pushing him and Rullin against the wall.

"Then who?" she said. "Who's been asking about where I'm going?"

The boy grinned and shook his head.

"Go right ahead," he rasped. "Do your worst. I've said all I'm going to."

This time when Loretta squeezed, Rullin's eyes watered, but he kept smiling. When Karl finally managed to twist his body and break Loretta's grip, she stepped back.

"To The Pit both of you," she said as she opened the door.

SHE PUSHED OPEN the splintery wooden door, vowing to never again sleep in a room she couldn't lock. Karl followed her down the narrow corridor toward Bill's cabin, one arm under the boy's ribs to hold his feet off the floor.

Karl wasn't even breathing hard.

No one else seemed to be stirring in this part of the ship, and no light showed under Bill's door. Loretta looked at Karl, hoping he'd come to his senses.

If they just dropped this asshole over the side, no one would be the wiser. A good headwind would keep even the navigator from hearing Rullin scream. The boy's face was drawn up like a fist, but he wasn't making a sound.

Karl nodded. Loretta knocked on the door. This one was smooth dark wood polished to a bright shine.

After several seconds, heavy footsteps sounded through the background noise of the airship. Loretta heard a lock of some kind turn, and Bill glared at them.

"When I said I'd give you passage, I wasn't inviting social calls in the middle of the night!"

"I'm afraid this isn't a social call, Bill."

Loretta stepped aside, and the pilot's face crumpled. The change would have been amusing in a less threatening situation.

"The Imp take you, Rullin," he said, his voice barely above a whisper. "Bring him in."

The space was huge compared to the smuggler's cabins, with room for a desk, two chairs, and a proper bed. The furniture, rug, and fabrics were fine without being showy, as was Bill's dark purple robe.

Karl carried Rullin to the far side of the room, dropping him hard enough that the boy's knees buckled before he stationed himself in front of the cabin door. Bill sat on the bed with his head in both hands for a long while.

"Are either of you hurt?" he said.

"No." Loretta sat in the chair closest to the door, still not convinced Karl was right.

"What did he do this time?"

"He invited himself into Loretta's room," Karl said. "With a knife."

Bill finally looked up into his younger brother's defiant eyes.

"Is this true, Rullin?"

"Why would you care?" the boy shouted. "You have no lack of women sharing your bed. If the crews get a few of the nastier spoils, it doesn't cut down on your supply."

Loretta had to force herself to sit still. The truth was Rullin hadn't made any effort to rape her. She had no idea what he was after or why.

She still had both knives, though, and she wanted to use them to find out. Very badly. The look on Bill's face was the only thing that stopped her.

"No one shares my bed who doesn't want to," Bill said. "If you were any kind of man, you're understand any other arrangement isn't worth the trouble."

He got up and walked over to his brother. They were the same height, but the years between them were stark in the handsome, well-groomed man and the raw, gangly boy.

"I thought our father went too far in trying to beat it out of you," Bill said. "Now I don't think he went far enough. Perhaps it can't be beaten out. Perhaps your mind will never be right. You might be destined for Joffrey Columns rather than Constable Law."

"I've seen what they do with men like you out at the Columns."

Karl leaned against the door and crossed his arms. "I've seen it with my own eyes. A few experimental treatments, maybe a surgery or two, and you'll never bother anyone else. Only the people who have to change your diapers."

"That 's exactly what you're heading for, Rullin." Bill squeezed his brother's chin, shaking his head. "And neither I nor anyone else will keep you from it if you can't stop this."

"You'll be lucky to live that long,' Loretta said, examining her knife. "I do appreciate Karl's assistance, but one second of wandering attention, and I would have put an end to you."

"Don't fool yourself that she couldn't have done it," Bill said. He turned to Karl and Loretta. Rullin continued to stare at the floor. "Perhaps she should have. Do you have brothers and sisters, Karl?"

"Several," he said. "I live away from home for a reason."

"You understand my dilemma, then," Bill said. "You understand why I'm in a terrible place here. I can't let his behavior keep getting worse, and I'd never be able to go home again if I execute my own brother, even this one."

He closed his eyes and sighed before he turned back to the younger man.

"This is your last chance with me, or with anyone else. You're on scullery duty for the next month, and you're back with the ground crews whenever we land. One more time, and I'll report you to Constable Law myself. And if they want to turn you over to Karl and treatments at Joffrey Columns, I will not stop them. Understood?"

Rullin looked up at his brother, and Loretta knew this wouldn't be the end of it. She'd seen that expression before, too many times.

This was a person who couldn't, or wouldn't, understand why his behavior was wrong. Something fundamental was missing inside of him, something that could never be made right.

She would do whatever it took to protect herself, but that didn't extend to hurting other people when she had no reason to. The boy stared for a moment longer before he dropped his gaze to the floor.

"I apologize for Rullin's behavior,' Bill said. "I'm glad you were there, Karl, and I thank both of you for not ending his worthless life.

He's my burden to deal with. He will not be leaving this room tonight. We'll discuss how he can make it up to you. Goodnight."

Loretta followed Karl out the door, thankful their rooms were across the long ship from this one. She didn't want to hear how that discussion went.

"Were you telling the truth, Karl? About the treatments and surgeries?"

"Sometimes criminals are sent there just for that purpose," he said. "To see if they can be reformed when everything else has failed. You probably don't want to know more than that. I used to be able to forget things like that, but I can't anymore. I wish I could."

"Would you..." Loretta surprised herself by having to take a deep breath. "I'd like you to sleep with me tonight. I don't think I'll be able to rest at all otherwise. We'll have to find a way to lock those blasted doors before tomorrow night."

He stared at her, his hazel eyes hard to read in the dim corridor light. She wasn't willing to beg him or anyone else to share her bed, but she hoped he would agree.

She wanted him, not just a warm body but his, more than she cared to admit to herself or anyone else. He reached around her and pushed the door open.

"Tell me why," he said.

Loretta blinked, not sure what he meant. She hadn't expected questions at all, only a yes or no.

Well, she'd expected a yes.

"What do you mean?" she said.

"Tell me why you want me in your bed tonight. Should be an easy enough question to answer. Do you want me to sleep by the door just in case our friend Rullin tries to come back after all?"

"No, Karl, I didn't mean by the door. I meant with me."

She wasn't wanting him quite so much now.

"For protection? Some kind of reward? Or because you actually want me?"

"I think the moment has passed." She brushed past him and stepped into the tiny room. "Maybe we'll talk about it tomorrow. Maybe we won't talk about it ever again."

"Makes sense to me. I already told you I wanted to be with you. But not as some kind of consolation prize." Karl smiled, pushing Loretta closer to wanting to slap him instead of sleep with him. "See the vents on the wall there? I opened those earlier. That's how I heard what was going on. I doubt anything else will happen tonight, but I'll hear if it does."

Chapter 25

Karl woke far earlier than he'd planned, but he knew his back
wouldn't tolerate the shifting bolts of fabric any longer. They were so
much harder than they looked.

He didn't see anyone else moving around in this part of the ship,
but he heard men talking and shouting above him. He hadn't wanted
to see anything when they left the ground last night, but he felt a lot
more confident after surviving even a disrupted night up in the air.

He pushed the door to Loretta's room open a tiny bit. She was still
asleep, brown sheets pulled up to her chin, or at least she looked like
it. If she was pretending, he was better off letting her.

He closed the door and headed toward the front of the ship,
wanting to find the way up to the deck. Nervous as he'd been about
flying, he was still excited to be so far from Waldron's Gate and getting
farther by the minute.

Once he was away from the cramped smuggler's rooms and the
narrow corridor he'd hauled Rullin through the night before, the cargo
hold opened out into a larger space than he'd expected. Most of it was
empty on this return trip, and Karl wondered just how much would fit
inside. He guessed it was easily two stories tall, but he had no guess
how long in the dim light.

He'd been too afraid of getting sick the night before to eat much. Right now his rumbling stomach hoped whatever food was available would turn out to be as well cared for as the rest of the ship.

Karl climbed the narrow metal stairs built against the outside wall of the ship, holding the rails against the swaying motion. The door at the top was made of heavy wood, but it swung open easily. He gasped at the view all around him.

They were over a vast, flat stretch of land, far larger than Karl had imagined existed in Alterra. He recognized huge farms with plants or trees in neat rows, but the great stretches of forest looked unreal to him. He walked toward the front of the ship, keeping one hand on the polished black rail beside him.

They were easily two hundred feet off the ground, and the wind was fierce and constant, making his eyes water terribly. The view at the front end of the narrow deck was even more spectacular.

Mountains bigger than Karl thought possible loomed far ahead, most of the peaks covered with snow. He hoped it would still be daylight when they were flying over them.

He heard voices above and to his left and climbed another set of stairs to the smaller level, much more conscious of his grip this time. This had to be the working deck of the ship.

Several men were busy adjusting the huge airbags overhead some scrambling up or down shifting rope ladders fast enough to make Karl's insides recoil. Others tended to the great propellers in the back or the smaller ones on the sides that controlled their direction. A few were cleaning or repairing the gleaming black ship itself. That's where he spotted Rullin with a mop in his hands, not looking nearly so sure of himself as the night before.

A few bruises were visible on the boy's arms and face, and he moved as if he were sore all over. Thoughts of what he'd do if he were in the same situation with his younger brother made Karl's stomach knot up despite his hunger.

Andy would never do such things, but someone probably thought the same of Rullin years ago. Karl couldn't quite manage to feel sorry for him, though, and that was only amplified when the boy glared at him.

"Good morning, Karl," Bill said from right beside him. "I hope you slept well the rest of the evening."

"I slept just fine, thank you. I hope you did the same."

Bill smiled and shook his head.

"I'm afraid I had a rather long night," Bill said. "I'm not sure it was a benefit to anyone. But sometimes these things can't be helped. I've never hired an enforcer like so many of the other pilots do. On the rare occasions that it's needed, the work falls to me. Have you eaten?"

"I was going to ask you about that. Where would I find food around here?"

"Across there to the port side," Bill said, pointing to the left. "Take those stairs down. That leads to the kitchens, such as they are. I hope you're not accustomed to fine dining."

Karl laughed out loud, surprising himself.

"Hardly. I generally eat out at the Columns. Unless I'm at my mother's house, I don't expect much more than fuel."

"So you were serious about that after all," Bill said, nodding slowly. "I'm not sure if I want to know more, but I'm tempted to ask you all the same. Perhaps later. Have you seen Loretta this morning?"

Bill's grin made it clear he'd made the same assumptions she had the night before about where Karl would end up sleeping.

"I peeked in on her before I came up," Karl said. "She's still out."

"Ah, well." Bill closed his eyes for a second. "I'm sure she needs her rest. I hope you'll both join me for dinner this evening. It would be my pleasure. On the unusual occasions that I do have passengers, they're rarely the sort I actually want to speak with."

"I'd be glad to. I'll let Loretta know when I see her."

"Well done last night, Karl. Though I wish it hadn't needed doing. Rullin can be an ass, but he's never tried to harm a passenger before. I'm truly sorry. He's always calmed down for weeks at a time after I've had to discipline him. He won't bother you or Loretta again. Enjoy your breakfast."

Karl did his best to enjoy it, but the porridge was far closer to fuel than gourmet fare, even if a step above the cafeteria at Joffrey Columns. At least the cafei was strong and plentiful.

Loretta walked in just as he was finishing his second cup. She didn't look nearly as bedraggled as he was sure he did.

"Quite a setup our friend Bill has here," she said, sitting at the rough wooden table across from Karl with her own bowl of thick stewed grains. No one else was in the compact dining room. She took a long drink of the cafei he handed to her. "He's made a lot of improvements since our paths last crossed."

"He invited both of us to join him for dinner tonight," Karl said. "I'd imagine he rates a little better setup than this."

"That he does. You won't likely see the pilot eating down here with the common folk. Or with the cargo."

Karl watched her, trying not to be obvious. He wondered if he'd made a mistake by refusing her the night before, but only for a second.

Something had shifted between them, a change in the balance of power he couldn't quite put his finger on. It wasn't so much in refusing to sleep with her. He'd done that back in his own apartment. This was more in his confidence, in his ability to take care of himself and of her when she needed it. He doubted she needed it all that often.

"What does an illegal shaw passenger do all day long?" he said.

"I honestly have no idea, Karl. When I first made this journey, I was nothing more than a fugitive, too afraid to show my face outside of the closet I was stowed in."

"Was that with Bill?"

She laughed, pouring more cafei for both of them.

"No, I wasn't that lucky. I hadn't met Bill yet. Rhysto brought me out of the Northlands."

"Oh. I...I didn't know you'd worked together before."

Despite his earlier confidence, heat rushed to Karl's face.

"I don't know that we worked together, exactly," she said. "We each had something the other wanted and happened to be in the right place."

"How did you meet him?"

Loretta watched Karl, her lips curving in a strange twisted smile that made him uncomfortable all over again.

"Sure you want to hear this?"

"No, but that's never stopped me from asking unwise questions before. I don't know a blasted thing about you, Loretta. You know just about everything there is to know about me. If we're going to spend the next couple of days either together or hiding out in those closet rooms, maybe we should at least make an effort."

She shrugged, staring into her cup.

"You asked," she said. "Where I came from, there weren't many options for women. I doubt there are now. I couldn't bring myself into line with the perversion of The Crown's followers, end up forced to be some asshole's wife and have his children until I dropped dead from it. The only other way..."

She sighed and looked into Karl's eyes.

"I could have been a scullery maid and died in filthy rags before I'd earned a single gray hair. Or what I did instead. I took care of other needs, usually what the wives didn't. Or couldn't."

Karl tried to force himself to keep breathing and not drop his gaze. Judging Loretta or any other woman for offering services he'd taken advantage of himself was more hypocritical than he could tolerate. Sitting here calmly discussing such things might turn out to be nearly as difficult.

"How did you end up in Waldron's Gate?"

"Well, I met Rhysto. He was, shall we say, a reliable customer back then. When he mentioned taking me away from such a life, I took him more seriously than I think he'd planned for. But he was true to his word, at least in that instance. When he returned the next time, he was ready to take me with him. Just a little bonus thrown in with all the potatoes."

"What did you..." Karl said, trying to grasp at a coherent thought. "When you got to the Gate, did you..."

"No. I'd decided to leave that line of work behind with my family and their backward views on the world. A woman has a great many more options in the city, and a lot more chances to make her own decisions. No one besides Rhysto knew that part of my life. Unfortunately, he was the only one who wanted to keep it going."

"What did you do about him?"

She smiled again. Karl was glad she wasn't thinking about him when she did. That was not a friendly smile.

"I paid him off. It took a few years, until after I built up my current line of work. By then I was able to save up enough to convince even him to forget about that. It worked for a long time. Until he showed up a few weeks ago, I hadn't seen or heard from Rhysto for almost ten years."

"And you have no idea why he showed up again," Karl said, almost to himself.

"I've been thinking a lot about that," Loretta said, scowling. "He claims he heard I was working with other shaws as suppliers, but that doesn't make a damned bit of sense. I've never needed that kind of supplier, and I've been in business too long for him to just now be figuring that out. Something else has to be going on."

"Does he know what you really do?"

"No one does. Not even my guards. No one besides you. It remains to be seen whether that was a mistake or not."

This time, Karl couldn't help smiling back at her. Both of them had gotten in way too deep to turn back easily now. And it wasn't as if either of them could get away on this airship.

"Well, I don't have any designs on your business," he said. "If that's what you're worried about. Assuming any of this works out, I'll leave you to it."

Loretta stared at him over the rim of her cup, her violet eyes curious. Karl felt that same stirring, one that went far past his unruly cock. He didn't trust her, and he was still drawn to her more than he had been to any other woman.

"Why do you want a Dragon, Karl?"

"I... I'm not sure. Just curious about it, I suppose. I've always wondered what Building was like."

She smiled and nodded, leaving no doubt she'd seen right through him.

"We'll do our best to see if it can work for you," she said. "I'm going upstairs to see where we are."

"I'll go with you." Karl stood. "Rullin's up there. I know you can take care of yourself, but I'd rather he knew he has to go through me."

"Why Karl Gilmore, what a gentleman you've turned out to be. From the looks of you, no one told you where the goggles are stored, did they?"

Karl fought the urge to rub at his still-irritated eyes. He hadn't given much thought to the other men on deck wearing them, but he remembered that now.

"No, but I'd be glad if you did."

Chapter 26

Loretta stood beside Karl, watching the approaching village. Jagged, rocky peaks soared above the airship, far too high for Bill or anyone else to navigate over safely. Countless sparkling blue streams gathered out of the mountains to form the river that sustained the village below them. If she followed the twisting course of that water, she could glimpse the Fog in the distance, the hard boundary around all of Alterra.

She'd had no plans to return to the Northlands, not for a long, long time. She'd hoped a few more years would have passed before she had to. The more she thought about it, though, having a spare compass and maybe a spare Dragon wasn't a bad idea at all. Even in such clean, idyllic settings, the air sharp and cold as ice in her lungs, people didn't live forever.

Bill spoke from right behind her, a habit she still hadn't gotten used to.

"I hope you'll reconsider letting us take you to your destination. We could easily moor just about anywhere, even in those mountains. The valleys grants us passage if we take care."

"I appreciate the offer, Bill," she said. "I truly do. I'm sure you understand my need for privacy. And Karl is desperate to learn how to work with horses. We can't deny him that experience."

Karl wrinkled his brow, the movement making his black goggles shift.

"Sure," he said. "I'm looking forward to that so much."

"I'll anchor here for two days," Bill said. "Three at the most. You believe you'll be able to leave by then? I don't want to strand you out here."

"Neither of us want you to have to wait any longer," Loretta said. "If we won't be able to leave, I'll send word. I promise."

"As you wish," Bill said. "We'll be anchored in half an hour. These rickety old wooden masts can be tricky."

Bill gave a grinning half bow, then walked back toward the busier middle of the deck.

"I'd still rather let him take us all the way there," Karl said. "Are you sure we can get back in time?"

"We'll simply have to, Karl. You're right about Rullin. He's paying far too much attention to us still. I need to protect this location if I possibly can. Someone like him knowing about it is as far from safe as you can get."

"I doubt I'm going to be safe anywhere near a horse."

"We'll see if they have wagons," Loretta said. "I'll handle the horses. You sit on the seat beside me and look handsome. And intimidating."

Karl rolled his eyes, but he did smile.

Once the airship was finally secured between two tall masts with an alarming number of ropes anchoring it to the ground, they walked down a shifting walkway into a crowd much like the ones that greeted shaws in Waldron's Gate. This one was a tiny percentage of the size but nearly the same volume.

Loretta doubted many of these local residents could afford what most shaw pilots took to cities far to the south of them. They were eager to welcome exotic visitors and sell their own wares. The thought of having a meal here, fresh-caught fish from the river and root vegetables expertly grown in the cool soil, nearly had Loretta convinced to stay the night.

Walton, the same man who kept a watch on things for her and always let her use his horses, for a price, was happy to provide the wagon she needed. Loretta was decidedly less happy to change into a shapeless, un-dyed shirt, long-sleeved and high-necked, and an equally boring flat yellow skirt. The pants she had packed away for the hard work at Gemma's would be a relief, but being forced to wear the uniform of her childhood in the village chafed her flesh and her mind.

Getting Karl to trust the animals or Loretta's guidance of them turned out to be an impossible task. Even after they were underway, he was fidgety and downright annoying.

"I'm not sure this is the best way to go," he said.

"It's done now." Loretta tried to keep her voice calm. "We have to get out of here before we run out of time. I don't want to waste a night camping out under these bloody cold stars with you."

"Is this the road that goes to her house? Whoever we're going to see?"

"Yes, Karl. This is the road to her house." Loretta shook her head, scowling at him. "What other road should I be on instead? One that leads in the opposite direction?"

"Yeah, maybe you should. Rullin was watching us the whole time, Loretta. He pretended to be securing the airship, but his eyes never left us. I don't care what Bill said about him calming down. I have no doubt Rullin's watching us right now. Is there another road we can take, even if it means we're out longer?"

Loretta slowed the horses, calling her knowledge of this area to mind. She didn't know that many of the roads. She'd only been up here a few times to get Gemma settled, and each time they'd gone directly to the house.

But she'd brought Karl for that very reason, to help her be as paranoid as necessary. He saw this place as an outsider, as far from his oddly sheltered life in an insane asylum as possible. Years in the capital city with predictable dangers may have dulled her senses a bit.

"We'll go back and see if Walton has a map we can have, or more likely buy," she said. "That way, we can go a different route. If Rullin bothers to ask, he should be thrown off the trail. Walton's the only one who knows where we're going, but he's kept my secrets for years now. I pay him well enough. Have you told anyone?"

"Of course not," Karl said. "Who would I tell? I don't have the slightest idea where we're going anyway."

They saw no evidence of the surly young man in the village, and the stall owner hadn't either, but the detour Loretta found looked like it would barely cost them an hour of travel time. That was easily worth avoiding more trouble with Bill's brother. The horses labored a bit over the steep passes, but they still managed to arrive before full dark.

Her grandmother's tiny stone house was high in the mountains, back in a small valley between two sheer stone faces. The ground was rich and green, with a small garden and a few stunted trees.

A small barn made of the same light stone with weathered timber supports sat close to the house. A copper fence with metal posts surrounded the barn, and a smaller pen inside held various sorts of livestock: chickens, a few sheep and goats, and one rather small horse. She was big enough to carry someone Loretta's size, but she looked like a toy compared to the four huge beasts that had brought them.

"Wait here," Loretta said. "I'll go in and talk to her. I doubt very much she's used to visitors."

"What about the horses?" Karl said, his eyes wide. "I don't have a damned clue how to drive this thing if they decide to take off."

Loretta forced a smile and reached back into the wagon.

"See this handbrake? They'll have a hard time going anywhere until it's released. If you want, you can wait on solid ground."

Karl climbed down fast enough that he almost fell. Loretta sighed and walked up the path.

The house looked even smaller than she remembered after years spent in Waldron's Gate. None of her clients would likely consider it a worthy servants' quarters, much less a house.

Two small chimneys stood at either end, with one spilling pale smoke out into the heavy air. That was one of the things about the Northlands that Loretta did miss: the smell of burning peat mixed with cool, damp air.

She reflexively checked the fuel supply stacked against the house and under the deep eaves of the barn. Helping cut and store the turf had been one of her most-hated jobs as a little girl, but it taught her to take cold weather seriously in a place like this with no gas lines within miles.

More importantly, those long hours taught Loretta how vital it was to keep herself prepared, no matter where she lived.

No one was stirring at the two windows at the front of the house, both covered with cheerful bright lavender curtains. The path to the barn was well worn, probably by Walton in his task of keeping an eye on the place and handling any supplies and deliveries. Otherwise it looked like no other human had set foot here for years.

She knocked on the heavy wooden door, taking care not to touch the metal strips set into the frame or stand on the metal grate. Before ten seconds passed, a small, gray-haired woman stood before her. She wore the same men's work shirt and pants that Loretta was eager to change into.

"Yes?" She smiled brightly, then tears filled her violet eyes. "Loretta? Is that you, my sweet bobbin?"

"It's me, Gemma. I'm here."

Loretta was surprised by the strength of the older woman's hug, especially now that she was into her seventies. Maybe the air in the mountains was as healthy as everyone said.

"I've brought a friend, Gemma, someone who wants to meet you. This is Karl Gilmore. He's from Waldron's Gate."

"Please to meet you, ma'am."

Karl flashed Loretta a puzzled look before he smiled and took Gemma's offered hands.

"Oh, the pleasure is all mine, Karl," Gemma said, beaming. "I'm so glad to see my Loretta not spending all of her time alone anymore. I adored my time in Waldron's Gate, but it was ever so crowded, it was."

This time Karl raised his eyebrows when he glanced at her. He had a point. She did have some questions to answer.

"We have a few things to bring in for you," Loretta said. "Supplies from the village. We'd love to stay with you a day or two if that's all right."

"Of course it is, bobbin," Gemma said. "You don't even have to ask. Just have this strong young man bring it in. I'll get tea ready. I'm afraid I'm all out of honey unless you've brought some with you."

"I didn't forget, Gemma. We brought jars full."

Chapter 27

KARL DID his best to keep his voice down as he and Loretta walked between the wagon and the house, hoping the woman inside wouldn't be near a window. Having to constantly drag his eyes away from Loretta's legs in the thin black pants she'd changed into only made his agitation worse. The brief outline of her shape against the dark fabric was somehow more enticing than her form-fitting leather.

"You should have told me we were visiting your mother, Loretta. Even I'm not thick enough to miss a family resemblance that strong."

"What difference would it have made?" she said. "Besides, she's not my mother. I'll die a happy woman if I never see that bitch again. This is my grandmother, my father's mother. One of the few people in my family worth staying in contact with."

"So we're up here on some kind of social call to your grandmother? Is that it? That would have made a huge damned difference." Karl picked up the heavy box full of jars of honey, reminding himself not to drop it on the ground too hard. He felt like pouring them over Loretta's head, one after the other. "Why did you spin the whole tale about getting your things repaired?"

"It wasn't a tale, Karl. My grandmother did build these things. Not like your family does, but she put them together."

"Based on what? Your designs? You use her like that?"

"Not my designs," Loretta said. She put a box full of spools of copper wire on the rock wall beside the house and faced Karl with her fists on her hips. "She dreams them. That's where they come from. She dreams of these things, then she knows how to make them work. I don't know how or why, but that's what she does. If you want to call that using, be my guest!"

Karl looked over his shoulder to make sure the door was still closed as he followed Loretta back out to the wagon. None of this was making sense.

"What do you mean, she dreams? Like daydreams, things she makes up in her mind?"

"I didn't say daydreams," she said. "She dreams when she sleeps. She closes her eyes, and she sees these things. I don't even know if she knows how to use them until she builds them. She's always done it though, since she was small."

Karl grabbed her arm, hoping her grandmother wasn't watching.

"You're making all of this up. No one sees things when they sleep, Loretta, not even out at the Columns. You close your eyes, and that's it."

She jerked her arm free and stepped toward him, her own eyes flashing.

"No one who takes Crumble," she said. "It steals your dreams away. I see things when I sleep all the time, Karl. Ever since I stopped that nonsense, shutting my own mind down just so I'd fit in a little better into Waldron's Gate's oh-so-perfect little society. The same society that's obsessed with the horrifying things I can provide for them!"

Karl backed up against the wagon, not sure he could believe any of this.

"She doesn't take it either?"

"Not for most of her life," Loretta said. She brushed loose strands of hair off her face and glanced toward the house. "That's part of why she's hidden away up here, and why I took her to the city with me. She had trouble with it when she was small, from what I'm told. It made her dull, barely awake. Like an empty-headed child. When she stopped, she could think again. Maybe it worked too well for her, who knows? But my great grandparents kept it secret as well as they could. Once she got older, she had to do that for herself."

"So you took her south with you," Karl said. "With Rhysto."

"No, I never would have exposed her to him." She shuddered and hunched her shoulders. "That was after I met Bill, on my return trip. That's how he knew where to bring us today. One of her neighbors in our old village realized she was off Crumble somehow, maybe something as simple as her never being seen taking it. Or maybe one of my father's brothers or sisters told, or mine. It doesn't matter. Once I got established a little bit in Waldron's Gate, I brought her there to get her away from them."

"And that's when she made the Dragon and your compass."

"Among other things, yes," she said. "Can we please finish this later? She's going to wonder where we disappeared to and get upset."

Karl followed her, his mind bristling with questions. Even after he decided whether he could accept this idea of dreaming or not, there was the matter of Gemma's mental state. He'd seen the look, heard the sound of the voice far too many times to mistake it.

She was at the very least naive, too much so to live out here on her own. If that was new since she'd returned from Waldron's Gate, she might not be able to help Loretta with repairs or anything else. And Karl might not be able to walk away and leave her up here in the middle of nowhere alone.

Just like it had since his little brother's anxious request to look into all of this, Karl's life was getting more complicated by the minute.

WHEN LORETTA OPENED THE DOOR, Karl was thankful he only had their relatively light bags in his arms instead of the heavy honey. The room was a blur of activity, more than even the busiest of medical experiment theaters he'd seen.

Pipes and belts and pulleys seemed to cover all of the walls and ceiling, dropping down here and there in shapes he couldn't understand.

He could see far more clearly than light from the fire or candles in such a remote location should have allowed. When he finally realized where the bright light was coming from, he knew his jaw dropped comically, but there wasn't a damned thing he could do about it.

"Gemma, you've been busy," Loretta said, trying her best not to laugh.

The older woman fairly preened before she launched into explanations.

"I'm making progress, yes, but such a long way to go. The electricity is certainly helping. So many tasks are easier when you can do such a simple thing as see clearly at night, don't you think, Karl?'

"Yes," Karl said, his eyes wide. "Yes, ma'am, I can see what you mean."

"Once I saw how the lights would work, the rest was fairly easy. Winding the copper wire just...so...is the hardest part. The steam keeps everything spinning and does all the rest."

Karl watched her nearly prance into one corner, to where most houses like this would surely have a normal fire burning. He could see the fire, and smell the strange flat mud burning, but the huge space above it was taken up by several odd cauldrons.

All of them had covers with tubes coming out the top, not like any cooking pot he knew of. The biggest one led to some kind of contraption that bristled with loops of more copper wire than he'd ever seen.

"Not all of it uses electricity, of course," Gemma said. "Some of it uses good old steam. Can't get gas up here, not like you do in Waldron's Gate. I dream of it often. The wonders I could do with gas..." She rubbed her upper arms. "But we all must make do with what we have."

"What's this one?" Loretta said.

She pointed to a complex pulley-and-gear mechanism anchored to the long stone countertop. Belts looped along the wall and ceiling and back down to another cauldron.

Gemma reached up to a high shelf and grabbed a whisk, the kind

Karl had seen his mother and her cooks using to beat egg whites. This one had bare, sharp metal at the top rather than a handle. When Gemma snapped it into place and adjusted a lever he hadn't noticed, he understood why. The whisk whirred in a tight circle, faster than even Karl's mother could manage.

"This is the heart of my kitchen," Gemma said. "Something every woman would have if I had my way. Every tedious task made easy. I can beat, whip, knead, all those chores that were making my old knuckles ache."

She reached up again, pulling down a flat metal square. What looked like several knives were attached to a bar at one end, and to a tiny crank at the other. She flipped the lever back down, stilling the whisk, and attached the metal box.

"Karl, would you fetch me a carrot from the larder there?"

He followed her eyes and saw a small wooden door with metal straps across it, set right into the stone wall at what would be Gemma's waist level. When he pulled the handle, he was amazed at the cool air flooding out all around him. This was every bit as cold as the modern coldbox in his mother's kitchen, with no trace of gears or pulleys to make it work. Several types of vegetables, a jug of water, and a bottle of what he thought must be milk were inside. He grabbed a thick carrot, not wanting to miss this demonstration.

"Thank you, dear," Loretta's grandmother said. "Now you must be careful with this chopper. Not for the faint of heart or those with curious children still underfoot."

She slid the carrot into the open end of the box until it was nearly all inside, then flipped the lever. After a blur too fast to see and a clatter too fast to understand, she turned the thing off. When she lifted it, the carrot looked intact. Gemma touched it with her finger, and it fell into perfect orange circles.

"I'm making one now that spins instead of chops. Anything I can figure out how to attach, I can make work."

All Karl could manage to do was nod. Gemma continued around the open room, showing them one device after another. One washed clothes; another spun them in a barrel over another fire pit until they were dry. A nearby sewing machine, not much different than the one Karl's mother used, attached to another pulley to save the user from having to pump the treadle.

He had to duck under what Gemma called a fan in the middle of the room, a series of elongated wooden blades attached in the middle. When she flipped the lever for that one, the blades spun, and a warm breeze filled the room.

"So much better than one corner broiling and the other freezing, isn't it?" she said. "And it's pure bliss on a warm day when the fire still needs to be going. I'm working on a smaller fan to blow the warm air right out the window at times like that. Still, I can see from my towering guest here that I need to make it adjustable. Easy enough."

She wasn't the least bit daunted by the idea of reworking what looked incredibly complex to Karl. A bright smile lit her features, and he couldn't help smiling in return.

"Where do you get all the materials for this, Gemma?" he said.

"Oh, that's part of what my lovely granddaughter takes care of for me. The same young man who brings my food and such takes the list and sends it off, usually to right where you live. Then a couple of weeks later, he brings everything back for me. I've been waiting ages for the wire you brought me today."

She reached out, and Loretta took her hand.

"I'm happy to take care of you, Gemma," Loretta said. "While we're here, just let me or Karl know if you need anything done that you aren't able to do. He's almost as clever as he is strong."

"Oh, handsome is what he is," Gemma said. "Looks like a fine match to me. Come sit with me. Tell me why an ordinary day brings such a wonderful surprise."

Karl followed the two women to the other side of the room where a surprisingly comfortable sofa and two chairs waited. One of the bright bulbs that should never be glowing so far past any city hung in the middle of the space, and a low table was covered with neat drawings on heavy paper.

Another table under the window held what looked like the new food chopper. This time, six blades were arranged almost exactly like the overhead fan. Comparing the two made Karl's flesh crawl at thoughts of a larger version.

"I'm happy to see you for any reason at all, Gemma," Loretta said. Karl was impressed at how honest she sounded. He hadn't gotten the impression she was glad to be here at all. "And I'm delighted for you to meet a friend of mine. But we do need your help."

The woman's strangely unlined face glowed nearly as bright as the electric lights.

"You know I'll do anything I can for you, bobbin."

Loretta sighed. "I'm afraid my gyro-compass has had a bit of an accident."

Loretta pulled it out of her bag, and Karl recognized the loops of copper, tiny as they were. This wasn't much different than the thing over the fire that produced such grand displays of electricity. Gemma frowned and took it in both hands.

"Oh dear, this has taken quite a knock," she said. "I might not be able to repair it. See how the wires are broken, there?" Karl nodded, trying to look like he understood. "I can take it apart to save some of the parts, but it would simply be easier to start over. That will take a few days. I'm sorry."

Loretta closed her eyes for a second, and Karl saw the hard line of her mouth.

"We may have to make some other kind of arrangement," she said.

"Was your Dragon damaged, bobbin?"

"No, it's fine, thank Jonah," Loretta said. "We were wondering about that too, though. Do you think you could make another? One tuned to Karl, so he can help me in my work?"

The fine wrinkles that had settled around Gemma's eyes and mouth vanished.

"Of course I can!" she said. "That won't be a quick job, but you must remember that from the first one. I'll have a list of the parts I need ready in the morning. Once those arrive, I can get started."

"That did take a while, didn't it?" Now Loretta seemed older than her grandmother, rubbing at the deep line between her eyebrows. She looked at Karl, exhaustion clear in her eyes. He was sure she was acting. Almost. "And we ll have to be here for you to tune it and make sure it works. We can't possibly stay here that long."

"I know I'm too tired for that tonight," Karl said, trying to take her cue. "Loretta bought fresh fish and greens in the village. Maybe we can have dinner, get some rest, and we'll work it all out tomorrow."

Now he wasn't sure which woman had the happiest smile, or the more relieved one.

Chapter 28

Karl turned over, trying to get comfortable enough to fall back asleep. The sofa was far newer and better made than his own, but his night had been long. To say his mind had been active was a painful understatement.

He imagined things were moving and shifting whether his eyes were open or closed. Stealthy footsteps and creatures scrambling on the thatched roof turned out to be his own breathing, or his foot pressing against the end of the couch. He put it down to sleeping in yet another strange room. He could barely see the fire, and the smell had died down quite a bit too.

His nose twitched, sure that scent was changing. That wasn't any kind of mud or fire. Karl was certain he smelled a beast, hairy and filthy and sweating, drooling with the chance to devour all of them before morning.

When he took another deep breath, it was gone.

Karl sat up, rubbing his face and his neck. As much as he was relieved by the less earthy air, he knew Gemma relied on steam to make the electricity that ran everything in this house. He'd hardly be a good guest if he didn't at least bring in more fuel for her.

His spine crackled when he finally stretched out, his hands flat against the ceiling. No one else was moving around in either of the tiny bedrooms, so he opened the front door as quietly as he could.

Loretta had explained how the peat was harvested and stored, but the whole idea of burning dirt didn't make any sense to him. Karl hoped he'd get to see how that worked someday. He gathered up an armload of brick-like mud from the pile beside the door, then glanced over his shoulder to see if the sun was up yet.

His involuntary step backward to grab for the door handle saved his toes from the heavy dried peat. Fog surrounded the house, Fog so thick he couldn't see the barn or trees or anything else.

Karl breathed in short, noisy rasps, no longer worried about waking the others. He'd never heard of Fog advancing so far overnight, never.

The pale wall shifted and moved, shapes forming and breaking apart right in front of him. He closed the door and nearly tripped over his own feet running to the small guest room Loretta slept in.

"Loretta, you need to wake up. Wake up!" He touched her shoulder and shook her, gently at first. "We need to get Gemma and get out of here."

"What're you talking 'bout?"

She pulled away from his hand and turned away.

"Listen to me, wake up! The Fog is all around us. The horses might be gone, but we've got to do something."

When he touched her shoulder again, she dug her fingers into his wrist and sat up.

"Don't shake me again. You're not making any sense, Karl."

"I just went outside to get more of that peat for the fire," he said, his words too fast. "The Fog is surrounding the house. We're not safe here anymore, and we can't leave your grandmother here. Come on."

She let go of his arm and ran both hands through her tangled hair.

"No, nothing bad has happened," she said. "I never thought to warn you. It's perfectly normal."

"That's what Parliament and the soldiers want you to think." Karl said. "But it's not true. I've seen some of the 'sters, Loretta. The ones in the Fog are even worse, and this is full of them."

"No, just wait a minute." Loretta covered a yawn with her hand.

"Let me wake up. It's all fine, trust me. I grew up in a place like this, remember?"

She rubbed her face, then grabbed her robe from the foot of the bed. The room was tiny, and Karl had to step back out into the living room.

"What is it, then?" he said. "It wasn't here last night."

"Shhh, you'll wake Gemma. Hang on, I'll go out there with you."

"No, Loretta, we all have to stay together. If the 'sters get us, *no one* will be able to help her."

Karl's heart pounded, and his hands shook. The need to keep everyone inside and get everyone away from here was not sitting well in his over-clocked brain.

"I don't know what you mean by stirs," Loretta said. "But I know this isn't what you think. I should have warned you, I'm sorry. I promise you, this is not going to hurt either one of us."

She yawned again and walked toward the front door, calmer than Karl could imagine himself being. He'd gotten close to the Fog as a boy, playing the same silly childhood games as everyone else in the Gate. He had no desire to actually step outside into that swarming hell as an adult.

"I mean monsters," he said. "Things you don't even want to imagine. They have to be all around us by now. Please don't go out there until we can all go together."

He touched her arm, and instead of pushing him away, Loretta covered his hand with her own.

"You're just going to have to trust me on this one," she said. "This is entirely my fault, mine and everyone who assumes Waldron's Gate is the center of the whole world. This is not the Fog you know, Karl. This is just harmless mist. We'll go out there together."

She checked a switch he hadn't noticed before she opened the door. Karl had to fight the urge to push her behind him. The Fog was just as thick and close, but it seemed brighter now. The twisting creatures inside it were every bit as active. Loretta didn't seem the least bit afraid. She rubbed her eyes and yawned again.

"Look," she said. "It's not the same as in Waldron's Gate. Not as solid. Can't you smell the difference?"

Some of the ghostly white drifted past them, and Karl forced himself not to recoil. If the Fog could get into the house, or pull them out, there was nothing left to struggle against. They were already lost.

Loretta took his hand, and Karl tried not to grip too tightly.

"Come on," she said. "We'll just go out a little way. This is just mist. It will seem to disappear all around us. Take a breath. It smells amazing."

She stepped out onto the first stone in the path, pulling his hand. Karl tried to look in every direction, waiting to see whatever would come screaming out after them. If they were lucky, it would be over quickly.

"Take a breath, Karl. Trust me."

He stepped out after her, wondering if she could feel how badly he was shaking. His feet felt like great blocks of wood, with no more agility or grace. He managed to draw in a breath through his nose instead of panting. This did have a scent, a sharp aroma almost like...

"It smells like water."

"Exactly," she said. "Now look how it moves around us. That's just the wind. There aren't any monsters out here. None that aren't human, anyway."

Karl saw the faint outline of a tree on his right and the house fading behind them.

"You said this is fog too?"

"Just normal fog," she said. "Nothing to be afraid of. It will probably burn off once the sun's up and the air is a bit warmer. It rarely gets cold enough in Waldron's Gate for anything this thick during the day. I've hardly ever seen it, and most of you are sound asleep when it would be there anyway."

They'd walked far enough that he couldn't see the house at all and he finally caught sight of the fence. One of the horses made a grumbling noise Karl had never heard before, and the sound had a dead, flat quality.

"Is there no Fog up here? Fog like back in the Gate, I mean?"

"There is, but it's a ways off, along the coast," she said. "I saw it from the ship today. I went out there years ago when it was farther out than normal. I could hear water, but I couldn't get close enough to see it like you can from Alseer sometimes. I've always wondered what's really beyond that Fog. Beyond this fog, nothing at all has changed. Okay?"

Karl finally caught a deep breath, letting his exhalation take as much of the fear with it as he could.

"Okay. I'm a little embarrassed. I was so sure I saw monsters out here."

"I wish you wouldn't be embarrassed." Loretta squeezed his hand, reminding him that she still held it. "I should've warned you, but it never crossed my mind. I am sorry."

"If you don't tell anyone about this," he said, "we'll call it even. Let's get back inside before your grandmother has to know how ignorant I am."

"It may not be ignorance, Karl. When did you last have Crumble?"

He stopped, his fears of being out in the open entirely forgotten.

"I haven't had all of even my low dose for a while now," he said. "Since all this creeping around at night started. Less and less since then. It's been...since before we got to the village since I had any at all. More than twenty-four hours."

"That could explain your reaction," she said. "Getting off that stuff isn't easy for anyone. We don't have any at this house at all, unless you brought your own. Gemma and I don't take it, so you may be off for a while. You might not want to go back."

She stopped at the front door.

"One thing I do need to warn you about is going outside during the night like that." She smiled. "Let's just say Gemma gave me my start in securing my home back in Waldron's Gate. If she'd activated everything before we went to sleep, you would have been in for an even bigger surprise when you opened that door."

Chapter 29

By the time they sat down to a very late dinner that night, Karl was feeling the effects of his restless night and early morning. Gemma and Loretta had kept him busy the whole day long, working in the barn and stable, tending to the horses, helping them put together the various lists of supplies.

The strange movements continued out of the corner of his eye all day long, along with sounds, smells, even crawling sensations on his flesh. From what he'd heard, and what Loretta told him, he'd done himself a tremendous favor by inadvertently cutting down his dose of Crumble for the past couple of weeks.

With the repeated outbursts from his pounding heart, Karl didn't want to find out what she meant by that. It was no wonder people felt like they were going insane if they stopped all at once. And no wonder that sometimes their minds truly did break under the strain. If he ever got through this, he'd never travel without his own supply again.

Maybe. Or maybe he'd never take it again.

He tried to keep his thoughts of staying off it from himself as much as everyone else. The fascination with starting to dream, visiting another world and life unknown to him, was hard to shake.

"Did you hear that?" Loretta said, her fork halfway to her mouth.

Karl tried not to laugh at the identical poses of the two women, brows drawn together, head slightly tilted. He probably looked the same.

"I thought I heard one of the horses," he said. "Want me to go check?"

Gemma was on her feet before Karl stopped speaking.

"No, that won't be necessary. That fence is active. I just need to get the door and we'll be perfectly safe and snug in here, too."

She pushed the same switch Loretta had checked that morning. The lights inside the house dimmed, and he was sure he heard a deep hum.

"What did you mean—"

The quiet was shredded by a scream, like a child in pain. All three were on their feet.

Karl's mind wanted to slide into panic, expecting the screaming 'ster George had told him about brought all the way up here to devour them. He didn't realize he was heading for the door until Loretta gripped his arm.

"Stay right here," she said. "No one's going to get inside unless we invite them."

"Who even knows we're up here?" he said.

Just as Karl's eyes met Loretta's, a second agonized scream rang out, this time from right outside the door.

The lights went even lower, fading to a brownish color. Karl heard an odd grinding sound, over and over again.

"That would be the alarm." Gemma was the calmest of all of them, nodding to herself before she turned back toward the door. "Karl, I hate to impose upon you after you worked so hard today, but would you be so kind as to step over here with me?"

"To step... What do you think I can do?"

He stood beside her, shaking almost as hard as that morning. No animal screamed like that. A man, very likely an angry one, was on the other side of that door.

Loretta handed the revolver and belt to him.

The revolver she hadn't yet taught him how to use.

"I doubt very much whoever that was will be awake," Gemma

said, still the image of calm. "We just need to make sure no one else is out there and see if anyone's hurt."

Loretta stood on the other side of her grandmother with her own blaster drawn. Gemma motioned for both of them to step back.

"What if someone charges through the door?" Karl said.

Much to his surprise, the woman laughed.

"Charges. Oh dear, Loretta. You didn't tell me he was clever, too.'

Gemma swung the door open, and Karl struggled to stay where he was. He couldn't imagine anywhere less safe in all of Alterra than right here.

A STORM RAGED OUTSIDE, one made no less terrifying by being confined between the door frames. Crackling blue light arced from one side to the other, starting at the bottom and rising to the top, then repeating. The grinding noise Karl had heard was loud enough to make his bones vibrate.

"Rullin." Loretta's voice was barely above a hiss, and Karl tore his gaze away from the light show. A man lay crumpled on the ground, his face turned toward them. Bill's brother. "Is he dead, Gemma?"

"No, not likely," she said. "Not unless he was before he encountered my door. Stay there for a second. I'll shut that down, and we'll investigate."

Before Karl could try to stop her, not that he would have understood how to do that, she adjusted the switch again. One final grinding arc twisted from bottom to top, and the light and noise stopped. Yet another odd smell hit him then, the singed burned hair smell that sometimes lingered in the experimental treatment rooms back at Joffrey Columns.

He didn't feel particularly brave about it, but he let Loretta and Gemma pass through the door first.

"I don't see anyone else out here," Loretta said. "I think he's still breathing. More's the pity."

Karl looked around the best he could in the fading light, then squatted beside the young man. Rullin was breathing, but he never stirred.

"What happened?" he said.

"I don't know what the first scream was," Gemma said. "The second was this young man trying to enter my house uninvited. He activated the alarm by touching it. If he stood on that grate, he took more than enough electricity to knock him out." Gemma nodded, not looking or sounding the least bit upset. "We need to see if anyone else is hurt. The barn has lights, but I *so* rarely get to use them."

She set out across the yard, with Karl and Loretta running to catch up. Gemma touched another switch set into a fence post, and light flooded the yard. Before Karl's eyes had quite adjusted, Loretta pointed to the base of the fence. A small form was crumpled on the grass.

"Is that still active, Gemma?" she said.

"Give me one quick moment, bobbin." The older woman crossed back over to the house and walked through the door, returning after only a few seconds. "It's safe now."

Loretta turned the body over.

"Oh, Imp burn you, Rullin," she said. "This is Morgan, the stable owner's son. Walton must be worried half to death. I don't think Morgan has more than ten years. He's still breathing, but he has burns on his arms. And bruises on his face."

"I'd imagine that brute back there threw him onto the fence," Gemma said. "Wasn't smart enough to think there might be electrified areas anywhere else. We'll bring the boy inside, and I suppose we should tie the other one up. Do either of you know how to make good, strong knots?"

"That's the first thing that's made sense to me since we got here," Karl said. "I know how to restrain him or anyone else. Mind if I use one of your sheets, Gemma, or something else I can tear? That and some good sturdy rope would do the trick."

"Of course, dear, get whatever you need. Loretta and I will fetch the rope. Can you carry this poor child inside for us first?"

Karl focused on the boy's face to keep from watching the shadows.

His sense of creatures moving in from all directions to attack them was growing worse by the second.

Morgan seemed to be eight or nine, and the pale skin around his eyes and mouth were definitely bruising. Karl brushed the fine brown hair back to see more around his thin neck and forehead. Blood was crusted around his mouth, nose, and both ears.

The boy was still breathing, but he might not be for long with a beating like that.

Holding one hand under Morgan's head to support his neck, Karl lifted him carefully, settling the boy's head against his own shoulder. A small wing at Joffrey Columns was set aside for children, but he'd never been inside.

He couldn't imagine having to tend to these small, delicate bodies every single day. He felt like he was carrying a warm bundle of twigs. By the time Karl got the boy inside, Gemma had covered the sofa with a blanket and was holding another.

"Let me check him while he's still out," Karl said. "Make sure nothing is broken."

He moved the boy's limbs, feet, and hands, marveling that none of the tiny bones seemed to be fractured. More bruises on his torso and back worried Karl, but he couldn't verify anything about the state of the child's organs. All they could do out here was make him comfortable and hope he woke up.

"Are there any healers we can get him to?" he said. "Any doctors?"

"None close enough to reach tonight." Gemma said. "I tended to five children of my own a long time ago. They're tougher than you think. We'll let him rest as long as he will." When Karl looked up, the older woman was holding a bundle of fabric, most of it already ripped in one way or another. "Use this to tie up the one who did this."

"Do not be kind," Loretta said, handing him a coil of thick, rough rope.

Chapter 30

RULLIN STARTED to stir while Karl was still working, but he was far past being a threat to any of them. He'd been less careful about straining limbs or cutting off circulation than he usually was.

Other than that, this was the same improvised restraint Karl had used more times than he cared to count. Find the body's natural points of weakness, the ways muscles and joints weren't used to moving. Secure limbs in that position. Simpler and more effective than most people imagined.

"Is that one injured?" Gemma said.

She stood beside him, and Karl realized she'd turned on yet another bright outdoor electric while he was working. Full dark surrounded the house and barn, dark with all the secrets and monsters he could imagine. The grinding blue fury that put Rullin into this state made him wonder just how much current Loretta's grandmother could draw upon if she needed to.

"He has some pretty good burns on his hands and face," he said. "Probably where he tangled with whatever you have set up on your door. We've run into him before, Gemma. I'm afraid he came up here because of that. I'm sorry."

"Don't you even pretend to apologize, Karl," Gemma said. She patted his shoulder. "These things happen from time to time. That's exactly why I have these little safeguards set up. I doubt he'll be the last."

"He's enough, though, Gemma." Loretta stood beside her grandmother, glaring into Rullin's bleary eyes. "We have no way to know how many people he'll tell, or how many he'll come back with. The world would be a better place if he never drew another breath. And even then, you're not safe up here alone."

"Wait, Loretta, we still need Bill to get us out of here." Karl pulled the last knot tight enough for Rullin to flinch, then got to his feet. "He made it clear he wants to deal with this asshole himself."

"He didn't do the best job of that, did he?" Loretta kicked the boy in the ribs before Karl could stop her, but Rullin only grunted. "This lovely example of brotherhood managed to get away, and he might have permanently hurt Morgan. Not to mention whatever he'd planned to do to all of us."

"I've been fine up here for a long time, you know." Gemma said in a low voice.

"Do you really think Bill won't figure out where he is?" Karl said. "The man has an airship, Loretta. He can search Alterra from end to end. You said Morgan is the stable owner's son? What makes you think Walton won't tell Bill what happened? He knew where we were headed. He or Bill will be up here before we could even manage to hide the body."

"So we take it apart and feed it to the bloody wolves then!" Loretta shouted. "I'm not going to look over my shoulder for this waste of human flesh for the rest of my life. Morgan's father isn't likely to agree to keep a watch on Gemma any longer, not after this. We either have to take her out of here or kill this bastard right now!"

"I am standing right here, and I'm not going to let you murder a man in my own yard!"

Karl and Loretta recoiled from Gemma's shout. Karl saw exactly where Loretta's temper came from. The tiny woman was leaning toward them, both fists clenched, eyes as fierce as her voice had been.

"Loretta, I raised your own father, such that he was, and I've managed up here just fine for a long time now."

"I know, Gemma," Loretta said. She reached for the older woman.

but Gemma pulled away. "I understand. But if people are finding you here, attacking you like this, it might not be safe anymore. How many times has this happened?"

Gemma crossed her arms and shrugged at the same time. The furious, confident woman had been replaced by a stubborn teenager right before their eyes.

"It doesn't matter," she said. "None of them have managed their mischief."

"But they're not stopping, are they?" Karl said.

He winced when Gemma turned to him. Tears stood in her eyes, and he was looking at a heartbroken little girl. Loretta put her arm around her grandmother.

"How many times, Gemma?" she said. "You know I can just ask Walton. I'm sure he helped you clean up the messes." Gemma stared at the ground and muttered something. "I'm sorry, I couldn't hear you."

"I said I don't know," Gemma said. "I stopped counting a long time ago."

Loretta closed her eyes and shook her head, and Karl saw muscles flexing in her jaw.

"What have I been paying blasted Walton for? He's never mentioned a word of this to me." She looked at Karl, the exhaustion he'd seen earlier clear on her face. "I can't leave her here. Not anymore."

Karl was torn between relief and sympathy for the two women. He'd thought the very same thing when he first saw Gemma. Rullin shifted on the ground, jarring Karl into action.

"We need to talk about this, but not right here," he said. "I don't want this piece of shit knowing any more than he already does."

He bent to grab the boy's shoulders, surprised to see Loretta and Gemma get his feet.

Loretta smiled at Karl. "I doubt he could do more than throw himself off the bed the way you've got him trussed up. We'll put him in the spare bedroom for now."

"You'll regret this, each and every one of you," Rullin whispered when Karl got a grip under his shoulders.

"I already regret not killing you when I had the chance," Loretta said, her voice somehow more menacing in its cheerful tone. "You're giving me motivation to eliminate that regret. Keep it up."

~

WITH RULLIN DUMPED none too gently on the floor and the door closed, any plans to argue Gemma's fate were interrupted by groans from the couch. Morgan tried to sit up, but Karl put a hand on his chest.

"Not so fast," he said. "You're fine right where you are. Can you speak?"

"I guess so." The boy's voice was terribly raspy. "How did I get in here?"

"A nasty piece of work threw you into my fence," Gemma said. "That's how."

Gemma sat down beside Morgan with a damp cloth, gently blotting at the blood on his face.

"Didn't throw me at all." He twisted one thin arm out from under the blanket and took the cloth, scrubbing at his own mouth. "I jumped."

"You did what?" Gemma said, her hand over her heart. "Why ever would you do such a thing, child? You knew about that fence. You've been up here with your father."

"That's *why* I did it," he said. "Can I have something to drink, please? I knew about your door, too, Ms. Gemma. He was going to make me try to open it. When he started dragging me off the horse, I jumped off and ran toward the fence. I figured I'd have a better chance with it, and maybe your door would kill him dead."

Loretta smiled at Karl, the satisfaction in her eyes a little frightening and a lot arousing.

"He's not quite dead," she said. "But he knocked himself out. Are you okay, Morgan? What hurts?"

"What doesn't hurt?" He moved to sit up again, and this time Gemma and Karl helped him move back against the cushions. "My head feels like it wants to split, but I think I'm fine."

"What happened?" Karl said. "How did he get you?"

"Same thing that always happens," Morgan said. "Just usually by other kids. He waited outside the school, followed me until he caught me alone. It's not all that hard."

"This has happened to you before?" Gemma said.

She handed the boy a cup of water, cool from her larder.

"Well, my father owns more than horses and wagons, you know. He owns a lot more houses than this one, and he treats you a lot better than most of his tenants. That doesn't make him a lot of friends. Me either."

"How old are you, Morgan?" Karl said.

"I'll be thirteen this summer. I know I look younger. I get that a lot."

"I'm sorry," Loretta said. "Other kids can be shits, especially when you're a little bit different. Or when your family is." Morgan giggled at her words, and her sad eyes didn't match her smile. "I appreciate you and your father taking such good care of Gemma, but what happens to you isn't fair."

"Nope, but what is?" Morgan said. "I'm sure he'll be beating down your door in the morning looking for me. Can we leave the alarm on for him?"

The twinkle in his swollen eyes left Karl not sure whether he should laugh or cry.

"We'll do no such thing, child," Gemma said. "What we must do is get you cleaned up and settled in for the night. If your previous visits are any indication, you're probably hungry."

Gemma was halfway to the kitchen before Morgan could respond.

"You bet I am! Can I help with the gadgets?"

Karl once again put a hand on the boy's narrow chest.

"You can see just fine from here," he said. "Listen, was anyone else with Rullin? The man who grabbed you?"

Morgan shook his head and winced. "Just him. He'd already grabbed the horse, probably right out of the stable. My father might be a jerk, but he's going to make this guy beg to hit that door again."

"We can throw him in the back of the wagon overnight." Gemma had an odd little smile on her face. "We're already in close quarters with our young guest here. No need for Rullin to take up a perfectly good bed."

"And if he gets loose and runs?" Loretta had brought a knife seemingly out of thin air, turning it so the reflection hit Karl's eyes. "I wasn't joking. I am not willing to keep my eye out for him around every dark corner for the rest of my life."

"He won't get loose," Karl said. "I've been keeping people a lot sicker and more twisted than him where they belong for a very long time."

"Great," Loretta said. "Gemma and I will help you carry him out."

"No, I can handle—"

"We'll help you carry him out," Loretta said again.

Morgan paused in his near-inhalation of Gemma's soup to roll his eyes.

"She's saying she wants to talk to you where I won't hear. Hard to believe you missed that one, Karl."

Loretta shrugged and tried to hide her smile, but the knife disappeared and she was on her feet.

Rullin had wormed his way under the bed. Karl grabbed the waist of his pants and hauled him back out.

"Don't know what you're trying to find under there," Karl said. "But you'll be disappointed. It's out to the wagon with you for the night."

Rullin snarled. "You leave me right where I am. If you throw me out there, I'll scream my head off all night long."

"Give it a try." Karl lifted Rullin up by his armpits, and Gemma and Loretta again caught his feet. "If you do, I'll show you another little trick I know. A scrap of this same cloth, soaked in just the right amount of whiskey, and you won't be able to catch your breath enough to scream. You could very well choke on that, though, so you might want to reconsider."

When he tried to twist out of their grip, Loretta somehow had the knife she'd taken from him in the hand still holding his bare foot. The blade pressed between his smallest toes.

"Keep thrashing around," she said sweetly. "And you'll have to deal with me."

The wagon was nearly at the end of the electrified fence around the small barnyard. The horse he'd stolen was eating calmly with the others. Rullin never made a sound, even when Karl secured him in the bed of the wagon. None of them spoke until they were back beside the house.

"He's not going anywhere unless someone, or something, carries him off," Karl said. "What was so important that we have to talk about it right now?"

Loretta turned to Gemma, taking her hands.

"Listen to me," she said. "I know you don't want to go anywhere. I understand. I love my house, too. But it's not safe up here anymore. Let us get you out of here, at least until things calm down a little."

Gemma wiped at her eyes. "Have you ever thought I might be getting tired of you dragging me here and there, Loretta? You just had to take me to Waldron's Gate, then you just had to bring me here, now you just have to drag me back down there. Does what I want even matter anymore?"

The sullen teenager was in charge, the one not that different from Rullin at his best. But Karl saw her eyes still brimming with tears, and worse, with confusion.

The reasons didn't matter. Loretta was right.

"We both need your help, Gemma," he said. "Loretta's compass is broken, and we can get the parts a lot more easily in Waldron's Gate. I'll tell you the truth, too. I'd really love to have a Dragon to help my patients. We tried it a few days ago on a man who was in a terrible state, and he calmed down for the first time in years."

"Truly?" she said. "It helped someone?"

"He's right, Gemma," Loretta said. "I saw it too. The man couldn't hold still for a second. After we used the Dragon, he went right to sleep."

She looked at Karl, and he knew neither of them would ever mention the other woman. The one who'd screamed.

"But all my things are here," she said. "Where would I live? Where would I keep my things?"

"You helped me set up my house," Loretta said. "You can stay there for now. Then we'll find somewhere close by where you'll be safe.

How long has this been going on, Gemma? People trying to get into your house like that?"

"On and off for a year or two," she said, staring at the ground. "More over the past few months. I'm sorry I didn't tell you. I didn't want you to worry."

"Didn't want..." Loretta pressed the heel of her hand just above her nose. "What happens to them? The ones who've tried?"

"I just stay inside until Walton gets here," she said. "He takes care of them. I think he locks them up in town."

"What if he doesn't come up here for a few days?" Karl said, not wanting to imagine Gemma cowering inside her own house.

Her broad, innocent smile made it clear she wasn't cowering at all. She didn't understand how dangerous this game was.

"I've done just fine," she said. "Every single time."

"And if several come at once next time?" Loretta took her grandmother's hand again. "If they see what your alarms are, all that electricity, they're just going to keep coming back until they get inside. We can't leave you here, Gemma. I won't."

The small woman looked from Loretta's eyes to Karl's, the tears in her own eyes spilling over. Karl took her other hand.

"Okay, then, I'll go with you," she said, her voice trembling. "For now. But only if we bring my things as soon as we can. Walton can bring all of it once I take it apart tomorrow."

"I'm quite sure he'll do anything we ask," Loretta said. She waited until her grandmother went inside the house to speak again. "As long as I have enough coin, that is."

Chapter 31

When Loretta opened the door, she saw Morgan jerk awake. He looked guilty when he saw her.

"I'm sorry," he said, rubbing carefully at his eyes. "Where do I need to sleep?"

"You're perfectly fine right where you are, young man," Gemma said. "You need to sleep the whole night through. You'll feel about a hundred times better in the morning."

Gemma closed the front door and turned the alarms back on. Loretta thought about arguing, but she knew she'd rest better if Rullin couldn't get inside. Assuming she rested at all.

"Then I'm going to bunk with you, Gemma," she said. "I'll just get my nightgown and things."

"Absolutely not," the older woman said. "If there's anything I've earned in a long life, it's the right to say who shares my bed. Especially on my last night in my own house." She smiled, jerking her chin toward the sofa. "He won't turn over until we wake him. That sleeping draught in a warm bowl of soup has never failed me yet. Rest well."

Before Loretta could say another word, Gemma closed her bedroom door. She didn't want to, but there was no way to avoid it. She turned to Karl.

He at least had the grace to blush.

"She believes she has everything neatly arranged, doesn't she?"

"Unless one of us wants to join Rullin or sleep in a chair," Loretta said, "she's right. We have a hard day ahead tomorrow. I doubt this would be the first time either of us slept in strange company. Give me five minutes to get ready?"

He inclined his head, then started clearing the kitchen table. None of them seemed eager to finish the interrupted meal.

Loretta eyed the bed while she got ready to get into it. It was fairly new and quite comfortable, one she'd bought and had delivered for her planned visits. She hadn't shared it with anyone. Tonight she was thankful she'd bought the largest one that would fit in the room. At least they wouldn't be on top of each other.

She caught her face in the mirror then, and smiled at how red her face was at the thought.

"He made it clear he wasn't interested last time you brought it up," she whispered. "So don't."

That wasn't quite true, though. Karl had said he was interested. Only that he didn't want to be some kind of compensation. Nothing about this evening seemed to fit that description. Loretta was in the decidedly uncomfortable position of wanting a man even more because he'd turned her down twice. Disliking it didn't change a thing.

She vowed to at least refuse to make the first move. She made sure her nightgown was as flattering as it could be but not too revealing. Loretta shook her head at such unusual shyness before she stepped into the living room. Karl already had his travel bag in hand.

"All yours," she said. "I'll wait out here. The water in the basin stays warm and clean. Another of Gemma's inventions."

Loretta sat watching Morgan sleep. The boy would probably be just fine, but she seethed with wanting to take his injuries out on Rullin. Bill might just have to learn how to let other people settle his problems from time to time. Just as she was painting quite the satisfying mental picture, Karl opened the door.

"May as well get this public sleepover started," he said. "Left or right side?"

"I'll take the left," Loretta said, unable to keep herself from smiling. "That gives me the best escape route."

"Good thinking."

Getting settled in took an unreasonable amount of time, surely longer than if they'd just gotten down to business and rutted. The bed seemed to be shrinking around them by the second. After much tossing and turning, they ended up in what had to be the most awkward possible arrangement: facing each other.

Loretta wished she'd already turned the light out. But then she wouldn't be able to see those lovely hazel eyes of his.

"Is this how you imagined finally getting me into bed?" Karl said, smiling.

"Not quite," she said. "Not with the crowd right outside the door."

"These things never happen at the best time, do they?" he said. "Your grandmother seems quite pleased with herself. I doubt she has any idea how long it's been since either of us was sleeping normally."

Loretta laughed. "She's quite pleased with her maneuvering. Gemma thinks I've been single long enough, and she likes you. I almost have to wonder if she paid Rullin to show up here tonight."

"Yeah," Karl said. "I've been hearing the same thing from my mother for a few years now. Listen, I know this is hardly going to...enhance the mood..."

"But that seems to be the way it goes for us."

Loretta was surprised to find the situation amusing rather than annoying. She'd never in all her life had such trouble getting a man to have sex with her. The opposite was far more often the case, especially when she still lived in a place like this.

"It does seem that way." Karl propped his head up on his hand. "I've been wondering about something Bill said. That first night on the ship, he said Rullin had never done anything like attacking a passenger before."

"And he said Rullin always settles down for a long time once Bill straightens him out. I've been thinking about that too. I'm sure Bill had a watch on him in the village. He had to sneak away. And what he did to Morgan can't be excused."

"No, I'm with you on that," Karl said. "Something got him stirred up. Then you told me Rhysto showed up out of the blue after you hadn't heard from him in years. Anything else strange happen lately?"

"Besides you tackling me in the middle of the night?" Loretta raised up on her own elbow to look into his eyes. She didn't like the direction her thoughts were taking, but she knew when fighting a thing like that wouldn't work. "My life had been pleasantly predictable for a long while before that. Except one thing, and it was the same day Rhysto showed up. I have a client, or I did have. Still might have. Anyway, this woman has been a regular for years now, one of my best. She's always ready with a request for something new she simply must have, and she pays extremely well."

"What changed?"

"The last time I was there to make a delivery, she brought out her husband for the first time. He kept trying to get me to come to a party with all their friends. He made me twitch in my skin, like I haven't since I got away from the assholes who raised me, and all their friends. I learned a long time ago never to ignore a warning like that. I made my excuses and got out of there. I was almost home before I noticed he'd given me an absurd amount of coin."

"And that night," Karl said, "Rhysto paid you a visit."

Loretta closed her eyes, hoping Karl wouldn't notice the flush in her face. That had been a night to despise, and to remember.

"He did," she said. "Carrying on about me working with other shaws. And then I had my little encounter with Rullin."

Karl turned onto his back, hands under his head. Loretta couldn't stop herself from wondering how good it would feel to curl up against him, her head on his chest. She wasn't used to the cold up here after years away.

She wondered how warm his body would be, how good he would smell after a day of hard work. She did manage to stop herself from moving toward him.

"We need to figure out if all those things are related, Loretta. Or none of them. I doubt any of them would willingly answer questions."

"I don't think they'll have to," she said. "Not answering them knowingly might be the key. If we can get Walton to participate, Bill's paranoia might come in very handy."

Karl nodded. "Neither of them are going to be happy with Rullin right now. Maybe not with each other."

"That's the beauty of my little plan," she said. "We use Rullin to get them on the same side."

"Want to tell me about this little plan?"

"You know," she said. "I think you were right about not getting enough sleep. If we're to get Gemma packed up tomorrow and get down this mountain, we'll have a long day tomorrow."

Loretta surprised herself by kissing Karl on the mouth. He blushed again, and a slow smile broke across his face.

"Night, Karl."

Chapter 32

Loretta's worries about getting Gemma packed and ready dissolved as soon as she opened the bedroom door. It was barely after sunrise, but the burner and most of the pipes and pulleys leading away from it were already dismantled. Morgan and her grandmother had been hard at work.

Karl spoke from behind her.

"Looks like we missed all the fun."

"Since the first day we met," she said, turning to face him.

His grin showed he was as well rested as she was. Waking up with her back warm against his had put her into a better mood than she wanted to admit to herself.

"Nothing lasts forever." he said. "I'll make sure Rullin didn't do himself in during the night."

Gemma walked in with Morgan hard on her heels before Karl could open the front door.

"Well, good morning!" she said. "I trust you slept well?"

"Like logs, Gemma," Karl said. "What can we do?"

"I was thinking about my poor animals," Gemma said, wringing her hands. "I can't just abandon them up here. Do you think Walton might take them?"

"I think Walton can pay you for them," Loretta said. "He's been paid very well over the years. Certainly after we bring in the criminal who did this to his son, you won't owe him a thing. How are you, Morgan?"

Bruises were more visible around the boy's face and neck, but he seemed to be moving just fine.

"I'm a little sore, but not too bad," he said. "It's worth it to miss a day of classes and get to see all of Ms. Gemma's electricity."

"That's all right for today," Gemma said. "You need school if you're going to make electricity for yourself." Gemma poured another cup of cafei and handed it to Morgan. "Go take this to Karl, and don't get too close to that wagon. That awful Rullin will get what he deserves soon enough."

"How much more goes with us today?" Loretta said, filling her own cup.

"The kitchen and my bedroom are packed. With the circuits taken apart, Walton can bring the rest into town."

Gemma stared at Loretta, the questions she was dying to ask with everyone else out of the house painfully obvious.

"No, we didn't do anything besides sleep," Loretta said. "I told you he's my friend. That's it. We really did sleep well."

"Your friend for now," Gemma said, nodding once. "That's the best way to start out. We saved breakfast for you. As soon as that's cleaned up, we'll be ready to go in an hour."

By the time everything was loaded and arranged, Rullin was perched on top of a towering pile of furniture and wires and pipes. Karl assured Loretta, out of Rullin's hearing, that everything was stable as long as the wagon itself didn't turn over.

With Gemma and Morgan fast asleep barely an hour into the journey, Loretta told Karl her plan. Before she finished, she knew from his eyes that he wished she hadn't started.

LORETTA BROUGHT the wagon slowly through the dirt roads of the village several hours later. The handful of shops and merchants, tiny and modest by city standards, each had at least a few people standing in the doorways and windows watching them go by. A good-sized crowd followed along behind. The horses grumbled at all the attention, and she kept expecting Karl to do the same on the seat beside her. Gemma and Morgan only stared.

She finally brought the wagon to a creaking halt in front of Walton's stable. Just as she'd expected, he stood outside with both fists clenched.

The red-and-black balloons of Bill's airship still loomed over the river's edge, so he wouldn't be far behind once word of who had attacked Morgan got out. Walton's face was bright red, the most upset Loretta had ever seen him.

"Do you have my son?" Walton said.

"He's with us, yes," she said. "And so is the man who attacked him yesterday."

At Loretta's words, a soft gasp went through the crowd. Morgan climbed down, moving far more slowly than he had been just a few hours before. Walton caught him up in a great hug.

"What happened, Son? Are you hurt? Where have you been?"

"I'm okay," Morgan said. "They took good care of me. That guy grabbed me on the way home from classes. He already had your horse, said he'd been asking around about the people who bought supplies the other day. He said I had to take him to that house or he'd burn the stable down. Our house, too."

Walton knelt and checked Morgan's injuries, more gently than Loretta would have believed possible.

"How did you get away?" he said.

"I... I jumped into Ms. Gemma's fence. That way he had to try the door himself."

Walton kissed his son on the head, then got to his feet. He pulled his black wool hat off and twisted it in his hands, the fringes of his gray hair standing up.

"Where is he?" he said. "I'll take care of this from here."

"We need to talk to you about that, if we may." Loretta accepted Karl's hand on the way down from the wagon. "I have an idea that may get to the bottom of this and get him out of your hair."

"I don't want that, Loretta," Walton said. "I don't have any blasted hair left. I want to settle with that monster myself."

"And you will," she said. "But please come inside. Let us share our idea."

Walton stared up at Rullin, who was foolish enough glare back. Loretta was about to try again when he turned and strode into his office.

By the time Loretta and Karl joined him, Walton paced across the creaky wooden floor, eyes on the wagon through the windows.

"Give me one reason why I shouldn't cut that bastard's throat for him."

"He's the shaw pilot's brother." Loretta sat in one of the chairs in front of the desk, arranging herself and her dress for the best effect. "We need him to get us back to Waldron's Gate, and you need him to buy your wool and bring your supplies."

"I'm not just going to let him go free after he kidnapped my son!"

"No one is suggesting that," Karl said, taking the other chair. "Loretta has an idea that will help all of us and possibly get him dealt with for good."

"And it involves you having him locked up here for at least a few hours," she said. "The best part is he won't know it's not for the rest of his life. Or until you hang him."

Walton stopped pacing and stared out at Gemma and Morgan, talking to the people who'd gathered. They all stood well away from the wagon.

"His mother's gone, you know," Walton said. "The rest of our children grown and moved away. I can't let anything happen to him."

"I know," Loretta said. "I'm afraid the shaw pilot feels the same way about his brother. Bill doesn't know what to do with Rullin, but this may just let all of us figure that out."

Walton turned around, not bothering to wipe his eyes.

"Bring the pilot here," he said. "If I can have a few hours alone with that...thing, we'll see what we can work out."

All of them jumped at a sharp knock on the door. Walton opened it before Karl or Loretta could move. She'd never seen Bill looking so badly put together outside of his own private quarters.

His hair stood on end, several buttons on his black dress uniform were undone, and his dark face was redder than she would have thought possible. She didn't want to upset either man even more, but she needed both on her side.

"Walton, this is the pilot of the shaw moored in your village,' she said. "Bill, this is the owner of this stable. And the father of the boy who was attacked."

All of the color and more disappeared from Bill's face until he was nearly as pale as Loretta herself.

Walton's voice sounded calm, but Loretta was afraid to breathe.

"Am I to understand it was your brother who did this to my son?"

"I'm sorry to say yes." Bill bowed his head and clasped his hands together. "We had him under guard, but he managed to escape. I am responsible for him, sir. What will be done with him?"

After several uncomfortable seconds, Walton took a deep breath.

"I'll be honest with you, sir," he said. "Since you were honest with me. What I would like to do is skin him alive and hang him in the village square for the birds to feast upon. He not only attacked my young son, but he was trying to attack this woman and her grandmother."

"That would be exactly what he deserves," Bill said. "My efforts to control his evil nature have failed."

Loretta felt sorry for manipulating Bill this way, but only for the seconds it took to glance outside and see Gemma and Morgan together.

"Our mutual friend has a suggestion that isn't quite so drastic," Walton said. "If you're willing to consider it, I would be as well."

Bill looked at Loretta, hope edging out desperation in his eyes.

"Since she was again the target of my brother's crime," he said. "I'm willing to consider whatever she has to say."

"I believe this may help all of us in the end," Loretta said. "What I propose is we leave Rullin locked up here in Walton's custody until they hang him. As far as he knows, anyway. We hope he'll get desperate enough to reveal why he's been behaving this way."

Karl hadn't moved or spoken since Bill walked in, but his voice cut through the silence.

"Wait." Loretta's annoyance turned to concern at his pale face and horrified expression. He wasn't meeting anyone's eyes, but he kept talking. "If this is going to work, he has to believe it. Don't give him any Crumble, Walton."

"What? Are you insane, man?" Walton was nearly as upset as when they'd arrived. Bill only bowed his head again. "I don't want a raving lunatic on my hands on top of everything else here!"

"I don't believe he'll get that bad," Karl said, and now Loretta could hear his voice shaking. He remembered the screaming woman at Joffrey Columns as well as she did. "He's been off overnight already. We had him tied up in that wagon. He'll likely believe he is going insane, though. And he'll be a lot more likely to believe Bill has left him here for good. He'll terrify himself a lot more effectively than any of us ever could."

Karl stood when Walton walked toward him. He was quite a bit taller than the stable owner, but Karl didn't seem at all sure of himself. Loretta was afraid to say a word to support her friend.

Walton put his hands on his hips, no more impressed with the younger man's stature than Karl was reassured by it.

"What makes you such an expert on being on or off of Crumble, Karl? You're the only one of this bunch I've never met before. Anything we need to know about you?"

Karl looked into the smaller man's eyes.

"No sir, nothing in particular. The only thing is I've worked out at Joffrey Columns for over ten years now. Rarely, only once in a great while, someone tries to go off Crumble. They forget or run short, or they just decide to. They do seem to go crazy, yes, and being off permanently would leave them that way forever." He took a deep breath. "Everyone needs it to stay sane. Everyone. But getting them right back on solves the problem. Those are the only ones we ever get to send back home."

Loretta stared at her hands, trying to force her face to stay neutral. She hadn't known Karl all that long, but she was certain she hadn't heard that many lies from him in all that time put together.

"Aye, I know about Joffrey Columns," Walton said, still staring into Karl's eyes. "We don't send as many that way as you people in Waldron's Gate, but it does happen."

"That kind of trouble is a lot more common there." Karl glanced at Loretta for an instant. "And I'm sure you understand why we can't be letting rumors get around that it's safe to go off Crumble even for a little while. It isn't. But keeping Rullin off can only help us here."

Walton watched Karl for a few more seconds, then he turned to Loretta. She nodded.

"I can't say it breaks my heart to let him suffer a bit," Walton said. "I'll keep him locked up the whole time. Now what exactly do you expect me to do if he does want to spill his secrets?"

Chapter 33

KARL JUMPED to his feet at Walton's words, glad to have something to do. Despite what he did for a living, or maybe because of it, he hated being in a room with so much tension. Especially when he'd made it so much worse with his little suggestion.

That kind of suggestion would get him fired and possibly locked up at the Columns himself back in Waldron's Gate. Hell, being off Crumble for nearly a week now would probably do the trick if word got out. But once the idea had taken shape in his mind, he'd known it was the only way to get information out of the boy.

His stomach rolled over at the idea of causing such distress, even to a criminal like Rullin.

The noise of the crowd died as soon as he opened the door, with every face turned his way. Karl kept walking, hoping no one would ask questions he'd have to ignore. That hope lasted about three strides.

"What's happening?" "Will there be a hanging?" "That man talked to me t'other day, thought he looked like trouble."

He kept his head down and kept moving. The only people he was willing to talk to waited beside the wagon.

"What's going on in there?" Morgan whispered, trying to look in every direction at once.

"That's not for you to worry about," Karl said. "Can you take Gemma somewhere close by, get the two of you something to drink?"

Karl handed the boy a handful of coin, whatever was in his pocket.

Morgan's eyes widened. "We could just about buy the pub for this much."

"Why don't you let me hold that for you?" Gemma was smiling, but her tone was serious. Morgan sighed and handed the ritterns over. "Is everything okay, Karl?"

"It might be in a little while," he said. "Go on. This isn't for you to see. Don't feel like you have to talk to anyone if you don't want to."

He leaned against the wagon with his arms crossed until the two of them decided he was serious. They crossed the dirt street, looking back every few steps. When they went inside a small wooden building that did look like a pub, Karl climbed up to the top of the load.

"Are we going to have a problem here, Rullin?"

The boy ignored him, staring up at the nearly midday sun. His wild eyes showed he was feeling the abrupt lack of Crumble. Karl didn't want to imagine how bad his night had been.

"One way to avoid trouble is if I just drop you over the side,' Karl said. "Depending on which way you land, you might not ever be trouble again."

When Karl moved to loosen the ropes, Rullin finally looked at him.

"Yeah, you'll have trouble," he said. "Trouble all around you. Never where you expect it."

"That's fine," Karl said. "I'm getting used to that. Right now you're going in there to face your brother and the father of the boy you attacked. Loretta too. That should be enough to keep you occupied for a while. I'll loosen your hands enough so you can climb down."

Once Rullin's feet where on the ground and his hands were retied, Karl got a grip on the back of his shirt.

"I think folks around here would enjoy seeing me break your neck," he said. "Don't tempt any of us."

For the first time, the boy knew when to keep his mouth shut. He shuffled forward with his head down until they got to the door of

Walton's office, ignoring the questions shouted at both of them now. He finally resisted at the door, pushing back against Karl.

"You can't get far tied up like this," Karl said. "We do have an airship, Rullin. You won't be able to hide. Get it over with. Face it like a man."

As soon as they were though the door, Walton crossed the room in three quick steps and punched Rullin in the stomach. Karl winced as the boy doubled over, wheezing. This was part of what they'd discussed, but it was still hard to watch.

Walton leaned down and nearly growled into Rullin's ear.

"You bloody monster, attacking a little boy like that. If I had my way, we'd string you up, roast you alive, and share you out to all the pigs and goats."

Rullin finally managed to catch enough air to stand up straight, but Bill now stood right in front of him.

"You bastard," he whispered. "Are you going to let him talk to me like that?"

"Yes, Rullin, I am," Bill said. "I told you before we landed that you'd had your last chance. You've pissed it away right proper. Whatever happens to you here is your own doing."

"Here?" Rullin said, his voice rising. "You're leaving me here, in the middle of blasted nowhere?"

The panic in Rullin's voice showed he was already more than half the way to outright terror.

"I am." Tears were brimming in Bill's eyes. Karl wished he could believe they were part of the act. "I'm leaving you here. I've wasted more than enough time and effort. You drew your fate around you. Now you have to live with it."

Rullin's narrow face went bright red, his shout deafening in the tiny room.

"When Father and Mother hear of this, they'll disown you!"

"You really think so?" Bill said. "They washed their hands of you when they sent you to me, remember? Could be true, though, if they ever heard of it. You see, Rullin, no one here knows our parents. And no one here cares. As far as they'll ever know, you'll just disappear overboard, exactly as I should have done with you myself a long time ago."

Loretta walked in a slow circle around Rullin. She didn't bother drawing her knives.

"If he doesn't want to stay here, you can just turn him over to me." The smooth tone of her voice was enough to keep the young man silent and starting straight ahead. "I'll take him back up to my grandmother's house, and the rest of you needn't be bothered. I'll return alone."

Rullin turned to Karl, still standing against the door. He sounded defiant, but his voice gave away how badly he was shaking.

"Nothing to say? Can't think of anything else to threaten me with?"

Karl's attacks had been made, all of them against the young man's already weakened mind.

"There's nothing I can add, Rullin. I was the one who kept Loretta from carving you up. Twice. I kept Gemma from electrifying you, and I have no doubt she could have. Thing is, I'm not standing in their way anymore. Neither is your brother. You had more chances than anyone deserves. You're on your own."

"Get out, then," Rullin said. "Go. Just leave me here to rot."

Rullin knelt, not easy with the way Karl had him bound, shifting until he sat on the floor. He refused to look up, even when everyone but Walton left the room.

Chapter 34

Karl stood beside Loretta, watching the village drop beneath them. The airship's circling angle of departure would be clearly visible from Rullin's cell.

"I wish you'd told me Bill would actually leave," Karl said. "I never would have said anything."

"And why is that, Karl?" she said. "As far as I can tell, you're still very much out of your element up here."

"I am, but—"

"But nothing. I know these people and how they think. The whole village has to believe it. What if one of them is reporting back to whoever's behind it all? This is the best chance we have of finding out who's pulling Rullin's strings. And you're the one who had the best idea of all."

He groaned. "Don't remind me. That might have been the worst idea I ever had. Nobody might be pulling his strings."

"If no one is, then he's out of everyone's hair permanently," she said. "Care to argue with that outcome?"

Karl watched the village a few seconds longer, then turned to Loretta. The afternoon light caught those amazing eyes, and the wind blew through her black hair.

He cursed himself for a fool for not making love to her the night before. Too much company in a small house, not to mention Morgan so badly beaten, had spoiled the mood before it ever really got started. But even when his mind was so jumbled and upset, he wanted her more than ever.

"No, I can't argue," he said. "This just seems...risky."

"If things are as connected as we both think," she said, "it's a huge risk. But not nearly as bad as not finding out at all."

A voice Karl had trouble recognizing spoke from right behind them.

"Excuse me." They turned to see Bill, clothes and hair properly arranged but still not his normal supremely confident self. "Our new passenger is a bit confused about why we're headed into the mountains rather than inland. I thought you might want to explain it."

Loretta put her gloved hand in his.

"I truly do hope this helps, Bill. If Rullin believes he's had his last chance, maybe he'll try to change his ways."

"I have no expectation of that happening," Bill said. "After he betrayed me by attacking you yet again, I'm afraid I must give him up as a bad job. If this gives you information you can use to protect yourself, it's worth it. Shall I bring your grandmother on deck?"

"Yes, thank you." Loretta held his hand for a second longer. She turned to Karl when the pilot walked away. "I want to skin Rullin alive myself, but I hate to see Bill so upset. Is there any chance you could help the boy?"

"Out at the Columns?" Karl looked out at the mountains to avoid her eyes. "It's never happened before, Loretta. You know I was lying about anyone going home, cured and back on Crumble. People never come back from Joffrey Columns."

"I did," she said, and this time she took Karl's hand.

"It remains to be seen whether that was a good idea or not."

They laughed together, and all Karl could think about was escaping from the rest of this day. Gemma would be upon them at any moment, but he didn't care about company anymore.

He leaned toward her, and Loretta met him more than halfway. Her mouth was warm against the cold wind. She squeezed his hand and pulled him closer.

Loretta's lips parted, pulling Karl in. She tasted as incredible as she smelled to him, like a spring breeze through the lilacs where he grew up. Warmth surged from his belly throughout his body at the thought of how the rest of her body would taste.

She drew back, laughing again.

"My grandmother..."

"I don't care who sees us."

He pulled her hard against him with both arms, kissing her more deeply. Her arms went around his waist. She whispered against his mouth.

"No, she told me this would happen. Just this morning."

Karl shook his head and put both hands into her hair.

"Your grandmother is a very intelligent woman," he said. "You need to hush, though."

Before he could stop kissing her long enough to gather his own intelligence, pick her up, and take her back to that tiny smuggler's cabin, someone very close by cleared her throat.

Loretta drew back again, smiling, her cheeks flushed and the purple of her eyes nearly vanished with dilated pupils.

"I do apologize for interrupting," Gemma said.

Karl didn't have to see Gemma to know she was not the least bit upset about catching the two of them. Loretta grabbed his hand again as they turned toward her.

"That's quite all right, Gemma." Her voice was deeper than normal, and Karl could hear she was breathing as hard as he was. "I've always been good at remembering where I left off."

"I certainly hope so, my dear. Our pilot tells me you can explain why we're heading the wrong way?"

Karl jumped in with their prepared explanation, the only thing he could manage to say. His brain was still lost in Loretta's kiss.

"We knew you didn't want to leave your things at your house any longer than you had to. We're going to pick everything up now, while we have men to help load it all."

Gemma's eyes lit up.

"My animals, too?"

"Yes, we're bringing them back into the village for Walton,'
Loretta said. "He agreed to a very reasonable price."

Gemma stepped forward and hugged both of them.

"Thank you both. I hate the idea of leaving at all, but knowing
thieves won't steal my things and eat my animals makes it ever so
much easier." She wiped her eyes, then winked at Karl. "I'll leave you
two alone, then."

"We'll...ah... We'll be right there," Loretta said. "We really should
help Bill find your house." Loretta pulled Karl's arm down and whispered close enough to send chills over his whole body. "Don't you
forget where we were."

WITH THE HELP of Loretta's memory and Walton's map, Bill had the
airship close to Gemma's little valley in less than an hour. The navigation
up narrow valleys and through the towering mountains didn't bother
Karl nearly as much as getting to the ground. He came to love the rickety,
swaying walkways and stairs attached to proper tethers that afternoon.

Several men slid down ropes at breakneck speed. They tied the
great ship to the barn, the house, the trees, whatever they could find to
pull her down and keep her steady. Karl avoided that terrifying
method of descent, but riding down on the clever rig of pulleys and a
platform was nearly as bad. Loretta and Gemma were delighted by the
slow drop. Karl felt far more like the animals: herded and held against
their better judgment until they were safely inside the cargo hold.

Loading the rest of Gemma's belongings onto the empty ship
didn't take long with all of Bill's crew loading and operating the lift.
The men were delighted to have something to do after a few days in a
very small village. They were again properly moored above that same
village before the sun started to set, out of view of the jail this time.

Bill prowled around the upper deck, barking orders at men already
working hard to look busy enough to avoid his attention. The ship was
in perfect, orderly condition. Everyone understood it was nerves, not
the imagined disorder, making the pilot so short-tempered.

He stopped in front of Loretta

"How long did you tell them we'd wait?"

Loretta glanced at Karl as she took her turn trying to reassure her friend.

"You were there, Bill. We said we'd wait until the morning, then speak to Walton. As far as I know, that's still the plan."

"This is a damned waste of time anyway," Bill said. "We should cast off now, get well south of here before it gets too late. My brother has been more trouble than he was worth since he was born."

Bill paced for a few more minutes before stopping in front of Karl.

"And if Walton kills him? Or doesn't send the messenger in time?"

"Walton seems like the type who'll keep his word," Karl said. "He has for years, taking care of Gemma."

Bill shook his head and kept walking. He kept his eyes on the village, barely visible with the sun behind the mountains now. He was the first one to spot the young girl running toward the shaw.

"Calder!" Bill yelled. "Bring any message she carries to me at once!"

A tall man with red hair caught back in a long ponytail turned and took the swaying stairs at breakneck speed. Bill stood beside Loretta and Karl, his knuckles white from his grip on the rail.

Karl wasn't sure what to do, or what message to hope for. He touched Loretta's shoulder, gratified when she leaned against him.

Bill climbed down several steps to meet Calder. When he returned to Karl and Loretta, he held a small, white envelope with a folded note underneath.

Karl hardly ever saw plain white anymore, outside of what Joffrey Columns used for official business. It was a lot less expensive, but hopelessly old-fashioned in his mother's opinion.

"Black seal," Loretta said, touching the waxy circle on the envelope. "Mourning."

"Rullin sent it, so he's probably alive." Bill's voice shook, but he sounded determined as he unfolded the note. "That's his handwriting. Loretta, my dear, your plan worked to perfection. After some time to think about it, time Walton says Rullin did not enjoy, he begged to be allowed to send just this one letter. He also begged for it to go out on the next shaw, horse, or beggar's cart. Anything but by his own brother's hand. Come, we'll do this in my quarters."

Karl followed, not sure why Bill needed to be so secretive about opening a letter on his own ship, especially after reading that note out loud. He and Loretta hung back as the pilot unlocked his desk and rolled the top up.

It was as fine as any back in Waldron's Gate, the dark wood polished to a gloss that seemed at odds with the rest of the shaw, at least outside of Bill's quarters. Karl wondered who'd been unfortunate enough to have to drag the heavy thing down here into the bowels of the airship.

Bill laid the envelope in the center of the dark green work surface, then used another key to open one of the tiny drawers. He pulled out what Karl thought was an odd sort of corkscrew at first glance. The carved wooden handle, dark with use, extended up from the thin copper blade instead of making a T.

Karl was drawing breath to ask how copper could be strong enough to pull a cork when he noticed the blade wasn't twisted.

Loretta winked at Karl, motioning for him to step closer. The pilot held the envelope up to the light, squeezing the top down just a little. He slid the copper end inside the gap there. Karl was sure Bill used his thumb to separate the blade into two parts. He angled it down, and when it was completely inside, Bill slowly twisted the handle.

The paper moved so gradually it didn't make enough sound to carry over the background noise of the ship. A small bulge formed at the top, and Bill pulled it out carefully. He unrolled a letter written on the same inexpensive white stationary beside the still-perfect envelope.

"Now that is a neat maneuver," Karl said.

He wondered if the guards out at the Columns did exactly the same thing.

"Well, you've both seen it. No need to keep the secret." Bill unfolded the paper carefully, pushing it flat against the wood. "Loretta is one of the few to know why I post letters and such for my crew for free, part of their compensation. They've never quite figured out how I know who's happy and who's not, and most importantly, who to keep and who to leave on the ground."

He fell silent. Before Karl could move away to give him privacy, the pilot got to his feet so quickly his chair creaked.

"This concerns you as much as me," he said. "I'd say my dear brother is far more concerned with everything besides his family."

He walked to the opposite side of the cabin, the only window Karl had seen on this level of the airship. Both he and Loretta stepped forward to read.

To My Kind and Gracious Benefactor:

The corruption and ruin around me is worse than I'd feared, with loyalties everywhere but where they rightly should be. In my efforts to correct the situation, I have fallen into a most dire predicament, one that may prove to be fatal. I still have so much to share, so much that will fill you with joy.

I beg of you, please allow me to help bring your wishes into reality. As has long been the case, you are far more of a father to me than my own, far more of a brother to me than my own has ever been. I will never be able to repay your kindness and generosity, but I deeply hope for the opportunity to try.

Yours, R

Loretta crossed the small room to stand beside Bill, and after a few seconds Karl did the same. The three of them watched the village disappear with the sunset. Only a few fires remained to let them know it hadn't winked out of existence.

Bill took a deep breath.

"I'll send Calder with a return message immediately. We pick him up in the morning. Keep a hood over his head. No one speaks after Walton tells him he's being sent to Constable Law or Joffrey Columns or sold as a slave or whatever he wants to bloody well say. Drop him in the darkest cargo hold, plug his ears so he won't know where he's landed. Karl, will he have permanent damage if we keep withholding Crumble?"

Karl held his breath for a second, wondering if he could go through with this. He'd already gone against everything he believed about helping people with Rullin.

On the other hand, he'd never met anyone who deserved his help less.

"He, ah, he won't have permanent damage from what I understand," Karl said. "I've heard if you give him just a little, maybe if Walton gives him a quarter dose, he'll have the hallucinations again in a few hours. That might make him more susceptible to whatever you tell him."

"I've heard the same thing, Bill," Loretta said. "Just a little now will send him back into it."

"It will be done," Bill said. "When we arrive in Waldron's Gate, we leave him with his blasted letter pinned to his chest. Let that person see what kind of unstable mess he's gotten wrapped up with. Once we find out who's pulling his strings, I no longer have a brother."

"I'm sorry I ever dragged you into this, Bill," Loretta said.

"No, you have nothing to be sorry for. Rullin has betrayed my family far more than he should have been allowed to. You coming to me for help exposed a threat neither of us were aware of." The pilot turned to Karl. "I am once again in your debt for protecting Loretta, and I must add her grandmother and a young boy to the list. Please let me know if I may ever repay you. Goodnight."

Neither Karl nor Loretta spoke on the way through the narrow, dark corridors back to their smuggler's cabins, but she did hold his hand the whole way. He tried to focus on the warmth of her fingers, the way they fit so well with his.

The past several days, all of it somehow related back to this woman, threatened to block out the rest of the world. Rullin's sneer, Morgan's scream, Gemma's tears. The baby 'ster's eyes, Rhysto's threats, Bill's broken voice. The terror of the patient forced off of Crumble, Karl's own terrors and hallucinations doing the same.

Karl was afraid he was going to spend the rest of this long night reliving every awful moment. He couldn't deny there'd been happiness, joy in his new surroundings. The thrill of learning of a wider world than he had ever imagined had been part of all of this, too. He just couldn't call any of that to mind.

When they got to the cabins, his mouth had the good sense to act without consulting his overheated brain.

"Want company tonight?" he said.

"I do, very much," Loretta said. "But not just anyone. I want you, Karl."

Loretta stepped into his arms, and everything that had been out of place between them vanished. He couldn't remember what had held him back even a few seconds before. He no longer cared to try.

This time, when Karl pushed the door to Loretta's cabin open, he followed her inside. He had no illusions that this was any sort of love, true or temporary. He simply needed to be with her and get away from everything he'd done. He'd deal with all the rest when the time came.

Chapter 35

Loretta woke, warm and comfortable enough that she had trouble remembering where she was. This wasn't her own bed or Gemma's house. She had to reach out and touch the rough wooden wall before she was convinced the smuggler's cabin on Bill's shaw could possibly feel so secure.

Karl stirred against her, turning onto his side with an arm around her waist. That was nearly as much of a surprise. After whatever ritual or routine he needed, they'd finally spent the night together, and not just sleeping back to back like they had at Gemma's.

The contrast to her first experience not far from her grandmother's house, and to her last experience with Rhysto, could not have been sharper. Karl had been the best lover she'd had for a long while. Not so rushed or inexperienced as those men who'd paid for her before she was old enough to leave school, and not nearly so close to violence and cruelty as Rhysto himself.

Well, best not to think about that right now. No one had ever lived up to the boss of the shaw pilots in a few memorable ways. The man beside her had done better than most who'd tried.

She got up slowly, wanting a little time to herself before Karl and everyone else woke. She dressed as quickly and quietly as she could, taking the excuse of moving around on the ship to wear her pants one last time before the return to Waldron's Gate's polite daytime society.

Rhysto. Loretta shouldn't have thought of him at all. If Rullin was telling the truth and it wasn't her former lover, who was behind all this nonsense? Even with Bess and all of her built-in security, Loretta couldn't possibly leave such interference unanswered. And the attack on Morgan, and the attempted attack on Gemma, was unforgivable.

Whoever it was would have to be stopped, at whatever cost it took. The calm, almost relaxed persona of the city dweller returning to visit country relatives was falling away with every mile they sped south.

Persona or not, Loretta wasn't returning after one of these visits as she normally did: with her grandmother seen to and some sort of new gadget ready to be installed in her house in Waldron's Gate. She had no idea when she'd get back to the normal, private life she'd worked so hard to build.

Gemma was not far from Bill himself, settled in and sleeping in Rullin's former quarters at everyone's insistence. She wasn't coming for a quick visit, or even an extended stay like when she helped design Loretta's house.

As far as anyone knew, Gemma was going to be a permanent resident. She might even be a permanent resident of the same small house. Loretta set her shoulders, pulled on her cloak, and slipped out of the room.

Karl could turn out to be a problem himself, another thing she simply wasn't used to dealing with. Loretta was afraid Karl would be like so many other men, and a few women. He'd start to want to see her more and more often, to stay with her, to eventually want to live with her and have way too much input into her life. She was afraid he'd want to fulfill the same fantasies of marriage and motherhood Gemma was forever holding out hope for.

Loretta opened the door to the top deck, the icy wind making her glad she'd fetched goggles on the way up. The day was barely dawning, the gray of Fog on the horizon tinged with pink around her.

No one else was on the upper deck so early, with the navigator out of sight in his room just under the prow of the airship. This solitude was exactly what she needed after days filled with so many people, with days full of people in her own house still to come.

Maybe she was underestimating Karl, or overestimating her own appeal. He'd resisted his mother's attempts to get him married off if his stories were to be believed. Maybe he would give her enough time and space.

The much larger problem was how he felt about what Loretta did for a living. That was going to be hard to avoid no matter who found out about it, as good a reason as any to guard her secret so closely.

But Karl had a more legitimate objection than most if she actually was sending people out to Joffrey Columns with her nocturnal activities. She didn't break minds on purpose, and learning how to avoid it would be a good thing to protect her suppliers if nothing else. And her paying clients.

She walked toward the front of the shaw, one hand brushing along the railing. Even with his surprising suggestion to keep Rullin off Crumble, Karl seemed too straitlaced to be accepting of her work even without the side effects. He hadn't been at all straitlaced in her makeshift bed, though, to a wonderfully surprising extent.

She stood at the front of the airship, watching the rolling countryside beneath them, mostly trees with a few dirt roads here and there.

Karl could come in handy, though, if he could get past any need to be overly involved in her life. He was the best protection Loretta had ever had besides Bess, and he was willing to do what was necessary.

He was damn smart, too, with a passion to learn nearly as fierce as her own. And she'd welcome such a skilled lover in her bed, on her own terms.

Alone, far above the ground in the middle of nowhere, Loretta whispered to herself that if they could somehow match up both of their terms, Karl might be good to have around for more than protection or sex.

For the first time on this trip or any other, she heard Bill walking up behind her before he spoke. Perhaps settling back to her Waldron's Gate self truly did make a difference.

"Good morning, my dear," Bill said. "I trust you slept well?"

"I did, very well," she said. "The best I've slept in a long while. And you?"

Bill smiled, his dark skin catching the reddish light of the sun.

"Not as well as you from the looks of you. Is this one a keeper?"

Loretta hoped her blush was hidden by that same light.

"As much as any of them are, Bill. I'm quite certain you understand."

"Indeed, I do," he said. "I speak true when I say you're the only one who could tempt me from my wandering ways."

He held out his hand, and Loretta squeezed tight.

"That's only because I would never do that," she said.

"You speak true as well, my lady." He kissed her hand. "Sadly, we're too well suited for each other, and that's the way we both prefer it. Karl does seem like a good man, Loretta. Maybe even a good one for you."

She smiled, trying to soften her abrupt change to an unpleasant topic.

"What will you do about Rullin? I shed my own family obligations, besides Gemma, many years ago. I know that's never an easy thing."

The pilot stared straight ahead before answering.

"I don't know. He's proved himself worthy of prison, or maybe Joffrey Columns, many times over. But if someone is behind this latest outburst, it doesn't feel fair to leave him to twist on his own. I'm as stupidly sentimental about family as I am unsentimental about lovers."

"Lovers are a lot easier to walk away from," Loretta said. "For anyone besides me. Please let us help any way we can. For whatever reason, I'm his target. I'd like to help resolve this mess if it's possible."

"I'll let you do that," he said. "I can't even read the damned address properly, or at least I can't tell where it is. I never did learn the Waldron's Gate way of navigating. So much trickier down there on the ground."

"That I can help you with, Bill. I'm more of an expert in that area than you know. I have a map at my house that will suit our purposes admirably."

"I thank you for that," he said. "We still have the problem of finding out why all of this is going on in the first place. I doubt someone who's worked so hard to keep this secret is going to just volunteer once my brother shows up on the doorstep."

"Well, that may be another area I can help with, my old friend. I happen to be expert in finding my way about Waldron's Gate, and its residents, late at night when secrets are most likely to be shared."

Chapter 36

KARL HELD the handle on the trolley, trying his best to keep from recoiling every time another person brushed up against him. He'd only been away from this sort of crowd for a few days, less than a week. But he felt like he was surrounded and hemmed in on all sides.

He glanced at Loretta, sitting a few rows down from him. She seemed to be more at ease in all this fuss and noise, not less. He'd have to ask what her secret was.

He watched the tall, colorful houses rolling by, wondering how he'd ever felt comfortable living in one of them. They very nearly rubbed shoulders as much as Karl was right now. He doubted a good, fresh wind could really get going in such close quarters, much less the heavy, wet breezes around Gemma's house.

Something about the peace in those mountains, the quiet, soothed a part of Karl he hadn't realized needed soothing.

Gemma sat beside Loretta, her bright eyes every bit as excited as Karl was anxious. He realized both women had caught him watching them, and both were smiling. At least he was certain Gemma wanted him around. He had no such certainty about her granddaughter.

When the trolley clanked to a halt, he nodded and stepped to the ground. Gemma looked alarmed for a second, until Loretta whispered into her ear. This was the same stop Karl had taken the last time he went to Loretta's house. He wasn't nearly as worried about being unobserved as that day, but the walk would do him good.

He could see the wagons parked in front of the house already, unloading Gemma's belongings. He assumed Rullin would not be among them. That delivery was scheduled for much later that night.

Maybe he was being too pessimistic about Loretta, and without even giving her a chance. She'd been more than friendly that morning, not standoffish and shy like women sometimes were after having sex for the first time.

She wasn't suggesting they move in together or anything like that either, something else Karl wasn't ready for. He, on the other hand, felt more unsettled than he was used to after being with a woman for the first time, no matter how he tried to think about it.

He turned onto the same street he'd watched Rhysto walking down what seemed like years ago. That problem was far from solved, and dealing with Rullin might only make everything worse. Karl wasn't exactly eager to worry about a violent ex who could show up at any time. He wasn't even sure if that would ever be a factor, with him not exactly willing to move and Loretta not able to live with him.

Some kind of match he'd made after a lifetime of his mother expecting him to settle down and start giving her more grandchildren.

"Karl," Bill said. "Didn't expect to see you walking toward this house alone."

He looked up to see the pilot walking down the porch steps, finally seeming to have regained most of his confidence and swagger.

"I needed a bit of fresh air," Karl said. "That trolley was crowded after a couple of days on your fine airship."

The pilot laughed, shaking his head.

"You sound as smooth with words as I do. Don't let that way of life overtake you. I do agree about conditions on the ground here. Far too close for my taste. Speaking of close, here's our lovely hostess.'

Loretta and Gemma turned up the sidewalk, the older woman beaming, Loretta looking far more cautious as she matched her grandmother's leisurely pace.

"Fancy meeting you two handsome gentlemen here," Loretta said, eyeing the piles of trunks and boxes on her porch and lawn. "I'll get the door open so we can get everything brought inside."

Karl kept watching the side of the porch, wondering if Bess was trying her best not to laugh at all the fuss. Loretta unlocked the door and motioned them all to go inside without so much as a glance that way. Perhaps she'd already gotten word to her guard.

Loretta sent Gemma to investigate her guest room and grabbed Karl's hand.

"Can you help me in the kitchen for a moment, Karl?"

When he let the door swing closed behind him, she stepped forward into his arms, much like she had the night before. As unsure as his mind and heart felt about where this might all end up, his body was quite sure it wanted more of hers.

She whispered into his ear. "All these people running around my house are going to drive me insane."

"I felt that way on the trolley," he said. "Like I was going to drown. Most of them will be gone before too long. I can go, too."

"You?" She put one hand behind his neck and pulled him down into a quick kiss. "You I wouldn't mind having around from time to time."

BILL'S MEN were as efficient on the ground as in the air, getting everything put away and disappearing before more than an hour had passed. With Gemma safely occupied setting up her equipment in the guest bedroom, Bill joined Karl and Loretta in the study. She'd already done whatever she needed to to bring out her map before anyone else came in.

Bill surprised Karl by handing the letter to him.

"Can you tell me where this place is, Karl? I'm not having much luck, and Loretta was certain you and her map would be able to work it out."

Karl scowled and shook his head, turning the white envelope over in his hands. It felt like Rullin's letter was already back inside.

"I don't know what you need me for," he said. "Just look at the street name and go from there."

"That's just the problem," Loretta said, sitting beside him. "It doesn't match any of the streets I know here. It says Waldron's Gate, but I've never heard of a Third Street here."

"Third Street?" he said. "There isn't one. It must be in some kind of...of code."

Karl stared at the address, trying to catch whatever was playing around the edges of his memory. A long time ago, something his mother had gotten quite upset about.

"Unless this is an old address," he said.

"How old?" Loretta reached for the envelope. "I've lived here for over ten years, and every street I know is named for some kind of plant or flower."

"This would be long before that," Karl said. "More than twenty years ago. I barely remember the change, but I remember my mother being furious. The streets used to be numbered, yeah, but I hadn't thought about that for a long, long time."

Bill turned from studying the map to face the two of them.

"Why did that upset your mother, Karl?"

"I'll just say she's a bit enthusiastic about the post," Karl said. "She loves few things as much as sending and receiving letters. She has a whole room dedicated to it. Every sort of wax and seal and paper you can imagine. Anyway, when they revised all the street names, she had to do the same with her drawers full of address cards. She has a lot of cards."

Bill grunted. "So how would my blasted brother know an old addressing pattern here? I don't even know the new one, and he's never lived in town either."

"I'd guess that was someone's way to work in code," Karl said. "Whoever Rullin was snooping around for probably taught it to him."

"Asking your mother may not be the best idea in this case, Karl," Loretta said in a strange, tight voice. "Do you remember well enough to tell us where this is? If we have to send it through the post, we'll never figure it out."

"I can give it a try," Karl said. He focused on the puzzle rather than Loretta's odd response. "I asked Mother what all the fuss was one afternoon. I hadn't even started school yet. She explained it all to me while she was rewriting her dozens of cards. Our address was...Number Seven on Twenty-First Street. Now the house is Number Three Lilac Row."

He walked over to the map.

"Here's the house," he said. "See how it was seventh if you count from this end, but third here? What was the address, Loretta?"

"It's Number Five on Third Street. What would my address have been then?"

"Yours wasn't here then," Karl said. "Nothing else was a few blocks in either. That was part of the problem, why they redid all of it. So many new houses went up about twenty-five years ago." Karl traced one finger along the map, avoiding the pins and string along with thinking about what they meant, counting the old streets down in his mind. "This one was, I mean it is, on Daylily Way now. It's Number Four."

Loretta was beside him, just short of pushing him out of the way.

"Four? Are you sure?"

"I'm as sure as I can be from so long ago," Karl said. "That's what it should be now. Why?"

Loretta looked up at him, her violet eyes flashing.

"The owner of that house would have absolutely no problem with the addresses, old or new. He's the Director of Posts for all of bloody Alterra. A client of mine called Olsen Norwood."

Chapter 37

LORETTA STRUGGLED to keep calm during dinner, a meal that seemed painfully crowded even with only four people. The food itself was perfectly acceptable, with Gemma, Bill, and even Karl helping with everything. Her house wasn't even as full as she'd feared. She had more room than she wanted to admit.

The problem wasn't even knowing none of them planned to leave until at least the next day. The problem was Bill and Karl being with her that night when she headed out to finally deal with Rullin.

She didn't mind the backup or the muscle, not at all, certainly not with who they had to visit. Olsen Norwood made her jump inside her own flesh like no one else ever had, not outside of the family she grew up with.

Loretta was glad Mr. Norwood would see she was hardly alone and defenseless. If she got the chance she'd show him just how capable she was of taking care of herself. Her supply of ritterns and other kinds of wealth was healthy and not likely to dwindle anytime soon, even while she waited for Gemma to complete the new compass.

Loretta was simply starting to miss Building. The little bit she'd done out at Joffrey Columns hadn't been enough, and that had been several days ago.

She wasn't comfortable admitting to herself how much she needed the sensations, the energy moving though her, the release that was often more satisfying than sex.

Just after sundown, Loretta tried to excuse herself to wait for Bess. Karl knowing about her guard was bad enough, and she hadn't been able to avoid that. Putting her grandmother at risk by knowing the same was a chance she wasn't willing to take.

Karl watched her trying to get away for a couple of minutes, dodging Gemma's and even Bill's questions, then came to her rescue.

"Loretta, I've been meaning to ask you about something," he said. "Step outside with me?"

The other two glanced at each other, looking for all the world like they'd just discovered the most amusing secret together with matching grins and eye rolls. Loretta kept smiling and kept walking.

"I don't much like needing a minder," she said when she closed the front door. "But I appreciate the assistance."

Loretta watched him, her eyes following the long line of his body, the way he sprawled confidently in the swing instead of pretending to like he had waiting for Rhysto. So many things had changed in just a few days' time.

He shrugged. "They'd be surprised to know they've stumbled upon the most non-romantic romance in the history of Alterra. I figured you needed to talk to someone out here. I'll go back inside and give you some privacy."

Non-romantic romance or not, she was enjoying having him around. She sat beside him, pleased when he moved his arm from the back of the swing to her shoulders.

"You don't have to go back inside," she said. "I'm meeting Bess. You two already know about each other. I wanted to make sure she knows all the adjustments going on around here."

"That's a rather long list," he said. "I won't be underfoot. I need to head back out to the Columns tomorrow evening. If we both feel like seeing each other after that, I'd be glad to head back next weekend. That would be a record number of visits for me in one month."

"Good to know I'm worth such a change of habit," Loretta said. She hoped the setting sun hid the flush in her cheeks at least a little bit. "I'd very much like to see you, Karl. Gemma will have a start on your Dragon by then."

"And your gyro-compass."

"Yes," she said. "And my compass."

Loretta had never been so relieved to see another person coming down her street as she was to see Bess just then. Discussions about her gyro-compass and how she intended to use it were not in her plans for the evening.

THE EVENING only got worse for Loretta as it wore on. She was relieved to finally be going out at night, the first time in weeks that she'd been able to. She wouldn't be taking her Dragon, no matter how badly she wanted to, and she wouldn't be going alone.

Sure, it might look like it, and for a few blocks it would feel like it, but she wouldn't be alone. She got dressed, trying to stay calm by going over the list of Builds she still had in her mind, the ones she had been in the middle of when Karl tackled her. Nothing had been the same since then except her clothes.

She wore the black skinsuit and low boots, with her hair pulled back, wondering what Bill would think of such a getup. Karl had seen it once before, but she'd be willing to bet he hadn't been paying much attention to her body.

These nights with a far-off Build usually started with a long, leisurely walk to prepare and get into the necessary mindset. Tonight Loretta was out front pacing long before Bill's wagon was due to arrive. Gemma had gone to bed earlier than expected, saving everyone that struggle.

"Everything ready?" she said when Karl joined her on the porch.

"As far as I know," he said. "Once Bill shows up, we're good. Rullin won't have much choice but cooperating, thanks to my skills with rope and yours with sedatives."

"Just stay close," Loretta said. "But not too close. I don't want to wake them or anyone else before we're ready."

No one spoke on the ride over to Daylily Way. Loretta kept

wanting to ask them to stop and let her out, even though she hadn't even brought her Dragon along. That was too much danger for Bill, and for her.

When they finally did stop a few blocks away, the houses were dark, the streetlights turned low. Odds were high no one would ever know they'd been here. No one outside the Norwood household, anyway.

"We'll leave him on the porch," Bill said, gripping Loretta's arm. "Then you're on. We won't be far away if there's any trouble."

She nodded and looked into Karl's worried eyes. Loretta smiled at him as she jumped to the ground. The small, dark wagon continued on past her.

She walked slowly until it stopped in front of the Norwood's sprawling house. Even though she strained to hear, Bill and Karl worked silently. The only noise Loretta heard was the creak of the wagon when it started moving again. She picked up her pace then, worried about what had to be the weakest part of their plan.

If Rullin made too much noise and woke everyone up, especially the Norwood's neighbors, everything would fall apart.

Loretta drew even with the house to see an unmoving lump on the porch. As unpleasant as the rest might turn out to be, that breaking point had passed. She resisted the strong urge to kick him in the face when she walked by. If she'd been wearing her high pointed boots instead of her silent night shoes, she might not have resisted.

She took a deep breath, then knocked on the front door. Not as loudly as she wanted to, not by any means. She wanted only the occupants of this house, not all of their neighbors.

After a few minutes, she knocked again. People slept so deeply when they were on a full dose of Crumble. Loretta had a few seconds to wish they could have tried Karl's idea of creating paranoia by somehow forcing Mr. Norwood off of it before a light moved down the front stairs.

She dropped the letter on the still-unconscious young man's chest as she stepped around the corner of the porch into the shadows.

"Who's out here?"

Olsen Norwood wore a quite proper striped robe tied most

improperly, and his hair stood around his head like a halo. He held a lamp in one hand, and held Mrs. Norwood behind him with the other. Loretta could hear her muttering, then exclaiming.

"What's that thing on the porch?"

Mr. Norwood drew back and reached for something before he pushed his wife inside and closed the door. He walked slowly toward Rullin, and now Loretta saw the heavy fireplace poker in his hand. When Mr. Norwood got close enough to see the boy's face, his shoulder slumped.

He dropped the poker and picked up the letter. The curtains in the door were pushed aside, but he didn't seem to notice. He was too busy reading the letter.

"Imp burn you," he said. "Worthless shaw scum."

Loretta stepped forward.

"Good evening, Mr. Norwood."

LORETTA WAS afraid the Mr. Norwood would scream out loud, or that she herself would laugh at the way he jumped backward. She walked toward him, stopping before his wife would see.

"I need to have a word with you," she said. "I'll leave it up to you whether your wife joins us or not."

"No, please. Just give me a minute."

He dropped the letter and nearly crashed into the door. Loretta leaned against the wall, trying to put proper Mrs. Norwood together with the language she was hearing. Those words were more appropriate for the collection hidden deep inside the house, or deep in the shaw camps in the middle of the night.

"I said go back upstairs, Roma. It's not him! No, I don't tell you what to do. That's why you're going to listen to me this one blasted time!"

Mr. Norwood stood inside the door watching his wife walk up the stairs, then closed it and leaned against it. Loretta shoved Rullin with her foot.

"Care to explain why this worthless shaw scum tried to kill me in my sleep, Mr. Norwood?"

He nearly dropped his lamp.

"That's not... I didn't... He wasn't supposed to do anything like that!"

Loretta stepped closer. "You need to consider what class of criminal you're hiring before you hand the rittern over. Whether he went outside of his job description or not doesn't matter to me. I want to know why he was bothering me in the first place."

"He was just..." he said. "I only wanted to know who your suppliers are. That's all. He was never supposed to try to hurt you."

Loretta walked closer, gratified when Mr. Norwood drew back.

"I find it interesting that two men attacked me in short order asking me the same questions. I don't suppose you hired any other criminals to inquire into my private business? Perhaps the same day you were last supporting that business, very generously, I might add?"

"I asked around," he said, nearly stammering. "I didn't hire anyone else. I swear it. I asked one of the shaw pilots. I can't... I don't remember what his name was."

Loretta's mind strained with trying to put this shivering coward together with the cold, arrogant Director she'd met right before her life got so damn messy. Mr. Norwood slumped against the side of his house, in danger of slipping down to the floor with Rullin. He was barely able to meet her gaze.

"Rhysto," she said. "A bigger criminal than Rullin could ever hope to be. He was waiting inside my bedroom closet that night, Mr. Norwood. He was not kind."

At that, he did slide to the floor, letting the lamp drop with a bang before covering his face with his hands.

"Rhysto," he wailed. "He is not kind. I didn't want that. I didn't want that."

After a few more repetitions, Loretta waved her right arm in the air. She felt absurd doing that with nothing to say, but questioning him further herself wasn't going to do any good.

It was time to frighten him a bit, make sure he understood she wasn't working alone anymore. Before Mr. Norwood looked up, Karl and Bill stood at the bottom of the steps.

"That may be, Mr. Norwood," Loretta said. "But you still haven t told me what you do want. Why should such a loyal client be so interested in my suppliers? Looking to cut out the middle woman and save yourself a bit of coin? You could simply stop buying such items altogether."

"I wanted to! I tried!" He lowered his hands and jumped when he saw the two men, knocking his head against the side of the house. "Roma, she wouldn't hear of it. She loves... You know how she loves such things."

"If you didn't want me to stop selling them," Loretta said, standing over the cowering man, "if your dear wife wouldn't hear of it, then why were you interfering with me in the first place? I am not looking for a partner.'

The man covered his face again, moaning and shaking his head. Loretta motioned Bill forward.

"Mr. Norwood, is it?" Bill said. "I'm one of those worthless shaw scum you were just referring to. This young man here, barely more than a boy himself?" He walked up onto the porch, fists opening and closing. "That's my younger brother. Whatever you got him mixed up in, whatever empty promises you made him, drove him to beat an even younger boy half to death. It will destroy my own mother, but I'll have to turn him in to Constable Law. Being a Director, you know as well as I do how easily they get people to give up their secrets. What makes you think my brother will protect you when he sold me out so easily?"

"No, please," Mr. Norwood said without lowering his hands.

"Please what, Mr. Norwood?" Loretta bent down, hands on her knees. "I'm afraid none of us can hear you."

"Please don't turn him in," he said. "We can find some other way. I know we can. My career won't survive such a scandal. I won't survive."

"Sir, you're giving us no other option." Bill stood beside Loretta, and Mr. Norwood shrank closer to the floor. "Unless we know what drove you to interfere in this lady's personal business, we'll have no alternative than letting the Ministry handle this."

Mr. Norwood lunged forward, grabbing Bill's leg.

"If you're a shaw pilot, you know what he's like," he whispered, tears running down his cheeks. "I had to do something to get him away from my home, from my family. He threatened the most horrible things to my wife."

Olsen Norwood didn't need to say another word, not for Loretta's sake. Of course. It all made sense now.

Bill pushed him away and brushed at the wrinkles on his pants.

"I know what who is like, Mr. Norwood?" Loretta said.

"Rhysto! I never should have contacted him, never!" The man was sitting forward, talking so loudly Loretta was afraid he would wake his neighbors. She didn't care quite as much anymore. "I only wanted to start up my own little side business, nothing to compete with you, just a tiny bit here and there. I can send things outside Waldron's Gate, that's all, and get things from there too. Our friends... Our friends started asking me if I knew any other purveyors of such items when you grew busier, when your visits were less frequent. I never wanted to hurt you, Ms. Schofield, the furthest thing from it. I never expected that beast to bother you."

He slumped back against the house. "I never, ever expected him to come here either."

LORETTA WATCHED Karl walking up the porch stairs, not sure what to do or say. If Rhysto was bold enough to attack others in town the way he'd attacked her, if he'd even attacked a Director's wife, the pilot had gotten even more out of control.

None of them would be safe, not as long as the man was drawing breath. Anything they did could make it all worse.

Karl stood beside her and mouthed one word to spur her into action.

Gemma.

"Mr. Norwood, listen to me." She squatted down beside him, and when he didn't respond she grabbed his chin. "Listen to me. You're right not to trust him. You need to tell me what he did. We might have to lock him up to stop him, but we can't do that unless we know what he's done."

He stared at her for several seconds, eyes wide.

"He came calling," he said. "A few days after you were here. While I was at the Ministry, while Roma was here. Alone. She came downstairs and found him sitting on the couch. When she screamed, he told her if I didn't do exactly what he said, she'd...spend the rest of her days screaming like that. He said she'd scream until she liked it or he died trying."

Loretta felt cold settle into her guts at Rhysto talking to Roma Norwood like that. Sick taste in curios or not, she was not a woman to even know such games existed, much less to have enjoyed playing.

Letting the pilot continue to draw breath might no longer be possible.

"What did he want, Mr. Norwood?" she said.

"He said there were other shaws," he said. "Pilots who didn't follow him. He told me I had to find out if they were behind your trade, that I had to figure out who was. He said if I didn't, he would keep his promises to my wife. The things he said..."

"I know what kinds of things he said, Mr. Norwood," Loretta said. "I'm telling you those are the things he does, and worse." She didn't flinch when the older man did. "What else?"

"He gave me names," Mr. Norwood said. "One man in every rebellious camp, he said. Told me I gave him the idea. He told me if I managed to persuade each of them to work with us, he'd leave my wife alone. And I did that! Your brother wasn't the only one, sir, he wasn't. None of them knew a damned thing."

Mr. Norwood straightened up, wiping his face.

"That's when he visited me at the Ministry, right in my own office. He said you left with another pilot, that you had disappeared. Rhysto thought, I'm sure he still thinks, that we worked out a deal together to cut him out. He told me in person exactly what would happen to Roma on his next visit if I didn't tell him the truth. He told me I'd have to watch."

Loretta closed her eyes, trying to stop images of what Rhysto would do to Roma Norwood if he ever returned. And what he'd do to Gemma if he ever caught her alone. She stood.

"Mr. Norwood, listen to me," she said. "I swear to you I have no suppliers among the shaws. None. I am sorry you've run afoul of Rhysto. I'm also disappointed you tried to interfere with me. Your wife doesn't deserve to suffer for your bad judgment. I suggest you get back inside, lock your doors, and do not answer no matter who knocks until morning. Take Roma with you when you leave. I don't care what your excuse is. Do not leave her here. We'll try to clean up this mess you've created."

She turned and walked toward the steps.

Mr. Norwood scrambled onto his knees, eyes wide and staring.

"Wait! You can't leave this boy here!"

"I'll take my brother, you coward," Bill said. "For your sake, I pray you never show your face at my camp again, or at the camps of the other independent shaws. We would all regret that."

When Mr. Norwood started to say something else, Karl spoke for the first time.

"That's enough. Go back inside, lock the door, and go upstairs." He held out the letter and envelope, and Mr. Norwood jerked away again. "You're taking this. You need to remember your actions have consequences. Now go."

Olsen Norwood got slowly to his feet and took the letter, holding it between his fingertips as if it would burn him. He turned without another word and went back inside the house.

No one moved until they heard the door lock and saw the lamp going back up the stairs. Bill hit the sidewalk at a run to fetch the wagon.

"You okay?" Loretta said, standing beside Karl. He stood with his hands on his hips, looking down at Rullin.

"No, not really," he said. "We have to stop him, and I don't even know how that begins. But I can't let him hurt anyone else. Least of all you or Gemma."

"Myself I can take care of," Loretta said. "Right now Gemma's safe with Bess. We'll make whatever arrangements we have to keep her safe."

Karl grunted as he picked Rullin up, and Loretta saw the boy beginning to stir. The last thing any of them needed was to deal with him conscious and raving. She stepped forward with a numbing hypodermic already in hand.

"Leave him, Loretta," Bill said, jumping out of the wagon. "I'll drop you two off, but I'm taking him with me. If Rhysto suspects I'm wrapped up in this, my airship isn't safe. Neither are my men."

"Bill, it's harmless. He won't even feel—"

"I said leave him." Bill helped Karl lift Rullin into the wagon, then climbed up to the seat. He never looked at Loretta. "Let's go. I need to get back."

When they stopped in front of Loretta's house, all was calm. Bill grasped Karl's hand before the larger man climbed down. Loretta stayed where she was, waiting until he looked at her.

"I don't know what this business of yours is," he said. "The one I'm supposedly mixed up in. I do know it's pulled me, my brother, that boy Morgan, and who knows who else into a terrible mess. Take care of your grandmother, Loretta. Let Karl take care of both of you. Leave my family out of it."

She touched his arm, desperate not to leave on such terms.

"I hope to see you again, Bill. I don't want to leave things like this, my old friend. I am sorry."

He finally looked at her, the crooked grin she knew so well on his face.

"Perhaps in time, my lady. Go now. Take care."

Bill clicked his tongue at the horses and disappeared into the night. Karl was already on the porch. When she walked up, Bess appeared beside them.

"No, Karl, no one has been here this evening," Bess said. "From your voice I gather you're expecting unpleasant company."

"The most unpleasant kind, Bess," Loretta said. "If Rhysto shows up, do not hesitate to solve the problem. Understood?"

"Yes, ma'am. Unless he has an army with him, you won't be bothered."

Chapter 38

Loretta swept out of her steaming kitchen, with the clear intention of ending the conversation. Karl decided he was up to her challenge. He followed her into the dining room.

"No, Karl, that's out of the question."

"You're not thinking clearly," he said. "From what you and Mr. Norwood said, Rhysto leads most of the shaw pilots. He pretty much does have a bloody army. I know Bess is loyal and strong, but you're crazy to risk yourself and Gemma like this."

Loretta slammed the bowl of greens she was carrying down and headed back to the kitchen.

"Keep your voice down," she said. "She's just in the bath."

"Then listen to me," Karl said. "At some point he will catch you gone, and I have to leave tonight. I can't afford to lose my job, even for all this wonderful adventure with you. Just for a little while, Loretta. I'm not talking forever."

She pushed by him. "I can't move myself and my grandmother out to Joffrey Columns, Karl. I'm not that crazy, no matter what you seem to think."

"Just hang on! I know that. I'm not asking you to check yourselves in. I have a friend who knows where all the empty rooms are. He's the same one who helped us before. This gets you and Gemma and even your guards out of Rhysto's path until we can figure out what to do about him. You said if he's bold enough now to walk into the Ministry to threaten Mr. Norwood, he's gotten even more out of control."

She whirled around, and Karl drew back from the look in her eyes. She didn't seem angry, not exactly. Loretta seemed like she was about to agree with him.

Somehow that made him more anxious.

"All right Karl, I'll promise to at least think about it, on one condition. Gemma's almost finished with my gyro-compass. Delays between visits are what got Mr. Norwood into this. I've had nothing but delays since you broke the first one. You said yourself that the Dragon calmed one patient down. Let me Build while I'm there."

"What? Now you *are* talking crazy!' he said. "Letting the two of you hide out for a little while is one thing, but you can't be roaming the grounds experimenting on the patients. They'll lock both of us up, and well they should!"

"Then what did you want your own Dragon for, Karl? Tell me. You said it was so you could figure out how to help them, right? Was that just a lie? I suddenly have potential business partners coming out of the bloody woodwork when I never wanted the first damned one."

Karl stared at her, his own eyes narrowing. That was what he'd said, yes. It was even partly what he really did want to do. But his own temptation, his desire to have the limitless power of Building, hadn't lessened in the slightest. Admitting that to Loretta right now seemed like one of his worst bad ideas.

"Yes, that's what I wanted it for," he said. "I have no idea if it will ever get approved, but I believe it will work. That has nothing to do with getting you and Gemma out of Rhysto's path."

Loretta crossed her arms, turning her head to the right, then the left.

"That's the condition," she said. "You tell me which ones. Go with me if you want. I'll even split the profits with you if this works out. But I'm not even willing to think about this if you expect me to sit and stare at the walls. If I do that, I *will* go insane."

Karl scrubbed his face with both hands, certain he was getting into trouble he couldn't foresee.

"Fine," he said. "Only the ones I say, and only when I say. I don't want a scrap of your profits. Put them away for Gemma."

"Gemma will be well cared for as long as I'm alive. You never have to doubt that. I'll consider your offer, Karl. I will."

She walked back into the dining room, and Karl heard her greeting her grandmother as if nothing else had happened. He stood with his head down, hoping he wouldn't regret his latest grand idea.

Chapter 39

THE IMPOSING stone wall and brick towers of Joffrey Columns looked even stranger to Karl than Waldron's Gate had. He might have been gone for ten years rather than living here that long. His eyes cringed away from the worn and drab corridors; his nose recoiled from antiseptic and illness. He couldn't imagine how he'd ever found his life here acceptable, much less felt like he was at home.

Karl jumped at George's voice, nearly dropping the keys to his apartment.

"Well, if it isn't Mr. Karl Gilmore, returned from mysterious family illness leave."

"Yeah, I'm back, Georgie. Not exactly back to normal, but back. Come on inside."

Karl wondered if his apartment had always smelled this musty and stale and he'd never noticed. He opened the bedroom window as wide as it would go. He pulled a heavy paper-wrapped package out of his bag, then tucked the whole thing onto the top shelf of the wardrobe. He'd forgotten to get rid of that damned revolver Loretta had yet to teach him to use.

George stood in the living room, his grin even broader when Karl handed him a full bottle of Northlands whiskey.

"What's this for?"

"Advance payment," Karl said. "I'm going to need your help for a little bit, more than I usually do. A lot more."

By the time Karl explained his plan to move Loretta and Gemma out to the Columns, they'd consumed several shots of the whiskey. And George was getting more incredulous by the second.

"Karl, I've heard of guys going to just about any length to get a steady supply of the fairer sex out here but never anything like this. You're going to get all of us locked up out there with the 'sters."

"This guy Rhysto *is* a monster," Karl said. "I'm not trying to get a steady supply of anything. I can't exactly send them to my mother's house, and I'd never get over it if something happens to them. This is the best thing I can come up with. Now come on, I know you know where they'd be safe."

George sat back and scrubbed his fingers through his already messy brown hair.

"The safest place isn't where I'd put anyone I cared to keep sane," he said. "There's an old caretaker's house, one that's been abandoned for a long time. No one ever goes out there."

"That sounds like exactly what we need." Karl got up and started pacing. "Can we move them in tomorrow?"

George crossed his arms over his belly. "Just like that, huh? No worries about where it is or maybe why it was abandoned?"

"Why, then?" Karl said. "What's the big problem?"

"It's out in the middle of where the oldest 'sters live. I'm telling you, no one goes out there unless they have to."

"So why were you there?" Karl said. "How do you know about this place?"

"I drew the short damned straw about five years ago," George said. "One of us lucky bastards has to go check the place out once a year, make sure it's still standing. I don't know why they bother. No one is ever going to live there again. I figure it got put on someone's maintenance list thirty years ago, and no one ever thinks to take it off. That's how most of my run of the mill busywork happens."

"Is it in bad shape now?"

"No, not especially," George said. "I don't think the 'sters ever manage to get inside the fence. It's more like a cage, really. But you're missing the essential piece of information, Karl. The house is in the middle of where the oldest monsters live. No one can control these at all, not that we can really control any of them. It's just a matter of waiting for whoever spawned the damned things to die. This is not a vacation house out in the countryside."

"That's exactly why it's perfect," Karl said. "This woman, she's a little different. She's fine keeping to herself. Better off, maybe. She's a wild Tinker. She dreams, Georgie. Real nighttime dreams. Then she builds what she dreams about."

"Bullshit. You're trying to smuggle some kind of sick Builder out here without letting anyone know, probably to show off for your girlfriend. No one dreams."

"This woman does, I'm telling you,' Karl said. He wondered yet again why his own sleep hadn't dissolved into strange visions after days off Crumble. "She doesn't Build, not like you're thinking. She sees things in her dreams, and she makes them with her hands. The most amazing things. Her house out in the middle of nowhere ran completely on electricity. If she sets up that fence anything like she had out there, the biggest 'ster ever born won't get through. All she needs is a little bit of copper and a fire to make the steam."

"An electric house out in the sticks, huh," George said. "Not dependent on Builders or the Ministry for any of it. I'd bet that little skill is what drew her to this prince charming Rhysto's attention."

George still sounded doubtful, but Karl knew he was going to help them. He felt sick to his stomach for lying to his friend about what Rhysto was after, but he was glad no one else would be drawn to the pilot's attention. And George made a terrible point Karl hadn't even considered.

If Rhysto, the scientists at Parliament, or the military out at Stensue knew even a tiny bit about what Gemma made, she wouldn't be safe anywhere in Alterra no matter where he tried to hide her.

"That's it, George. He wants to get out from under the Builders, cover both ends of the supply chain is how he put it. I'd be the last one to argue about escaping from a house full of them, but I didn't put an old woman at risk in the process."

"Or your girlfriend," George said. "Have you thought about this long term, Karl, my buddy? Once this little hideout has served its usefulness, where is this talented lady going to live?"

"If we can deal with the shaw pilot, we can keep her hidden in plain sight. Loretta kept her hidden away for a long time before Rhysto caught on. She can do the same thing, just here where she can keep an eye on her."

George sighed and got to his feet. He only swayed a little bit.

"I don't know what it is about this woman, Gilmore. For more than ten years, you're the most boring asshole in all of Joffrey Columns. Even I look like a socialite by comparison. Now all of a sudden, you're dragging me into yet another bad idea of yours that could get me fired. Or worse."

"So you'll help us?" Karl said.

"Yeah, yeah, I'll help you," George said. "I should get my own damned head examined for even thinking about it, but I guess I'm in the right place for that. You owe me, Karl. Again."

"More than I could ever repay, Georgie. I'll talk to you later."

Karl kept pacing after his friend left, searching for a single idea of how he was going to break this to Loretta or Gemma. He couldn't imagine either of them finding an abandoned house in the middle of 'ster country to be an acceptable place to hide, even for a few days. But he couldn't think of anything else to do, either.

He'd been feeling that way far too often lately.

And the end was nowhere in sight.

Chapter 40

Loretta squeezed her eyes closed, irritated at the growing light. She hadn't been asleep nearly long enough for the sun to be rising. Or maybe it had just been too long since she'd slept alone in her own damned bed.

She turned over and took a deep breath, hoping to be able to get back to sleep, and froze. This was her own bed. The sheets and pillowcase were far too soft to be at Gemma's, Karl's, or certainly on Bill's shaw.

The sun didn't come in her bedroom window.

Keeping her eyes closed, Loretta drew in another slow breath. Her imagination wasn't running away with her in her sleep. In fact, her mind had let things go way too far, and her guards had too. If her guards were still alive.

Rhysto's distinctive aroma of whiskey, cigars, and perfume were all around her. Pretending to sleep wouldn't save her now.

"Ah, sleeping beauty opens those gorgeous eyes at last."

He was sitting on her bench, drawn up close beside the bed. He'd been turning the lamp up gradually.

"Rhysto. Should I point out that I have not invited you into my house, much less my bedroom?"

"Point it out all you want to, darlin'. That won't change the fact that I'm here. And that you're finally here after your little adventure in the Northlands."

Loretta sat up slowly, moving back against her pillows. She thanked a Crown she no longer believed in that the pilot hadn't found the weapons hidden in that headboard on his last unexpected visit.

"I was visiting family," she said. "You know where I come from, as you're so fond of pointing out. I'm not sure why that concerns you."

"I've already paid a visit to your family," he said. "Quite an array of toys she has in her room. Making something special for you?"

"If you've hurt her, one of us dies tonight. I'll do my damnedest to make sure it's you."

Rhysto threw back his head and laughed, the movement of his throat making Loretta ache to bury her knife there. This same bastard would have laughed no matter how loudly Roma Norwood screamed. No matter how loud Gemma screamed.

"Don't worry your head about your guest," he said. "She's still sound asleep. As far as I know, your guards are, too."

"Tell me why you don't know," she whispered.

"Well now, the dose of gas is a bit harder to regulate when the tank is full." He patted a small gray tank on the floor beside him, with a long tube coiled on top of it. A black gas mask lay alongside. "I'm afraid the little girl at the back door had a bit more than I'd planned. The lovely woman at the front should be just fine in a few hours."

"Why didn't you just use it on me, you bastard?"

"You can't tell me what I want to know if you're not awake. And you have plenty to tell me." The pilot grinned and leaned closer. "Depending on what shape you're in after that, maybe we'll have a little fun, Loretta. I've missed you."

"The same kind of fun you planned to have with Roma Norwood?"

"Oh no, not at all," he said. "You know I prefer my partners to enjoy themselves as much as I do." He grabbed her headboard with both hands and shook it, but none of the compartments gave up their secrets. "This will do nicely. I've returned to you over the years because you're the only woman I've ever found who's a match for my appetites."

"You've had your last fun with me," Loretta said. "And I don't have a damned thing to tell you. That all ended when your little friend Rullin tried to attack me."

He shook his head and sighed, moving onto the bed. Loretta moved as far away as she dared. She didn't want to get out of reach of her weapons.

"You know as well as I do that I didn't hire that boy," he said. "You're well acquainted with Mr. and Mrs. Norwood, so you know that was his bad decision making. He's soft like so many others in the Ministry these days, babbling the same absurd rumors about Aerchead and elves and haunted houses."

Rhysto put one arm around her, pulling her against him. She didn't need to see the revolver he kept in a holster on the other side. She knew it was there, and loaded. He brought out the little black knife she remembered too well in his free hand.

"From the looks of your little meeting in the middle of the night," he said, "you and your friends have a nice little arrangement worked out."

"There's nothing to arrange," Loretta said. "Mr. Norwood is just as mistaken about my private business as you are. I have no control over the rumors he spreads. What I told you about where I find my goods the last time you broke into my house was the truth. I'm sorry if it's not what you were hoping for."

She inched her arm behind him, aiming for one of her hidden compartments.

"So sorry to disagree with you," he said. "I told you not to lie to me about this. That soft gut asks me about your suppliers, then next thing I know you're off to the Northlands with one of the scab shaws. Darlin', you know I'm not stupid enough to believe that. Where's your rather large companion this evening? He's not doing much of a job protecting you."

When his rough hand slipped under her gown to her bare breast, Loretta drew in a breath and flinched away. The motion and noise might encourage him, but it covered her pressing on the tiny door. She felt the cool glass curve of a hypo inside. Not the lethal weapon she would have preferred, but it would do. He'd never feel the needle until it was too late.

She held the hypo against her wrist, once again reduced to watching for him to drop that damned knife.

"He'll be here early in the morning," she said. "I'm sure he'll be most interested in hearing about your visit."

"I'd be happy to return so he can watch," Rhysto said, squeezing her nipple. All Loretta felt was pain. "Once you've recovered, of course."

The risk she was about to take might backfire with this man, especially with Bess unconscious. Loretta had never forgotten how he'd beaten one of his crewmen years ago, on that first voyage out of The Pit of her childhood to Waldron's Gate. That man had never worked for Rhysto or anyone else again. Rhysto's passions were impossible for him to control, and anger worked as well desire.

He had no more reason or restraint than a cornered animal when either took control of him. Loretta may be cornered, but she would not be so mindless and weak

"If you're so damn worried about the other pilots," she said, "why don't you question them? Leave me be."

"I will question whoever it is," Rhysto said, his eyes dark and burning. "Never doubt that. Bringing each of them in is such a waste of time and energy. Perhaps I should start with your friend Bill."

"Bill has nothing to do with this." Loretta let her voice quiver. "Rullin betrayed him over and over again, and betrayed Mr. Norwood as well."

Rhysto transferred the knife to the hand around Loretta's shoulders, turning it slowly in front of her eyes. He pulled a thin, rough rope out of his pocket, more than enough to bind her hands and feet. Or her mouth.

"That just gives me more reason to help Bill understand his place," he said. "If he can't run his shaw any better than that, he doesn't deserve to have it. He'll be one less scab pilot causing trouble for the rest of us by the time I'm finished."

Loretta breathed deeply, forcing her mind away from Bill's furious eyes and voice when she last saw him. Letting that distract her now would get both of them killed, or worse.

"Is controlling every single shaw the only way you'll feel secure, Rhysto? Same as causing a woman pain is the only way you feel like a man?"

"You can't tell me you don't like the pain I cause," he said, breathing against her ear. He held the rope in both hands now, a few inches from her eyes. And still, he held the knife. "You're too damn good at causing pain of your own. You play that game better than any woman I've ever known."

"Whether I do or not doesn't matter here. You've moved on to softer targets over the years, haven't you?" She glanced at his neck while he focused on the rope, noting where his collar fell loose. The numbing spray wouldn't work without bare flesh. "Olsen Norwood. Roma Norwood. My *grandmother*. Perhaps it's not Parliament that's gone soft. Perhaps it's you."

He laughed, but the sound of it chilled Loretta to her bones.

"Keep that up," he said. "I'll show you how far from soft I am. That pretty little mouth will be too busy to spout such nonsense."

Loretta could see he was telling the truth, and how well her dangerous game was working. One weakness or the other would give her the chance she needed.

If she survived.

"Then show me," she said, turning her face up to his. "Get it over with so I can get back to sleep. I have nothing more to tell you, about Bill or anyone else. If you can't control your shaws, you have no one to blame but yourself."

He pulled her into a rough kiss. Too brief for her to get the needle into place, but she moved her arm higher on his back.

"Sleep is the last thing you'll get," he said. "And that not for a long time. When I'm finished with you, we'll go wake up your aged friend and see if she takes her punishment as well as you do. I'll make sure you get to watch."

Loretta pulled him down into a deeper whiskey-scented kiss with her free hand, throwing her lot with desire after all. She whispered against his lips.

"What I get to watch is you drawing your last." She heard the faint hiss of numbing steam as she pressed the hypo against his neck. "Before The Imp drags you back to The Pit."

~

RHYSTO JERKED TOWARD HER. She'd already injected the full dose of sedative before he understood anything was wrong. He tried to drag the knife across her neck but caught her forearm instead.

Loretta pulled her other arm from behind him and jabbed the empty hypo into the back of his hand. He screamed and dropped the knife into her lap. Her palm was already slick with blood when she picked it up, so she gripped the copper-wrapped hilt with both hands.

"What's the matter, Rhysto?" She pushed the tip against the hollow of his throat, pushing until he moved back onto his hands and knees. "Not so eager to punish me anymore?"

He tried to reach for his revolver, but she jabbed hard enough to break the skin. With that much of the drug inside his body, and probably more than a little booze from the fumes of his breath, she only had to keep him away for another minute or so.

"You're just...just fooling yourself. Stupid wo-woman." He shifted onto one hip, and she moved with him, still holding the blade against his bleeding throat. "You... Regret. Promise I...I keep."

"Yes, I'm sure you believe that, you sadistic bastard." He slumped farther, and Loretta slipped his revolver out of its holster and showed it to him. "You've made and broken your last promise. You've crossed me for the last...bloody...time."

Rhysto groaned and collapsed onto the bed. Loretta watched him, certain he was only pretending, waiting for her to drop her guard so he could finish what he'd started. She prodded at his chest with one bare foot, but he didn't move.

A growl started deep in her own chest, more like that cornered animal than she realized. That growl rose to a scream when she braced herself and kicked with both feet, shoving him onto the floor. The pilot never moved. He was perfectly still with one arm caught underneath him at a terribly awkward angle, his neck twisted so he snored with every breath louder than he ever did in sleep.

Loretta got to her feet, her legs trembling, her throbbing arm held against her chest. She bound her wound the best she could, wrapping a scarf held in her bloody hand tightly around her forearm. Not perfect, but it would do until the job before her was finished.

The only question she could see was whether to end this life with his own knife or his own gun. She went as far as making sure the revolver was loaded and aiming it at Rhysto's chest before she managed to stop herself.

Putting several bullets into Rhysto might be satisfying, and she would do it without hesitation if she had no other choice. But right now she could catch her breath and think this through. He would be out for at least a few hours, possibly more.

She laughed out loud at what was stopping her. It wasn't wondering whether he deserved to die or not, or wondering if she could go through with it. It wasn't worry about disposing of the body. Even if Bess was not able to help for a while, there were plenty of options there.

Loretta simply didn't want to deal with the bloody mess of blasts or a slit throat in her own bedroom. There were neater ways.

She grabbed her robe and dropped the black knife and gun into the pockets. Before she did anything else, she had to check on Gemma and her guards. The thing she had in mind was in her kitchen anyway. She knocked, then pushed her grandmother's door open.

The older woman was still in bed and still breathing. She didn't wake when Loretta shook her, so Rhysto had likely gassed her. Gemma's color and breathing seemed normal. Without knowing exactly what the gas was, Loretta could only wait and hope she woke.

Bess was in similar condition, slumped over her chair but breathing normally. The young woman guarding the back door, barely out of her teens and new to working for Loretta, was not. Sophie's flesh was as cool as the night air, and she'd long since breathed her last.

"Burn you, Rhysto. She never did a damned thing to you. Neither did Gemma or Roma Norwood."

Loretta thought about waiting for Bess to recover, or even of trying to reach Karl or Bill. But the truth of it was none of these people, save Bill, would have likely crossed paths with Rhysto if it weren't for Loretta. And Bill's interaction would have stayed on the same level as the other independent shaw pilots: unpleasant and annoying but not deadly.

Getting help with disposing of the body was one thing. Loretta needed to kill the man herself.

She locked all the doors, knowing Bess would be able to get inside if she woke up sooner than expected. The much stronger sedative she needed was behind a false wall in her pantry, hidden behind a shelf that seemed to be loaded with spices. Turning five of the bottles in sequence tripped the mechanism, and the whole shelf slid to the side.

Loretta pulled out one vial and a larger hypodermic. This one lacked the numbing steam, but any need for avoiding pain was over. She thought for a second, then retrieved a second vial.

Even with Rhysto already drunk and sedated, she didn't want to take any chances.

He hadn't moved when she returned to her bedroom, closing the door in case Gemma woke. Loretta shoved the pilot onto his back so she could get to the big veins in his throat. She turned the black knife several times, watching the glints off the copper wrapped around the handle. She wiped her blood on his shirt and slipped the blade back into the sheath around his waist.

Part of her mind replayed their history, pleasant and erotic memories contrasted with cruelty and pain. This was the surest way to make sure he never broke through any of her defenses again as long as she lived.

As she knelt beside him, she wished he were awake. He'd go from sleep to death without ever knowing who was responsible for the last beat of his heart.

In the end, Loretta injected both vials and sat cross-legged on the floor to wait. Faster than she'd expected, the motions of his chest slowed. He gasped the last several breaths, taking longer and longer to move again. She counted to one hundred, then touched the reddened injection site.

Loretta's fingers sank into the flesh. She smelled his bladder releasing, but she wanted to feel the truth for herself. After nearly twenty years of knowing this man, half of that hoping she'd never see him again, and the last few weeks hoping for this very moment, Rhysto was dead.

Chapter 41

LORETTA SIPPED her cafei and nodded at the appropriate pauses, letting her grandmother's words wash over her. She wasn't awake enough to interact, but she didn't want to be rude. She'd worked out how to appear interested many years ago.

Her back ached and her arms trembled from dragging two bodies out to her conventional cellar and dumping them inside. Her arm felt swollen and tender where Bess had helped her bandage it properly before she went home. Long sleeves kept it from her grandmother's eyes. When she reached out to pour herself yet another cup, a bit of Gemma's chatter broke through.

"Is your guard quite all right?" she said. "The young woman out front?"

"My guard? Gemma, what are you talking about?"

"I know, I know. I'm not supposed to know anything about that. But I saw her clear as day in my dreams last night. Tall, beautiful, gorgeous red hair. What's her name, bobbin?"

"Her name is Bess." Loretta had never quite gotten used to these Seeing dreams, and she'd never had one herself. She knew to pay attention to them whether she understood or not. "What did you dream?"

"Is Bess doing well this morning?"

Loretta was afraid her guard would have a terrible headache from whatever Rhysto had used on her, but she'd seemed recovered once she'd woken.

"She's fine," Loretta said. "She went home for the day already. Why do you ask? What did you dream?"

"Well, Bess is a perfectly capable guard," Gemma said. "The others are too. But they don't see the gas before it hits them. I'd like to speak to them about an improvement we need to make to the doors and windows."

Loretta sat back, all worries about cafei forgotten.

"The gas," was all she could manage.

"There's a perfectly awful man, one you've met before. He's a pilot, but he's nothing like Bill. This one is cruel. He won't stop until he has whatever it is he wants."

"Rhysto," Loretta whispered.

"That sounds right, yes," Gemma said, beaming. "This Rhysto, he has a sort of gas. It's not like what you use for lights here. He carries it with him, with a long tube he can use to put it into a house. We never planned for anything like that in your defenses, bobbin. I think it must be new."

"What does the gas do, Gemma?"

"I saw your guard fall asleep, so she couldn't warn you. Then he used it to fill up my room too. He had knives, Loretta, and the most awful things in mind to do with them. We simply need to modify your doors and windows. He'll get the surprise of his life when he tries his little trick with the gas."

Loretta drank the whole cup of cafei, wondering how badly she'd just burned her mouth.

"We can't exactly do that here," she said. "Not in Waldron's Gate. Someone will notice if people start getting electrocuted." She pushed her chair back with a loud scrape. "I'm sorry. I'll be right back."

Loretta tapped the transmitter beside the front door, the short, rapid code that let her guards know she needed to speak with them. The system, like most of the others in her house, was simple in the extreme. That was a huge part of what kept them so effective.

A tiny hammer was tripped by the plate she tapped on, and the tones of the hammer striking a small pipe sounded inside her guard's hidden room. By the time she opened the door, her day guard was waiting.

"Good morning, ma'am."

"Good morning, David. Gemma and I are going to visit Karl for a few days, maybe a week or so, until we can figure out how to deal with Rhysto and anyone else he may be working with. Once we leave, I want you and the other guards to stay away until I return. It's not worth the risk. Do you understand?"

"I do," he said. "When will you be leaving, ma'am?"

Loretta took a deep breath, looking around the house and the yard, the morning sunlight coming through the wisteria along her fence. She hadn't planned to ever leave here, not permanently. Something about dumping Rhysto's body into the cellar and closing the door brought reality crashing around her.

The disappearance of the ringleader of the shaw pilots would bring too many questions and investigations for her to have any chance of keeping Gemma hidden or both of them safe. If Gemma decided to electrify the windows and doors without telling Loretta, the outcome would be just as bad.

They had to accept Karl's offer whether she liked it or not. Loretta had to make sure as few people as possible knew the truth.

"We're leaving tomorrow night," she said. "I'll keep up all of your pay, so please don't worry about that. But if he shows back up here with his sleeping gas or whatever else he digs up, he'll find no one to use it on."

Chapter 42

KARL SLOWED when he turned the corner toward Loretta's house.
Bill's dark brown wagon was already parked out front. It seemed she'd
patched things up with the shaw pilot after all.

Karl wondered if Bill had gotten the same sort of urgent letter he
had. The purple envelope was in his jacket pocket, but he'd read it
enough to commit it to memory.

Dear Karl,

*I know you've only just settled in, and I'm so sorry to disturb you
again. The illness has returned. You won't need the day off, but please do
call on us this evening. Your trusted assistance is most important in our
hour of need.*

Love, Mother

He hadn't yet had a chance to investigate George's abandoned
caretaker's cottage, but he had a feeling time had run out. Now he
only had a few minutes to get ready for whatever was heading his way.
Bill opened the door, looking as resigned and uncertain as Karl felt.

"Good evening, Karl. What a lovely surprise to see you again so
soon." He rolled his eyes and winked. "The gang's all here, Loretta.
Think you can tell us why now?"

She surprised Karl with a quick kiss on the mouth.

"Thank you both. We've had unexpected events here that I'm

afraid have accelerated everything. Don't worry, Gemma is busy in her room. Working on a project for you, as a matter of fact, Karl."

Bill looked confused, but he didn't ask questions. Karl wouldn't have had any idea how to answer.

"What is it I won't need the day off for?" he said. "Taking more time won't be an option for at least a few months, no matter what it is."

Loretta stood and walked from one end of her living room to the other.

"Rhysto showed up here last night. He used gas to kill one of my guards and knock the other one out, and he knocked Gemma out too. He was going to attack her after he'd finished with me."

Karl's stomach turned to a cold rock inside of him, blocking his ability to breathe or move.

"What did you do?" Bill said, his own face pale.

"I distracted him until I could get to one of my hypodermics, but not before he cut me." She lifted her sleeve, revealing a thick white bandage covering most of her forearm. "I meant to sedate him so I could get us away, but he must have had more to drink than he usually does. The shot, it stopped his heart. He's dead."

Karl caught his head in both hands, wishing once again that he could turn back whatever clock had put his life on such an insane course.

He wasn't the least bit upset the man was dead, not after knowing he'd attacked Loretta yet again and planned to attack Gemma. He simply wished he didn't have to deal with it.

Bill spoke before Karl could find even a ghost of his own voice.

"Where is he?"

Loretta continued to pace. "I dumped him and Sophie in the cellar around back. To be honest, that's the main thing I need your help with. I've been trying to figure out what to do all day yesterday and today, and I think I might have an idea that would work. We can use your wagon, Bill, and dump him in the Fog. Every trace of him should be gone before the morning."

"Wait, just calm down and wait," Karl said. "Why would we dump his body anywhere, or your guard's? We need to report this so the Ministry will..."

Karl's brain locked up solid, like he'd seen gears do when they weren't maintained. Or when they were overworked.

"Will what, Karl?" she said, stopping in front of him. "Come here and question me, question Gemma? We've been seen together, so they'll question both of you. Then I'm quite sure they'll get around to Olsen and Roma Norwood. Do you think any of those have a chance of going well? Which one of us won't be exposed?"

"She has a point," Bill said, rubbing the back of his neck. "The best thing is if Rhysto disappears. He was a right bastard on a personal level, and I have to admit I'm glad he's dead. But he managed to keep most of the shaws in line. No one had managed that before, not in living memory. Most pilots aren't as gentlemanly as I. If it gets out that he's dead, that will bring his supporters down on Loretta, and his rivals into a disastrous struggle to take over. The longer people think he can just return at any time, the better."

Karl knew what they were saying made sense, but his brain still refused to accept what he was going to have to do.

"Isn't his airship still here?" he said. "No one's going to think he left without that."

"That's unfortunate, but not unprecedented," Bill said. "He's gone missing for days at a time before. A lot of us think he does that just to keep the shaws, and the Ministry, off balance. It works. All of that balance falls apart if people find out he's dead."

Loretta took Karl's hand.

"As much of a bastard as he was," she said, "people in Waldron's Gate will never take kindly to murder. And if what I used to do for a living gets out, I won't stand a chance. Even if that doesn't happen, they wouldn't decide I had no choice and let me walk away. Just having something like sedatives here will be enough. I won't have any way to protect Gemma, either. Once Parliament gets their hands on her, we'll never see her again."

"That much I worked out for myself," Karl said. "What about your guard? Won't people be looking for her?"

"No, not this one." Loretta looked down and shook her head.

"Sophie was a lot like me. Came here from the wilderness, ended up caught out at the Convenience for a long time. Working for me was her first chance to earn a living not on her back. No family close by, and the ones she got away from aren't likely to care."

Karl breathed out sharply through his lips.

"So we just haul them out in Bill's wagon, dump them in the Fog, and pretend it never happened?"

"Yes. That's exactly what we do." Loretta started pacing again. "Then Gemma and I come stay with you for a while. That's the best way to keep her safe. If Rhysto just drops out of sight and no one puts him together with me, the heat will eventually die down."

Karl stared at her, wondering if she had any idea how cold she sounded, how inhuman. He'd moved bodies, more than he cared to count or remember. That was part of the job out at the Columns for a guy his size, whether he liked it or not. But even after so many years, he'd never thought it was no big deal, no different than taking out the garbage.

Would Loretta speak that calmly about dumping Bill's body? Or his own?

"I don't like this any more than you do, Karl." Bill spoke quietly, but his eyes and mouth were firm. "We all have too much to lose to walk away. Loretta and I could probably manage, but it would go a lot faster if you help."

"I'll help," Karl said. "I'm not sure this is the best idea, but I can't think of anything else. Listen, this gets one bad guy out of the way, and I'm sorry about how this sounds, but where's Rullin?"

"No, that sounds exactly right," Bill said. "My brother brings suspicion wherever he goes. He's in our cargo hold, in the closest thing I have to a dungeon. Two of my best men guarding him. They know if he gets away, it means their skins. I don't know what I'm going to do with him after that."

"Fair enough," Karl said. He couldn't ever remember feeling more weary. "Let's get this over with."

In the end, it took less than half an hour with the three of them and the wagon. Rhysto didn't smell particularly pleasant, but that didn't bother Karl. Carrying the slender body of the guard did.

Sophie looked barely into her late teens, far too young to under-stand the danger she was putting herself into selling herself out at the Convenience or working for someone like Loretta. And now she would never learn any better.

The Fog itself was only a few minutes away from Loretta's house, less than a quarter mile. No one else was out so late into the evening, and hardly anyone would come out that far anyway. Karl didn't like standing so close to that boundary, though he was a little less afraid after his experience with natural fog in the Northlands.

From barely three feet away, he could hear things in there. Things that did not sound remotely human.

"Will they be eaten?" he said, trying to keep his stomach under control.

"That's what I think will happen," Loretta said. She sounded like she knew more than she let on. "Even if they don't, no one's going to go in there looking for them."

Bill stared into the Fog. "The soldiers go in there to kill monsters, but I hear they never get all of them. Whatever's in there is probably hungry."

"Hopefully Rhysto won't make them sick," Loretta said, shudder-ing. "If you throw them in far enough, no one's going to see them even if the Fog recedes a little."

Loretta stood by the wagon for a few seconds, staring at the pilot and the girl. She darted forward and grabbed a knife with a solid black blade from somewhere near his waist. Their lanterns caught coppery flashes as she tucked it into her own belt.

After that signal no one realized they'd been waiting for, Karl grabbed Rhysto's shoulders while Bill got the feet. After a couple of swings, they launched the corpse out into the Fog. Karl guessed he went several feet.

The girl went quite a bit farther.

The noise level rose immediately.

Chapter 43

Karl met George for lunch in the crowded cafeteria the next day, wondering how he was going to ask yet another favor of his friend. Loretta and Gemma planning to arrive that same night didn't give him much choice, but he still had no idea how to bring it up.

"Spill it, Gilmore," George finally said. "Playing with food this bad only makes it worse."

"Okay, you asked for it. Can you get me out to that house? Sooner rather than later?"

George sat back and crossed his arms. "Everyone's in such a hurry to get into this place all of a sudden. Never would have expected that. I won't really have a chance until the weekend. Can your folks stay put until then? Stash their fine furniture and party clothes in one of the empty sheds by the docks?"

"They can," Karl said. "Not sure how long we'll be able to stand quarters as close as mine, but we'll have to manage. Is this something I can find myself?"

"Well sure, once I show you how to get out there. You never quite lost the habit of using the tunnels to get around, did you?"

Karl raised his eyebrows, not wanting to admit he'd already smuggled Loretta through them.

"I still use them," he said. "Do they go all the way out there?"

"Sure do. There's no other way to get where you're talking about. These are locked corridors though, and they're in even worse shape than the ones on this side. The 'sters never seem to get in, if that's what you're worried about."

Karl groaned. "I hadn't thought of that. Thanks, buddy. I was more worried about me or someone else getting lost under there and wandering around until they have to add us to the list of permanent residents."

"You've got a good memory," George said. "Too good for your own good. Think everyone else does, too?"

"I think one will stay at the house. The other probably has a better memory than I do. I appreciate your help, Georgie, I do. Are the tunnels sound enough to push a cart through?"

"Mostly. We'd have to pick it up in a few places. You need a cart all the time or just for moving day?"

"Just for moving day, I think," Karl said. "We'll have a bit of equipment to deal with. Nothing too big, but a lot of it."

"Making something special?"

Karl blinked, remembering something Loretta had said the night before. Gemma was working on his project now, not Loretta's. That must mean the new gyro-compass was ready.

He wouldn't be able to pretend Loretta didn't use people the way she did anymore, that her stealing didn't send people out here sometimes. People she used to keep her profit margins high. He shook his head.

"Just a bit of Tinkering to keep everyone busy," he said. "Listen, let me know what time you can make it out there. We'll all be raring to go after a few days together."

"Yeah, togetherness does that to me, too," George said. "With anyone. That's why it's best for everyone that I live alone."

Chapter 44

Loretta wished she could be as excited as her grandmother still was at the idea of using a shared bath, one they had to sneak around to use. Camping out here in Karl's rather spartan apartment hadn't sounded like much fun in the first place. The reality several days in was wearing on her nerves, and her patience, even more than she expected.

"Your turn in the bath, Gemma."

"Thank you, bobbin. I'll be as quick as a flash!"

Loretta watched Gemma open the door, look left and right with exaggerated care, then grin before she closed the door behind her. She sighed and walked into the bedroom.

"You're awake early," Karl said, stretching.

"We both needed our turn in the bath. Just as easy to do that early instead of late."

"None of this has been easy," he said. "George will be here in a couple of hours. We'll finally see if his idea of a hideout is better or worse than being cramped in here together."

"About that, Karl." Loretta sat beside him, enjoying how warm he still was from sleep when he put his arms around her. "How much does your friend know about all of this? Gemma has never been particularly good at keeping things to herself. If I have an idea what the secrets are, I might have a better chance at keeping them."

"He doesn't know much, honestly. He knows one of you has a good bit of equipment to take out there but not why. He knows Gemma will likely stay put if the place is at all tolerable, but you'll be coming and going. And he knows you and I have something going on, but he doesn't know what any more than I do."

Loretta wasn't able to stop herself from laughing, and she hugged Karl's face against her breasts to make up for it.

"If it helps, I don't know either. The fact that we haven't killed each other after being cooped up in here for five days has to be a good thing."

"So far, no. We'll see if that holds up once you see your new digs. It's hardly any kind of grand estate, and the locals aren't exactly friendly."

When Karl's friend showed up, Loretta was surprised at how he looked and acted. She wasn't sure what she'd been expecting, but a small, well-mannered, polite man wasn't it.

George barely came up to Karl's shoulder, and something about his messy brown hair, glasses, and round features and belly didn't exactly scream competence. She had a feeling his warm brown eyes didn't miss a damned thing, though. Maybe this wouldn't be quite the disaster she'd been afraid of.

"You have a lot of stuff with you," George said. "Why don't we head out there and check it out first? You might run screaming, and it would be a real shame to have to run and push the cart at the same time."

"Sounds good to me, Georgie," Karl said. "We'll just follow your lead." He turned to Loretta's grandmother, taking her hands. "Gemma, we have to be careful now. Your doctor's clothes will help, but you have to look bored. I'm glad you're excited, but you'd stand out like a torch around here. If anyone stops us, just let me and George handle it."

"I'll do that." Gemma's smile didn't reassure Loretta. "I am excited. Thank you for doing this, George."

"You're welcome," George said. "Don't thank me until you see the place. Really."

THE EARLY HOUR on a weekend morning worked as well as it possibly could have. They didn't encounter a single person on the silent walk through the commons and the wood-walled corridors. Loretta and everyone else breathed a little easier once they were in the dank brick-lined tunnel two flights of stairs below the surface.

George handed out folded pieces of paper.

"I made maps for all of you, but you can't be letting anyone else see those. That would mean all of us rounded up and wishing we'd never met. For now, just follow me and watch where we turn. Oh, I have copies of the keys, too, but I'll give you those in order as we get to the gates. Karl, you have a light?"

He held up a lantern, the same kind George was carrying.

After several minutes of walking and avoiding the larger puddles, they turned down a darker passage. The floor was still damp, but the bricks seemed to be a lot less worn than what Loretta had seen before.

"I've never been in this section," Karl said. "I think we're going under the fence to where the 'sters live."

Loretta frowned. "Stirs?"

George glanced back at them, glaring at Karl before he smiled at Loretta.

"Monsters. Your host forgot to tell you who your neighbors will be?"

"He told us," Loretta said. "I forgot you called them 'sters. These are the oldest ones?"

"That's right," George said. "They're all at least forty years old right now, some a lot older. They don't seem to get weaker the way people do, present company excepted."

"Of course," Gemma said, grinning.

"They stop growing around the same time as people do," George said. "They get stronger, though. More substantial, at least, more confident. A lot harder to control, but they don't seem to care as much about us, either. So when they hit about thirty-five or forty, they're brought out here. Some of them, anyway. Some have to be kept locked up in the towers. The area's still fenced in, but it's a lot more open in the middle. That way they can move around a lot more."

"Don't they hurt each other?" Karl said.

Loretta wasn't reassured by Karl's question, or by the fact he had to ask it. What had he agreed to get them into here?

"They do sometimes, but it's usually not fatal." George paused to unlock a black metal gate, then handed each of them a brass key with a large number one on it. "As long as they don't actually kill each other, everyone seems to be fine."

The tunnel continued, with fewer ladders or stairs to the top than when they first started and not as many corridors or doors branching off to the side. Stretches of the bricks underfoot were buckled and heaved, and brick had fallen out of the roof in a couple of places The lanterns saved everyone's ankles more than once as the gaslights grew dimmer and less frequent.

George unlocked gates on three of those corridors, providing a key for each. At a nearly solid metal gate, he stopped.

"End of the line here," he said. "I don't have a key to that gate, never even seen one. It's not on any map I know of, either. We have two ways we can go. This ladder's in pretty good shape, but it's slick as glass." He tapped the dark metal rungs with the last set of keys. "This door goes to a tunnel to the surface, steep but passable. Both come out inside the house, no worries about that. As long as the fence holds up. '

"Let's try the tunnel," Karl said, glancing at Gemma. "We'd need that to bring supplies in anyway."

George nodded and handed out the keys.

"I'll go first to make sure it's safe," he said. "Stay close behind me."

Loretta watched Gemma dart behind George.

"She'll be fine with him." Karl gestured for Loretta to go next. "If anyone needs help, I'll be back here."

"Great. I suppose I should be reassured by that?"

"You might as well be," Karl said. "We don't have much choice right now."

The tunnel looped back on itself three times, and Loretta found herself reassured Karl was behind her after all. The steep footing was more treacherous than she liked, even without Gemma making the climb.

"Here we are." George handed his lantern to Gemma, who held it steady in both hands. "That last key I gave you will open this door. Give me a minute."

Dim light came through glass near the top of the door, but Loretta was grateful for the lanterns. She was even more grateful for George going ahead of them. A smell she'd barely noticed farther back was making her eyes water closer to the surface.

At first she'd thought someone must have relieved themselves in the corridor, just too damn lazy to wait until they were outside. But this was horrible and getting worse. The nastiest toilet combined with a filthy operating room mixed with a refuse pile.

If that stench was coming from the house, she would not be leaving her grandmother or anyone else out here.

GEORGE PEERED through the glass in the door before he unlocked it and stepped through. Loretta coughed and covered her nose, watching Gemma do the same.

When she looked back at Karl, he was breathing normally. He looked upset, but he made no move to protect himself. Before she could ask why, George ducked back in.

"Come on. It's all clear," he said. "I'm sorry about that smell. If you don't get used to it, I can bring gas masks. That's the 'sters, though, not the house. It's clean enough."

The air seemed to get thicker as Loretta walked toward the door. She wanted to grab Gemma and turn around and get her out of there. Neither of them could possibly tolerate whatever made that smell.

"Oh, it's perfectly lovely!" Gemma exclaimed.

Loretta was surprised enough when she followed her grandmother that she gasped without thinking. The horrible odor seemed to be coating the back of her throat now, but Gemma was right.

The caretaker's house was a simple stone building, not a whole lot larger than the house Gemma had left behind in the Northland mountains. Four doors stood open, revealing three bedrooms and a bathroom. There was only one hearth, but it was an old-fashioned open one, several feet across and lined with fire brick. Plenty of room for her grandmother's cauldrons and power generators.

"How long has this place been empty?" Karl said, walking over to one of the large windows.

"About thirty years, I think," George said. "At least that's the closest anyone can guess."

"I can understand why with this stench," Loretta said.

"Yeah, that was part of it." George tried to smile, but his eyes were watering. "The people who work with the 'sters say you get used to it pretty quickly. I don't know if I believe that."

Gemma stood beside Karl at the window.

"The yard is small," she said. "But I'd have enough space for a garden. Maybe even a few animals."

"I wouldn't recommend the animals, Gemma," George said, shaking his head. "I'm sorry, but they'd probably draw the monsters right to this place."

"Won't that happen anyway once they notice us?" Gemma said.

Loretta glanced out the windows, then stopped for a longer look. The yard was overgrown with weeds, but it was level with plenty of space. A black metal fence surrounded everything, arching up and out of sight above the house.

"That's what the fence is for," George said. "I'm afraid animals would get them too upset. I doubt the animals would be happy out here, either."

"This isn't as bad as I thought it would be," Karl said. "Except for the smell." He was still looking out the window, Gemma at his side. "Georgie, why was it abandoned? We can't leave anyone out here if it's not safe."

"I wouldn't have suggested it if I didn't think it was safe, Karl. I've never been able to track down the records, but the story is the last caretaker kept saying there was no point in living all the way out here. He couldn't control the 'sters, and they hadn't managed to really hurt each other for a long time. When he finished his turn, no one was sent back."

"That doesn't make any sense," Loretta said. "Why maintain it, then?"

"Sometimes I don't think they know why." George was moving around the house, checking the windows and fittings. "But I wonder if it all might change depending on what 'sters are out here. If it's more important that they be kept healthy, you know?"

Karl shook his head at George, just for a second, but Loretta caught it. She was sure there was plenty she wasn't supposed to know. She wouldn't forget the slip.

Beyond the fence, the landscape was nearly as open as around Gemma's house in the Northlands. A few trees broke up the grasslands, and she could see the spiraling brick towers of Jeffrey Columns not far off. Nothing was moving, but at least nothing out there looked like a monster.

"Well, what do you think?" Karl said.

He spoke to Gemma, but his gaze met Loretta's.

Gemma clasped her hands between her breasts. "I think I could do perfectly wonderful things out here once I have my supplies. That hearth should be big enough once I have everything set back up."

"I'll have to double check the chimney for you," George said. "I'd hold off on fires for a little while. At least wait until we're all out here with you." He leaned into the hearth, looking up with his lantern held high. "I don't think the 'sters will be drawn to it. I'm not sure, though. I'm quite sure a lot of smoke will catch more attention than you want. Can you have your fires more at night for whatever you need?"

"I need it mostly at night, I suppose," Gemma said. "Do you have peat here, or will I have to use wood?"

"Pete?" George shook his head, but Karl jumped in.

"We'll have to see about that," he said. "It might be wood for a while, maybe coal. George, let's go check the fence, make sure it's secure before everyone else comes outside."

Both of them looked at Loretta, as if she were going to scold them for keeping their little secrets. She rolled her eyes and waved her hand at the door.

"You want to get closer to that smell, be my guest. We'll see what needs to be done in here."

Chapter 45

Karl wanted to hold his breath when he stepped outside, but he knew it wouldn't help. Dry grassy weeds brushed against his knees, broken only by an old flattened path from the door to around the edge of the yard. He tried to imagine how his mother or anyone else at the Ministry of Decorum would react to such chaos. The spiraling brick columns were closer than he liked, even knowing some of the 'sters were loose out here.

"You were right about one thing, Georgie. The smell is about a thousand times worse out here."

"I know," George said. "I'm sorry about that. People swear they get used to it. We'll see."

"The thing about Gemma is if it can be solved, she'll solve it," Karl said. "She'll probably dream it up tonight. Listen, what did you mean about someone living out here depends on who the 'sters came from?"

The two men walked across the yard to the fence. The black metal was straight until a couple of feet above Karl's head. It arched inward all around, meeting in the middle like an upside down bowl.

"It might just be my paranoia playing tricks on me again." George tried to shake the fence with both hands every few feet as they walked, but it held firm. "They keep records when they can figure out who the 'sters come from. Lots of times they can't, but sometimes...well, you remember that part."

"I do," Karl said. "Wish I didn't."

"Yeah, me too. When we started digging into all of this, I looked at those records for when this place was abandoned. There were a bunch of 'sters that seemed to be connected to some pretty high-ranking folks in the Ministry for a long time. I always wondered why they were all bunched together like that. Anyway, when the last of that group died, the humans, I mean, they never sent another person to live out here."

Karl frowned. "So you think it was just to make sure those 'sters were safe."

"That or maybe those 'sters were particularly nasty, you know? I've wondered about that, if they weren't running around murdering the rest. Now they really don't seem to hurt each other all that much."

"I don't think this will have to go on too long," Karl said. "At least I hope not."

Too late, Karl realized what subject he'd led George right to.

"Has this Rhysto shown up again?"

"He did show up in the middle of the night," Karl said. "First night I came back out here. He used gas, knocked Gemma out. He was trying to do the same to Loretta, but she woke up. Thank The Crown she had a knife, but he's the one who sliced up her arm before she stopped him. He told Loretta when he came back, he'd...have his way with her, then do the same to Gemma."

George shook his head, and Karl focused on the fence. Lying about why the pilot had been bothering them was one thing. Now he was covering up when a man had been killed. And a young woman.

"Sounds like a fine gentleman," George said. "Any way you'd consider reporting him, for the gas if nothing else? You have no way to know when he'll show up again."

"I'm afraid if we report him, word of what Gemma does will get out. Like you said, she can give people a way to get around the Ministry for almost anything. Even hiding her out here might not keep her safe if that happens."

George didn't say anything, just kept testing the fence. They were at the back of the house now, surrounded by more of the open grassland. Karl was afraid to look his friend in the eye.

He was a little horrified at how easily he seemed to be able to lie now.

"We'll keep them here for now, then," George said. "Unless something really bad happens that brings someone out here, no one's going to know."

"So far we're lucky none of the 'sters know."

Karl was surprised to hear his friend laugh quietly.

"You think so?" he said. "You're not looking in the right direction, buddy. Try again."

KARL'S SHOULDERS and back were instantly tense, and the last thing he wanted to do was turn around. He forced his hands to let go of the fence. His neck creaked when he turned.

The yard was still empty, and he couldn't see anything along the fence. He took a step forward to check the front of the house and froze.

"How long has that damned thing been there?" he whispered.

"Since we started checking the fence," George said. "I've seen that one before. Never tried to hurt me, but I've never gone up there to try to shake its hand, either."

A creature was crouched at the very top of the fence, right above the house. It looked like one of the demons described in the holy books of The Crown, maybe The Imp himself, with one important difference. This demon had a tail and wings and arms and even small curved horns, but instead of red it was pure white. And it was huge, bigger than Karl himself.

"I never heard a thing," he said. "Did it just climb up there?"

"It flew," George said. "I think it hangs out up there the whole time I'm checking things over." The 'ster watched the two of them intently as they continued to check the fence, its head turning this way and that as they spoke. "That one seems smart enough to make me nervous."

"That's what makes you nervous?"

The 'ster turned its body to keep them in sight, and it didn't make a single sound. What disturbed Karl the most, besides seeing terrifying stories from his childhood come to life, was the creature's eyes.

They were deep blue and utterly human. George was right. This one looked more intelligent than most people did.

"Will it tell the other 'sters we're out here?" Karl said.

"Good question. I only see others sometimes, but this one's always keeping watch over me. I have no idea if it can talk or not."

The creature rustled its wings, and Karl drew back. George didn't seem to notice.

"Why doesn't it just fly away?" Karl said. "There's no fence big enough to keep it in here."

"Now that is an excellent question." George smiled as he looked up at the creature. "One I asked a few times when I first got sent out here. I was told a 'ster with wings would never be sent out here under the clear blue sky for that very reason. When I explained that I saw this handsome devil every time I was out here, I was informed that there's no record of that. The monster with wings isn't in the files, therefore it didn't come from the Ministry, and they would never send one with wings out here. So it doesn't exist."

Karl snorted, staring into the 'ster's blue eyes.

"Bureaucracy at its finest."

"All in a day's work, my friend." George stopped testing the fence and glanced at Karl. "The truth is no one besides me had been out here for a few years until today. Rotten as the smell is, I don't mind coming out here by myself. Maybe I'm the first to see this one. It either really likes me, or it plans to eat me."

"If it didn't come from the Ministry..."

"Another excellent point," George said. "Who knows? Maybe it came from the Fog and just likes the company. Karl, I'm not going to point this out to Gemma or Loretta, but there is a gate in the fence. See it, just beyond where the tunnel entrance goes into the house?"

Karl saw the thicker border around a square section of the fence. He hoped the 'ster wasn't paying attention.

"Do you have a key to that?" he said.

"I do, but only one. Sorry to do this to you, buddy, but it's yours.'

George held out a key, this one marked with an *F*. Karl wished he hadn't done that where the creature could see, but he put the key in his pocket with the others.

"Yeah, thanks for that," Karl said. "Anything else I need to know?"

George held both arms out. "You know everything I do about this place. I really do think she'll be okay out here for a while, but I'll rest easier when she can move back out to the Gate."

"Me too. The fence seems sound enough, as long as none of them can squeeze through it."

"Not so far," George said. "At least not out here. If I hear of a new transfer, I'll be sure to let you know."

Karl wished he could feel as confident as George's smile.

"We have a problem here, Georgie, besides all the obvious ones. But it could help us. If at least one 'ster knows we're here, we can't just not tell Gemma and Loretta. Think we should bring them out and see what happens?"

George blinked and raised his eyebrows.

"You want to do some kind of test and see if they notice?" he said. "Or if they panic?"

"Yeah, that's what I was thinking," Karl said. "I really do think Gemma will be fine. A bunch of people tried to break into her house in the Northlands, and she just turned on her security and waited it out. She's pretty damn tough, but we can't just assume she'll be calm about your friend up there."

George crossed his arms. "Hang on, what kind of security? You know we can't let her kill any of the 'sters. I mean, I don't want her or Loretta hurt, but killing one of them would bring the whole damned world down on our heads."

Karl closed his eyes and rubbed his temples. That wasn't an easy promise to make.

"I'll tell you the truth," he said. "Her security up there was electricity strong enough to knock a grown man out cold and burn his hands pretty badly. I know that's hard to believe, but I saw it with my own eyes. She's perfectly capable of generating enough to give anything that touches this fence a hell of a shock. Even worse for the door."

George was shaking his head before Karl stopped talking.

"She can't do that, Karl. I'm not sure who the 'ster in the sky is linked to, assuming it's linked to anyone, but it's up there a lot. We can't risk giving some random person back in the Gate seizures or worse. Even if her handiwork didn't kill people, we don't know what will happen here."

"I know," Karl said. "I hadn't thought about that. I'll have to talk to her about the fence. I don't have any problem with her covering the doors or windows, though. Do you?"

"No, if something happens there we need to know the fence isn't secure."

"None of this will matter," Karl said. "Not if Gemma sees one of them and refuses to hang around. You with me?"

"As long as they know it was your idea if it all goes to hell, be my guest."

They walked inside under watchful blue eyes.

"We checked the fence if you want to take a look at the yard," Karl said, watching Gemma closely.

Loretta could hide out with him a bit longer if she needed to. The true concern was leaving her grandmother out here alone.

"Oh yes!" Gemma said. "Even if I can't have animals, I want to see how the space would work for a garden."

"Is the smell worse out there?" Loretta said.

"To be honest, I think I have been getting used to it a little bit." Karl wrinkled his nose, surprised at the lowered distress he'd been feeling. "But it is thicker out there, yeah."

The two women followed George out the front door, and Gemma immediately looked up.

"Is that the welcoming committee?" she said.

She didn't sound the least bit afraid. More curious and happy.

"You could say that, I suppose." George smiled at Karl. "That one's up there pretty often."

Gemma looked at Loretta, who half shrugged and nodded.

"He's lovely, isn't he?" the older woman said.

"Sure. Nice eyes," Loretta said. "Any friends hanging around?"

"Not so far," Karl said. "George says nothing out here can get through the fence. I think it's more curious than anything."

Loretta caught her grandmother's hands.

"We won't test that any more than we have to. Right, Gemma?"

Gemma smiled in a way that didn't do a thing to calm Karl's nerves.

"Of course not, bobbin. I'll have plenty to do getting the house ready and working on Karl's project, not to mention your next one."

Loretta put her arm around Gemma, taking care not to look at Karl.

"Yes, let's not mention that," she said. "Let's get back so we can move your things out here to paradise."

Chapter 46

Faster than any of them would have believed possible, Gemma settled into the house, and Karl and Loretta settled into a routine. After a couple of weeks, her staying in his apartment on weekends and him visiting the old caretaker's house a night or two during the week started to feel normal.

He caught himself wondering when they would pass from not knowing what was going on between them to figuring out what the next step was. Long-term plans he'd never imagined with anyone else drifted though his mind when he wasn't keeping such things under control.

One thing that never quite felt normal was smuggling Loretta and her repaired gyro-compass and Dragon in to visit patients on the weekends.

"Can you feel a difference in any of them?" Karl said several days into their experiments. "How they work with you, I mean?"

He and Loretta were leaving Mr. Otis's room after their third time Building with him.

"He's more, I don't know, receptive, maybe?" she said. "He was always cooperative, but he's halfway into a Builder's trance the second he sees me. And he's been influencing the Builds."

"Builders never do that when they're awake," Karl said. "At least that's what I hear from my family. Is that unusual during the night?"

"The only time they really do that, or did, was when it was the thing they'd ordered. Then I could feel them making tiny adjustments, things they hadn't thought to mention to me. If it was just a Build for someone else, they just Built it as I sent it."

"How is it with Mr. Otis?" Karl said.

"So far we've just done simple things like jewelry," she said. "You've seen it. We haven't lost a Build since Gemma set up her target at her house. Mr. Otis likes to adjust the colors, mainly. He'll change ruby earrings to sapphire, or make the shape more symmetrical. Should I try to enforce the rules like I do with the others?"

Karl concentrated on his feet, trying to dodge puddles in the wetter-than-usual tunnel. He didn't want to force anything on Mr Otis or any of the other patients. He was already worried enough about how patients in close-by rooms seemed more upset, not less, when he and Loretta visited.

So far every single person they'd focused on had been helped by Building, mania or madness held at bay for a time. They had never revisited Mrs. Labine or any of the others he suspected were sent here by Loretta's nighttime visits. He'd been wondering how he could possibly present any of this to the medical staff, especially with such large gaps in their research.

"Not just yet," he said. "I want to learn how to try it myself first, just to see if another person can do it."

"Have other people noticed the changes in them?" Loretta said. "Since we started all of this?"

"Sure. I have. Other nurses, too." Karl nodded, ticking through all their subjects in his mind. "The doctors are fairly predictable in thinking a change in medication they never actually made is suddenly working. But yeah, other nurses have talked about how much calmer all of them are."

Loretta stopped, catching Karl's hand and pulling him into a kiss. His breathing and his body responded as strongly as the first time, far in the air above the Northlands.

"I'm glad of that, Karl, truly. I'd bet we'll see the same when you get started."

"When do you think that will be?" He'd resisted asking so far, but his impatience was getting the best of him.

"I think Gemma will be done in a day or two," she said. "Once she got the fire going and the air cleaned up, she's been working nonstop on your Dragon. It won't be long. I promise."

Karl climbed up the ladder closest to his rooms, stopping long enough to check the corridor.

"All clear," he said. "Do we need to get lunch for Gemma today?"

"She's eaten just about everything in that house, so that would be a great help. Listen, Karl, have you seen anything? Any investigations?"

"Nothing so far," he said. "Not after those reports that he was missing in the gossip pages. Nothing on the talkbox yet. I'm sure if they'd found traces we would have heard about it by now."

"They're not going to find any traces," Loretta said. "Bess has gone by the house a few times to check, but no one's been inside." She closed the door to Karl's rooms, then sat on the couch. "I need to talk to you about something before you get lunch."

Karl sat beside her, and he wasn't quite reassured when she took his hand.

"Why does that sound ominous to me?"

"Don't panic. This is just business." Loretta kissed his cheek. "I need to make some deliveries, Karl. A few of these orders have been out for almost a month now. You heard what Mr. Norwood said. That was what got him stirred up in the first place."

"Deliveries you've already Built?" he said. "I didn't think you were making those kinds of things out here."

Karl was dismayed at how completely he'd put Loretta's normal work out of his mind. Reality lodged there now like a sharp rock in his shoe.

"No, I haven't been," she said. "I still think it would be fine if we tried it. These are things I Built before my gyro-compass got broken. I could sell the jewelry and such we've been Building lately. There's a good market for that, too. People with the most horrifying collections usually want to show off with the normal things they have and gifts they give."

"What were you thinking?" Karl said. "Leave during the day and come back? Will that be safe with people looking for Rhysto?"

"I'd have to take Bess with me. I doubt many people would put me together with him, besides Mr. Norwood, but we may have to pay him a visit to make sure he keeps his mouth shut. We don't know who Rhysto may have told about where he was going, though, before his little visit that night."

Karl didn't miss her evading part of his question, about her returning at night. If things were calm enough for her to stay at her house, keeping Gemma out in 'ster territory alone didn't make any sense.

But he was already growing too fond of both of them to suggest that.

"I know Bess will watch out for you," he said. "And I know you can take care of yourself. Getting in and out of here is tougher than you think except on the weekends."

Loretta nodded. "We may have to try to schedule several over the weekend to see how it goes. Between that and visiting Mr. Norwood, we'll have a pretty good idea of how things stand in Waldron's Gate."

"And you'll keep your client base happy."

Karl immediately wished he could take that last bit back. He didn't want to start some kind of fight and give her an excuse to leave. Her voice was calm, but her flashing eyes let him know she'd heard him.

"You knew that was the deal with me going in. Are you going to try to tell me you won't be Building anything? If so, there's no real reason for Gemma to finish your Dragon."

"I haven't really thought about that." Karl hoped he could defuse the tension by admitting his lack of planning. "I suppose I can go with whatever they want to Build, within reason."

"I'm not sure it works that way," she said, sounding more curious than angry now. "I think you'll at least have to suggest a starting point. But we'll figure that out when we get there."

"You want to make deliveries tomorrow," Karl said. "Then sneak back in."

She squeezed Karl's hand and moved closer. He put his arm around her, breathing in her scent. It hadn't gotten any less intoxicating with familiarity, any more than her body had. Or her mind.

Getting in over his head with a woman set off the usual alarm bells, but for the first time in his life he managed to ignore them.

"That's what I want," she said, leaning her head on his shoulder. "If you have stationery, I'll send Bess a note right now. Safer than the talkboxes out here from what you tell me."

"I do. Klia Gilmore would never, ever send one of her children out into the world without a huge supply. Even one as hopeless at using it as me."

Chapter 47

Karl forced himself to stop fidgeting, but the tickling only got worse. He couldn't imagine how the soft leather straps he'd brought so Gemma could make his headgear suddenly felt like they were full of ants. He looked around the room again, focusing on the remarkable transformation since Gemma and Loretta had brought in bright cushions and rugs, curtains, and tablecloths. Even his mother might have believed this was a holiday cottage rather than an abandoned caretaker's house.

"Hold still now," Gemma said. "Or I'll end up cutting this wrong, and we'll have to start over."

She shifted the straps a millimeter at a time, over and over again. Just when he thought he was going to scream from all the adjustments, she made her final cut and took the whole thing off.

"There. Only a few more steps, and it will be ready."

Karl scratched his scalp, doing his best not to groan. Gemma carried the leather to her workbench and started punching holes in it. Karl walked over to the window to avoid peering over her shoulder yet again.

The whole yard was taken up with garden plots, from just outside the door to a safe distance from the fence. Most of the space had tiny green plants springing up, a lovely contrast to the brown of the grass-lands beyond.

"It smells so much better in here, Gemma. I wonder if they'd pay you to install the same thing over in the hospital wing."

"I'd be glad to help," she said. "But they'd have to pay me a pretty coin to drag me away from my real work."

Karl wasn't quite sure he understood how she used something as sooty as charcoal to scrub the rotten aroma of the 'sters out of the air inside the house. He appreciated it every time he visited, though. The second combustion chamber for the hearth made a little more sense, but he was still amazed at how the smoke from the constant fire was invisible now.

"So all you have left is this?" he said. "The gyro-compass and the Dragon are finished?"

He walked back over to the table to examine his smaller, sturdier version of the compass. Gemma had explained how she'd reinforced the thin bits of Loretta's that snapped, but he picked it up with extreme care.

"That's all that's left, dear. Well, once you learn to use it, of course, but Loretta will be the one to help with that. Are her deliveries going well this week?"

"She seems quite happy," he said. "So they must be. She's almost caught up and through what we had here as well."

"Good," Gemma said, nodding. "She's a lot like me in that. I never could stand to have nothing to do for more than a little while at a time. Now sit, and let me make sure I have this fitted correctly before I attach the rest. It won't tickle as much, I promise."

Karl sat and waited, and after a few seconds he realized the straps were on his head.

"It feels like nothing's there at all."

"Of course it does," she said. "That's why it took so long to fit, dear. As long as you don't make drastic changes with your lovely curly hair, it will stay that way. I had to refit Loretta's with her hair braided once she decided to do that."

Karl snorted. "I won't be braiding mine anytime soon. What will you be working on next once this is done? To keep from getting bored?"

Gemma was threading fine wires onto the leather. A cord much like the one he'd seen on Loretta's headgear waited on the table.

"I've been dreaming of a kind of a machine to help with talking to the monsters," she said in an airy voice. "Sort of a translator. I'm quite certain some of them can speak, no matter what you and your friend George say."

"That's what you're doing next?" Karl tried, but he couldn't keep the worried tone out of his own voice. He sounded far too much like his mother for comfort. "They really can be dangerous, Gemma. The ones out here are the smartest and strongest."

She waved one hand at him without looking up from her work.

"I know, none of you want me to get too close," she said. "I remember that. The lovely white one that perches outside all the time especially seems to want to talk with me. If this machine lets me do that, it might even help the people where you work deal with the other poor creatures. Wouldn't that be worth it?"

Karl blinked. "I...yeah, I'm sure it would. Your dream about, what did you call it, galvanic steam treatments? That would probably be a big help to some of the most ill patients someday too. Just don't jump into talking to the 'sters too quickly, okay? Maybe only when George or I are here."

She pushed the last wires into the cable and squeezed the connection closed with delicate pliers before she turned to Karl.

"Don't worry," she said. "I'm not going to do that one next anyway. I'll be busy for a while."

Karl had a flash of memory from the first day they'd come out here.

"Working on something for Loretta next, right?"

Her cheeks turned red, and he was glad he'd taken the chance.

"I'm not really supposed to talk to anyone about that, not until she says it's okay." She scowled in the way she had that made her look like a rebellious teenager. "I don't know why, though. It's nothing I haven't made before. Nothing more than a glorified version of what I've made for both of you."

Karl looked up from his own Dragon, directly into Gemma's violet eyes. So like her granddaughter's.

"You're making another Dragon? She already has one."

"That's exactly what I said, exactly," Gemma said. "I already know how to make that." She sighed, then reached for Karl's Dragon. She started connecting the tiny wires to the other end of the cable. "Loretta is convinced a larger one will make a difference somehow."

"Why?" he said. "Is there a limit to these smaller ones?"

"I'm sure there is. I've seen that massive one-sided Blunderbuss all the Builders use. It's far larger than these. She's not asking for one that big, thank goodness."

Karl hoped his cheeks weren't as red as Gemma's had been. Loretta wouldn't appreciate him prying into her plans like this, not one bit. But the idea of a larger Dragon made his skin crawl.

"How big will it be?" he said.

"Oh, probably almost as long as she is once all is said and done."

Karl stood behind Gemma after all, but he was only pretending to peer over her shoulder. He wanted to be sure he could hear any hints in her voice.

"She won't be able to move something like that easily."

"No, I tried to explain that to her," Gemma said. "She said she has a solution in mind. It won't take me a terribly long time, certainly not right after making yours. It's fresh in my mind, you know. But I was hoping to move on to something new."

Karl walked back over to the window, not wanting her to see his face. He tried to convince himself it would be like a pulley lifting a heavier load than he could himself. That a larger Dragon would be less drain on the Builders, not more.

That justification wasn't holding up in his mind.

He didn't know much more about the Blunderbuss than any other non-Builder, but he did know many Builders worked together. His training had gone that far before it was obvious he'd never have the talent, and he had a lifetime of listening to his family talk about their work.

He watched the white monster circling above the house for a few seconds before he turned to Gemma.

"Maybe she wants both of us to use it. After she's trained me, of course."

"Maybe so," she said, smiling. "That would make it a lot more fun for me, having to figure out how to connect two users at the same time. I'll have this ready to go in a couple of hours. When she gets back, you can get started learning right away."

Chapter 48

Loretta and Bess walked into Loretta's blessedly quiet house. Loretta went into the bedroom to empty her very full purse before going out on the last run of the day. She never had to fear Rhysto searching for her safe again, but she was determined not to lose her good habits.

Neither woman wore her usual, and preferred, dark and practical clothing. Loretta was readjusting to the pressure of steel boning and leather against her ribs, though she was enjoying the movement of her voluminous black skirts. Bess was unrecognizable in a surprisingly appropriate and fashionable dark green gown of her own.

Loretta's absence only made the desire for her services grow stronger. She had the longest Build list she'd ever had to keep up with stored away in her mind, and her payments reflected gratitude for her return. Bess's lifetime in Waldron's Gate, and her resulting knowledge of gossip and intrigue even Loretta hadn't suspected, had Loretta wondering if she should make this arrangement permanent.

Bess came out of her kitchen with one last black leather bag and a raised eyebrow.

"Who's left for deliveries, Bess?"

"I see how this got put off until last," she said. "This little item was made especially for Mrs. Klia Gilmore."

Loretta took a deep breath and sat on the sofa.

"You're right," she said. "I've been dreading that one for a while now."

"Besides the obvious problem of her son, doesn't she work at the Ministry of Decorum?"

"She does," Loretta said. "High up the ranks. She was after me for quite a while before I agreed to work with her."

Bess sat beside Loretta, her arms crossed.

"You know your own business," she said. "And I appreciate you trusting me to meet so many of your clients. But isn't there a risk of her being a spy? Or just turning you in because she feels like it?"

"That's why it took her so long to convince me." Loretta stared at the floor. "I still wouldn't agree to see her until several of my other clients vouched for her. Seems she's been traveling in these circles almost as long as I have, but she was afraid to approach me too. Mrs. Gilmore has been a reliable and discrete buyer for a few years now."

Bess scowled. "Even if you can trust the woman, how can you possibly trust her not to tell her son? He made it pretty clear he wanted you to leave his family out of it, didn't he?"

"He did, from the first night." Loretta rubbed her shoulders, tired from carrying so many of those bags. "The thing is if I just never go back to Mrs. Gilmore's house with this, that might be what gets her to turn me in. She'll know all of her friends finally got their long-delayed curios. You don't know that crowd as well as I do. They're already planning their rounds of showoff parties. Mrs. Gilmore would certainly wonder why she was the only one left out."

"What are you going to do about Karl?"

"I can't do a thing about Karl, much as I want to sometimes. I have to trust his mother to be as circumspect with him as she must be at the Ministry. And I'll tell you my little secret rationalization, but you have to promise never to tell him."

Bess smiled, and her pale cheeks flushed in the sweet way Loretta knew so well.

"You know where my loyalties lie," she said. "I'm fond of him, and I'm grateful he's doing so much to keep you and Gemma safe. I'm glad to see you so happy with him. But I'm not about to give him a damned thing to use against you."

Loretta squeezed Bess's hand, trying her best to keep tears from showing in her eyes.

"I never should have asked for your promise, Bess. What I told Karl is I'd never use his family for Building again, though that's a real shame with all of them being so strong. And, I was telling him the truth that his sister was never a client of mine. He never asked whether his mother was."

"Works for me if you can live with it." Bess got to her feet, nodding once. "If we can get this visit wrapped up quickly, we might still be able to swing by and make your last stop before you head back to Joffrey Columns. I'm quite eager to meet this Mr. Norwood."

Loretta smiled her unkind smile. "I'm eager for him to meet you. He needs to understand that he'll never know who's with me or when one of you will show up or be watching him from around the corner."

Loretta reset all of the security devices on the door and joined Bess on the sidewalk.

"Speaking of someone showing up," Bess said. "What have you heard of Rullin?"

"That's a much harder situation than Karl or Mr. Norwood. Bill sent me a note saying the boy is basically working as slave labor, often chained, with guards on him at all times. His attitude isn't much improved. He doubts it will be. I'm afraid he's right."

"Why doesn't Bill just turn him in?" Bess said. "Constable Law and even Stensue have plenty of practice dealing with his sort. Or you could send him to Karl."

"I agree with you, Bess. From what Karl's said, Joffrey Columns would at least be able to make use of him, even if he was never quite the same afterward. I think Bill is reluctant to do something like that while his parents still live. They sent him to Bill as a last resort, but they're not ready to give up on Rullin just yet."

"Will he have to murder someone before they understand what a monster he is?"

Bess again had a flush in her face, but this was darker and decidedly more threatening. No one would take this for desire, except for violence.

"Possibly," Loretta said. "Bill says his brother and sisters understand, so once the parents are gone he'll be free to do as he will. Thankfully they're both well advanced in years and not in the best of health."

"Thank The Crown for small favors."

Loretta slowed as they approached the Gilmore house. With such a large and well-connected family, arranging time for a private meeting with Klia was not easy. The woman's correspondence room that Karl remembered so clearly, though more than a little obsessive to Loretta's eyes, provided the perfect hideaway.

Bess touched her shoulder before they started up the stairs.

"Listen, this may be the furthest thing from your mind, but I wouldn't be doing my job if I didn't at least ask." She paused, chewing on her lip, then spoke quickly. "What if you and Karl continue to get along so well? At some point, you won't be able to avoid meeting his parents. That would be awkward to say the least."

This time Loretta felt her own cheeks coloring. That had been much on her mind lately, but she wasn't about to admit it to Bess. At least not until she was ready to admit it to Karl. Or herself.

"Karl and I haven't talked about anything like that, but you have a good point. I'm fond of him, and I have to admit I like his mother." Loretta glanced up at that high, rounded turret where Karl said he still slept when he was here. She wondered what his room looked like, what it felt like. "I'm, well, if that ever comes up, I hadn't considered much past doing whatever I could to warn Mrs. Gilmore in advance. I know she'd keep her own secrets. I'd have to trust Karl to do the same."

KLIA GILMORE OPENED the dark blue door seconds after Loretta knocked, a sure sign she'd been anticipating their visit. Even though it was late Saturday afternoon, her pink silk dress was as formal, if less revealing, than what Loretta and Bess wore. Loretta suspected that was simply who Mrs. Gilmore was rather than any attempt to impress her.

"Ms. Schofield!" Klia took Loretta's hand in both of hers. "What a pleasure to see you after such a long absence. Please do come inside."

"Mrs. Gilmore, I'm delighted to see you as well. One reason I try to avoid these long delays is I do miss seeing everyone, especially people as pleasant as yourself."

Loretta stepped inside and turned to her guard.

"This is my sister, Bess. I trust her with my life. She's been thinking of partnering with me in my business, partly to help keep these problems from coming up. I hope it's acceptable for her to join us?"

As every other client had done, Klia was quick to agree. She held Bess's hand the same way she had Loretta's.

"Of course, and I'm very pleased to meet you. We'll go through into my correspondence room, Bess, for a bit of privacy." She opened a door to the left of the entryway. "I've already prepared tea, and we have service enough for three."

Loretta watched Klia Gilmore bustle around the small room, seeing her differently than on her last visit over a month ago. Whether she wanted to or not, her mind noted the strong resemblance between Karl and his mother.

Mrs. Gilmore wore her hair caught up in the current style, but the same curl Karl fought with was obvious. She had a similar shape to her face and the same easily tanned complexion. Karl must have gotten his size and those striking eyes from his father. Klia was only a little taller than Loretta herself, and her eyes were light brown.

Loretta glanced around the room, trying to match this aspect of Mrs. Gilmore with her son. Her desk was large and fairly plain, though the legs were elaborately carved and the whole thing polished to a high shine. The fine fabrics on the modern loveseat and chairs and the expensive floral rug certainly didn't match anything in Karl's apartment.

The shelves, though, that she recognized. Every wall space that wasn't a window, door, or fireplace was covered with them, and they were loaded with books, appropriate curios, and odd handmade gifts that must have come from her children.

The shelves around her desk were full of paper, envelopes, pens, and sealing wax. Now that she focused on them for the first time, Loretta realized she'd never imagined so many varieties and colors existed, much less that one person would have all of them.

"We won't be bothered in here," Klia said. "I've made sure everyone knows I have a private meeting. Would you both like cream and sugar with your tea?"

"Thank you, both would be fine," Loretta said. She waited for Klia to finish with the tea. "I am truly sorry for the delay, but I hope your item will prove worth it."

Bess loosened the drawstring and pulled out a large glass box framed with bronze. Klia's eye's lit up as she took it and turned toward the window. Beneath the glass was a tiny fetus, one that would have been conjoined twins if carried to full term. And if it were genuine.

The thing was a bit longer than Loretta's hand, skin pale and leathery. She could easily make out fingers on four hands, toes on two feet. Karl's mother acted as though she were holding a jeweled tiara.

"Ms. Schofield, this is perfect," she said in a breathless voice. "Exactly what I asked for. Do they truly come from Aerohead? I'd never be brave enough to get close to there."

Loretta suppressed a shudder, remembering she'd used Mrs. Gilmore's daughter Rethia to Build this hideous thing. Her pregnant daughter. Some things were far worse than a haunted city.

"Oh, you know I must respect the privacy of my suppliers, Mrs. Gilmore. The same way I respect the privacy of all of my clients."

"But of course," Klia said. "I appreciate that very much. This truly is a treasure. I only hate that I must keep it so hidden away."

"That's too often the case with the things we love," Bess said, not looking at Loretta.

"It is indeed." Klia tilted her head, looking intently at both women. "I know this will seem a bit forward, but may I ask if either of you are single?"

Loretta closed her eyes for a second, wishing she could disappear.

This was something she hadn't anticipated in all her worry about this visit.

"Yes, ma'am," Bess said. "Loretta and I both are."

Loretta glared at Bess as she turned to Mrs. Gilmore.

"My sister's right. We both are."

"Well, I do have a son who's nearly marriage age," she said. "The age for a Builder, I mean, thirty. He's not a Builder himself, but he has a good, steady job. He's very smart and handsome. I wonder if either of you would be interested in meeting him?"

Loretta realized it wasn't just the secrecy and awkwardness of having had sex with Karl just the night before that bothered her at that moment.

Mrs. Gilmore knowing very well what Loretta did for a living and wanting to match her with her son was disturbing. Every bit as much as her keeping where Karl's good, steady job happened to be to herself.

"I'm afraid I must decline," she said. "Though that is a generous offer. This sort of work does make it difficult to date, with all that privacy we were just talking about. I simply wouldn't be comfortable dating the relative of a client. Bess, though, she's only learning about this business."

Bess winked at Loretta.

"Our mother has partners in mind for both of us," Bess said. "Back in Yon where we came from. If we dated here before we agreed to at least try her matchmaking, she'd be heartbroken. I hope you understand."

Mrs. Gilmore sighed. "Oh, I do indeed. I worry for my son, working so much and living alone like he does. I only want to see him happy. But I suppose he'll have to make that decision when the time comes. I like your mother's strategy of matching you up herself. No one could know you better."

"You have a point there." Loretta kept her feelings about her own mother to herself. "I'm glad the item is to your liking, Mrs. Gilmore. May we begin the search for something else special for you?"

"Only if you call me Klia," Mrs. Gilmore said, reaching into a small wooden drawer to pull out a purse. The wall beside her desk had a section that wasn't shelves but more of the drawers, most of them small. Loretta suspected these were the address drawers that helped Karl lead them to Mr. Norwood. "Please make sure the correct amount is there."

Bess sorted quickly through the coin, then nodded as she dropped it into Loretta's purse.

"Thank you very much, Klia," Loretta said. "It is a delight working with you."

"You're quite welcome, Loretta, and Bess. Now, I do have something in mind for your next search."

Chapter 49

Karl walked away from his supervisor's office, knowing his burning face was not hiding a damned thing in the brightly lit administration corridor. He could only hope he didn't run into someone who was paying attention. He could only hope anyone he passed was being as damn careless as he'd become over the past few weeks.

The hell of it was he couldn't find a single thing to disagree with Ms. Curtis about.

He had been sleepwalking through the days, half-sleep deprived and half worrying too much over the complicated mess that was his life. A couple of doctors had had to try several times to get his attention, something that had never happened to Karl before. And just because his behavior hadn't endangered a patient or one of his coworkers, he knew if he kept trying to lead this insane dual life it would only be a matter of time.

Whether he, or more accurately his cock, wanted to or not, it was time to change his arrangement with Loretta. Now was not the time to worry about whether more than one of his unruly organs was going to resist the change. His heart, for example.

His brain was already bubbling over with a list of justifications for keeping things as they were, an internal argument he couldn't afford to pay attention to.

He turned the corner into the cafeteria and tried to force himself not to wince. That was something else that had never happened before: flinching away when he saw his best friend in this crazy place. George was sitting at a table close to the doors, a sure sign he wanted to talk to Karl about something.

George stood and gestured toward the empty tables by the windows. All Karl could do was nod and turn to get his lunch. He couldn't exactly refuse to talk to George after all he'd done for him lately.

"You look about the way I feel, buddy," George said when Karl joined him.

George didn't have anything in front of him except a glass of water. Karl wondered for a second if it was Crumblewater, if he shouldn't try to drown himself in the stuff in an effort to get his own head out of his ass.

"It's been a rotten day, Georgie. What's up?"

When Karl finally looked into his friend's eyes, all worries and thoughts of his own messed up situation evaporated.

"Don't jump to conclusions," he said. "At least not because of... It might not mean anything. Karl, the baby 'ster, the one that you saw?' Karl nodded, and his mind and body froze solid. "It died today. A couple of hours ago."

"What happened?"

"I wasn't there," George said. "I can't say for sure, but the guy who told me has never lied about anything. He said he was in there cleaning up like usual, and the 'ster woke up, like usual. Instead of burning itself but not making a sound, it started crying." George took a deep breath and stared out the window. "It cried, then it screamed. And when it... When it burned this time, it just kept burning. They tried blankets, water, nothing worked. It died, Karl."

Karl squeezed his eyes closed, holding his own breath, trying to find a way to get around hearing this, understanding it. By the time he realized it was hopeless and opened his eyes, he was thankful he hadn't touched a bite of the dubious pinkish casserole in front of him.

He clenched his jaws, trying not to dry heave. The cramping

nausea was spreading to his ribs and down into his guts, threatening to take over his whole body.

"George, that means Rethia, she might be..."

"We don't know for sure it was linked to her."

Karl remembered he'd never told George about Loretta's map, the pattern that passed right through his sister's house. Or about Rethia's restless night when Loretta was Building.

"I have to get out of here," Karl said. Maybe if he got his body moving, his brain would stop. "Don't say anything to Loretta, okay? Let me figure this out."

"Slow down, just wait a minute. It could have been anyone, some other family. Don't assume that. Not until we know more."

"That's why you told me in the first place," Karl said. "The eyes. I saw them with my own. There's no way it wasn't linked to someone in my family. This might lose me this damned job after all, but I need to get home."

"I'm afraid that's about to be taken care of," George said under his breath, jerking his chin toward the doors.

Karl turned to see Ms. Curtis walking toward them, her face as pale and grim as George's. Normally none of the doctors or supervisors would be caught dead eating in the general cafeteria. Either she'd come to her senses and decided to fire Karl after all, or his day was about to get even worse. She stopped beside the table, taking a deep breath before she spoke.

Karl's jaw dropped when the light through the windows caught the strand of dark blue pearls she was wearing, one he'd been too upset to notice earlier in her office. Mr. Otis's lost first Build with Loretta.

"Mr. Wood," she said. "Karl, may I speak to you alone for a moment?"

George put a hand on Karl's shoulder as he stood.

"Ms. Curtis. I'll talk to you later, Karl." He started to walk away, then turned back. "Almost forgot, this letter came for you today. Sorry to... Talk to you later."

Karl glanced at the lilac envelope long enough to pick out his mother's elaborate seal in the darkest angry green wax he'd ever seen her use. Just another load of shit to add to his day.

He slipped it into his chest pocket and turned to Ms. Curtis. She sat and pulled yet another letter out of her own pocket.

"I have some terrible news," she said. "I didn't want to just forward you a letter like this. Your mother finally got through on the talkbox, but it took the switchboard a while to forward the message to me."

She put the envelope on the table. Karl tried not to confirm it, knowing what he'd see, but he couldn't stop himself. He turned it over. The seal was black.

"What's happened to Rethia?"

"No, not that. She's as well as can be expected. The baby, Karl, the baby was born this morning. Something went wrong, though. He died not long after. A courier brought this. That usually takes—"

"About two hours."

Karl covered his face, the grinding of his teeth sounding throughout his skull. Loretta hadn't been using Rethia. Not at all.

Loretta had been using the baby.

"Well, yes, that's right," Ms. Curtis said. "Never mind what we talked about earlier. You need to go. You're excused for the rest of the week. We'll deal with the rest when you return. I'm truly sorry for your loss, Karl."

She held out her hand, and Karl shook it, hoping she took his trembling and refusing to meet her gaze as sorrow. He'd never been more furious in his life.

"Thank you. I'll let you know how it's going." Karl stood, but before he could get his feet moving his mouth took over. "Ms. Curtis, I need to know something. You taught medical history before you came here. Do you know why women aren't supposed to Build late in pregnancy? I don't mean the usual reasons we hear, but the truth. Can you please tell me?"

She tilted her head, watching him for a second before she spoke.

"No matter what else may be going on, you're a fine nurse, Karl. You know as well as I do why some things aren't common knowledge, and why they need to stay that way. What we think happens is the baby starts Building in the womb if the mother does, if it's to have the talent. We think the brain isn't ready for that until adolescence when children normally start to show the ability. The strain may be why they're so agitated. If that starts, the mother must take time away from Building."

"What happens if the mother doesn't take time off? Rethia did, as soon as the trouble started. I just need to know."

Ms. Curtis looked down at her hands, then back up at Karl.

"Years ago, long before we even started to understand such things, live birth rates were low for women who were Builders. When they did have children, they were frequently without the talent. For a time, it was thought women should never be allowed to Build during pregnancy lest Builders die out. Some wanted to take it further and ban women from Building altogether to protect from an undetected pregnancy, even though the trouble doesn't start until they're well advanced. Thankfully taking leave when the problem started was adopted instead."

She didn't say the conversation was over, and Karl had an idea she would have told him more if he asked. About what exactly she thought had gone wrong with his lost nephew, or why Mrs. Labine was being denied Crumble, perhaps.

Between the look in her eyes and his mind's screams that he had to get home, he let it go.

"Thank you, Ms. Curtis. Don't worry. I understand why this is sensitive. I'll be in touch."

KARL REALIZED his mistake when he got on the trolley into his neighborhood in Waldron's Gate. No one on the train or in the busy train station paid him any attention, or maybe he'd been too upset and furious to notice. Now on the quieter, more residential route, people kept glancing at his gray uniform and looking away. He remembered that fear from when he lived on the outside, as if just seeing someone from the Columns would doom you to end up there. He couldn't remember ever leaving without changing clothes first, partly for that reason.

This time he'd been too worried about running into Loretta to take the chance of going back to his own blasted apartment.

He stared at his feet at the stop for Loretta's house. If her Building had caused this, or at least contributed, that had happened weeks ago. He couldn't blame her for that, and there wasn't even any way to know for certain.

But she'd been gone more and more lately, even after the deliveries she had stacked up should have been finished. Karl had started to suspect she wasn't spending the night out at Gemma's during the week after all.

He had a terrible suspicion she'd been Building again, outside of the Builds they did together with patients. He was in too deep with her already, too afraid to ask any of the questions blazing through his mind.

Unless she'd changed her spiral pattern, something he didn't think Loretta was likely to do, she'd likely passed close by Rethia's house again over the last couple of nights. That shouldn't make any difference if she hadn't aimed her blasted Dragon at his sister, but he couldn't dismiss the horrible possibility.

When Karl stepped off the trolley, he tried to convince himself the other passengers weren't relieved, but he didn't pay close attention. That was just another truth he didn't want to risk seeing. Standing on the porch of his parents' house, he'd run out of time to avoid anything at all.

He knocked before he realized that was yet another thing he'd never done before. He started to open the door, but his mother beat him to it.

"Oh, Karl."

Klia Gilmore pulled him into a hug, but not before Karl saw her red eyes, her blotchy face. Her curly graying hair hung loose almost to her waist, just about long enough to touch the full black skirt she wore. The same kind of skirt Loretta often wore.

"Mother, what happened? Is Rethia okay?"

She drew back, wiping at her eyes with a lacy black handkerchief.

"She's sleeping right now, poor thing, just going to pieces. Of course I understand why." She stopped, covering her eyes and reaching out for Karl's hand. He held tight. "She woke up this morning in labor. It's a little early, but no one thought it was anything to worry about. The doctor was there before everything got started. He screamed so loud when he was born."

Karl had known that was coming from the letter, that the baby would be a boy, but his heart stopped anyway. He stepped forward to close the door, then took his mother's arm to walk her into her correspondence room. He hoped she'd draw comfort from her own private space.

"He was absolutely perfect, Karl," she said, sitting on the loveseat beside him. "The cord wasn't round his neck, no marks or bruises, nothing. He was smaller than he should have been, but he looked as normal as you did. He was fine, for a little while. Then he stopped moving. We thought he was asleep, but he stopped breathing before the doctor even left."

"Did the doctor have any idea what happened?"

"No, except that he'd seen it a few times," she said. "Almost like the baby got so far and something stopped developing. Maybe his brain, but they're not sure. He was okay as long as Rethia's body was supporting him. He couldn't make it on his own."

Karl was relieved she covered her eyes again. He had no illusions he'd be able to keep up the appearance of mourning and worry. He didn't have to ask the doctor or anyone else if the trouble had been in his nephew's brain, or when it had stopped developing.

He knew. Down to the day and the hour.

He knew.

"I'm so sorry, Mother. Did that cause any trouble for Rethia?"

"Oh no, the doctor said she's going to be fine, thank The Crown. Physically, anyway. I'm more worried about Gerald than her. He's not doing well at all."

"Is he here?" Karl said. "I can try to talk to him."

She shook her head, her normal brisk motion. As was so often the case, a suggestion she thought inappropriate helped bring her back to herself.

"He's with Rethia, and just as well. He was nearly passing out on his feet." She started to get to her feet, then she froze, starting at Karl's chest. "Please tell me you didn't read that."

Karl looked down, with no idea what she was talking about. He reached for the envelope with the dark green seal, but she plucked it away.

"I sent that yesterday," she said, wincing. "I said the most horrible things, certainly with what's happened. Hard to believe I was upset about something as minor as you not visiting for a while when everything was about to fall apart."

Karl clenched his free hand into a painful fist, trying to give his aching jaws a break. It had been way past his normal pathetic schedule of once a month, and he hadn't even bothered to let his mother know why. Mainly because he'd lost all track of the days and nights.

"Well, I didn't read it," he said. "I deserved it in any case. I'm sorry. It's been a little crazy at work. Listen, what can I do to help?"

She smiled a tiny bit.

"Everything is calm for now with the two of them asleep," she said. "I'm sure Andy would appreciate the company upstairs. He's been a dear watching all the younger ones and the cousins for me all day His patience only goes so far, though."

"I'll go right now, but only if you promise to get some rest, too."

She smiled and patted his hand.

"I will now that you're here, I promise. This is probably the best chance I'll get for a few days."

Chapter 50

LORETTA PUSHED the door to Gemma's house open, glad to be out of the sour-smelling tunnel. She'd helped her grandmother install the charcoal air cleaner, but she wasn't quite sure why it worked. She didn't care. Anything that removed the foul stink of the monsters was worth it.

"Gemma?"

The main room was empty, and the doors to the smaller rooms were open. Loretta tried to keep calm, but she'd never gotten comfortable enough with this place to be here alone. Not even with her grandmother's belongings and gadgets set up and running. Even Karl and George were uneasy out here.

She went to the front window, puzzled by the addition of a narrow row of horizontal bars in front of it. George and Karl constantly reassured her the fence out there was enough.

The bars shifted, and she realized it was a ladder. Gemma walked into view then, arms crossed, looking up at the sky. Loretta tried to prepare herself for the smell every time she stepped outside. It never seemed to work. She held up the perfumed handkerchief she always kept with her for these visits and joined her grandmother.

"What are you doing out here?" she said.

"Oh, bobbin, you're just in time! George is making the last connections on my talking machine."

George was coming down the ladder now, the top rung lodged against the arching top of the fence.

"What talking machine?" Loretta said. "Weren't you working on that project for me?"

Gemma patted Loretta's arm, then reached up to steady George.

"I haven't forgotten. Don't worry," she said. "I kept dreaming of this, several times every night. When that happens, the only way to get a good night's sleep is to make whatever it is and get it out of my system. I'll be finished with yours in a few days."

"Good to see you, Loretta," George said, stepping to the ground and wiping sweat off of his face. "Good to be down here, too."

Loretta looked up to the top of the fence, where a bright metal bowl shaped like the end of her Dragon, or the much larger Blunderbuss, was attached. A black cable ran down the fence, along the ground, and into one of the windows.

"George. But what is this, Gemma? Who are you trying to talk to?"

"Why, the monsters, of course," she said. Her eyes and voice neatly scolded Loretta for such silliness. "Especially the big white one. You can tell that one is just dying to talk to us."

Loretta scanned the cloudy sky for the creature before turning back to her grandmother.

"Dying, huh?" she said. "Can you tell me the rest inside? I'm not out here enough to get used to that stench."

"You know, I didn't think it was possible," George said. "I hardly notice it anymore." He compressed the ladder much like Loretta did her tripod before he hung it just under the roof. "We'll get that cable buried for you, and no one will ever be the wiser."

Inside, Loretta spotted the other end of the device on a table beside the biggest window. It had a similar curving open end and part of the middle tube structure of the Dragon. Gemma beamed as she sat down beside it. She picked up headgear that matched Loretta's and Karl's.

"Shall we try it?" she said.

"It wasn't out there," Loretta said, glancing out the window. "You're not going to call it, are you?"

The white demon stared at her any time she was here. Even when she stayed inside, she caught it hanging on to the fence and watching.

"I'd bet it came right back once we were inside," George said. "I doubt it liked me being up on that ladder." He opened the door for a second. "Yep, it's up there, checking out my handiwork. Want to show us what I set up?"

Gemma grinned and nodded.

"It's much like the Blunderbuss, and the Dragon... The same thing Builders use in their work." She pulled the headgear on. "I should be able to use this to focus and send out my thoughts."

"How will it answer?" Loretta said.

She wanted to try it for herself, but maybe on other humans. Talking to monsters was low on her list of interests. Gemma tapped a second silvery bell-shaped device, larger than the first.

"This will send the reply back," Gemma said. "As words with any luck. It's sort of like a megaphone. The shape should amplify the signal."

"And you just dream these things," George said, his forehead wrinkled as he peered over his glasses at the headgear. "Did you dream whether it would work or not?"

Gemma giggled when he touched the soft leather around her hair, sounding about sixteen years old.

"Well, it worked in my dream, but nothing is guaranteed, is it? We'll just test it and see if we need to make any adjustments." Gemma closed her eyes, tilting her head to one side, then the other, a gesture Loretta recognized as gathering her thoughts.

"Hello there," Gemma said. "Do you understand me?"

SEVERAL SECONDS PASSED before a dissonant scratching sound, like a spoon dragging across a rough empty bowl, tore through the small space. Gemma jumped, leaning forward to adjust several knobs, one after another. The noise dropped to a less painful volume, but the pitch was still unpleasant. It wavered without a pattern Loretta could detect.

"Try again now," Gemma said. "I can't quite understand you. I'm very close by. You don't have to shout."

The screech modulated, sounding more like harsh birdsong than the awful scraping. The sounds picked up a rhythm almost like speech. Gemma turned one more knob. All three of them gasped at scratchy but clear words.

"Hear you."

"How can it possibly talk?" Loretta said, staring at George. 'How could a monster know how to talk like a person?"

His cheeks turned red.

"I can't... We're not supposed to say. The 'sters, they're not as far from humans as you might think. I've never heard one talk, but I wouldn't be surprised."

Gemma laughed. "I'm glad you can hear me! I live here, right below you. Do you have a name?"

The scratching sound started up after a few seconds, then slowly resolved into words.

"Name. No name. All have names?"

"You mean all people?" Gemma said. "We all have names. Do all of you have names?"

"No names," the monster said, its voice gaining clarity as Gemma made further adjustments. "Some want names."

"Oh, I'd be delighted to give you names," Gemma said, clapping her hands. "Can you bring the others so I can name them, too?"

"Don't tell it to bring others," Loretta said. Her flesh was cold and clammy with a growing dread she couldn't explain. George looked as bad as she felt. "Maybe you've said enough already."

"Not give names. Tell names. Tell names of their people?"

The question was clear, and George's face went pale. Gemma didn't notice.

"My name is Gemma. I live right here. You see me every day. Is that what you mean?"

"Gemma. Glad to see you. Tell people's names? For others?"

George grimaced. "Tell it we don't know. We hardly ever know, unless... We don't know."

Gemma looked at George with her eyebrows together, but she answered.

"I don't know what you mean by your person, but I live here. Do you have a person?"

"Gemma, do you have to speak out loud," Loretta said. "Or can it hear your thoughts? Can it hear all our thoughts?"

Gemma covered the speaking bell with her hand.

"It may very well hear our thoughts. I don't want to be rude to my guest." She moved her hand aside. "I see others outside sometimes. Do you know them?"

"Maybe Loretta's right," George said, increasing her unease. "Let's take a break."

"Know them," the scratchy voice said. "Some can't speak. Many can. Others with you?"

"Yes, two others," Gemma said. "They've been here before."

The voice drew the next word out into a hiss, making the hair on Loretta's arms stand on end.

"Sssssssseee them?"

Gemma turned to them, her eyes large and radiant.

"He wants to see you! George, can you help me carry this outside?"

"That might not be a good idea," he said, meeting Loretta's gaze and shaking his head. "That lets the smell in."

Loretta put her hand against the front door. Her heart was beating faster with every passing minute.

"George has a point," she said. "I'm not sure we should go out there. It might be looking for a meal."

Gemma stood, arms crossed, eyes furious.

"Loretta! I'm sure it wants no such thing. George, please help me take this outside. I don't want to drop anything."

"We have no way to know that," Loretta said. "Not after a few words. I'm just trying to keep you safe, Gemma."

George stepped forward to pick up the equipment when Gemma tried to.

"That one can't get through the fence," he said. "Stay close to the house anyway. I'll get these things if you'll get the door, Loretta."

"Sssssseeeeeeeeee you."

"We'll be right there," Gemma said, motioning toward the door. "So sorry to keep you waiting."

Loretta wished Bess or Karl were out here to either help put a stop to this or keep it from getting too far out of hand.

The white monster was at the highest part of the cage, crouched beside the bell-ended device. It turned to watch them. George braced the heavy black box against the windowsill, held the talking bell up, and nodded.

"I'm Gemma. This is George and my granddaughter, Loretta. Isn't there anything we can call you?"

The monster tilted its head back and forth at her words.

"Death."

Loretta's stomach knotted, and she had to force herself not to run back inside.

"Your name is Death?" Gemma said.

"Not me. Not name. Sssseeeee death."

George looked around the yard, his face twisted with worry, then shrugged. Nothing was there but Gemma's thriving garden.

"Where do you see death?" Gemma said. "I don't understand."

The creature rustled its wings and shifted around to face them more directly.

"Death. Today. Death. Now. Sssseeeee death."

George seemed to shrink in on himself, nearly dropping Gemma's equipment.

"George?" Loretta walked to his side. "What is it?"

He shook his head, but she saw tears in his eyes.

"Where is other?" the monster said.

Now George tried to reach toward Gemma with his free hand, but she spoke quickly.

"Other?" she said. "You mean Karl?"

"Other death came to. Not here with you. Not now."

Loretta grabbed George's arm. Her heart contracted with worry over Karl, far more than she would have ever imagined or admitted.

"George, what the hell is that thing talking about?"

"I don't know where Karl is," Gemma said, sounding afraid for the first time. "What do you mean, death came to him?"

"Death here now. Sssseeeee death."

All three of them looked up at the monster. Loretta was frozen to the spot, afraid to even breathe. She would have sworn those blue eyes were locked onto hers.

"Here..." Gemma said. "I don't understand!"

Gemma was crying, but Loretta made no move to comfort her. Something she couldn't comprehend was going wrong all around her. Her heart pounded so hard her head pulsed with it, but she still couldn't move.

"Gemma, go inside," George said, tears streaming down his face. "We can't get into this, not out here. Karl is with his family. He's fine."

He pulled away from Loretta and tried to follow Gemma into the house. She stepped in front of him, ducking down to look into his eyes.

"Tell me what's going on!"

He squeezed his eyes closed and turned away from her.

"Go back to Waldron's Gate, Loretta. Just go. I'll keep an eye on Gemma. He'll find you when he's ready."

Loretta didn't resist when he moved around her. The monster rustled its wings again, and Loretta turned on numb feet and legs. George had taken the equipment inside, but she could still hear the crackling speaker over Gemma's crying. The creature leaned down until its face was nearly against the bars of the fence.

Now she knew it was staring at her.

"Death."

Chapter 51

When Karl walked into the family room on the second floor, Andy smiled and rolled his eyes at the same time. Seven kids ranging from their youngest niece in diapers to their younger sister Janie, twelve and looking put upon to be required to have an older brother watching her, took up almost the whole toy-and-book-cluttered space. Two of his aunts and one uncle sat in the adult area, deep in conversation.

Andy got up and hugged Karl.

"I'm so glad you're here, big Brother. Rotten situation, but I'm glad to see you."

"Same here, little Brother. Are the ankle biters behaving?"

Janie gasped, drawing back in an imitation of their mother that would have been funny on any other day.

"I am not an ankle biter!"

"No, I didn't say you were," Karl said. "That was about the little ones. Listen, Janie, I need to talk to Andy for a minute. Can you watch them for us?"

This time Janie seemed to actually expand. She looked around at the smaller kids, all occupied with some kind of group project with painted wooden blocks, and nodded gravely.

"I'll watch the ankle biters for you."

Karl and Andy walked over to the window, far enough from the kids to have at least a little privacy, not close enough to the older relatives to draw their attention.

"Where have you been for so long, Karl? I've been stuck here with the savages for weeks now."

"I know. I'm sorry," Karl said. "Busy at work, life just out of control in general. I don't have any excuse. How's it been going here?"

Andy swiped at his eyes and stared out the window at the heavy clouds overhead.

"Today's been awful," he said. "I don't know what to say to anybody. I volunteered to watch them just to get out of the way."

"Yeah, no one knows what to say when things like this happen. Mother said you've been a big help."

"Nice of her to say, at least," Andy said. "What's been going on with you? Got a girlfriend Mother doesn't know about? Or one she wouldn't approve of?"

It was Karl's turn to stare out the window. His worries about introducing Loretta to his family felt absurd now.

"I don't know," he said. "Maybe something like that. I have been checking into what you told me, about too many people from here going out to the Columns. Has that calmed down at all?"

Andy scratched his head, frowning.

"I hadn't thought about it for a couple of weeks, but that answers the question. It's been pretty calm around here lately. The first person I've heard of for a while went yesterday. Mr. Gosander over on Apple Lane. Did you find something?"

"I may have."

Karl tried to stop it, but his mind brought Loretta's map into sharp focus.

Apple Lane was in the next sweep of her spiral. He could point to Mr. Gosander's house as accurately as Mr. Norwood could have. Karl knew exactly where the next target would be.

That wasn't the worst part, bad as it was. The pattern doubled, then tripled, and Karl gasped before he could stop himself. The ones he couldn't explain, Builders who'd ended up out at the Columns but were never under one of Loretta's enameled pins. They were all at the intersection of those larger, sweeping circuits.

More broken minds caught in the fallout. Just like Rethia's baby.

"I'll see what I can find out about him," Karl said. "I'm glad it s calmed down out here."

Someone tugged at the back of his shirt.

"Unka Karl?"

He turned to see Sally, another of his nieces. Janie was stomping toward them with both fists clenched.

"What's up, Sally?"

Karl picked the girl up, trying not to smile as Janie stopped and crossed her arms.

"Did you see it?" Sally said.

"See what?"

"The twins," she whispered, leaning close to his ear.

"I don't know any twins. Do you, Andy?"

The boy shrugged again, shaking his head.

"Not alive twins, silly," Sally said. "These are too little. And they're together."

"A doll?" he said. "Are they up here?"

"Uh-uh. In Gramma's room. But they're a secret." She leaned closer and whispered again. "A big, big secret, but Janie showed me."

All the noise in the room faded, leaving Karl with only the pounding of his own heart.

He didn't want to see. He didn't need to see. He had to see.

If what he was thinking was true, several decisions had just been made for him.

"Okay, Sally." he said. "I want to see. Can you take me, or does Janie need to?"

Sally looked around, her hazel eyes huge, but Karl didn't have the heart left to smile.

"Janie can take you. I don't wanna get in trouble."

"Smart girl,' Karl said. "Stay here with Uncle Andy, then. I'll be back in a bit."

Karl stood, struggled to find his balance, and somehow managed to walk over to Janie. He took a deep breath, not wanting to scare her with how he was twisting inside.

"Janie, Sally tells me there's a big secret in Mother's room. Want to tell me about that?"

The girl's face went white, and she clapped both hands over her mouth. Karl knelt beside her, looking up at her.

"I'm not mad," he said. "No one's in trouble. I just want to see. I'm curious too, you know."

"But you're a grown-up. Sally never should have told you, not one word of it."

"No, don't be mad at Sally," Karl said. "I don't think she sees me as much more than a big kid. She's probably right. Please, Janie? I want to see."

The girl shifted from one foot to the other, twisting her curly ponytail through her fingers. She glared at Sally for a second, then looked back at Karl.

"Fine, I'll take you," she said. "But you have to swear not to tell Mother or Father. And really swear, not pretend like Sally did."

Karl held out his hand, and Janie shook it.

"I swear, Janie. A real swear." He stood and turned back to Andy. "Will you be all right for a little while? I'll come back up as soon as I can."

"Yeah, go ahead. Getting her out of here will help."

Janie stuck out her tongue at Andy, but she grabbed Karl's hand again.

"We have to make sure Mother's not in there first," she said. "Can you be quiet on the stairs?"

"I'll do my best."

Karl glanced down the hall to make sure their parents' bedroom door was closed. That usually meant one of them was in there. With any luck, it would be their mother taking that nap.

He wished for just a second that he could turn the other way, climb to his old room in the turret, and do the same. Curl up with a pillow over his head and forget about all of this, pretend none of it ever happened, at least for a little while.

Janie pulled at his hand, so he followed her down the stairs instead.

No one seemed to be on the ground floor. Janie took big, careful steps to their Mother's correspondence room.

"Knock," she whispered.

"What?"

"Knock," she said again. "Make sure no one's in there."

Karl knocked softly and turned the handle at the same time, only then wondering what he'd say if their mother was in there after all. The room was empty, and Janie sighed as dramatically as she'd been walking.

"The coast is clear," he said. "What's the big, exciting secret, Janie?"

Janie held one finger to her lips, then walked toward the wall opposite the desk. She squatted down behind the sofa and pushed on a floorboard until the end popped up.

As she pulled it loose and reached down into the space, Karl wanted to stop her. He wanted to grab her arm and pull her back up the stairs.

Once he saw whatever it was, there would be no turning back.

He should turn back right now.

"Look," Janie whispered.

Chapter 52

Loretta walked out of her study, mind lost in the map of Waldron's Gate she'd just been poring over. Taking George's advice to get away from that horrible white creature had been easy enough. Building was the best way she knew of to keep her worry for Karl—and her guilt over what might have happened to Rethia's baby—from taking over her mind once she was alone.

With Karl so occupied with his family and Gemma safe in her strange way, she'd eventually allowed herself to enjoy her solitude. She'd missed her house and her own life more than she realized.

Loretta was deep enough into anticipating her Builder's trance that she didn't see Bess sitting on the sofa until she cleared her throat.

"Bess! You scared the life out of me."

Loretta was instantly drenched in sweat and trembling with delayed readiness. She'd been away from her normal routines and awareness for far too long.

"I didn't mean to do that, ma'am," Bess said. "But that's something you may want to think about. I'll admit I'm curious why you didn't let me know you were staying here for the last couple of days. Planning to go out this evening?"

"I am, but we're not making deliveries this late. Nothing to worry yourself about."

The guard wore her normal black work clothes, not much different than Loretta's Building skinsuit. Bess chewed her bottom lip, then took a deep breath.

"I know I'm way out of line. I may end up losing myself a job that means a lot to me. If you don't want me to worry, you shouldn't show up at my house white as a sheet, more upset than I've ever seen you, and tell me about some kind of monster that says you're death."

"That thing isn't even in Waldron's—"

"No, but that's not something any sane person would ignore, either. Do you know about what happened to Karl's sister? To her baby?"

Loretta sat, hands clasped between knees, staring at the floor. Finding out what George had been so upset about had been painfully easy.

"Of course I do," she whispered. "It isn't exactly a secret."

"Then why aren't you with Karl?"

"You know why!" Loretta gritted her teeth and forced her voice into a quieter range. "You pointed out exactly why I can't just show up at his mother's house, Bess."

"Right. So unless I'm missing something, we have you promising not to involve his family right before you deliver one of your lovely items to his mother. A creature out of the Fog or maybe The Pit watches you and calls you death. An infant at a house you've visited in the middle of the night dies. You show up at my door so upset you're barely able to talk, but you don't bother to mention that you'll be staying here with no protection after years of keeping guards at all times. Tell me again how I shouldn't worry myself about all of this."

Loretta looked into Bess's blue eyes, the eyes of the person she trusted most in all of Alterra. She was indeed crossing the line as an employee, but Loretta knew that line had ceased to exist long years ago.

"I'm not heartless, Bess. I don't know if my Builds with Rethia caused this. I hope not. I'm being more careful about that."

Bess leaned forward, hands on her thighs.

"Then why are you going out at all?" she said. "Much less alone? I know you can take care of yourself, but you can also take too damn many risks with no one there to protect you or even know where you are. Why don't you just do your Builds out at the Columns instead? Those people are crazy already."

"I can't do that. Certainly not once I finish training Karl. He knows exactly what I Build already. They go right to Gemma's house. And he's not... He isn't exactly supportive of that side of my life, anyway."

Bess scowled and got to her feet.

"And now you're letting a man make your decisions for you, to the point that you're going out at night again when you know people are on the lookout for Rhysto. Or his murderer."

Loretta had no intention of getting into a discussion about relationships with Bess or anyone else if she could help it. Her own thoughts and feelings about Karl were too jumbled to even know where to begin.

"Listen, Bess, I've already been going out. For the past couple of weeks." Her guard grimaced, shaking her head. "Yes, I should have let someone know. I should have yet *you* know. I'm sorry. I needed some time to myself, and I decided I should do something constructive while I was at it."

"Do you have any idea how that sounds? Putting yourself at risk to get some privacy, which you should have without clearing it with anyone?"

Loretta knew pointing out that Bess was making quite a dent in her privacy by showing up in her living room would not be in anyone's best interests.

"I know how it sounds," Loretta said. "The important thing is I have been Building, and I haven't run into any problems at all. No one is out searching for Rhysto in the wee hours of the morning. You might have forgotten he was a bastard who not many people are going to miss. I'd wager most people would reward his killer rather than demand any kind of punishment."

"You don't know that, Loretta." Bess knelt in front of Loretta, looking into her eyes. "You didn't grow up here. I did. Murder is almost nonexistent, sure, but it does happen. Sophie didn't grow up here either, but she learned that lesson in the worst possible way. No one in Waldron's Gate is happy about it when anyone is killed. Even an asshole. If the slightest rumor gets out that he's dead, you'll think Karl and me paying too much attention to what you're up to was child's play. Any secrets you hope to keep *will* be fair game."

Loretta stared at the floor again, her face pale and cold. Bess knew very little about her past, and Rhysto's death eliminated the only person besides her grandmother who knew more.

Fair or not, the reminder of Sophie hurt.

"I understand. One thing I don't think *you* understand is doing this keeps me sane, Bess. Getting out on my own, concentrating so hard, making something new that never would have existed otherwise, even if they're not fine art by anyone's standards. Nothing else in my life is normal anymore. I can't give this up, too. I'd end up one of Karl's patients instead of his lover."

Bess stood, shaking her head.

"That's more or less what I thought you'd say. I'll leave you to it. Assuming I'm still employed, when will you need my services again, ma'am?"

"You're still employed." Loretta stood and grasped Bess's shoulders. "Mainly because you're absolutely right. I am taking risks I shouldn't be, far too many to think about all at once. I appreciate your concern more than you know."

"I'm sure I don't have to tell you I don't believe one word of that. Tomorrow afternoon, then. Take care, Loretta."

Loretta watched her guard walk away, darkness thickening around her as the streetlights adjusted to their lowest setting. When Bess disappeared from view, Loretta followed her into the night.

Loretta's target Builder was only a few blocks away, leaving her wishing for more time to clear her head after such a difficult conversation. The example of her parents and especially her grandparents, not to mention her own past attempts, had given her more than enough reason to avoid the very situation she was in. Worrying about what a man would think.

Gemma had not been the happy, kind woman she was now when Loretta's grandfather was alive. He grudgingly kept her secret life off of Crumble to himself in return for a larger dowry than usual, but only if she promised to never make any of the things she dreamed of.

Loretta hadn't been lying about Building keeping her sane and calm. Gemma had been neither when she lived under such restrictions. Loretta often wondered if that torment had left her grandmother with her sometimes filtered grasp of reality.

She walked down the middle of the darkened street, watching the house for any signs of movement. During the day, this small, tidy one-story was a bright pink with pale blue accents, one of the more cheerful houses in the row. The muddy gray in the dim light made it hard to recognize, but Loretta never needed such obvious guides. She almost knew the number of steps it would take after studying her map.

This Builder wasn't a client. She'd have to have a strong focus, a challenge when her mind was so unsettled.

Her next path took her into the yard, a silent circuit to examine all the windows and doors. No one was about, and only her soft footsteps broke the silence. She didn't like setting up in the front of a house where she was so visible, but the man's bedroom wasn't accessible from anywhere else.

Loretta thought of Karl seeing her from the high turret in his parents' house, several blocks from here. None of the less grand houses surrounding her held such threats. She moved as close as her sightlines would allow and shrugged off her pack.

The noise, quieter than her own breathing, alerted her as she took out the case holding her Dragon and gyro-compass. With Bess's warning about murder investigations, her nerves were on a sharp edge. Loretta's hands kept moving, adjusting the tripod and putting the case as far under the bush in front of her as she could.

She stood and stared at the house with her head tilted, shifting her body so she could reach for the weighted club in the opposite direction the breathy sound had come from.

Loretta drew the club and turned in the same motion, and froze.

Karl stood a few feet away from her, several of his long strides from any kind of cover. He held his hands up and lowered his head. Loretta had to grit her teeth to keep from using the club on him anyway. She crossed the distance between them.

"What the hell are you doing out here?" she whispered. "How did you even know—"

"I haven't been sleeping well lately," he said. "Didn't take much deep thought to figure out where to find you."

Loretta forced her breathing to slow, trying to keep her anger from driving her on.

"You remembered the blasted map that well, did you?"

"Just one of those things," he said. "I don't want to ask what you're doing out here."

"Then don't. What do you want, Karl?" Now that her heart was slowing, an ache set in, one she was terribly uncomfortable with. That ache demanded a sympathy Loretta wasn't sure she was capable of. "I... I'm sorry about the baby. I wish I could be with you for the funeral."

Karl lowered his hands, then held one out.

"Take the night off? I could use some company. Your company, to be painfully honest."

"The night?" she said. "This doesn't mean..."

"No, nothing like that. All this means is I don't want to be alone tonight. I need you, Loretta."

Her traitorous heart pushed her forward, and Loretta took Karl's hand. He pulled her into a trembling embrace. All she could do was hold tight. Wanting to make him feel better, wanting the awful shaking to stop, was unknown territory.

She was afraid to make a wrong move and blow everything apart.

He pulled back and kissed her, bringing demands from her body firmly into the whirling mess in her head.

"I'll help you pack up. I promise, I won't break anything this time."

A soft laugh escaped Loretta before she could stop herself. She let the one thing she could make sense of, her body, take over, and kissed him long and hard.

"That's fine, you clumsy oaf," she whispered against his lips. "I know where you keep the spares."

The walk back to her house was silent, with Karl carrying her pack and holding her hand. Loretta hoped it would stay that way. She didn't have words for the way she was feeling, an uneasy mix of desire, fear, and a sadness she couldn't define. At least she wouldn't have to explain any of this to a disapproving Bess.

Karl hugged her as soon as she locked the door, groaning with his face against her neck. That ache was back in her heart, so deep it brought tears to her eyes.

"Come to bed," she whispered.

He nodded and followed her. Loretta unbuttoned his shirt, kissing him as she pushed it off of his shoulders. She moved down his jaw to his throat, his chest, his delightfully sensitive nipples, using her lips, tongue, and teeth while her hands were busy with his belt and pants.

He stood naked before her, the odd distance in his eyes evident nowhere else in his body. His wasn't so thick as Rhysto's, but more than satisfying. She was never sore after making love with Karl.

He took his turn with her more challenging skinsuit, undoing the buckles and catches as expertly as she ever did but taking his sweet time. He lowered her to the bed, his mouth following his hands, leaving Loretta with a deeper ache to match the one in her heart.

When Karl lay down beside her at last, Loretta pushed him onto his back. She thought she saw tears in his lovely hazel eyes for just a second before he pulled her down into a kiss.

Loretta gasped when he raised his hips and slipped inside her. He moved underneath her, his hands on her hips, rising and falling according to his rhythm that somehow matched her own.

Days away from him and her interrupted anticipation for Building brought Loretta to the brink of climax sooner than she would have liked, but stopping wasn't a possibility. She leaned forward with her hands on Karl's shoulders, and he stopped moving.

She rocked her own hips, grinding against him, fingers digging into his flesh. She couldn't look away from him or close her eyes, not even at the end. Karl put his hands into her hair and watched, breath quickening with hers, his mouth opening when hers did. Even when she cried out, he watched her through half-closed eyes.

None of her partners, consensual or not, had ever left Loretta feeling so exposed.

Karl grabbed her hips again, moving her less gently than before. He raised her body with his when he came, his deep moan and tight grip nearly enough to send Loretta over the edge once more. He finally drew in a sharp breath and relaxed, closing his eyes and smiling when she moved beside him.

She could feel his heart pounding under her cheek. He shifted enough to pull the blankets over both of them. When his breathing, and hers, calmed, Loretta raised up on one elbow. She pushed damp curls off his forehead, noticing for the first time that his hair was getting longer. She started to say so, but he leaned up to kiss her.

"We'll talk in the morning," he said. "Right now I just want to go to sleep with you in my arms and forget about everything."

That empty ache broke through, and Loretta hoped he'd forget whatever was making his eyes so sad while they slept. She didn't want to face one more painful or confusing thing, not for a long, long time.

Chapter 53

Karl got off the trolley in the main Mercantile District the next morning, only a few feet away from the clothiers he needed to visit later. Several other shops were close by, all of them full of a variety of fabrics and colors and stylish new designs that made his head hurt. Those Ministry of Decorum-approved shops had a steady stream of men and women passing through their doors.

This one was far more traditional and quiet, even predictable. Karl had never gone to any other, not even for events as formal as weddings. He didn't want to get comfortable with someone new and have to make too many decisions for such a difficult day as his nephew's funeral.

He started to walk past and peer into the other windows anyway in case anyone was watching before he realized what he was doing.

He'd gotten off several stops early to avoid the unlikely event of someone seeing him, and the even more unlikely event of that person caring. The habit of sneaking around, living this strange double life, was deeper than he'd imagined. He stopped so abruptly that an older woman bumped into him.

"I'm so sorry," he said. "Wasn't paying attention."

"I'll say you weren't! If you want to stare into space, at least move out of the way."

Karl drew back at her angry response. He watched her walk away, brown-hatted head held high. He shrugged and turned toward the shaw camps several blocks away. Karl couldn't fit worry about one more person into his aching and weary mind.

His night with Loretta and his cowardly predawn escape only made his stubborn indecision worse. His mother couldn't possibly have gotten the horrifying...thing anywhere else. Janie swore him to secrecy, not that he would have known who to tell, and she insisted the glass box had only been there for a week or so. That was a lot to trust from such a young child, but she had no reason to lie to him.

Apparently Loretta had, and he had no way to know how many times. That combined with the death of Rethia's baby was too much. No matter how badly it hurt.

The change in the shaw camps from his first trip out here might have seemed subtle if Karl didn't know the reason for it. The noise level was noticeably higher, for one thing. Where most of the camps had been grouped evenly together and organized, now there were several clusters with spaces in between.

The neat aisles between the camps had deteriorated too, with stacks of goods and equipment making travel difficult. Despite Rhysto's clear flaws as a man, he'd somehow managed to keep large groups of men from fighting with each other for a long time.

One camp toward the middle had several pilots and crew milling around pretending not to look at each other, and Karl wondered if the massive rectangular block of wood, rounded on one end, was Rhysto's ship. The dark gray airbag above was sleek and pointed on both ends, more like the military ships from Stensue than a normal balloon. It also looked it was overdue for repairs, with flattened areas all around.

Karl knew he'd imagined the general air of menace and danger on that first trip to meet Bill. Compared to now, it simply hadn't been there. Today he wished he had that damned revolver, still tucked away in his wardrobe.

Particularly in that teeming space where he was sure Rhysto formerly held strict control, he would have sworn he could smell the tension. He breathed much more easily as he approached the far end where the independent shaws still anchored. The chaos stayed behind him.

Karl recognized Calder standing guard outside Bill's immaculate camp. The slender red-haired man nodded at Karl, then stepped into the red-and-black tent. Karl tried not to think of Rullin doing the same thing on that first day. Bill's younger brother was nowhere in sight.

After several seconds, Calder stepped out and held the tent flap open. Karl shook his hand as he ducked inside. Bill stood in the middle of a room lit only by hanging gas lamps, beside a low, round table and several huge pillows on a thick wool rug.

"Karl Gilmore," Bill said. "I was sure Calder's eyes were deceiving him. Good to see you." Bill stepped past Karl's outstretched hand into a quick hug. "Please have a seat. I expect you have a most interesting reason for braving the madness out there alone."

THE THICK PILLOW on the ground wasn't what Karl expected, but it was more comfortable than it looked. Bill poured each of them a generous serving of what smelled like Northlands whiskey, setting the dark green tumblers on the table between them. An earthy scent Karl couldn't identify drifted from a bronze pyramid on the table.

It was hard to believe he'd just walked through the outskirts of Waldron's Gate rather than into some exotic land from an old storybook. They each held their glasses high.

"To adventure!" Bill said with a wicked half grin Karl couldn't help returning.

"And to routine," Karl said.

"Indeed. Now, what brings you to my most humble camp?"

"I don't know if I'd call it humble," Karl said. "It's certainly one of the more organized camps these days."

Bill laughed and poured each of them another.

"I never expected to give Rhysto any measure of respect, certainly in death. But he did keep the savages more or less in line as it turns out. The absence of leadership has been great for business, for the independents, at least. Even the worst of pilots have enough commissions to keep themselves occupied most days."

"Anyone suspect what's really going on yet?" Karl said.

"No, no one to be worried about," Bill said. "Parliament doesn't appreciate the dear man's absence, and I'd imagine at least a few of them are afraid he'll try to cash in on whatever favors they owe when he returns. Thus far everyone is assuming he'll come back from his bender at some point. We're not even up to his longest disappearing act yet. Meanwhile, they squabble. We profit."

"I'm glad to hear it. How've you been otherwise, Bill?"

The pilot smiled, but it was not a happy expression.

"Not as well as I'd hoped. About as well as I expected. My brother continues to defy me at every turn. I do at least seem to have him confined and properly guarded. I'm certain you know what my turn at a difficult question will be."

Karl drained his glass and stared at one of the lamps through it.

"Gemma's doing well," he said. "She's a pleasure to have around, if a little hard to keep up with."

"And her granddaughter?"

The pilot didn't sound or look like he was teasing. He sounded sympathetic. Especially with Bill's surprisingly warm welcome, Karl knew his instinct to come here was a good one.

He still hated every word he was about to say.

"Loretta is doing quite well herself. Her business is thriving. A lot more than I'd like."

"You don't strike me as the woman-locked-at-home-in-the-kitchen type," Bill said.

"No. My mother would have my hide for that. My aunts and sisters, too."

"Tell me what brings you out here, my friend."

Karl drew his knees close to his chest and wrapped his arms around them.

"She's broken at least one promise," he said. "Probably more than one that impacts my family. And something she did might have... I have a funeral to attend tomorrow. Loretta's actions probably helped bring it about. Before she made that promise, but the timing makes no difference in this case."

Bill closed his eyes, nodding.

"Family I understand, better than I'd like to," he said. "If only we could trade. Rullin is more terrified of you than he'll ever be of me. So you're furious with her and who she is, and you'll be heartbroken without her."

"That about sums it up. I know I can never live with her when I can't live with what she does, how she affects other people. I don't know what I could do that would have any effect on her. I doubt she cares much about me except as an easy mark."

Bill laughed and refilled both their glasses.

"That's where I come in," he said. "I'll tell you first that I've never seen her so taken with a man, and I've known her for a long time. Now, before I say another word, is this broken promise one you can forgive? I'm single for a reason, but I have more experience in these things than I care to admit. Think about it before you act, my friend. Loretta is an extraordinary woman."

Karl raised his eyebrows, then hid his face against his knees. None of his brief relationships, going back to when he was younger than Rullin, had ever gotten so deeply into his heart or his mind as this one.

He might never find another who fit him so well.

And if he was a lucky man, he'd never find another who could betray him and everything he believed so deeply as long as he lived.

"Whether I can forgive her or not isn't the question," he said, looking at Bill. "I can never trust her again. Getting my family involved in all of this isn't something I can get past. And yeah, she may have done some things I can't forgive. I have no doubt she will again."

"Just so," Bill said, nodding. "If you decide to go through with this, the way to get to Loretta is her past. It's more unpleasant than either of us want to imagine. Only Gemma was worth considering as family. She's worked hard to put it behind her and keep anyone else from learning about it."

"I might just make her angry enough to turn all of us in, Bill.

She'd cast a wide net if she wanted to. I don't want her in prison, but I don't think I could stand running into her on the street."

Karl didn't want to tell the pilot the truth. He knew he'd search for her in the middle of the night, trying to stop her from destroying anyone else's mind. Trying to distract her with lovemaking, convincing himself it was only to protect others in Waldron's Gate.

Knowing it would never be enough for either of them and never able to stop.

"She could hurt a great many people if she wanted to," the pilot said. "Or if she had to. That's why the threat of an investigation might be exactly what you need. If you can get her to leave before she manages to take us all down, that may be our best chance. Starting over somewhere else without a murder hanging over her head might even be a good thing."

Karl shook his head. "I can't just turn her in for Rhysto's murder. That would catch both of us, too."

Bill swallowed his whiskey, and Karl did the same.

"No, nothing so uncivilized as all that," Bill said. "All you need is someone to make it look like she's being investigated. Someone who has enough power to make her believe it. You already know a man like this, one who'd probably be quite happy to get back at our dear lady and rid himself of her at the same time."

"Mr. Norwood," Karl said. "I'd have to convince him, but he probably does know more than enough people to pull this off."

"As Director of the Posts, I'd imagine he has more inside information than anyone else in Waldron's Gate, maybe more than anyone else in Alterra. I can't imagine he doesn't use at least some of the same methods I do to obtain information."

Karl grunted, remembering how easily Bill extracted Rollin's letter. Mr. Norwood undoubtedly had faster and easier ways to gather dirt while keeping his perfectly manicured fingernails clean.

"That may be exactly what I needed, Bill. Well, except for the courage to go through with this."

Bill held up the bottle, but Karl shook his head.

"Courage does not seem to be a quality you lack," Bill said. "Once you make your decision, all will be clear. Not easy, I'm sure, but clear."

"This is probably far too much for me to ask," Karl said. "I've had just about enough to drink now to manage. If Loretta comes to you, will you help her? Take her away from here?"

Bill smiled.

"Only if you answer me now, and answer me truly. Will you follow behind, begging me to take you to her?"

Karl closed his eyes, trying to see into a future he didn't want to imagine.

"No, Bill. I won't. And when I ask, please don't tell me where she is."

Chapter 54

Karl looked up and down the street the next morning, wanting to be sure he had the correct house. He'd only been here once, and that at night. The address matched in the bright sunlight, at least what he remembered after such an unbelievable few weeks.

It would have to do. He didn't have long to get this over with and get back home for the funeral. He knocked on the cheerful yellow door.

Mr. and Mrs. Norwood both stood before him, neither dressed for company early on a weekend morning. Mrs. Norwood smiled at him, and Karl remembered she'd never seen his face that night.

Mr. Norwood glanced around the yard as he moved in front of his wife. He was not smiling.

"What do you want?" Mr. Norwood said.

"I need to speak with you for a few minutes, sir," Karl said. "I have another engagement, so I won't take up much of your time."

Mrs. Norwood leaned around her husband's arm.

"Would you like to come inside?" she said. "We've just finished breakfast, but I have cookies and cafei."

"No, thank you for the kind offer. I wouldn't like to disturb you as much as that, ma'am."

"Exactly, Roma," Mr. Norwood said. "This young man obviously has somewhere else to be. I'll be inside in a bit." He smiled at her, touching her shoulder. "I'd love to have cookies and cafei with you."

She blushed, then stepped back inside. Olsen Norwood stepped onto the porch and closed the door.

"If any of your friends are with you," he said, "you're wasting your time. Loretta's already been round here with her guard trying to shut me up."

Karl shook his head.

"No, only me. I don't know who my friends are anymore."

"I'll help you out, then," the older man said. "I'm not one of them. Why are you here?"

"I'm here because I know you don't like the way Loretta treated you," Karl said. "I have an idea that might solve both of our problems, but I'll need help."

"I'm listening."

Karl sat on the wide rail of the porch. Mr. Norwood took one of the rocking chairs with cushions covered in fabric that matched the door. Karl knew he was yet again out of his depth dealing with someone so powerful, and yet again left with no other choice.

"All of us, including you," Karl said, "are too caught up in all of this to actually turn Loretta in to any kind of authorities. The thing is, she's more afraid of being questioned than anything else. If you know a couple of soldiers or constables who owe you a favor, we can make this seem real enough to work."

The older man sat back, rubbing his chin.

"I know a few who can be trusted to keep their mouths shut," he said. "They'll follow my lead. What are you suggesting?" He scowled and shook his head. "And what's your name?"

"Karl. I'm from here, but I haven't lived here for a long time. That will have to do." Mr. Norwood stared at him for a moment, then nodded. Karl hoped he could get the words out around his aching heart. "If you help me, if this works, we'll convince Loretta to leave. To go away and not return."

"Why in the world would she do that?" Mr. Norwood said, hitting the arms of the rocker with his open palms. "Do you have any idea how much coin she makes here, from us alone?"

Karl stared at the pastel, flower-shaped rugs on the green painted floor. "No, not really. I know she's not poor. She'll do that because she could be a suspect in a crime. Whether she's innocent or not doesn't matter for our purposes. She doesn't want the investigation. If she thinks she's a suspect but doesn't suspect either of us, I believe she'll go."

"What do you get out of this, Karl?" Mr. Norwood said.

"Same thing you do, Olsen," Karl said, meeting the other man's gaze. "Loretta out of my life. You know how much trouble that will save both of us."

Mr. Norwood rocked, staring down at the rugs the same way Karl had. He spoke without looking up.

"What about Rhysto?"

Karl took a deep breath. This was probably even riskier than confronting Loretta. If he messed up here, he could end up the subject of any investigation himself.

"Rhysto is no longer a danger to you or anyone else," he said. "I give you my word, sir."

Karl forced himself not to turn away when Mr. Norwood looked up.

"And how do I know I can trust you?" he said. "You're tangled up with her somehow."

Karl let out a soft laugh, staring down the street to hide his face until he could get it under control.

"Being tangled up with her means I'm taking a bigger risk than you are. If we work together, this may all turn out for the best."

Mr. Norwood stood, hesitated, then held out his hand. Karl shook it.

"Sounds like we have an agreement," Mr. Norwood said. "If it turns out she's guilty or there's any hint of this business affecting my family, all bets are off. I'll find out who you are and what I can do about it."

"I feel exactly the same way about my family, Mr. Norwood. She's not guilty of this crime. Others, I'm sure, but not this one. If she does end up getting arrested because of something you or your people do, I will not be happy. Understand me?" Karl stood at his full height, watching Olsen Norwood draw back and nod. "Can you have everything arranged this evening? I know it's short notice, but we need to move quickly."

"Give me the details," Mr. Norwood said. "Let me know where they need to be, and I'll make it happen a lot sooner than that. The faster Loretta Schofield is out of our lives, the better."

Chapter 55

Loretta jumped at the chime sounding through her house, one she hadn't heard for a long time. The booming single note sounded like an ordinary clock striking the hour, but Bess would never trigger the urgent alarm without a damn good reason.

She locked and set security on her study door, glancing into her pantry to make sure everything was hidden before heading into the living room. Loretta flipped the round portrait of a stranger she claimed as her mother aside and spoke into the opening.

"What is it?"

"Constable Law," Bess said. "Three, in uniform. Not heavily armed, walking with a purpose."

"Let me talk to them, but listen in," Loretta said. "This might just be random questioning. Hold tight unless I signal."

She closed the speaking port and glanced around the living room. Everything was as it should be: perfectly normal to the outsider's eye and armed to the teeth. The small knife in her corset wouldn't be worth drawing against three people, but the small revolver hidden behind the sofa might. She wished she'd remembered to replace the one in the bookcase that she'd given to Karl.

Loretta slowed her breathing, using the time to arrange her hair and dress. She'd been hoping Karl would stop by that evening, so she'd chosen a bit more of a feminine look than she sometimes did. Flowing hair and enhanced cleavage might come in handy even before her lover arrived.

She waited several seconds after the sharp knocks to open the door. Two young men and a middle-aged woman waited. All three wore dark blue uniforms and carried the distinctive Bronzed Revolvers, far more powerful than Loretta's hidden illicit gun.

"Loretta Schofield?" the woman said.

"Yes, that's me. Can I help you?"

"Good afternoon. I'm Constable Law Detective Warstan. My deputies and I are investigating the disappearance of a young woman, Sophie Jeddason. May we ask you a few questions? We won't take up much of your time."

Loretta's heart pounded, but relief tempered the fear. Sophie was bad, especially since someone had obviously followed the trail here. Rhysto and any number of other secrets would have been far worse.

"Of course, please come in."

She held the door open and watched as they arranged themselves on the long sofa. The men examined the room, then kept their eyes on their leader. The detective never looked away from Loretta.

"Do you know someone by that name?" Detective Warstan said, opening a small notebook.

"I employed Ms. Jeddason for a brief time, yes," Loretta said. "Just a bit of cleaning and such. I haven't heard from her for a while now."

"Did she say anything to you about leaving?"

Loretta's mind raced, trying to find the safest path. Leaving would be a convenient story, but only if no one else had said otherwise.

"Not that I remember. She was the private sort, kept herself to herself. I was disappointed when she stopped turning up, but she was very young. I hope nothing's happened to her."

"That's what we're going to find out," the detective said. "How did you come to hire Ms. Jeddason? Did you know her family?"

"No, I'm not even sure where she's from. I found her the usual way with such things, by asking around of other girls in her line of work."

Detective Warstan raised her eyebrows as she made a note.

"That's interesting, Ms. Schofield. It seems this young woman wasn't employed in this part of Waldron's Gate at all before a couple of months ago. She was a working girl, though. Out at the Convenience."

"Then I'm glad I gave her a way out of that sort of life," Loretta said. "Even for a brief time. I'm sure you've spoken to people who knew her there. They probably know more of her background."

"We've spoken to several people in that part of the city, people of various backgrounds. A few from far north of here, much like Ms. Jeddason. That's how we found our way to you."

Loretta stared at the detective, trying not to let her imagination get the best of her. She didn't dare look at the two men and show her unease, but she couldn't let this line of questioning continue.

"I'm glad to help in any way I can," she said. "I'm afraid I simply don't have much to tell. Sophie worked hard, and she was a pleasure to have around. If something has happened to her, I regret not informing you when she first missed her arranged time with me."

"We regret that as well, ma'am," one of the young men said. "I'm sorry if I'm out of line, Detective, but with Ms. Schofield living alone here, I think we should tell her the rest."

Detective Warstan stared hard at him for several seconds, nodded, and turned to Loretta.

"It seems Ms. Jeddason was known to frequent the shaw camps during her previous employment. In questioning the pilots and other crew, we learned of another disappearance at around the same time. Are you familiar with a pilot called Rhysto? No one seems to know what his surname is."

"Or they won't admit it," the other man said.

Loretta chewed on her tongue to keep her nerves from blurting out that she'd never known, either. The room seemed to be shrinking around her, the chair turning into an interrogation cage.

"I've heard the name Rhysto in the gossip rags," Loretta said. "I can't help you more than that."

This time Detective Warstan made a note while still watching Loretta's eyes.

"That's also quite interesting," she said. "More than one person at the shaw camps suggested you should be our next visit." She closed the notebook and leaned forward. "Any idea why several people in less desirable parts of the city have mentioned you, Ms. Schofield?"

Loretta waited long enough to breathe once, hoping to calm her heartbeat enough to speak normally.

"Other than visiting when the shaws arrive to see what goods they carry, I'm no more familiar with them than anyone else. May I ask if I'm being accused of something, please?"

"We're not accusing anyone," Detective Warstan said. "Besides our suspicions of this Rhysto. We've heard more than enough about him to be cautious. With so many people linking you with Ms. Jeddason, you should be cautious, too." She stood, and the men joined her. "We won't bother you anymore today, ma'am. But I would like to speak with you again in a few days' time. We need to follow up with anyone who has a similar background in cases like this."

Loretta stood, knowing her full skirt would cover her shaking knees and cold sweat. She hoped none of them would want to shake her hand. That would hide neither.

"I'd planned to be out of town later in the week," she said.

The detective shook her head once.

"We'd prefer it if you didn't leave town just now, Ms. Schofield. I certainly hope your plans can be postponed."

Loretta tried to smile. "I'll see what I can do."

"Thank you for your time, and we'll be in touch in a couple of days. Please be sure your houseguest from the Northlands is here. Your grandmother, I believe? I'd like to speak to her as well."

All three of them left without looking back.

Loretta stood, one hand on the doorknob, one on her stomach, breathing as slowly as she could.

Too much. They knew far too much. And she would have bet her life they knew much more than they'd let on. The thought of anyone knowing where she came from, maybe even involving her family, stopped her brain cold.

She finally opened the door. Bess was there before Loretta finished speaking her name.

"Go back inside, Loretta. I heard."

"They know, Bess. They know everything."

"Sit down, catch your breath. They probably know more than they're admitting, but beyond that you're just guessing." Bess brought two glasses and the nearly empty bottle of whiskey from Joffrey Columns, the bottle Karl brought to her a lifetime ago. "Don't make it worse than it already is."

"Worse?" Loretta said. "They know about Sophie and Rhysto, my links to the shaws and the Convenience, even about the Northlands and Gemma. What can make this worse?"

Loretta swallowed the harsh, clear liquid without taking a breath. Bess refilled the glass.

"We don't know how much they know about any of those things," she said. "They're trying to rattle you, Loretta. That's standard when they don't have much to go on. Don't do their jobs for them."

"Who did this? Who told them about me?"

Loretta forced herself to drink a small sip instead of the entire shot.

"That's not worth guessing about, is it?" Bess said. "You do know several people in both places. I know I didn't meet all of your clients, either, so that's no help. Trying to figure that out is a waste of our time."

"But not a waste of their time!"

Loretta finished her drink as she walked in a circle around the room. Bess was right about one thing. Her heart was pounding harder than before.

"Stop, listen to me," Bess said. "You can always get away for a little while. You did that before, and no one was the wiser."

"Bess, they knew about Gemma. Bloody Rhysto knew when I went north with Bill. What makes you think I can leave now without the whole of Constable Law right behind me?"

The guard took a deep breath, then swallowed her own whiskey.

"They never mentioned Joffrey Columns, did they?" she said. "No one knows about Gemma's house out there, and no one seems to know about Karl. Not even his own mother. I don't like it any more than I did before, but as long as you stay away from that white beast, that's where you go."

Loretta let out a breath she felt like she'd been holding since the alert chime not twenty minutes ago. Joffrey Columns was the only place she could be safe until she figured out what to do next, and she wanted to keep up with Gemma's progress on the larger Dragon anyway.

No matter what Detective Warstan said, she was not about to sit and wait for some kind of net to close around her. Or worse, for her past to catch up to her at last and drag her north into The Pit.

"You're right, Bess, as you so often are. Strange as it sounds, that might be the safest place in Alterra for me right now."

Chapter 56

Karl turned at a hand on his shoulder. He was glad of any excuse that let him look away from the tiny, freshly filled grave. George was standing behind him, nearly unrecognizable in a dark suit with his unruly brown hair tamed down. He stepped forward and shook Arthur Gilmore's hand.

"I'm sorry for your loss, sir," George said. "But I'm glad to see you again."

"George Wood," Karl's father said, nodding. "I don't think I've seen you since you and Karl here were in training together. Are your parents well?"

"Yes sir. They both send their condolences. When everything calms down, they'd love to have the two of you over for dinner. Mind if I borrow Karl for a few minutes?"

"Not at all," Karl's father said. "He needs a break from all of this. He's all that's kept Klia and Rethia from falling apart." The older man pulled Karl into a one-armed hug. "Comes from everything he's learned over the past ten years, taking care of people. I'm damn proud of him."

"Thank you, Father,' Karl said. "I'll be right over here."

Karl managed to walk several feet before his jaw dropped and his eyes widened. George stood against the elaborate wrought-iron fence of the small cemetery with his back turned, apparently looking at the stand of oak trees just beyond, but Karl saw his shoulders shaking.

"What was that?" George said, wiping tears from his eyes.

"Damned if I know." Karl was amazed at how good laughter felt, even if he was doing everything he could to keep it quiet. "If you hadn't been standing right there, no one could convince me I didn't hallucinate the whole thing."

"Well, I'll back you up with whoever you need me to. That's the best thing I've heard in years, buddy. You doing okay?"

Karl finally caught his breath and managed a small smile. There were so many things George didn't know, things he wasn't ready to talk to anyone about yet. Maybe never.

"It's been a rough few days. We're getting through. I really do appreciate you coming all the way out here, Georgie. That means a lot to me. Things calm out at the Columns?"

"No matter what else is going on, I hate this for Rethia," George said. "She was nicer to me than my own sisters ever were. Wish I could do more." He shook his head slowly. "This might not be the best time to get into the rest. We can talk later."

"My father's right about me needing a break from thinking about this." Karl hoped he wasn't making a mistake, letting himself in for more stress and nonsense when he had more than he could deal with already. "Talk to me now."

"Things are calm enough, mostly," George said. "The 'sters are a little restless. Some of the patients too, but nothing to worry about. Gemma's the one I'm worried about."

Karl tried to ignore the lurch in his guts, that deep certainty that he'd overlooked something crucial.

"Tell me, George."

"I was out there yesterday, taking her food like you asked. She looks ten years older, like she hasn't slept in a month. She was wandering around and sort of muttering to herself the whole time I was there."

"Could you tell what had her so upset?" Karl said.

"She kept looking at her workroom," George said. "The bedroom with all her tools in it. I think she was determined to wait until I left, but I'd bet a month's salary she was right back in there as soon as I did."

Karl rubbed his temples, trying his best to sort through what his friend knew and didn't know. He'd forgotten all about the larger Dragon Gemma was building for Loretta. If she took that with her, she'd do even more damage with no one to stop her. He couldn't tell George about this, either.

He was in the middle of driving away a woman he was well over halfway in love with, probably right this second, in part because she hid so much from him.

Since she'd come into his life, Karl wasn't behaving any better.

"Thanks for checking on Gemma," Karl said. "We probably need to get her to a doctor. Spending time out there might not be good for her. We don't know how someone who dreams is affected by being around all those 'sters. Do you think you can get her to stay in my rooms for a day, until I get back out there?"

"Not asking for much, are you?" George smiled when he said it, but Karl's guilt drove even deeper into his belly. "Yeah, that shouldn't be any problem. She seems to like me for some reason. It's been a long damned time since anyone lived out there, so something strange could be going on."

"The ones they were hiding from in the first place are still around," Karl said. "This will help me out more than you know. I've got a few things to wrap up here, but I'll be there as soon as I can."

"Sure thing, Karl. Any idea what I should tell her about why I'm dragging her back to your palatial estate?"

"Not really. Tell her you have to repair something, maybe that her well is going dry. Just don't let anyone know where she is, George. No one. If she is sick, we don't want it to get out why."

George shook his head and clapped Karl on the back.

"Brilliant as always. I'll take care of her."

Karl watched George walk away, opening his mouth to call his friend back more than once. If this worked, the latest phase of this horrible plan of his, he'd just managed to put himself in charge of Loretta's grandmother once she was gone.

A woman nearly as innocent as any of his youngest family

members, who loved her bobbin very much. A woman who would not be the least bit happy with Karl for deceiving her or her granddaughter.

What he would tell Gemma might not be as hard to work out as where she was supposed to live after all of this. Worst of all, he had no intention of admitting any of it to anyone who didn't already know.

Karl actually drew breath to call out, then held it until George turned out of sight.

His plan was in motion, for better or for worse. Karl hoped he could live with the fallout.

Chapter 57

Loretta stood with the men and women between the rocky coast and the iron fence around Joffrey Columns, watching many of the same couples pair up and walk inside. The matches were clear and long-lasting, at least compared to how such things usually went.

She'd gone in on her own more often than Karl would have approved of, frequently during the week when almost no one else waited. Seeking out and paying one of the more desperate fishermen had been well worth her time, and her coin. The man never hesitated to bring her day or night. More importantly, he never asked questions.

She'd never even needed George's badge, but she'd made sure to keep it with her for every trip out here. Loretta worked her way over to the side as each person left the group, closer to the deep shadows of a huge oak tree with every departure.

No one ever had a problem getting in or leaving, but she felt terribly exposed. The detective hadn't mentioned her visits out here, but she'd been involved in this line of work long enough to know raids and arrests were always a possibility. She waited several minutes after the last two joined up and disappeared through the gap in the fence before she followed.

The paradox of feeling safer inside the gray stone walls of the asylum was not lost on Loretta, but that didn't change how much more easily she breathed. This was a routine she knew, almost as well as the one she left behind in Waldron's Gate. Even if the detectives did know she was here, finding her wouldn't be an easy matter.

She crossed the dark lawn and let herself into Karl's building. Loretta paused outside the door to his apartment, thinking about staying there for the night. He'd be in Waldron's Gate for at least one more day. The brick tunnel was unpleasant enough even when she knew the sun was only a short climb away. At night, the moldy air inside was thick and heavy against her skin, and the smell lingered almost as badly as the reek of the monsters.

She touched the scuffed door with her fingertips, considering. She'd had her own key for a few weeks now, and she could be warm in Karl's bed, even if by herself, within a few minutes. The dreary hike out to Gemma's took almost half an hour.

The shared bath here was a far less pleasant prospect. Gemma, true to form, had the large tub at her house supplied with more hot water than everyone here was forced to share. A long, hot bath finally outweighed an early bedtime, and Loretta continued on.

Her doctor's dress and forged identification had never been tested, and this night was no exception. Loretta made it into the tunnels without seeing another person.

She sent a mental thank you to George for keeping the lanterns restocked at this end. The brighter tunnel suggested he might have repaired and cleaned some of the dim lights as well.

And she sent thanks to herself for keeping so many supplies at her grandmother's house. She carried her backpack with only a few weeks' worth of coin, her Dragon and tripod, her skinsuit, and her normal supply of weapons. Trying to drag a heavy case out here by herself would have kept her in Karl's rooms for certain.

The puzzle of who'd turned her in, or at least linked her to Sophie and Rhysto, gnawed at her mind as she walked. Bess was right about the daunting number of possibilities. Loretta's stomach churned at the thought of disappearing when the detective had all but told her not to.

The risk of increasing the intensity of the search by dropping out of sight rested uneasily against her fear of exposure. She couldn't imagine that balance shifting anytime soon.

Loretta turned to the last key on her ring and froze, her hand a few inches away from the door at the top of the last tunnel. Nothing looked different by the shifting lantern light, and she didn't hear or smell anything unusual.

Her flesh crawled anyway.

She turned in a circle, all her senses on high, but still found nothing. Maybe she'd spent too long living on suspicion and paranoia. This routine would seem insane to just about everyone else, but for whatever reason, it worked. She smiled, wondering if the stability itself was what made her uncomfortable.

She opened the door to her grandmother's house.

"Gemma?"

The house was warm with a few lights on, but her grandmother was nowhere to be seen, or heard. Loretta turned the lights up, hand on her knife despite her fleeting confidence. Gemma hadn't ventured back to Karl's apartment, Loretta's house, or anywhere else since she settled in here.

For whatever reason, she loved this place. And yet she wasn't here.

Loretta walked over to the windows, knowing the failing light wasn't going to reveal much. She could barely see the fence and yard outlined in deep pink. Going outside and getting a full blast of the stench wasn't on her list of evening activities, no matter where her grandmother had gotten herself to.

Unless...unless Gemma had managed to hurt herself out in the yard. Nothing like that had ever happened before, but she was nearly forty years Loretta's senior.

She glanced around one more time, noticing her larger Dragon through the workroom's open door. It looked like it was very nearly complete. Loretta had been pushing harder on this project than she had on any other, anxious to have it in her hands.

The concentrated groups of Builders here would be the ideal place for testing, as long as she could keep it to herself. She tapped her foot, tempted to investigate and wait for Gemma to come back from wherever she'd gone.

The idea of the older woman wounded and needing help pushed her out the door with her hand over her nose. The lantern didn't light much of the yard, but what she could see was as empty as the house.

Loretta detoured around the garden until she saw the edge of the fence. No one was out here, either. She'd never seen Gemma behind the house, so she turned to go back inside and wait.

Loretta almost dropped the lantern at the sight of a man standing in the open door.

LORETTA RECOGNIZED KARL'S SHAPE, his shoulders, his hair, his long limbs. He didn't move, only stood there watching her, arms at his sides. The hand on her chest, over her thundering heart, wanted to curl into a fist and beat him until he begged her to stop.

"Why are you so damn determined to scare the life out of me everywhere I go lately?"

He didn't move or speak. Loretta walked toward him, then stopped in her tracks. The unease, the certainty that something was wrong, was back full force.

Her flesh again seemed to crawl all over her body. She'd never felt that warning so strongly when nothing was actually threatening her.

"Did you follow me out here?" she said.

"No. I was here already."

His voice sounded odd, strained and deeper than normal. Loretta finally remembered the door to the guest room being closed when she walked in.

That was exactly what a safe routine did. She was too bloody soft and trusting.

"Where's Gemma, Karl? What's going on?"

She moved forward again, much more slowly.

"Gemma's fine," he said. "She's safe."

"Safe from what? Has someone been out here? Is she hurt?"

He shook his head. She was close enough to see his face in the lantern light. He looked like he hadn't slept the whole time he'd been back in Waldron's Gate, face puffy and eyes red, but his expression was too blank. Too neutral.

"She's not hurt," Karl said. "But she was well on her way. She's been working much too hard, Loretta. Care to tell me why?"

"I don't know what I'd say," she said. "Gemma gets into phases like that sometimes, when she has an idea that won't let her rest. Then she sleeps for a day or two. Where is she?"

He finally moved, crossing his arms and leaning against the door frame.

"She's safe," he said. "She's getting some rest. That's enough."

"No, that's not enough. What's going on here? She's my grand-mother, Karl."

"You're right, she is," he said, nodding. "That makes this whole thing worse. What critical project was worth pushing herself to exhaustion? Or you pushing her?"

"Karl, please," she whispered, reaching toward him. He didn't move. "What's going on? What's happened?"

"I'm not the one who needs to be answering questions, Loretta. This game has gone on long enough."

"What game? At least tell me what I've done."

But she knew. Whoever set the detectives on her trail had said one too many things to Karl, if it hadn't been those same detectives.

This man knew more about her than almost anyone alive. She had to figure out how bad the damage was.

"Things will go a lot easier for both of us," he said, "if *you* tell *me* what you've done. I don't think you can, though. Do you know what killed the baby? My nephew?"

"No," she whispered.

"I spoke to the doctor yesterday," Karl said. "Turns out his brain stopped developing several weeks ago. Remarkably close to the night we met, don't you think?"

"If that was me, sorry doesn't even come close." Loretta struggled to keep the idea from taking root in her mind. "Sometimes those things just happen with babies."

"Sorry isn't going to make a damned bit of difference," Karl said. "Even if you did actually mean it. I'm afraid I've lost my ability to believe in coincidence since I got to know you. There was another baby, a baby monster, born the same night you were outside my sister's house. That baby burned itself, over and over again. Any time it opened its eyes. The second my nephew died, that baby burned itself to death. It died screaming, Loretta."

"If I..." Loretta swallowed, fighting her rising gorge. "I'd never do anything like that on purpose. You have to know that."

"I don't believe you," he said. "I told you your Building was driving people insane, remember? Sending them out here for a permanent stay. Turns out one of the newest residents of this asylum lived only a few blocks away from my parents. That's how I knew where to find you the other night. Still going to tell me you haven't been Building again? That you'd never hurt anyone on purpose?"

"No, Karl, I'm not. I have been Building." Loretta finally knew the truth, and the fear of telling it, might be a smaller risk than losing him. Or the risk of him turning on her, turning her in. "Gemma's been making something to keep me from having to do that so much, something we can use here. I won't have to go out there anymore."

Karl shook his head slowly. "Forget it. I haven't been completely honest with you, either. Sorry about that. The people we work with, one at a time? Those people do stay calmer, sure. But the monsters and the other patients, not so much. What you do to them bleeds through, just like out in Waldron's Gate. You sweep everyone up in your path, and you don't give a damn who you hurt. I wasn't going to let it go on much longer."

The anger she'd been waiting for finally pushed the fear and sadness to the side.

"What, once I'd finished training you?" she nearly shouted. "Is that it?"

"Sure, if that's what it takes to bring all of this to an end. Let's go with that. Yes, Loretta. I was using you."

Cold deeper than the tunnel flooded up from her belly, taking over her whole body in an instant.

At least it soothed her shattered heart.

"Bring it to an end?" she said. "You should have said so first thing. I wouldn't have wasted so much of your time." She walked forward, meaning to push past him into the house. "I'll get my things, collect Gemma, and we'll leave you in peace."

Karl held one arm across the door.

"No. You're not taking her anywhere. She probably needs a doctor, and she needs rest more than anything. You can go." He took a deep breath. "You *should* go, but she's staying."

"Get out of my way, Karl. I can't go anywhere until I get back to the tunnel. And I will be taking my grandmother." Loretta couldn't find her anger in the cold. She'd have to do the best she could from memory. "Move, or I'll move you myself."

"Be my guest. You'll have to kill me."

Loretta drew her knife, horrified at how badly her hand was shaking. Her voice was worse.

"At least tell me who did this, Karl. Who turned you against me?"

He laughed. The hollow, desolate sound nearly stopped Loretta's heart.

"That's easy," Karl said. "On top of everything else, on the same day my nephew died, my youngest sister found that thing you sold to my mother behind my back. My *twelve-year-old* sister. You turned me against you, Loretta. Take your Dragon, your weapons, whatever you need. Just go."

He stepped back into the house, leaving her way clear. Loretta managed to get her knife back into the sheath.

She hoped he would look away or maybe stare at the floor. Karl's icy gaze never wavered as he watched her walk past.

She glanced into the workroom again, but the larger Dragon was still in several pieces. No one besides Gemma would be able to finish it. It would have to wait for another day.

She picked up her pack and tripod, then turned back. Karl was still watching her.

"Karl, I... I thought we... Leaving wasn't what I expected between us."

He shrugged.

"Yeah, me neither. And yet here we are."

She nodded and closed her eyes for a few beats of her heart.

"Goodbye, Karl."

Chapter 58

LORETTA MADE it as far as back into the tunnel. When her boots caught on the uneven bricks, she stopped with one hand on the rough wall. Her chest felt full of water, heavy and hot, and the burning pressure rose into her throat.

She swallowed a few times, trying to stop everything from bursting out of her too fast to survive, or stop. She held her breath, but that only let her gasp turn into a moan.

"No, I will not give in to this," she whispered, walking a few steps. "Not over anyone. Not over any man. Not over Karl..."

His name was too much, and Loretta leaned against the wall with her face in her hands. She hadn't cried like this for years, not since she'd finally gotten away from the evil people who raised her.

She'd never thought anything would push the fear of seeing them again aside, make it seem like a child's game. Karl's words and his cold eyes did both.

She could hate the idea all she wanted to, but Loretta needed to get herself away and trust Karl to take care of Gemma. She would return and settle that matter when the time was right.

The last thing she wanted was for him to come down into the tunnel and find her like this. She wasn't sure if his sympathy or his pity would be worse, and she had no intention of finding out. Loretta kept going.

Her tears didn't slow, but her hands' shaking did as she unlocked each of the gates. If she couldn't stay out here, she had to clear her head enough to figure out where to go next. Letting the detective drag her further into her past or into jail was not an option.

Her clients might owe her some sort of loyalty for the risks she took for them, but Loretta didn't fool herself. That loyalty would not go so far as hiding a fugitive being investigated for a murder.

The Ministry of Decorum would find some way to make short work of the lot of them, even if new laws had to be forced through in record speed. The number of various sorts of Ministry workers who did business with her wouldn't matter if a scandal like this went public.

She locked the last gate behind her and stood still, breathing deeply to try to stop her tears. Keeping her mind off of Karl was helping, even if her dread of the next few days was only getting worse.

The only reasonable thing she could imagine was asking Bill for help. The last time she'd felt like this, cornered with nowhere else to go, he was only one person she could turn to. Bill had never let her down, and he was fond enough of Gemma to help get her away once things calmed down.

Loretta knew she'd drawn on his good will more than she ever had over the past few weeks, but this was a chance worth taking. Her coin and treasure soothed the way with so many things. The only more effective method she knew for that was her body, and sharing Bill's bed was a pleasure.

Not nearly as pleasant as Karl, but he had to stay out of her mind. She didn't need that unexpected awful pain jumbling her thinking right now.

Loretta opened the door at the top of the ladder, listening and watching. All was quiet in the hallway. She headed toward the exit, and toward Karl's apartment.

As far as she knew, Rullin was still part of Bill's camp. She wasn't sure she could trust her own restraint around Bill's brother if he came anywhere near her.

Taking her anger at Karl, and her heartache, out on the young man might not be fair, but it certainly would be satisfying.

Lost in soothing contemplation of exactly how she'd deprive Rullin of what little sanity he had, she turned the corner and nearly ran into two people.

"Oh, excuse us, doctor."

"So sorry. We weren't paying attention."

The man and woman were both wearing the same gray clothing she was, and both seemed scared to death that she was about to beat them. Letting them see just how badly she was startled could only make things worse.

"You certainly weren't paying attention," Loretta said. "You could have knocked me down! Get to where you're going, now, and keep your eyes open along the way. Or if you prefer, I could assign you extra duties this weekend?"

They both shook their heads and nearly ran down the hall without looking back. Loretta managed to keep herself from smiling until they were out of sight. Childish it may have been, but she felt a tiny bit better.

When she walked by Karl's door, she paused again.

No, thinking about the time she'd spent there with him wouldn't do, not one bit. She still had to get out of here, not an easy thing even with hardly any guards during the week and none on the weekend. She could go back to the patient wing, perhaps spend a restless night in the still-empty room across from Mr. Otis. For all she'd be likely to sleep, Loretta would be just as well off waiting in the empty shed down by the docks.

Going into Karl's room now could only cause harm, especially if he walked in and found her there.

That heat and heaviness started up in her chest again, trying to squeeze her heart into a million pieces.

Maybe being able to get in at all wasn't a good thing. Loretta pulled her keys out, slipped the room key off the ring, and knelt. The gap under the door was small, but she should be able to manage.

She took a deep breath when the ache rose into her throat again.

He hadn't left any space for a future between them. She needed to do the same.

"Goodbye, Karl," she whispered, pushing the key under the door and out of reach.

She nearly ran down the hall toward the exit, not wanting the ridiculous tears to take over her body yet again. Loretta closed the outside door and leaned against it, breathing in the cool night air until she was calmer. The only thing that might keep her calm would be the waves against the rocks. And no chance of anyone walking in on her. Early boats were always willing to ferry more than cargo back to Swan's Gate.

Now was the time for getting herself away and safe. Falling into an irrational emotional pit wouldn't do anyone any good.

She couldn't see or hear anyone else on the lawn, not a big surprise since it must be near midnight. Loretta would send a courier to Bill the second she got back to Waldron's Gate, before Constable Law ever noticed she'd been gone.

She laughed under her breath as she walked, imagining using the posts instead and sending Mr. Norwood into some kind of frenzy. Just a few letters saying she was retreating for now, that she'd return with allies to seek her revenge upon him and everyone he held dear, should give the man fits.

Halfway between Karl s building and the iron fence, Loretta froze.

This part of the lawn was pitch dark, right between two weak lights. It was silent, too, but she was positive she'd heard something moving.

She drew both of her belt knives and turned to her right, skin rippling with gooseflesh. That sounded like...fabric, like a sheet rippled across a bed.

She held the knives in front of her face, expecting a sack thrown across her head at any second.

Loretta whirled, hearing the same thing from behind her and higher up.

Was she hearing more than one of them, or were her nerves more frayed than she'd realized? This useless dress didn't have anywhere to carry her revolver, and she was afraid to take the time to dig into her pack.

Rullin flashed through her mind again, somehow escaped from Bill and bringing his own allies to force her into submission at last.

The fabric rustled again, this time much closer and directly overhead.

"Come on, then, damn you! What are you waiting for!"

Strong arms grabbed Loretta from behind, squeezing too tight for her to turn.

Before she could swing the knives back, her feet left the ground, and she dropped one of the blades. Some kind of harness, her attacker suspended in the trees, it had to be.

Only she was above the trees and getting higher, the noise of the fabric flapping all around her.

Loretta looked down and saw thick, muscled arms holding her. Pure white arms, glowing in the faint light of a crescent moon, arms that ended in hands with heavy claws.

Loretta screamed, holding the knife she hadn't dropped above the monster's arm but too afraid to use it. They had to be over a hundred feet off the ground already.

She could see the buildings of Joffrey Columns dropping away, the lights of the village beyond the lake in the distance. If she hurt the thing, it might drop her.

Why hadn't the reek of the monster warned her?

Now they were higher than any airship and rising. She'd never survive the fall. The roaring wind made it hard to breathe, but she shouted as loud as she could.

"Stop, please! Someone help!"

The creature banked, heading away from the lights, and Loretta screamed again.

The Fog rose up before her, faint in the darkness but making a barricade around the water as far as she could see.

She wouldn't survive in there; no one could.

As the white wall drew closer, she tried to pull the monster's hands away despite the fall.

It was like trying to move stone.
She screamed one last time as the Fog swallowed them.

Chapter 59

Karl opened the front door of Loretta's house to Gemma humming
and talking to herself in the kitchen. He grunted, shaking his head a
little. No, this was Gemma's house now, not Loretta's.

Thinking anything else wasn't going to help him get over those
violet eyes.

"Mind if I work around you, Karl?" George said from behind him.
"Wouldn't want to interrupt your staring-into-thin-air time."

George pushed the bundle he was carrying against Karl's back.
Karl walked into Gemma's workroom, found one of the few remaining
empty spaces, and waited for his friend to do the same.

"Is that what she was doing before, Georgie? The way she's talking
to herself?"

"No, not even close," George said. "She sounded like one of the
patients that day, like she couldn't stop herself. If my own grandmother is any indication, she's working up a hell of a to-do list for us
in there."

Karl stretched with his hands pressed against the small of his
back.

"Is that the last of it?" he said.

"That's it. Unless someone bothers to inspect the chimney enough
to find her filters, no one will ever know she was there. The 'sters will

have some nice, fat rabbits once they get done with what's left of her garden."

Gemma spoke from the doorway.

"Oh, thank you for bringing all of this inside!"

Her good color and high spirits went a long way toward convincing Karl that she'd recovered. Sometimes a few days of sleep, and less stress, was enough.

"I'm sorry we had to move you again," George said, sitting down and wiping sweat from his face. "Once that well started to fail, the repairs were more than I could handle."

"It's just as well, dears," Gemma said. "Someone really should keep up Loretta's lovely house until she gets back."

She bustled out of the room, already muttering again. George raised his eyebrows and half smiled at Karl.

"I guess *someone* should be optimistic around here," he said. "Sorry, Karl. I know this only makes it worse."

"Have they found anything yet?" Karl said.

Karl didn't want to admit what he was really asking.

Had they found a body? Her body?

"They might not find her or anyone else," George said. "You know that. People scream out there all the damned time."

"Yeah, but not right outside the residences like that," Karl said. "And not half an hour after she left the house. You told me yourself someone pushed a key under my door just a couple of minutes before the scream. The 'sters went crazy that night, and the patients did too. They even found her knife."

George scowled. "They found a knife, man. Solid black, copper wire, no initials or anything on it. And you told me you set it up so she'd have to leave, then made sure she knew you weren't kidding. I know this stinks, but don't let your mind make it worse than it already is." Karl shook his head and looked away. "Come on. Let's go see how long our list is going to be."

Gemma hadn't been daunted by the small hearths once she figured out how the gas lines worked. Karl and George had already carried her electrical supplies into the kitchen, and she was well on the way to getting everything reassembled.

She looked up when they walked in, and she did indeed have a long handwritten list on the counter. Karl knew it would keep his mind off of sending Loretta away that night at the caretaker's house, likely to her death.

"This is quite a list you have here, Gemma," George said, shaking his head.

"I don't know how we can afford all of this," Karl said, reading over George's shoulder. "We need to pay the guards to stay on, too, at least part of the time. I don't earn this many ritterns in a month."

Gemma patted Karl's shoulder.

"Oh, you don't know my granddaughter as well as you think," she said. "She'll have plenty of coin, especially since she had to leave in a hurry."

"She probably did," Karl said. "Does, I mean. That doesn't mean we can get to it."

Gemma put her hands on her hips.

"You just haven't asked the right person. Who do you think designed this cozy little house? I know where all the secrets are, at least as well as my bobbin does." She crossed the small room and went into the pantry. "Well, come along. I'll need someone to help carry things."

"How much coin could she possibly have stashed in a pantry?" George said.

Karl shrugged and followed George into the tiny room. Both men stared as Gemma pulled the lamp down and adjusted part of it. Both gaped when she sank into the floor.

"Don't worry," she said. "This is exactly how it's supposed to work." She grinned as the floorboards continued to sink and lights came on in the basement Karl had never suspected existed. "George should go next, I think. He doesn't weigh a lot more than I do."

"What could that possibly have to do with it?" Karl said, hoping she didn't expect them to follow her down there.

"Did you know this place had a basement, Karl?" George said.

"Not a clue," Karl said. "All I ever saw was a cellar." The floor slid back into place. "I think that's your ride."

"What, I'm supposed to just stand on the floor and hope nothing bad happens?"

The smaller man was laughing, but he stepped back from the movable boards.

"If you want to see this treasure chest, you do," Karl said. "And I'm damn sure not going first if it works by weight."

George stepped forward, holding the shelves for balance, until he stood on the same spot Gemma had. The boards floated down just as smoothly as they had before. In less than a minute, George stood beside Gemma.

"If you designed this place," George said, "why didn't you put in something to hold onto?"

"Don't be silly, George," Gemma said. "How would I hide a handrail in the middle of the pantry?" She moved out of sight, and Karl heard metallic thumps and jingles. "Karl, I believe this is close to your weight now."

"And if it's not?"

Karl looked around again, though he knew there was no door in the pantry.

"If it's too far off, the floor won't move at all," Gemma said. "That's how it's designed to work, so no one can get down here uninvited."

Karl watched the floor move back up, thinking back on the things Gemma designed that did work. Pretty much everything, at least that he'd seen.

None of them involved him dropping onto a basement floor, one he couldn't then get back out of. Even if he didn't break both legs, he'd be trapped down there with George and Gemma.

That might not be the best thing to dwell on. He couldn't stop himself from grabbing for the shelves when he moved downward.

As soon as his eyes cleared the pantry floor, Karl forgot about being afraid. The whole space glowed, as if they were inside one of his mother's finest cooking pots. Copper shelves lined the walls, and a huge table made of different metals took up the center.

"What is this, Gemma?" he said when he caught his breath.

"It's a target, of course," she said. "For the Dragon."

"Same as the one at your place, just a lot more powerful," Karl said, tracing the circles on the table. "So this would work from a lot farther away."

"What are you two talking about?" George said.

George looked confused, and Karl realized his friend knew nothing about what Loretta and he could do. Too late to keep that secret now.

"We'll have to explain a few things to you, Georgie. If I can figure out how."

"I hope you do," George said. "Look, the metal down here would help a lot if we sold all of it, but I'm guessing whatever this target is wouldn't work then. Where's all the treasure to pay for your improvements, Gemma?"

She pointed to one of the walls.

"The safe is through there," she said. "We could always sell some of the things Loretta already Built."

Karl wanted to stop George from looking at those shelves, but that was more explaining he wasn't ready to do just yet. He followed Gemma instead.

She reached under one of the shelves, and Karl's jaw dropped when the wall folded in upon itself, revealing yet another small room.

"Stay out here for just a moment, dear," she said. "This part is a little bit trickier. Wouldn't want to trigger the gas." Karl took a couple of steps back, trying to see what she was doing. "This part is keyed to weight again, but I'm afraid I can't adjust it. We might be able to reconfigure something later."

This time Karl gasped when Gemma opened the massive safe in the small room. The shelves were piled high with more coin and treasure than he'd ever seen. More than he would have earned in a year, in a lifetime of working out at the Columns. Maybe more than the doctors earned.

Gemma motioned him forward.

"This is all from her Builds?" he said.

"As far as I know, though she may have other means. I told you she would be prepared. Now we must keep her home ready for her return."

Karl glanced at George, still investigating whatever horrors waited on the shelves.

"Gemma, I have to tell you something, especially since you're sharing all of this with me. We weren't completely honest about why you had to move. It's not the well. It's an investigation. The night George came to get you, a lot of people heard screams outside my building. And they found a knife that looked a lot like one I saw Loretta carrying."

Gemma continued to bustle around the space, adjusting the files, moving stray coins or jewels or rings into the right place.

"Karl, would you be a dear and fetch a few of those bags?" she said. "And don't worry so much. My bobbin is just fine, wherever she is."

Karl shook his head as he got three of the black leather bags stacked just outside the safe door.

"How can you know that, Gemma? No one has seen or heard from her, not even Bill. You know there are dangerous creatures out there."

She started filling one of the bags.

"Of course, but there are good ones, too," she said "That's how I know she's not dead."

Karl held his breath for a second, trying to make sense of the surreal conversation.

"From a good monster?" he said. "I don't understand what you mean, Gemma."

"The big white one I can talk to, remember? When we were out there packing up my things, I took the time to say goodbye and thank you."

"What did it say?"

"I told it why I was leaving," she said. "And that I was terribly worried about my granddaughter. It said, now let me make sure I have this right. It said, 'No worry, other safe. Across water, all are safe.' Yes. I believe that was it."

Karl's body alternated between too hot and too cold, and he nearly dropped the heavy bag of coin Gemma gave him. He looked around the room, at the glittering wealth he never would have imagined.

"If Loretta is alive," Karl whispered, "she'd never leave all of this behind. Not for anything."

"Well, I'd say people matter more than coin in the end," Gemma said. "She'll come back to you, dear. Don't you worry."

ABOUT KARI

Kari Kilgore's wanderlust and imagination lead her all over the world on grand adventures. Her heart and family bring her home to her native Appalachian Mountains of Virginia. From that solid base, she and her husband Jason A. Adams bring those adventures to life in fiction.

Kari writes science fiction, fantasy, and horror, and she's happiest when she surprises herself. She lives at the end of a long dirt road in the middle of the woods with Jason, various house critters, and wildlife they're better off not knowing more about.

The Confidential Adventure Club

Want more fiction from Kari, including stories, discounts, and box sets not available anywhere else? Want to hear about locations, research, and other cool things that inspired this story and beyond? All that and adorable pet photos, too?

Join The Confidential Adventure Club and get a thank you gift of a free short story and a whole lot more at www.smarturl.it/c-a-club.

Hope to see you there!

www.karikilgore.com
www.spiralpublishing.net

ALSO BY KARI KILGORE

I hope you enjoyed reading *The Dream Thief* as much as I enjoyed writing it. Check out more of my fiction at www.karikilgore.com.

The Confidential Adventure Club

Want more fiction from Kari, including stories, discounts, and box sets not available anywhere else? Want to hear about locations, research, and other cool things that inspired this story and beyond? All that and adorable pet photos, too?

Join The Confidential Adventure Club and get a thank you gift of a free short story and a whole lot more at www.smarturl.it/c-a-club.

Hope to see you there!

Novels:

Until Death

Dreaming the Storm: Book One of the Storms of Future Past Series

Joining the Storm: Book Two of the Storms of Future Past Series

Fighting the Storm: Book Four of the Storms of Future Past Series

Novellas:

Songs in the Mountain

Legacy of the Land

Restricted Species

The Becalmed

In the Pines

Into the Storm: Book Three of the Storms of Future Past Series

Short Stories:

Renovations

Intentions

The Garbage Belt

The Seeds of Love

Wicked Bone

The Sound of Murder

Terminalia

Little Five: A Terminalia Story

Reflections

Collections:

Fantastic Women: A Dark Fantasy Novella Trio

Fantastic Shorts: Volume 1 - A Fantasy Short Story Collection

> "Kari Kilgore is an author to watch—her lyrical voice a siren song; her insight, conjured voodoo."
>
> —Richard Thomas, author of *Breaker* and *Tribulations*